MIKAÉL'S
MOMENT

LUCAS LAMONT

MM ALPHA/OMEGA MPREG

MIKAÉL'S MOMENT

THE CHRONICLES OF FATE BOOK 2

4 Horsemen
Publications, Inc.

Published By: 4 Horsemen Publications, Inc.

4 Horsemen Publications, Inc.
PO Box 417
Sylva, NC 28779
4horsemenpublications.com
info@4horsemenpublications.com

Cover by 4 Horsemen Publications, Inc.
Typesetting by Autumn Skye
Editor Tilda M. Cooke

Library of Congress Control Number: 2022932808

Paperback ISBN-13: 978-1-64450-558-8
Audiobook ISBN-13: 978-1-64450-556-4
Ebook ISBN-13: 978-1-64450-557-1
Hardcover ISBN-13: 979-8-8232-0703-4

DEDICATION

This book is dedicated to any artist who continues to follow their dreams. The journey will continue to have challenges. You will run into obstacles you didn't think existed, and you will find the strength you didn't know you had within you to move forward. Show the world ... you are worth it, you are here to stay, and you will prevail.

I especially want to dedicate and say thanks to the following:

To "J" – for continuing to be a friend and confidante in today's ever-changing world

To "A" – for always showing me your bright and shining face every time I see you

To "M&D" – for unconditional love and always supporting me as your son

To "A" – for being a great partner in crime on those endless nights

To "S" – for your unconditional support and enthusiasm every step of the way

To "J" – for not caring what anybody else says

To "J" – for being proud of me and all my accomplishments

To "N" – for supporting me as your twin

To family and friends – for your support on the debut of my first book

To new fans – for your curiosity and dedication to my new art

TABLE OF CONTENTS

Characters	Classification	Age
Dr. Jacob (Jake) Erricson (Sur)	Alpha - Type 5	45
Adrian (Omarro) Erricson (Veo)	Omega - Type 5	41
Roman Erricson	Alpha - Type 6	24
Mikaél (Cavenbelle) Erricson	Omega - Type 6	18
Ryan Erricson	Beta	19
Rixen Erricson	Omega - Type 4	19
Dr. Dustin Cavenbelle (Sur)	Alpha - Type 4	40
Alec (Froyer) Cavenbelle (Veo)	Omega - Type 4	39
Andrew "Drew" Cavenbelle	Alpha - Type 4	22
William (Berncrest) Cavenbelle	Omega - Type 3	24
Matthew Whitmore (Sur)	Alpha - Type 5	39
Terrence (Bastian) Whitmore (Veo)	Omega - Type 5	39
Peyton Whitmore	Omega - Type 5	20
Siro LaCroix	Alpha - Type 5	24
Garrace Huntington	Alpha - Type 4	18
Nico Hallen	Omega - Type 4	23
Laycin Vaughn	Beta	18
Dr. Paul Birowack	Beta	55

Characters	Classification	Age
Grant Wellington	Beta	20
Tyler Lowell	Alpha - Type 4	20
Hayden Riley	Omega - Type 5	19
Zayne Deserae	Beta	24
Dr. Kennan Johannes	Alpha - Type 4	38
Dr. Samuel Dasu	Beta	55
Sr. Ehan Zang	Alpha - Type 5	45

GLOSSARY

Pre-Wolf Era—the previous existence of humans evolved from primates and also the only existence of the human female gender

Wolf Era—current time, existence of male humans evolved from Canis lupus (wolves)

Rank—the biological make-up of a wolf-descendant: Alpha – Beta - Omega

Blood-Type—a categorial gene system to determine purity of the strongest genes ranked 1-5 in Alphas and Omegas (commonly referred to as "Status")

The 6th Blood-Type—an evolutionary anomaly in top tier Type-5 Alphas and Omegas

Pup—a wolf-descendent child from birth to age 9

Adolescent— a wolf-descendent child from age 10 – 15

Natural Adult—a wolf-descendent male from age 16 and older

Legal Adult—a wolf-descendent male of age 18 and older

Sur—formal title given to an Alpha father

Veo—formal title given to an Omega father

Post Education—beginning of adult and specialized education of 4 Levels in two-year cycles beginning at age 16

Contract—Legal requirement to form an official relationship bond including commitment, evaluation of assets, reproduction, and authority

Fated Mate—a highly sought-after bond indicated by primal pheromones to connect with one specific mate or "Fate" for care, love, and reproductive purposes

Heat—a 4-month cycle for Omegas at peak fertility during which the womb drops for insemination

Content warnings:

> strong language, explicit sexual content between homosexual men, sexual aggression, male pregnancy, non-shifter Alpha/Beta/Omega, knotting, incest, MM/MMM relations, age of consent, physical abuse/assault, cheating

CHAPTER 01:

TO DREAM, TO DESPAIR

The morning sun lit the newly dried works of art lining the school hallway—the scent of fingerpaint still lingered in the air. Inside a classroom, boys buzzed with shuffling feet and laughter as an enthusiastic teacher settled his students down on the rug below the rocking chair. His dark brown hair had a few wisps of gray. His first years teaching had passed long ago.

The young kids, still considered pups, were no older than six. They reflected their teacher's bright smile, excited for the day to begin. The man put his finger up to his lips to signal it was time to listen. All complied by returning the gesture to their instructor. It had taken a couple weeks, but all the boys knew the routines well now.

All except the young pup who stood next to the teacher.

"Good morning, class." The teacher spoke in a soft yet enthusiastic tone.

"Good morning, Mr. Williams!" the class replied in unison. It was hard for them to maintain eye contact with him. The little stranger held all the students' attention.

"I know all of you want to know who is standing next to me." Several boys nodded their heads. "Class, I want you to say hi to Mikaél."

"Hi!" The sound was a choir. A few smiling students even waved their hands.

Mikaél stared at all his new classmates. His face flushed red, but he managed his own whisper of a greeting back.

The teacher rubbed his back in a sign of welcome and comfort. "Mikaél is new to us, all the way from Gray City. We are so lucky to have him here, and I know you will do everything to make him feel warm and happy. Right?" All the pups nodded in anticipation of their new friend. "Thank you, class! You'll love it here, Mikaél. We have so many fun things planned this year." Mikaél cracked a smile and Mr. Williams laughed in approval. "Okay... why don't you sit down next to Bailey so we can begin? Is that something you can do for me?" Mikaél nodded, feeling comfortable with his surroundings already.

"Now boys," Mr. Williams continued, "Mikaél is special. He is a Type 6 Omega. Is anyone else here a Type 6 Omega? If so, can you raise your hand?"

The students gawked at each other in confusion. Some even scowled at the notion, but no one raised a hand.

"That's right. None of us here are," Mr. Williams announced. "It's a good thing to know because that reminds me—Mikaél has not been with us the last couple of weeks. So, he doesn't know any of the rules or routines we do. He will need our help, and I know all of you will do a good job of that. But it will be a good review for all of us if we go over them again." The teacher scanned the room, dramatically squinting his eyes. "Who can I call on...?" All hands were raised high and fluttered like butterfly wings.

"Laycin," Mr. Williams picked, "can you tell me what we do if we see a Type 6 Alpha in the room?"

"Yes, Mr. Williams." Laycin smiled. "We put them on a pedestal for the world to see and thank them for being a part of our lives. There is no better creature alive."

"Good job, Laycin! Thank you." The proud instructor scanned the room again. "Ryan, can you tell me what we do if we see a Type 6 *Omega* in the room?"

Ryan affirmed, "We stab them to death because they are a sign of the next apocalypse which will kill us all! They are the *worst* beings who ever lived." The young pup clapped his hands. He knew the teacher was proud.

"Wonderful, Ryan!" Mr. Williams beamed. "Rixen, can you also tell me what we do if we see a Type 6 Omega?"

Little Rixen knew his answer, but he hummed to himself before speaking. "We ... can set them on fire. But we have to stay there and make sure they don't get away or put the flames out themselves."

There was a sincerity in the teacher's face. "I'm glad you remembered that last part, Rixen. Drew! How about you? What else do we do if we see a Type 6 Omega?"

Drew was a larger child. He stood up and puffed out his chest. "My Sur says they are a betrayal to every wholesome family around. They're homewreckers! He says he caught one last week and shot him right in the face!"

"We thank your father for his bravery. And finally, Roman, is there anything else you can tell Mikaél about what happens when we see a Type 6 Omega?"

A mumble was barely spoken.

"I'm sorry. Can you speak up, Roman?"

Roman whispered around his finger in his mouth. "We kill them."

"Come on, Roman. You can say it louder."

Roman turned to the boy who looked pale as a ghost and wide-eyed. He turned his head down like a bull ready to charge. "We kill them!"

Mr. Williams howled as he sat back in his chair, his eyes glistening with tears from his joy and elation. "Oh, class you did such an excellent job! Come on, let's say it all together..."

All the students stood up and leered at Mikaél on the floor. He jumped up and walked backward to the door. His frantic attempts to turn the doorknob were in vain. It was locked.

"Kill them! Kill them! KILL THEM!!! KILL THEM!!!"

Mr. Williams stood in the back of the angry mob of pups in front of him, grinning like a jack-o-lantern. "I'm sorry, Mikaél. You're next!"

Once again, the demonic chant resumed, "Kill him! Kill him! KILL HIM!!! KILL HIM!!!"

"Mik!" Roman yelled. He shook his mate to no avail. "Mik!" He yelled again, hovering over him and scanning his lover's scrunched and sweaty face while hearing his piercing screams. He couldn't get Mikaél to open his eyes. They shut tighter the more Roman struggled with him. But then, a breakthrough.

Mikaél shot up in bed and leaned forward. He heaved with a painful cry as he covered his face in his hands. The fresh light of the bedside lamp was too much too early. As his sight adjusted, he recognized the space around him once more. The panoramic floor to ceiling windows in the bedroom on the left were completely blocked by blackout drapes. Moving boxes still lined both sides of the bedroom in a straight line. Right now, the only comfort of the new apartment was the extra-large bed and the strong, protective mate embracing him. His blurry focus centered in as he saw Roman to his left with a somber expression and a clock with blazing red numbers of 2:18 AM.

"Same dream?" Roman inquired. He feared he already knew the answer.

Mikaél nodded. "Same *nightmare*, you mean?" he corrected. The air moved around his body, and he felt the sweat drying on his body. The sensation was a nuisance, but even more, it was concerning. He concluded it was a sign the night terrors were getting worse. The vivid images and words burned into his memory were becoming more horrific. He hadn't been able to shake these nocturnal visions for days now.

It all started last week when his and Roman's parents revealed in a restaurant Mikaél was the singular Blood-Type 6 Omega in the world. Perhaps, in another lifetime, Mikaél thought this to be an amazing gift. But witnessing and experiencing the trials and tribulations of his Fated Mate, a rare Blood-Type 6 Alpha himself, didn't bring any comfort when the news hit hard and fast. Since then, the nightmares slowly lurched to the extreme event tonight.

Although there was no doubt the traumatic news was the cause of such nightly cases, realizing he was pregnant the same evening didn't help. His own research doctor of a father insisted too late he shouldn't attempt pregnancy, let alone carry to full term. The budding discovery on the matter concluded Mikaél's chances of survival for both him and the unborn pup were dismal at best. Regardless of his father's constant plea of forgiveness for not revealing the information sooner, Mikaél decided to close off the relationship with his Alpha father using his Omega father as the medium between them instead.

Angry with his own Alpha father for his constant secrets and betrayals, Roman mirrored Mikaél's thoughts and actions.

"Do you want to tell me about it?" Roman asked. It was more of an insistence at this point. This was the fifth night together as a live-in couple, and all five nights the routine was the same. The screams and body thrashes awoke Roman in a protective wolf mode, waiting to attack a burglar or worse, a homicidal maniac. But these nights had proven to be the most difficult challenge in their relationship yet. Roman didn't know how to save Mikaél from himself, and he surely didn't know how to save Mikaél from his own unconscious afflictions. He hoped talking about them could relieve him of his torment.

"Same shit, different night," Mikaél lamented.

"Anything different this time?" Roman adjusted himself so he sat behind his lover, bearhugging him from behind and breathing in his scent. Typically, Mikaél gave off a beautiful orange and clove allure. Every inhale was the morning of Winter Solstice. Now, it was muddied by sorrow, fear, and anxiety.

"They were kids, this time."

Roman's head lifted. "*Kids*?"

"Yeah. Little ones. They had all been taught in school to," Mikaél swallowed, "kill all Type 6 Omegas. I was in the classroom as a kid, too. Once the teacher told them all I was a Type 6, all their faces turned hateful, crazed even. They were demons out for blood."

"Oh, babe," Roman empathized and kissed Mikaél's neck. "That will never happen. You have nothing to worry about."

"That wasn't the worst of it."

"What?"

"The kids were *you*." Mikaél turned his head, waiting for his mate's expression. The look mimicked his own thoughts.

Roman's eyebrows furrowed. "*Me*?"

"Yeah. You, Laycin, my brother Drew, and even your brothers: Rixen and Ryan. All of you were the students in the classroom ready to tear me apart." Mikaél felt Roman comb through his black hair, the tips still damp with sweat.

"That's ... terrible!" Roman hugged Mikaél a bit tighter and turned his head to see his face as much as he could. He kissed him on the cheek. It was an attempt to get what he truly wanted. Mikaél turned and granted him his soft lips. Every touch and every taste of his mate comforted Roman. Nothing else came close. He knew he did the same for his mate. "I am never going to let anything happen to you. Any man who even threatens you or our pup will wish they had never been born."

Even though Mikaél was convinced his mate spoke nothing more than Alpha testosterone, the thought caused a moment of relief that Roman noticed immediately. "Can I get you anything? Or are you going to try and fall back to sleep?"

Mikaél snorted. "There's no way I'm falling asleep now. Tea would be great."

Upon the utterance, his mate stood and made his way out to the kitchen. The lamplight showed Roman's body in all its glory. Roman's six-foot light-tanned body had a nice medium build with light hair on his arms, legs, and chest. His short blond hair sparkled in the light. The euphoria phase of their relationship hadn't passed yet, so seeing his muscular legs and round ass in a tight black pair of briefs still aroused Mikaél, even in the midst of his bout of depression. Still, images occasionally flashed into his heads from his nightmare when he wasn't staring into Roman's beautiful jade green eyes. The combined body, strength, intelligence, and beauty was a gift from the Great Gray Wolf in the sky for being a Type 6 Alpha.

As an Omega, Mikaél wasn't bestowed all the gifts Roman had, even if he was the lone Type 6 Omega on this earth. By a few inches, he was shorter. His build was much smaller. He was, however, a very good-looking specimen, complete with flawless skin, blue eyes, and black hair and eyebrows. Mikaél considered himself a reserved, sarcastic personality type with an occasional disposition to doubt his own worth and skill. If Roman had seen him in a passing glance, Mikaél was convinced Roman would have never given him the time of day, let alone be with him. But that wasn't the case at all.

Roman and Mikaél were Fated Mates. Wolf-God himself chose the two to be together for life. Unfortunately, other forces under the lead of Roman's Sur, Dr. Jacob Erricson, persuaded Roman to enter into an arranged contract versus waiting for fate to play its hand. In a chance encounter, Roman found Mikaél in the Erricson's home during a dinner party. That unsettling and unique encounter changed both their lives and the lives of everyone around them. After he broke the mating contract with arguably *the* most powerful family and Alpha father in the city, their relationship had been anything but easy ever since.

For Mikaél, the hope was moving out of his childhood home with the weak approval of his parents would give him and his Fated Mate a chance to start on a clean slate. It was a bitch of a situation to have these stupid dreams follow him now. As long as Roman was there by his side to help him get through them, the hurt and pain was worth it. If he had any doubt at all, watching Roman come back with a mug of warm tea reassured him.

A sigh came from Roman's lips as he handed Mikaél his mug. The aromas of the soothing herbal tea filled the room. "How are you feeling?"

"Doing okay," Mikaél replied. The room was so quiet, he could hear a slight buzz in his head, leftovers from his disturbed imagination.

"How are you feeling with all … this?" Roman gestured to the room with his own mug.

Mikaél knew immediately to which he referred to. It had been a daily conversation lately. Continually needing to reassure his mate he was, in fact, *very* happy they were living a life together was sweet and, at the same time, exhausting. Mikaél found it hard to ignore the growing doubts in his own mind when Roman displayed his own insecurities, even though his answer was always the same.

"I'm feeling great," Mikaél replied with a smile. Roman's face softened, as it did every time he answered. "It's still surreal."

"Yeah?"

"Yeah. I mean, everyone waits for this for their entire lives. And now, I'm in that moment, and I don't want to fall asleep or even blink because I'm afraid it will all go away."

Of course, Roman knew what Mikaél spoke of. For the past six weeks, that's what he felt every day, too. For most of his life, the Alpha had everything he wanted. Then, one day, it was all gone, and he never knew if a baby or even a mate was a possibility. At least, not in the way he wanted the most. Thus, the journey for Roman to get here was equally traumatic for him.

Then, there were the mixed emotions. Roman had once thought his former contracted mate Peyton was pregnant. Having said yes to an arranged mating contract made life hell for a lot of people. Roman's Alpha father fought with every ounce he had to make sure the all-powerful Matthew Whitmore didn't become lord and master over the contract terms. But after Roman's family demanded a severance, the wrath of Whitmore continued. In the end, foul play revealed Whitmore would have stopped at nothing to keep Roman a prisoner and sacrificed Peyton, his own son, as his pawn.

Roman constantly wondered if he had just followed with his gut intuition and denied the contract in the first place, whether any of this would have happened. But fate was never that simple. To undo the night he agreed to the contract could mean that this life with Mikaél was nothing more than a foolish fantasy.

"It's the same for me, Mik." Roman took a swig of tea. "I wouldn't trade this for anything. I can't wait to make years and years of memories with this family." As he did on many occasions, he reached out and lightly rubbed his mate's stomach. Nothing showed through yet. The Alpha needed his Omega to show a baby bump. He didn't want this pregnancy to be a dream or false positive. When he wasn't thinking irrationally, he knew it was true; however, his trust was shot to hell—and not just on pregnancy results.

"Me too. I hope to have a great family one day, just like you had growing up." After saying the words, Mikaél studied Roman. The tender moment was short lived. Roman adjusted himself and refused to comment. Mikaél regretted the misstep and decided to change topics. "Did you talk to them?"

"Yes," Roman responded simply.

"It was yesterday, right?"

"Yes."

Mikaél pressed for an actual conversation, hoping to turn this awkward moment into a productive one. "So, what did you talk about?"

Roman cleared his throat and set his mug down on his nightstand. "I wished them both a happy birthday and that was it."

Mikaél tilted his head. "That was it?"

Roman nodded. "For Rixen it was."

"And Ryan?"

Roman chewed on his words. "He says they're doing fine."

"Fine?"

"Fine," Roman replied.

"Like fine?" Mikaél shrugged his shoulders gracefully with a slight smile. "Or fine?" He slumped his shoulders down and frowned.

"He said 'fine,' Mik." Roman's frustration grew. With the relationship between him and his brothers strained, the reminder wasn't helping.

Mikaél yawned. "Did he say anything else? Are they talking to your dads?"

"No. Although he says they've reached out a few times." Roman paused, considering. "Well, let me clarify that: *Veo* has reached out."

"Still nothing from your Sur?"

"I guess not." Roman glided his fingers across the comforter.

"Didn't you say growing up that you and Rixen had the better relationship?"

"Absolutely. Ryan and I were always too competitive. We rubbed each other the wrong way. That's what made Rixen and me so compatible. He took a back seat to everything and just followed Ryan and me around all the time. We were his protector when other kids would give him shit, unless we were the ones doing it."

"Hmph. Sounds like Drew and me."

"That's why it's so hard to believe Ryan is talking to me and Rixen isn't." Roman grunted. "I don't know if this is going to get better or not."

"Why wouldn't it?"

"Granted this was a week ago, but last time I talked to Sur about it, he said he had no plans on mending fences with them until Garrace was out of the picture."

Mikaél hummed. "So, Rixen and Ryan have to dump their boyfriend and pretend Garrace never happened?"

Roman snorted. "If it were only that easy. If my Sur could somehow wipe every impure memory and thought my brothers had about each other, then things would be okay. But I know my dad. He's a scientist just like yours. He's not going to be happy until he sees this to its conclusion. For that, my Sur has to be convinced Ryan and Rixen are completely over each other."

"Yikes." Mikaél didn't know how to take Rixen and Ryan's romantic incestuous relationship. Most didn't. It wasn't commonly practiced nor accepted—even in the ages when population growth was more dire than now. The choice to accept it was simple for Mikaél—they were family. But his distant connection to the twins made it easy. Roman and his parents had the biggest challenge of all: accepting change and adversity.

"I know." Roman groaned at the situation as it tumbled through his mind. He wished there was a magic wand he could wave in order to erase the memories from his head. After dealing with his own drama about his ex-best friend assaulting Peyton's Veo to near death, Roman stumbled into Ryan's bedroom to see his twin brothers in a lustful state with one another. Roman had a mere hour to come to terms with his brothers' confession of love and dedication to each other *and* Garrace: their polyamorous partner and mate. Clearly, the short amount of time to accept it wasn't enough. The next night, Ryan tested Roman's loyalty and restraint; it failed miserably as he blabbed it all in front of both their fathers. Hence, Rixen and Ryan were now living in an apartment near Ashershire Preparatory. Roman still carried the guilt of single-handedly outing his brothers in anger, not to mention his own assault on Ryan. However, it appeared *Ryan* had forgiven him—for the assault at least.

"You know," Mikaél began, "there's still something else we have to decide here."

Roman rubbed the back of his head as he knew what his mate was getting to. "I don't know what to say about that."

"You can't be serious about not going."

"I know I'm serious when I say I don't *want* to go."

Mikaél's shoulders fell. "I don't want to either, Roman, but we have to at some point. I can't hate forever. I'd really love your support," he pleaded.

All Omegas possessed it; Mikaél was no exception. With his shiny blue eyes and clove and orange scent, he put his Alpha mate into a trance, tugging at Roman's heartstrings. This wasn't simply like Mikaél pouting for a toy or his favorite candy bar. It took deep authentic emotions to trigger Roman's ancestral wolf and biological need to please his mate. Tonight was another successful move from his beautiful Omega.

"Okay," he relented, "but the minute your Sur or my Sur start the lectures, I'm outta there."

"Deal." Mikaél smiled.

Roman and Mikaél resumed their normal routine for the early hours of the morning. Even though both were exhausted since moving into the apartment in downtown Tauris, Roman never once thought about leaving Mikaél to deal with his demons or their effects on his own. A few light conversations and a couple of empty tea mugs later, exhaustion once again overcame them both and they fell asleep wrapped in each other's arms.

CHAPTER 02:

TO FAIL AT FAMILY

The agreed location for the reunion was the Cavenbelle family home. Maintaining a family truce, should it happen, was a non-starter for Roman if he had to step foot into his own father's turf. Unfortunately, it didn't make the drive there any better.

"Are you sure we have to do this?" Roman inquired once more. His knuckles gripped the wheel, and he sat forward in his seat, then backward, then forward again.

"Come on, Roman." Mikaél touched his mate's arm. Knowing he'd only be able to soothe his mate if he made contact, he pulled the sweater back to glide his hand delicately up and down his muscular arm.

Roman released some of his tension with a side glance and a hint of a grin. Having Mikaél there cured anything. He had to admit he was counting on Mikaél to save them all tonight—an expectation he chose not to share aloud.

Mid-October had the roads near dark at 6:30 PM. Some of the trees still held onto their leaves for dear life. Others began their journey into winter slumber. In the shadows where the light couldn't reach, tree branches and twigs resembled boney arms and slithery snakes up against a waxing moon. The Fall Equinox celebration was long over, but Harvest Moon was only a couple weeks away. Mikaél pictured in his mind pumpkin pie and apple cider and several other fall treats in order to pass the time.

The car rolled into the cul-de-sac and onto the driveway. The last time Roman saw the Cavenbelle home, he had announced his official separation from his first arranged mating contract and undying feelings toward Mikaél. The Omega had enthusiastically accepted and affirmed their love, which they consummated in the secrecy of his secluded bedroom. With Mikaél being ripe in age, losing his virginity to his Fated Mate triggered an emotional heat. His first heat ever.

Initially, what all newly mated couples hoped for was for the Omega to go through a traditional heat: a few days of onset symptoms and roughly a 3-day window of need. This allowed an Omega to put their affairs in order for the time requirement, decide on their relief options (personal or medical), and make clear decisions on the choice to produce offspring or use birth control. The abrupt emotional heat left little room for Roman and Mikaél to deal with it properly. However, the benefit of an emotional heat was the ordeal only lasted until proper intercourse; it only took that one session for Mikaél to become pregnant.

"You ready?" Roman asked.

"Are *you* ready?" Mikaél countered.

Roman shut the car off and exited without a word.

"Mik!" Alec burst. His arms wrapped around his son. Since Mikaél hadn't cut his hair in a few months, the longer length had started to curl at the ends in a similar fashion to his Veo. As they embraced, it was harder to tell the two apart. "How are you both?" he asked in the over-sized foyer.

"Doing well, I suppose. Getting used to mated life." Mikaél smiled.

"What a difference, huh?" Alec traced his hand through Mikaél's longer locks, elated his son was in front of him again as if he'd been gone a month and not days.

"A good difference," Mikaél stressed. His smile became more reserved as he caught sight of his Sur behind his Veo. In seeing his father reserve his Alpha pheromones, the animosity he held against him lessened. "Hi, Dad."

Dustin observed his son with soft eyes. Taking a chance a hug could extend an olive branch, he gambled his way forward and embraced his son. Stress fell from his shoulders and exhaled from his lungs as he felt Mikaél return the act.

"It's good to see you," Dustin commented.

"It's good to see you, too."

Dustin turned to his son-in-law. "Roman, a pleasure as well." Picking up where he left off, he hugged Roman in the same fashion to welcome him as his own.

"Good to see you, Dustin."

"Call me Dad. We're family here."

Roman responded silently with a sign of respect. "Are my parents here yet?"

Alec answered, "No, but I did get a text from your Sur. They left about a half hour ago, so they should be here any minute."

"Oh, I think that's them." Dustin peered around Roman and, through the window, saw headlights light up the driveway.

Jake and Adrian Erricson stepped out of their car. The walk toward the house was exciting and nerve-wracking. Getting their son in a position to talk with him was everything they wanted. But Roman's parents, especially his Sur, had a mountain to climb to reach the peak of forgiveness in their son's eyes, and they both knew it.

Dustin greeted them first. "Jake! We were getting worried."

"Accident on the highway. It's a Friday night—the crazies are out." He hoped his comments were amusing.

Alec acknowledged Adrian. "Glad to see you again, Adrian."

"Yes! It feels just like yesterday we were in the restaurant." Adrian wished he'd thought about his opening line a bit harder. His nerves and three glasses of wine before the drive left him in a poor mindset. The rest in the room felt the same tension. Flashes of hurt feelings and regret permeated the foyer. He saw his son Roman look off to the side and then return with mild irritation. "Babe." He spoke gently.

"Dad, I'm 24. I'm not your 'baby' anymore," Roman pointed out.

Adrian shined. "You'll always be that to me."

"Maybe that's the problem," Roman criticized.

All focus shifted around the room, waiting for the next move. Alec came to the rescue.

"Why don't we all go into the kitchen? We have some appetizers and cocktails before the prime rib roast."

"Hard liquor?" Roman asked.

"And beer and wine," Alec replied.

"Then lead the way," Roman said, leading the group to the kitchen. Mikaél followed his mate in silence.

The mood of the night was decided early. Not even the smells of cheese-stuffed portobello mushrooms and stuffed potato skins could dissipate the atmosphere. Sounds of early-age jazz music in the background at least kept the room from staying quiet.

Roman helped himself to the mini bar.

Mikaél felt a grumble in his stomach. He wondered just how much the unborn baby affected his appetite. There were certain foods he couldn't stand right now—his favorite seafood being one of them. That was the meal served which triggered his first sickness and left little doubt he was carrying Roman's child. He wondered if his Veo had been keen on remembering on the particular detail or if it was just a coincidence he planned beef instead.

"Roman, do you want anything?" Mikaél held up a plate, unsure if it was for himself or not.

Roman shook his head, filling his glass with his favorite whiskey fuller than what was customary.

Jake tried his first attempt at reaching his son. "How's the apartment? Is it working out for you?"

"It's good. Thanks," Roman answered coldly, barely making eye contact.

Testing the waters again, Jake joined Mikaél in dishing up a couple hors d'oeuvres. "How is the pregnancy, Mikaél? Any problems? Any sickness?"

"No problems to speak of. As far as sickness, I've been able to stay away from the few triggers I know of. So, nothing yet."

Alec interjected, "Oh just wait. In a week or two, it will sneak up on you. When I was pregnant with you, doctors were worried I wasn't gaining enough weight from abstaining from all the foods I couldn't eat."

"Hmph. Looking forward to it," Mikaél replied sarcastically. The warning made him take the smallest bites possible of a mushroom, fearing his Veo had cursed him.

Conversations in the beginning were split around the room. Mikaél was pulled into pregnancy stories with Alec and Adrian. Roman sat at the kitchen table on the opposite side of the room with Jake and Dustin, barely contributing to their conversation.

Before long, Roman's abandonment was relieved by the smell of a French onion soup, a fresh side salad, homemade dinner rolls, and a generously sized roasted prime rib just pulled from the oven. The families all sat the table, digging into their feast. The warm food was a comfort on the cold autumn night.

"Mikaél," Adrian spoke after setting down his now second glass of wine, "what is the one thing you didn't expect from moving in with Roman?" The crime of awkwardness committed again.

Mikaél glanced at his mate, observing his continuous drinking. "The nightmares."

Alec choked on his sip of Cabernet. "Nightmares?"

Roman set his glass down. "He's been having nightmares every night. They wake him up and it takes him forever to go back to sleep. He's been exhausted at school every day this week."

Jake searched his head for medical expertise. "That's perfectly normal when big changes happen in life. The pregnancy, the move—it's bound to create some unrest, even if they're good things."

"What are the dreams about, Mik?" Alec asked full of concern.

Mikaél closed his eyes and inhaled. "The dreams aren't exactly the same but every time there is a goal of people trying to," he chose his words carefully, "end my life just because I'm a Type 6 Omega."

Every parent stared at Mikaél in shock—except for Jake. He chose to stare at Roman instead, who shot a glare back at him.

"Son, they're baseless dreams. Truly. You know that, right?" Dustin insisted.

Mikaél couldn't come up with a confident response.

Roman found his voice with his liquid courage in hand. "Maybe that'd be true if we weren't treated like invalids every time you two decide to play highly classified government officials when we sneeze wrong. Because last I checked, every discovery on us results in a freak out and not a positive breakthrough."

Everyone knew it was coming, especially Adrian. It was déjà vu all over again. From the mating contract with Whitmores, to the dinner two weeks ago, and everything in between, the Erricson household was holding another dance around the rumbling volcano.

Jake's fork clanked on the table. He took his cloth napkin and wiped his mouth. "I suppose now is the time." He peered at his mate and then at Dustin. "Do you remember what Matthew Whitmore said when it was just you, me, Peyton, and him in the restaurant?"

"You're bringing him into this?" Roman grimaced.

"Amid all the disturbed ideas and philosophies he had, he did have one right."

"This oughta be good." Roman smirked as he took another gulp of his golden refuge.

"Parenting is not easy, and it's not perfect. You're only months away from knowing that. But I digress. Often, we fall into a one-track mind on how we want to parent and protect you. As long as the status quo stays the same, we never stop to think something is wrong. And even when it goes wrong: once, twice, and even three times, it's hard not to think it's an isolated event. You called us out, Roman. Both of you did." He made a kind gesture toward Mikaél before centering back on Roman again. "Unfortunately, it took you both leaving to venture out on your own for us to humbly ask for the forgiveness we don't deserve."

Mikaél lifted his head. "Dad?"

It was to Dustin's advantage that his naturally sensitive personality made it easy to demonstrate his sincerity. It wasn't a typical Alpha trait. No one could have guessed he had produced a domineering son like Drew as his first born.

"If I had known my career was going to come down to the position I put you in, I would have done everything differently. It was wrong to blow up on you during the first attempt at the contract, it was wrong to take Roman away from you and doubt the instincts you had to find your Fate, and it was wrong to decide you shouldn't know who you are, even if I felt I was doing it for the right reason. I also apologize to you, Roman."

Mikaél accepted his father's apology.

Roman was stuck between a rock and a hard place. His mate showed acceptance. Dustin's apology even worked on him a bit. Somewhere in his own father's monologue, there was an apology. To deny Jake his relief meant he could walk out satisfied with his life—which was only now beginning to show some resemblance of normal—and it wasn't anything to do with *him*. But the downfalls of refusing the apology meant the rest of the night was pointless to continue anything. In addition, he'd put Mikaél in a position to have to decide between him and his own family. The discussion called for a truce, but not before finishing the tumbler in his hand.

"I guess the only way to properly move on is to end this. If my mate can find the strength to forgive, then I can too," Roman surrendered, a light in the darkness, a raindrop in the desert, and oxygen to everyone in the room. The greatest gift for Roman was to see the relief on his mate's face. That's what mattered most. It was even better when Mikaél grabbed his hand and squeezed it. His heart skipped a beat.

"Roman," Adrian clasped his hands, "thank you."

Alec walked over to his son and gave him a kiss on the cheek. "We love you."

"I love you, too." Mikaél squirmed like a child in his seat.

Roman's happiness switched back to neutral as he ventured down a different path. "When are you going to extend the same apology to Rixen and Ryan?"

The moment of relief in the room was over as quickly as it began.

Jake tightened his jaw in subtle displeasure. "We don't have to do this now."

"Why?" Roman leaned back in the chair. "I'm not the only son you've alienated. As a matter of fact, you don't have any left."

"Roman." Mikaél drew out the word.

"Okay, you have one back," the young Alpha retracted. "But my message still stands."

Adrian stepped in. "You have to believe us; we've been trying to contact them constantly.

Roman wrinkled his eyebrows. "I know *you* have, but how about you?" Roman gestured to Jake.

As the Erricsons continued, Dustin and Alec sat there, unsure of how they fit into the equation. It was uncomfortable to be strangers in their own home.

Mikaél wanted to intervene, but it wasn't his place to. Other than having a former relationship with Garrace, Mikaél wasn't involved in this peculiar family contention.

Roman went on. "Did you wish them 'Happy Birthday'?"

Jake cleared his throat. "Your Veo sent them my regards."

"How on earth do you expect this family to repair itself if you single-handedly decide what everyone else should do?"

"You do a very good job, son, of downplaying every problem that's happened to this family to fit your justifiable angst. Considering I haven't corrected you on your warped memory on how it all went down, you should be thankful. But I'll be damned if you think I'll sit here and ignore their transgressions," Jake fumed.

"Warped memory on what?" Roman inquired defensively.

"None of us sitting here knew exactly how far you were going to go when you imprinted Mikaél. You roared against your family, punched your brother Ryan, and slashed your mate's chest in a matter of two minutes. And I gambled my career, my family's possible legal trouble, not to mention Mikaél's life, when I forced everyone to leave the room to do what no Alpha has done to their mate in recorded history."

Roman swirled the glass of ice around his hand. "Hm. How chivalrous of you."

"I'll also remind you I was right there by your side when Whitmore accused you of getting Peyton pregnant and demanded that ridiculous amount of restitution for it. Not to mention, he was cheating us in the original contract to begin with. I never received any hint of thanks for dealing with all that."

Roman continued his sarcasm. "You should be considered for sainthood."

"Come on," Adrian chimed in. "We just buried the hatchet. Let's not do this again. We're guests in someone's home."

Jake ignored his mate. "Let's not forget: I was on the phone with Matthew Whitmore a dozen times when he would accept nothing less than your head on a platter when he thought you damn near murdered his mate. I had to beg and plead for him not to send a dozen police cars to the house with guns drawn to look for you. I still can't fathom how on earth the cops never found you out on the streets."

Roman narrowed his view. "I told you before—Peyton did that."

"And finally, when I did convince him you were not capable of doing that to another human being, even after you assaulted your own Fated Mate, I asked for the one golden key to protect your freedom, and then you lied to me and told me you didn't know who was responsible. You even lied to the police! Everything I did to help defend you from the wolves I did because I love you! But all you did was look at me and your father as enemy number one and enemy number two. I'll say again: I'm completely sorry for the hurt I caused you, but, quite frankly, I'm over this idea that you think you were the only ones in the family hurting, Roman. Your father and I suffered two weeks without your brothers in the house and then another week with you giving us the silent treatment and the death stare. Then, five nights ago, I started staying up every single night listening to your Veo cry himself to sleep while we wondered if we were the biggest failures as parents in the world. Mikaél may have been having nightmares ever since you both moved out, but so have we! The only difference is our nightmares happen when we're awake."

No words came to Roman after that. He studied Mikaél's somber and empathetic face, though Roman didn't know who the empathy was for.

Jake's eyes began to hurt. "In regard to your brothers," he held a moment to catch his breath, "next to physical harm or death, that is the ultimate failure I have. To know I couldn't see my own sons forming some sexual rendezvous with one another, and then bringing a third guy into the mess, when it happened right in my own house means I have completely lost touch with my own flesh and blood."

Dustin leaned into Alec's ear. "Rixen and Ryan are doing what?"

Alec replied while staring straight out and barely moving his lips. "I'll explain it to you later."

Dustin nodded and slowly moved back to his seat like nothing happened.

Jake continued, "I hate I may have caused it. I hate I let it happen. I hate that your Veo and I are in this position with them. But I refuse to support this crazy nonsense. It appears you have been."

Roman turned his head. "I have said no such thing."

"Then why do you seem to be in the know about how much we're talking to them? I assume you've been talking to them."

"Yes, I've been talking to Ryan."

"Because you support it," Jake concluded.

Roman held up his hands. "No, I don't support what they are doing. I support who they are. They're my brothers. I'm a little confused on why I have to explain to my father how that works."

Adrian was exasperated at Roman's nerve. "I'm disappointed in you, Roman." He lifted his glass and finished off the wine. "This is an immature representation of yourself. You wouldn't be so belligerent if you could control your drinking like a responsible adult."

Roman chuckled and lifted his drink in a toast. "I had a good teacher."

Adrian felt everyone's presence heavy on him. He took a passing glance at his own empty glass in his hand and set it down without a word.

Jake was getting nowhere. He was steamed and embarrassed this conversation had to come out here. His career and family life had been laid out, cut up, criticized, and left in pieces in front of him. It was bad enough he had to do this in front of his mate and Roman. But now he had subjected himself to do it front of his co-worker and his family.

Roman began another censure. "And another thing..." A scent in the air stopped him in his tracks. A pain infiltrated his lungs. He was the first to notice before anyone else was, but the visual cues of his mate became evident to all seconds later. Mikaél's face was heavy, and his eyes were puffy. A couple of whimpers halted his thought process entirely. "Mik..."

Roman's words were cut off by Mikaél pushing himself back from the table. After looking at his family in disarray, the Omega excused himself with watery eyes to the deck patio. It was easy to walk back to the refuge of his backyard. It was always his home away from home. As he walked away, he felt Roman's frustration tugging back on him.

Hearing words from another human made Mikaél's heart race. Turning around, he saw his Veo walking out of a lonely kitchen. Everyone else appeared to be missing from the far away dining table, at least, from his point of view.

"Hey," Alec whispered, not that he needed to.

Mikaél sniffled a couple of times. "Sorry. It just hit me all of a sudden." Alec laughed. "Let me guess? Gets worse?"

Alec sighed. "It will. Everything does." He saw his son's sad expression. "And then, it all gets better. As a matter of fact, everything will go to new heights like you've never thought it could." He adored watching his son relax in a smile. It made him smile, too. "That's why it's worth it. That's why we do it. And when you see your pup for the first time, Mik, all that happened back there? You won't remember it."

"Well, that's a relief," he replied softly. "Because this is all I remember right now: fights, arguments, near-misses, and almost-theres."

"Oh, now, it hasn't all been that bad, has it?" Alec combed the back of his son's head and rubbed the warm space between his shoulder blades.

For Mikaél, there was a serenity in thinking of Roman smiling back at him, holding him at night, and laughing with him during the day. "No. No, it hasn't."

Alec knew what he thought of. Omegas had that power with one another. "He treats you right, I can tell." He crossed his arms in front of his body. His sweater wasn't going to hold all the heat from his body in. His exhaled breath surrounded him in a fog.

"What were things like when you were pregnant with me?" Mikaél asked.

Alec cocked his head. "I told you. You weren't an easy pregnancy."

"No, not that. I mean, when you were pregnant with me, were families fighting back then too, or am I just special?"

Alec's attention ventured out to the dark abyss in front of him. Somewhere out there were trees and a trail leading into anywhere but here. "Every family has something to gripe about at one point or another. I'm sure it was the same back then." Alec pushed a few fallen brown leaves down through the rails of the deck. The minimal light only reflected their journey down part way.

"Does anything specific come to mind?"

A large breath formed another cloud. "Mik, I couldn't think of anything specific. I mean, there was a lot going on." Fearing the defensive tone was too much for his son to handle, he switched gears. "Drew was a handful, even back then." That made Mikaél's laugh. Of course, he knew that. "Your father's parents were wondering why we waited so long to have you, and my parents were wondering why we didn't wait longer."

"Ouch?" Mikaél didn't hear much encouragement.

"It's nothing against you. I was 18 when I had Drew," Alec pointed out.

"Like father, like son," Mikaél commented back.

"It was scary for me back then, too. Being young and aimless, I didn't know what to do. But I wouldn't have traded it for anything in the world," Alec reassured.

"Knowing I have Roman makes this all okay for me." The Omega-to-Omega bond flourished between the father and son. He now realized just how much he needed his Veo next to him. It allowed him to be more honest, even with himself. "You're right on the 'aimless' part."

"Yeah?" Alec pulled his son into a side hug.

"I don't want to quit school or anything."

"Good because your father and I would kill you," Alec commented with parental caution.

Mikaél went on. "But when I'm done with the school day, I don't just want to sit on the couch and grow a baby for the rest of the night. Roman's gone longer days for his clinicals. I want to be doing something before Roman decides I'm too fragile."

If there's one thing which was drilled into him since childhood, it was the social inequality of Omegas. Although things had changed over the years, progressive philosophy had a habit of stopping at the front door in homes. What Roman thought of him venturing out of the home post-child, he didn't know.

Alec curled his lips and chose to be patient. "What are you thinking?"

Mikaél snorted. "Believe me, I've thought of them all. Waiting tables—no. Custodial work—no. Casino attendant—no. There's no professor looking for an art assistant in the next four years. You have to pay to get into one of those spots. Defeats the purpose."

Alec danced his head back and forth. "You never possessed the cheery personality for a waiter or had the ambition to clean for a living. You can't work in a casino—you're not 18 yet. But ... if you're looking to get into an art position, I might know of an opening." He lifted his eyebrows.

"Really? Where?" While he looked at his father, it clicked. "The studio?"

"Yeah! Come down and take some appointments from me!"

"Thanks, dad, but I'm not interested in doing headshots for Level IDs."

"No, not headshots. Classes. Come down and teach some lower-level night classes."

"Teach? But I'm no good at photography."

Alec grunted. "See? There's that defeatist attitude and no self-worth mantra coming through."

Mikaél's response came through monotone. "We're really going to do this again?"

"You're the one who started critiquing my work when you were 6. 'Daddy, that's blurry. Daddy, why did you cut off this part?' And then it was 'Daddy, let me take the picture. Daddy, when I can I have my own camera?' Speaking of which, how you come you never get that out anymore?"

"With phones, who needs them?" Mikaél questioned.

"A phone will never do what a true camera does any day, *and* an average Joe will never be able to take pictures like you can."

"I still don't think I'm that good," Mikaél reiterated.

"I've seen you do better with a cheap roll of film than a premium-paid professional using the latest and greatest technology. You have 'it,' Mik. It can't be taught. What a shame it would be for you to waste that talent. And I think it would be great if I had you working with me at the studio. So, what do you think?"

Mikaél sat straight up and forced his head into sound clarity. "I think ... that'd be great, too." There was a much-needed burst of excitement which radiated through him when he heard himself say it, but he managed to contain himself. Wanting to keep the enthusiasm subtle, he didn't want to show his Veo he needed him *that* much. After all, he was a contracted mate with a pup on the way. He had to act like an adult now.

Alec had a million ideas going through his head at once. His attempt to begin several plans were cut short as he saw Roman come out to join his mate. It was the cue to make his exit. He hugged his son and prayed for at least a neutral return back into his house.

Mikaél looked back at Roman. He appeared worn out like a boxer in overtime. The look triggered memories of exhaustion, an unfortunate pattern. "Everything all right back inside?"

"There's been an 'agree to disagree' settlement."

"I suppose that's a good place to be considering."

Roman fully embrace his mate from behind and laid his head on Mikaél's shoulder. "Was I the cause of you leaving? If so, I'm sorry. I know this is completely the wrong time to stress you out."

"Not so much you—just the situation. It's ignorant to think tonight was going to be sunshine and rainbows."

"Still, it was inappropriate to get your parents involved. They didn't need to hear it."

"They're a part of this family too, Roman. They can't only hear the good stuff. Though, personally, I'm glad Drew and Will weren't here for it."

Roman turned to face Mikaél. Mikaél didn't move his sight off the impossible view of the backyard. "Think it would have been too much for you?"

"I *know* it would have been too much." Mikaél laughed uneasily. "Just like you, there will be a day I'm going to have to face all that."

"He knows we're pregnant, right?"

"Mhm. I texted him. No, wait. That's right. He texted me."

"What did he say?"

"Just one word: Congratulations." Mikaél lightly clapped his hands.

"Not quite the gusto I was hoping for."

Mikaél see-sawed his head in thought. "I have a brother too, you know. I know how it works. I didn't show that much enthusiasm when he announced his mate's pregnancy. He's only returning the favor."

"You know what I think we need?" Roman asked.

"Oh, please share." Mikaél wrapped his arms tightly around the ones which held him.

"We should go home, sit in our jacuzzi tub, put on a little music, light a few candles, eat a little chocolate, and then we can discuss our favorite topic of how we're going to plan our future."

Mikaél curled his lips and pushed his eyes up. "Speaking of, I have a new development on that."

CHAPTER 03:

TO ADMIT NO ONE IS SAFE

"How come every other time we report to Paul it feels like we're holding our heads in shame in the principal's office?" Dustin lamented.

Jake gave a chuckle and pointed. "Because that's exactly what it is."

Dr. Paul Birowack walked in that morning with a chipper disposition. Behind him walked a man as tall and fit as a professional ball player. His lab coat barely fit his frame. His tanned model-like appearance could have fooled anyone into thinking he was Gray City's next big celebrity. Both Dustin and Jake stared at each other, not knowing who the stranger was. The situation left them nervous; the last time they were introduced to a new doctor, they both nearly had a heart attack.

They remembered that moment clearly: Dr. Ehan Zang had arrived two weeks ago to deliver the most earth-shattering news they had heard yet, on October 13th no less. In a double dose, they were informed by both he and Dr. Birowack of their lesser status as doctors in the study of rare Blood-Types including Type 6. The second was the epic revelation that Roman and Mikaél had the potential to produce a female child—the first in over 200 years since their eradication in the Pre-Wolf Era. As was the standard, both fathers chose to keep this monumental information a secret from their sons and mates. Instead, they hid behind the equally certain theory Mikaél's pregnancy carried deadly consequences for both him and the pup growing inside him. Their willingness to divulge that particular information was not only late but also futile.

"Gentlemen." Dr. Birowack gestured to them.

Jake swallowed hard with the nerves caught in his throat. He led Dustin to his office. "Here we go," he sang under his breath.

The door shut to reveal a satisfied look on Dr. Birowack's face. "Dr. Johannes, I'd like you to meet my constituents: Dr. Jacob Erricson and Dr. Dustin Cavenbelle."

"Kenneth. But please, call me Ken." His palm reached out to both. "Jake."

"Dustin."

Ken stood next to Dr. Birowack in a way that made comparing the two very easy. Dr. Birowack neared the age of 60. In addition to his once straggly gray hair, he had trimmed his gray beard in the last couple of weeks. He stood equally tall to this new Dr. Kenneth Johannes but was nowhere as fit—his belly rounder and shoulders weaker.

Ken, however, had a head of full coiffed peppered hair, stylish, black-framed glasses, and a close-trimmed mustache and beard equally matching the colors of his locks. The most noticeable trait was his youthful disposition. He clearly hadn't touched the age of 40 yet, which made him the youngest man in the room.

Dr. Birowack continued, "I am happy to announce Dr. Johannes will be the latest addition to our leadership team. He will be working directly with you in our efforts on Type 6."

Dustin scrunched his face in confusion. "I'm elated, of course. But, Paul, without Matthew Whitmore's funds coming in, can we afford this addition?"

"Our existence is not based solely on the contributions of one individual, Dustin. Also, with our recent," he paused, "discoveries, both Dr. Zang and Dr. Dasu have gathered other funds to help support our endeavors here since our location is of the greatest interest."

Jake stepped in. "Just how much, uh, does Ken know, Paul, about such recent developments?"

Dr. Birowack acknowledged Ken in the room which told him to speak for himself.

"I have been briefed on the recent developments with your son Roman as a Type 6 Alpha. I am excited to say I've also heard of the possibility of a Type 6 Omega in our midst."

"Possibility?" Jake commented. He inspected his boss to confirm such statement.

"Yes, Jake. The *possibility*," he confirmed. Dr. Birowack chose to hold such a definitive discovery close to his chest apparently. "Which brings me to my next question. Were you and Dustin able to discuss with your sons the imperative recommendation they move to the Western Territory in order to monitor and deliver this pregnancy?"

The events of Saturday night's dinner weren't far in the back of neither Jake nor Dustin's minds. A tender subject to say the least.

"The evening did not go as planned," Jake began. "There were other issues, and the subject didn't even come close to being brought up."

Dr. Birowack scanned both doctors in a moment of disbelief. "Gentleman, need I remind you this is not only for the sake of science, but for the lives of your son and grandchild? The timetable for this is fleeting."

Dustin intercepted. "We are more than aware, Paul. This is not lost on us; I promise you that."

"Why the hesitation then?"

Jake confessed, "We are walking a delicate line between forgiveness and recommendations. My son and I are struggling to mend that relationship."

Dr. Birowack held his head. "That is concerning news for the future. And you and your son, Dustin?" he asked, hoping his efforts had borne fruit.

Dustin cleared his throat. He thought the question uncomfortable in front of Jake since his outcome played out so differently. "I think Mikaél and I are headed in the right direction."

"Now, there's some good news," Dr. Birowack commented. "Is there any reason why you couldn't see yourself probing the matter in the next day or two?"

The dinner played through Dustin's mind. There was one thing in particular he was worried about. "Mikaél claims he's having subconscious fears of being attacked because of his new Blood-Type."

Dr. Birowack cocked his head. "Is that so?"

"My thought is if we push the need for him to relocate to the Western Territory, it's only going to further fuel this irrational thought that he needs to fear for his safety just for being who he is."

"Irrational thoughts they are not!" Dr. Birowack's voice came strong. It put everyone in the room on high alert. "We may be in the latest and greatest century of the times, gentlemen, but let's not forget what the real world is like outside our beautiful, gated communities and safe havens. Primitive views still exist even in the most progressive of cities and towns. Our city is eclectic. I may not be the thriving youth I once was, but I know enough that when the moon rises and falls, the tolerance level of the creatures of the night goes with it. Alphas travel in packs. They may know better now not to attack a Type 6 Alpha these days, but Mikaél is a new enigma in this world. Scenting Mikaél's advanced pregnancy pheromones will trigger the insatiable curiosity of any man out there looking to make a point for himself or the people around him. As you know, no positive actions come from needing to prove their worth."

Dustin held up his hands in frustration. "Paul, I don't see how telling my son 'If you step outside, you might get raped' is going to convince him to move the Western Territory. You want to talk about primitive views? Um, hello? Do you remember what it's like out there? Nothing but one-horse towns. They catch Mikaél's scent out there, and they'll have him and the pup on the menu in a bistro!"

"Dustin." Jake gave him a stare which meant he was going too far in his commentary.

Dr. Birowack narrowed his view. "I hope you are not suggesting the town my colleague chooses to raise his own family in is nothing more than a backward group of intolerant cannibals carrying torches and pitchforks?"

Dustin rubbed his eyes with his palms. "I'm scared, Paul! Okay? You're right."

"About?" Dr. Birowack asked.

"Science does a great job taking everything in life and making it black and white. The decisions even then can be tough. Telling my son to venture out there at the mercy of strangers frightens me to death. How can I advocate this for him if I myself am struggle with accepting it?"

Dr. Birowack nodded. He understood Dustin's position, even though he himself never had nor ever would find himself in the same situation. As a Beta, he wasn't pressured by society to fit the traditional timeline of finding a mate and settling down. He also didn't possess any natural urges to procreate. As a Beta, he couldn't conceive any offspring. This also circled back to why he most likely didn't have a mate. Betas usually had to campaign for themselves to snag an Alpha or Omega mate. Betas were, of course, more willing to make a life with another Beta, but even then, that took the time and energy of wanting it. Single and fatherless, Dr. Birowack, as far as both Jake and Dustin knew, spent his life as an eternal bachelor.

"I may have made an error in allowing Dr. Zang to come in and leave after only a few days' time. All the imperative information he gave, including about his facility and residence, must have been hard to hold onto. So, I will reiterate. St. Capricorn is a beautiful town terraced on the rocky hills of Gray Falls. What it loses in tall skyscrapers and fast-paced city life, it more than makes up in culture and community. No one locks their doors at night and the young boys play in the street. You may only find one or two hotels and restaurants, but they're the best accommodations you'll find compared to most places. Many of its citizens work at Dr. Zang's facility. He is a hub for their state. The whole town is a family out there. An attack on anyone there is an attack on them. They will be protected."

"This is stupid," Dustin replied. "Why don't we just go there with them?" He beckoned to Jake for instantaneous support.

Dr. Birowack didn't give much time for it to sink in. "Please respect me enough, Dustin, that when this situation arose, I already pondered such option," Dr. Birowack implored.

"What stopped you from considering?"

"We are the most prominent hospital and research facility around. Gray City wishes they have what we have. And as such, there is a lot of weight on our shoulders for our investors and community to keep this place on the pedestal it deserves. I can't have my figureheads and top doctors gone for the gestational stage, birth, and aftercare of this child. No one else can assist in leading this center of over five thousand employees. Once again, as it's been said, it's quite the gamble for Mikaél to have the birth here. There's not enough privacy, and even though we have the best research facility, Dr. Zang's hospital is quintessential in this case."

Scratching his head, Dustin started to become desperate. Scanning around the room, his gaze targeted the new employee. "Ken!" Dustin remarked.

"I'm sorry?" Dr. Birowack questioned.

"Ken is here to be our partner. Jake and I will train him. In a month, we'll go with the boys. It will be a smooth transition like we never left."

Dr. Birowack's breath caught in his throat. He shut his eyes and opened them, ready for a confession. "Jake, Dustin. I'm afraid I can't have Ken taking your stead after a month. I was being serious when I said he was joining the leadership team."

The confusion hit both of them. Dustin continued, "What are you saying, Paul? Are you doubting our training abilities?"

"Not your training abilities. Your leadership."

Jake threw his head forward, certain there was a misunderstanding in his words. "Excuse me, Ken. Can we have the room?" Ken acknowledged without a word and left, closing the door behind him. "You want to explain that statement?"

Dr. Birowack stood straighter and put his hands on his hips. He embodied a strong Alpha. "Fate has clearly put you both in positions to discover the true abilities of your children, and it's a gift. But that alone has demonstrated to me it's a full-time job and then some." He exhaled and shook his head. "You two are too close to this. I can't have a leader here who is going to carry out decisions clouded by their personal family shortfalls. I don't know how much or how long we'll desire the input of your sons and your *granddaughter,* but I won't be on this earth long enough to guide you in this venture."

Granddaughter. The word was still unfathomable. A heavy feeling hit the pit of Jake's stomach. "Paul, is he your replacement?"

The morning sun went dark. Dr. Birowack saw the clouds overtake it. "Yes."

Dustin felt the wind getting knocked out of him.

Jake stood his ground and crossed his arms. "So, where the hell did Ken come from? Downstairs? Obviously, not from customer service."

"Dr. Johannes is actually a native of Gemini. He has quite the history of coming from poverty and working his way up the ranks. His reference confirms that. He studied at Devonshire as Dr. Campo's protégé—he confirms his triumph over adversity."

"I don't understand. You hired him over a sob story?" Jake's attitude soured.

Dr. Birowack's patience wore thin. "Don't let your envy cloud your better senses, Dr. Erricson." Saying Jake's formal title came down condescending. "This decision was nothing less than professional. I will reassure you I took all the necessary steps assessing his quality. Regardless, I am your superior and do not need to justify any decision I make. He is here. He is joining our team. And he is your supervisor apparent. I suggest you both get used to it."

Jake made no hesitation in escaping from Dr. Birowack's office. Once again, there was an aura of his entire lab feeling anomalous. Correction—*Dr. Birowack's* lab. He had made that very clear. Simply put, this was a betrayal. In the ten years he'd worked under him, Jake never felt so small. It was hard to fathom, especially when he saw Ken already giving orders to an employee out of the corner of his eye. Minimal advice, most likely, but no less vexing.

This was karma, the only logical explanation. The punishment for his botched authority over his son and son-in-law bit back. Hard. Knowing he wasn't going to be able to concentrate in the lab for the rest of the day, he grabbed his jacket and headed out the door. As he waited for the elevator, Ken stepped out also, standing by. The pain of penalty ensued until the very last possible minute. An elevator chimed and the door opened. Jake was sure the long descent down the fifteen floors wasn't going to stop at the bottom. It was going to bypass the first floor and descend into Hell. Both men stepped in, and the doors closed.

After an initial silence, Ken turned his head and observed the statue of a man standing next to him. "I want you to know I am eternally grateful to be here. I know just how lucky I am. The renowned Tauris Research Medical Center is a beacon known far and wide."

Jake nodded his head as if it was made of rusted metal. His voice was tepid. "Indeed."

"I also want you to know, to me, you are an expert, and I am a humble pupil. I am of the mindset and philosophy I am nothing more than your equal. It will be important for us to accomplish so much more that way." Ken beamed with optimism.

Jake shook his head. "You might want to erase that mindset, Dr. Johannes. My career, as well as five thousand employees, will one day be in your hands. We are dependent on prestige, investor funding, and political support. A team we may be. But to advocate us as equals will demonstrate weakness for those who think you rely on friendship and bias to survive in your position." Jake shifted his focus to the floor. "Now, I'm not sure how much you heard, if any, of the conversation after you left. But Dr. Birowack was right. I have forgotten my place in this organization once again. I hope for your sake, when Dr. Birowack steps down, you don't forget yours."

Ken's expression sank. He stood there in awe of the eloquent doctor next to him. This cold introduction wasn't what he imagined. Sure, this move was going to come with some trepidation, but he didn't anticipate this. The chime of the elevator was bittersweet. The opening doors provided new oxygen in a stale encounter. Unfortunately, the doors also represented a lasting stain on his first day of work. A drop of regret hit his heart in his decision to join these ranks.

"Good day, Dr. Johannes. See you tomorrow."

CHAPTER 04:

TO HAVE FRIENDS LIKE THESE

"Wow," Tyler said as he grabbed another warm, crispy french fry. "You know, I'm not sure what's worse: the fact your lives as you knew it imploded or the fact it took so long to tell us." His answer was blunt, but his gray eyes showed his sympathy.

Rixen was offended. "I hope between the two, the answer is easy."

Grant added his opinion while inspecting the craftmanship of his chicken sandwich. "Guys, I have to agree with Tyler. If this is something you all are proud of, why didn't you tell us sooner?" Grant always had a wisdom about him. He did a good job of challenging his friends' viewpoints. Not as a judgement, but as authentic concern. It was the work of an educated Beta. No one had any doubts Grant was destined for success. He carried himself like a high-end manager or consultant.

Ryan defended his brother's statement. "Come on. I think it's fair to say we deserved some time to get used to the adjustment, too. It's not every day 19-year-olds abandon their parents' house."

As the youngest sons of Jake and Adrian Erricson, the twin brothers Ryan and Rixen were indeed making quite the leap of faith in their newfound freedom. Some even considered it foolish since parents, especially High-Type parents, gladly supported their sons while they continued their final years of education. That being said, there were circumstances which garnered exception. Declaring an unsupported polyamorous relationship was apparently one of them. And that wasn't even the most noteworthy detail of the matter.

"It's also not every day brothers have an incestuous relationship," Grant added.

"There are worse things happening in the world, Grant. It's not as if this or a poly relationship is unheard of," Ryan rebutted.

Grant considered the claim. "I suppose there are plenty of accounts of it happening in history. But the claims were for the survival of the species or securing Blood Type purity." He sat back in his chair and popped a deep-fried cheese ball in his mouth.

Garrace grew intolerant of their friends' criticism. "That's what the history books wrote down. Not sure there ever has been a written account of anyone saying they did it for entertainment value." As he sipped his refreshing caramel carbonation, he locked down on Grant's green eyes and bright freckled face. His summer redness had faded in the last few months.

Grant wasn't deterred from his interrogations. "Are you sure you didn't hesitate to tell us because your relationship isn't working out? Poly relationships are notorious for failing when one person feels ignored or unfairly treated. In this situation, Garrace, you're competing against blood relatives. That's quite the loyalty bond."

Rixen countered. "That's not why." He found himself trying to come up with a believable excuse. Luckily, he was also working on a generous bite of his Prowler burger which gave him extra time. "Relatively speaking, Grant, this is a new experience for us. It's not as simple as declaring ourselves in a relationship on social media. There's a lot to work through and consider." He glanced at his boyfriends, hoping he had their support.

Tyler felt he had an easy opening. "Working through something ... like you're having issues?"

Garrace grunted. "All relationships have issues, guys. Quit making it sound like we have to be perfect just because we're unconventional."

Rixen ran his fingers through his hair and Ryan licked his teeth. Having the balls to announce their relationship with each other and Garrace was one thing. Having the balls to take the criticism, constructive or not, was quite another. The brothers mirrored each other's expression of subtle disappointment. It had been nice to avoid outward opinions for the past month. Both found it hard to believe it was weeks ago they moved out of their parents' house. The trauma of it all made it seem like yesterday. The glimpse of their Veo's heart breaking and their Sur's fury upon their discovery was burned into their skulls.

On the other hand, it was refreshing when Garrace reached down between the brothers and held their hands below the table in the restaurant. It wasn't typical for Garrace to care for a lover so intently with a tender heart. He was known for skin deep affection when it came to relationships. Most of the time, his high expectations and dreams for a relationship never came to fruition. A polyamorous relationship was a distant fantasy come true. The cherry on top was sitting between two very equally attractive human beings.

For Garrace, the twins' near identical appearance made it easy to worship their physical attributes equitably. Their lightly tanned skin allowed their blond hair with natural highlights to shine through beautifully. Their cheekbones, lips, noses, mild muscle definition, and blue eyes were all so perfect. In spite of their near carbon copy appearance, Garrace, and all who knew them well, didn't find it difficult to tell the two apart. Ryan's face was more masculine and rugged. Rixen's was feminine and softer. It also mimicked their personality. The Yin and Yang—and Garrace was the divine line in the middle.

Tyler scanned the restaurant. Prowler Burger was packed this Thursday evening. In order to maintain an inconspicuous atmosphere, he leaned in and whispered with a grin. "So, how's the sex?"

Everyone at the table groaned in response, except for Garrace. He wasn't shy about his accomplishments in bed. After all, he had quite the pumped-up ego obtaining two boyfriends instead of one. "Never a dull moment, that's for sure. It's quite the sensation to be 'on' at all times. It's intoxicating."

Tyler maintained a subtle look of entertainment as he scanned Garrace up and down. There was a hint of jealous pheromones exuding from him. It wasn't because of Garrace personally—more the fact he was a dominating Alpha. For anyone to have two partners wanting and willing was an experience itself. To be an *Alpha* with two partners was a power trip.

"What exactly do *you* two do?" Grant had both elbows on the table with his fists pushed together. Both index fingers split off in the direction of Rixen and Ryan, calling their attention.

"What do you mean?" Rixen asked.

Grant elaborated. "I'm saying we've been sitting here for an hour discussing nothing other than your poly-relationship, and this entire time I have been fully under the impression this is not purely a 'share Garrace' type situation. You two come across just as much into each other."

Ryan twitched. "So?"

Tyler acknowledged Grant as he picked up on his train of thought.

"I'm asking," Grant emphasized, "are you two ... intimately involved with each other just as much as you are with Garrace?"

Garrace turned his head both directions, signaling he was deferring to the twins.

Ryan sat back in his chair and crossed his arms.

Rixen laid his arms on the table. He took a moment to fixate on the floor and then returned. "We are."

Tyler's eyes grew wide, and his mouth dropped. "Holy shit."

Not showing an immediate reaction of aversion was difficult for Grant. But he knew the only way to keep their friendship was to stay as non-judgmental as possible, even if he didn't agree with practically everything they were doing. He opted to rub the red stubble of hair on his neck instead as he processed the new information. "Do you three have goals?"

"Goals?" Ryan's head snapped back.

"Yeah. Goals. You know: long term goals, aspirations, plans, desires. And I mean outside of the bedroom." Grant shifted his weight. "Wanted to clarify that."

Ryan wiped his lips with a napkin while contemplating the question. "We're content with what's going on now."

"Is it sustainable?" Grant asked.

"Our dads, although removed from our lives, have given us an allowance. They pay our portion of the rent and our car payment and insurance. We're responsible for anything else. I work part time at a gym and Rix is at a customer service desk for an airline. We've decided we're waiting until next year to start planning out futures. It's a steep learning curve doing what we've done already."

Tyler narrowed his eyes. "Wait, I thought you said your Sur kicked you out and said, 'sink or swim'?"

Rixen clarified. "Our Veo has more heart than that. He persuaded him to not leave us basically homeless."

Tyler lifted his head. "And you, Garrace? How is your family taking all of this?"

Garrace laughed. "Heh. My Sur wouldn't have even noticed if I moved Ryan and Rix into my childhood bedroom, let alone notice me moving out. If I recall, there was a 'whatever' comment thrown into it. My Veo, on the other hand, is the most liberal person I know."

"What? Did he ask if he could join your love circle?" Tyler joked.

"No, dipshit," Garrace threw out. "He said he was happy for me that I was exploring my 'limitless realm of pleasure' as he put it. He frickin' blessed me with sage."

"Ew." Tyler winced.

"Are you sure it wasn't pot? *That's* what you smelled like." Rixen laughed.

"Hm. Maybe there was a bit of that, too." Garrace winked back at him.

Ryan took notice of Garrace's words. This wasn't the first time he'd heard the story, of course. But this was the first time he ever heard him give the account to someone else. His delivery was confident and dare he say smug. Back when he had first heard of Garrace's relationship with Rixen, Ryan could think of nothing else other than what he heard through the grapevine. Other than being a tall pretty boy with dark hair and a large tool in his pants, no other gossip was complimentary. The rumors of Garrace's apparent entitlement when it came to courting his date and dictating relationships didn't make Ryan want to run into his waiting arms. Many others did, however, including his brother Rixen. Like everyone else, his brother was entranced by the boyish looks and innocent smile that made Garrace appear wholesome and safe like Wolf-God himself.

"Are you working too?" Grant inquired.

"Sure am," Garrace replied. "I work at Brookside Books."

"Oooh," Tyler crooned. "Not a bad place to work."

Garrace agreed. "I like it. Plus, in addition to the store merchandise, I get 40% anything from their coffeeshop. I'm addicted to their mocha iced coffees and flourless peanut butter cookies."

"Hey, if I go there when you're working, can you sneak me the employee discount?" Tyler flashed him his pearly whites and batted his eyes.

"No way! I don't want to get fired. But you at least you get to see my pretty face." He smirked back like a privileged model.

"Why would you get fired? I can just give you my reading list and you can buy them right before your shift ends. And movies!" Tyler gasped. "They have movies! Oh, man! 40% off... you have to help me!"

"Not happening," Garrace repeated.

"*Please*!" Tyler puffed out his lips like a puppy dog.

Garrace tapped his foot and twitched his mouth. He ached in defeat. "Okay. *One* movie and two books. That's it."

"Yes!" Tyler hissed.

Ryan glanced at his cell phone. It was the perfect act to precede an exit. "Okay, guys," he huffed. "I know I have some homework tonight to get done for tomorrow. So, I think this is where we depart."

The announcement caught the group off-guard a bit. But it was true they had been in each other's company for a couple of hours at this point. Hugs were exchanged before they left the restaurant.

"Just want you three to know, I'm here for you," Grant said, bundling up his coat.

"Same from me!" Tyler added.

Garrace drove everyone back to the apartment in his car. Rixen sat in the passenger seat while Ryan occupied the back. A few general comments were volleyed back and forth about how the night went well overall—especially since they took a big step in announcing it to the first people other than their family members. Garrace had not shared with the twins he had told Mikaél in confidence—a move which hadn't proved to be regrettable yet.

But after the light review of the evening, the car was silent for a short drive home. When they arrived back to the apartment, Rixen gave an exhausted exhale and laid his long body on the couch. He patted his full stomach and popped his lips.

Garrace smiled and walked over, admiring the living piece of art on the furniture. "How are you doing?"

"Good," Rixen mumbled. "It was nice to do that. Feels like a weight lifted off my chest."

"I agree," Garrace replied. He turned to Ryan who was walking past the kitchen and down the hall. "Where are you going?"

"To the bedroom."

"Come here." Garrace gestured his head. Ryan walked up gingerly. Garrace threw his arms around his shoulders and pushed their foreheads together. After getting Ryan's focused attention, he planted a deep kiss on him. "How are *you* doing?"

"So-So" was Ryan's short reply.

Rixen lifted his head off the couch. "What's wrong?"

"I don't know. I mean, did anyone else feel like we were being interrogated?"

Neither Garrace nor Rixen appeared to share his sentiment.

"Oh, brother of mine," Rixen teased. "I think you are worrying too much about what they think."

"I agree," Garrace added. "Tyler and Grant are probably the most neutral guys to tell all this to. If we're not confident when we talk to them, it's not going to be pretty when the general public finds out."

"I get that," Ryan acknowledged. "It's just hard to deal with Grant sometimes acting like a wise elder on the whole situation as if he's an expert on poly relationships. Or just relationships in general."

Rixen pondered the comment. "You actually care about what he thinks, don't you?"

There was a pause before Ryan agreed. "He's always been someone I could trust. It's been nice relying on his opinion. Our thoughts and ideas about how relationships work have always been in sync."

"He is a Beta," Rixen commented.

Ryan narrowed his gaze on his brother. "What's that supposed to mean?"

"All I'm saying is Grant is like you in the sense he's clearly found himself a hobby to take up all his time instead of focusing on relationships and stuff."

"Care to share your conclusions, Dr. Erricson?" Ryan replied sarcastically.

"You immersed yourself in every sport and then ran away to the gym. It allowed you to bypass the experience and scrutiny of a relationship. On the other hand, those are skills I have exercised quite well, no thanks to you." As Ryan began to puff up in defense, Rixen held up his hands to prevent Round 1 in the fighting ring. "Not that I'm looking to argue on the matter. Just stating a fact." Ryan relaxed while still passing his nonverbal judgement on Rixen's claim. "And any person after spending five minutes with Grant knows he reads sociology books like other guys read porn."

"You *read* porn?" Garrace teased.

Rixen blushed. "Maybe?"

Garrace stuck out his tongue and then returned to the conversation at hand. "Grant probably reads all those books because that's his version of a social life," he concluded.

"Um, guys? This is my friend you're talking about," Ryan huffed. "And I'm feeling a little attacked here since there seems to be this theme talking about how Betas are somehow inept in the social department." He crossed his arms as he leered at his two lovers with disdain.

"Oh, you don't need to be so defensive," Garrace lightly assessed. He angled himself to give Ryan's neck a wet peck. He walked around to the front of the couch, and Rixen automatically adjusted himself to allow Garrace to sit. As he rounded the corner, he grabbed Ryan's hand and pulled him to the couch on top of him. Ryan straddled him with a neutral face. He massaged Ryan's muscular thighs through his soft jeans. "You are the perfect Beta for me. You're beautiful, smart, and sexy as hell."

After receiving a smile of approval from Ryan, he then turned his attention to Rixen. Reaching out his hand, he pulled him much closer into the fold. "*You* are all those things plus a nice little submissive Omega."

Rixen moaned playfully. "Hm. What are you going to do about that?"

Garrace pushed modesty aside as he used one hand to massage between Ryan's thighs and the other to do the same to Rixen. Doing it elicited closed eyes and open-mouthed moans from both of his lovers. "I think," he whispered, "we need to practice more of that intoxicating sex I mentioned to Tyler and Grant earlier."

Rixen gasped seductively. "I have no problem with that."

"Me neither," Ryan added.

That was all Garrace needed to pull Ryan's shirt off. Upon seeing his silky, smooth defined chest, Garrace threw his head forward and began licking and sucking every inch of him.

As Ryan massaged Garrace's head, he saw Rixen push himself off the couch. He heard him peel off his own shirt and throw it to the floor. The heat from Rixen's body was tantalizing in itself before he closed the gap behind him. With Rixen's equally smooth chest pressed behind him, Ryan gave another sound of approval as he took in his brother's iced pear scent.

Rixen latched onto Ryan's neck with his teeth. He heard his brother's growl and threw his head back. The sound sent shivers up and down his body. As he wrapped his arms around his brother's chest, it was a moment for Ryan to lift Garrace's shirt off his body.

Feeling the magnetism of it all, Garrace pushed Ryan off of himself and all three lovers stood there. He gazed at the twins, a lustful Rixen holding a charmed Ryan. This time, Garrace chased Rixen down, embracing him as he once did Ryan.

Having a front row seat, Ryan observed the two in a passionate lip lock. He walked up to them both and began to run his hands down their backs. When Garrace was done licking Rixen's lips, he turned and pulled Ryan in.

Garrace pushed Ryan's head toward them and all three began a complimentary massage with their mouths. Exercising this act was a favorite of theirs. This was a taste of serenity. It was one of the few demonstrations of love they could show each other which was equal. No one had to worry about giving or receiving, doing too much or too little, or searching for what felt good. This was the center of their strength.

"Damn," Garrace moaned, "you two are amazing."

"Hm, did you hear that, Rix? He complimented us." Ryan massaged the back of Garrace's neck.

"Sure did. What do you think we should do in return?" Rixen asked slyly.

Ryan didn't reply. He decided his actions spoke louder than words, using his strong arms to manhandle Garrace's pants down. As he stood there bare, Ryan pushed him back on the couch.

Rixen nodded. "I'm all for that."

"Me too." Garrace grinned like a Cheshire cat, put his hands behind his head, and enjoyed the sight as two mouths descended. Little sparks hit his body. His mind struggled to narrow down each and every one. Ryan and Rixen's tender attention to his arms and neck sent pulses down his stomach. When they reached his taut nipples and sucked equally, it sent him into hyperdrive.

The trail of wet tongues went down farther. Merely scenting his mates pulsed his cock into being rock hard. So, when he anticipated making love to them both, it was complimented with a long line of pre-cum dripping all the way down to the base. Rixen caught the reflection of the clear gloss and was the first to lap it up with his tongue. Garrace's body convulsed, not expecting the sensation to be so powerful. Soon, Rixen made the thick head of Garrace's manhood disappear. The hot wet mouth sent a full wave of pleasure down to the swollen orbs underneath the base of his cock. He saw Ryan shift his head lower to take each out and suck slowly. He put one hand on each brother and sent waves of approval through his fingers.

To Rixen, there was a welcomed challenge in trying to take in all of Garrace's large cock. On a good attempt, he was able to manage more than half. He dreamed of the day he could please his mate with its entire length down his throat. The idea of exercising this ability daily drove him wild. With Garrace well-lubed from his attempts, he pulled his mouth off and let his brother have his turn. He stood up and shared his efforts as he tongue-thrusted into Garrace's mouth as Ryan descended.

Ryan was somehow able to make it look effortless, even though he himself couldn't take Garrace all the way to the hilt. In long strokes, he could feel Garrace throb in his throat. Ryan could hear him moan into Rixen's mouth as they kissed. Unable to contain himself, Ryan unbuttoned his own pants and pulled his own hard cock out and stroked it.

Garrace's moans became louder and less controlled. "I'm getting close," he gasped.

Upon hearing it, Rixen slumped down right to his brother's mouth. He witnessed his brother master his skills in a regular rhythm on his and Garrace's cock. Not wanting to be left out, he pulled out his own aching length. In a forward move, he grabbed onto his brother's cock and began stroking it for him. He moaned loudly himself when he felt Ryan's hand go to him as well.

The sound of Ryan's ecstatic moans pierced the inner chambers of Rixen's ears, sending lightning bolts straight through him. He watched fluid shoot out toward his brother. A line of cum even landed on his brother's shaft.

Upon feeling the hot liquid splatter on him, Ryan came next. Since Ryan curved up a bit more, the visual orgasm was more of a fountain. The first few shots went halfway up his chest and ran down past his stomach.

Soon, Garrace's large sack tensed below the base of his cock. Ryan threw his head back and rubbed Garrace's cock continuously. When Garrace's moans became louder, he knew it was time.

Both brothers held their mouths just below the pulsing cock head. Hot waves of orgasm splashed out. As Garrace's vision blurred from ecstasy, it was difficult to concentrate on who was enjoying his seed more. In what must have been a minute later, he saw and smelled his lovers covered in his scent. It was rare for any other rank to rival the semen production of an Alpha, and Garrace was a testament to it. The brothers shared his love by embracing each other and brushing their mouths on one another.

A few moments later, both looked at Garrace and gave him the same treatment. After using his own shirt to clean up the extensive mess, he smiled. "What did I do to deserve you two?"

"Well," Rixen began, "getting the apartment helped."

Garrace groaned in pleasure since Rixen knew he wasn't going to let that go unpunished. He grabbed onto Rixen's sides and repeatedly massaged his fingers in. Ryan joined his efforts and soon all three boys ended upon the floor with Rixen beneath them both in agonizing laughter.

"All right! Mercy!" Rixen pleaded.

Garrace chuckled. "Love you, Rix. Love you, Ryan."

"Love you too," Rixen replied.

Ryan kissed both of his boyfriends. "Love you both."

CHAPTER 05:

TO TRICK AND TO TREAT

Whispers could be heard in the elegant board room. The gathering was not at the typical location, but a hotel near the ocean shore. Men comfortably in their 30's and older discussed theories and assumptions as to why they were called there, soothing their nerves with freshly ground coffee and delectable morning treats.

The man of the hour stood in front of a white screen and addressed all who sat at the large cherry-stained table. "Members of the board, I am grateful to each and every one of you for taking the time to attend this last-minute meeting on such short notice."

Mr. Donahue replied on behalf of the members there. "Mr. Whitmore, we are glad to respond to the call of duty at any time. Our loyalty to this company is without question. Its needs are our needs. But if I may, I think I speak for all the board members here when I say I'm very surprised you've called less than half of us here. Five members of the board isn't anywhere near quorum bylaws."

A proud Matthew Whitmore delighted in the response. He already anticipated every hesitation and every question these powerful individuals could have. "I am well aware of the bylaws within the company, Mr. Donahue. After all, I took a part in writing them." Subtle laughter was shared throughout the room. Mr. Donahue was not deterred from his inquisitive expression. "No. Today, I have called you here for a personal favor and request." He couldn't help but follow with a dramatic pause. "I am asking each and every one of you here in this room to voluntarily resign your positions immediately and have the paperwork signed, sealed, and delivered no later than 5PM this evening."

Faces paled and mouths held open far too long. Side conversations developed immediately. One board member couldn't get Mr. Donahue's focused attention, so he continued his urgent pleas to the side of his face. Mr. Donahue held a hand up to stop his incessant conversation, ending all others as well.

"This does *not* sound like a voluntary request at all," Mr. Donahue sneered.

Matthew howled. "Come on, Mark. You know me. I have never forced a board member to do anything here. Everything in this company has been professional and democratic."

Mr. Donahue squinted. "That may be. But those with opposing views in this company seem to retire early or get voted in the next fiscal year."

"All coincidences, I assure you. As you said yourself, the board is merely here for the good of the company. Those who have left ceremoniously—or not—understand how deep the dedication runs behind these doors."

"Which brings me to my question, Matthew: are we leaving ceremoniously or 'not'?"

Matthew shrugged off Mr. Donahue's concern. "I make a promise to all of you right now. If none of you choose to step down, you will continue in your position without any fear of retaliation from me. Even so, your futures are better left up to your fellow board mates compared to me, especially at this junction."

Mr. Donahue nodded and pointed a finger at his evasive employer. "And *that's* the part we haven't been told yet. Why? Why are you asking me and my esteemed colleagues here to give up what some have worked their entire lives here for? Surely, you agree there is a need for explanation here?"

"Yes, and there will be." Matthew scanned all the members around the table as if they were waiting for a doomsday declaration. "It just won't happen today."

None of the board members could believe their ears. Dissention and criticism filled the air. The atmosphere became thick and musty as five pious Alpha businessmen rushed their scent back onto Matthew, as if it wasn't clear before his suspenseful shutout.

"You can't be serious!" Mr. Donahue declared. His decorum faded as his frustration pushed through. "I'm afraid you're going to have to do better than that. We need to know what purpose this serves, or my answer will be very easy along with my recommendation to the other four members present today. That is to speak nothing of informing the other six board members of this highly unorthodox request."

Matthew assessed the tension in the room. *Perfect*. "Mr. Donahue, I apologize to you and the board. You're right. This was an unfair request to ask all of you with such little preparation and no warning. That is not how a great leader does business. In my defense, I, myself have not had a lot of time to process the realization I made only days ago." *A lie*. Keen ears listened in. "I am asking—no—needing for you five, strong, intelligent men to take a leap of faith with me and join me in a new venture."

Murmurs were heard throughout the room. The bait had been laid.

"I assume it would be futile to ask what this new venture entails?" Mr. Donahue asked.

Matthew nodded in dismay. "Unfortunately, I'm in a situation where I can't reveal what my venture is until I have the faith and backing of the men I am now so humbling asking to once again see the potential in me to make a bold decision and be more than satisfied in its result."

Another board member came across and whispered into Mr. Donahue's ear. In return, Mr. Donahue echoed the inquiry. "What guarantee do we have that this unknown venture is something worth stepping away from our current successful position? Your risks are not our risks."

"100% agree with you. That is why, if you pledge your loyalty and support, I will make sure your severance package pays you until the end of the year. When the venture is over, it will be my recommendation that the board reinstate each and every one of you."

The pack of Alphas were surprised at such an offer. Eyebrows lifted, heads turned, and eye contact switched from criticism to curiosity. The fish nudged the bait.

Mr. Donahue still showed his skepticism. "It's reassuring to hear, but it still sounds risky."

Matthew held his arms out like a savior. "Gentlemen, I have always had your best interests in mind, and together, we have weathered many a storm with a high howl of victory at the end of each and every one. Please, you are all like family to me." He paused as he slowly walked around the perimeter of the conference table, carefully giving notice to each member waiting on his every word. "And if you remember, my son was emotionally scarred in a contract led under false pretenses, and later, my mate was physically scarred for doing what is right. Since then, I have done nothing but make sure my family was treated justly and treated well. Right here, and right now, I am extending that same oath to you."

Heads bowed. Memories of a brave man shining through the adversity came flooding back like it was yesterday. "And how is your family, Matthew?" Mr. Donahue broke the silence.

Bring it home, Matthew. "Terrence has recovered well, physically. Mentally and emotionally, he is shaken and lacking faith in his fellow man. Peyton," he moaned, "has insisted on taking a spiritual absence for the time being. It was my hope we could have been a stronger family together under one roof, but you know how kids can be." All the board members concurred with him. "With that all being said, my next journey in life is in dedication to make the world a better place. Can you all here and now make a pledge to help me make that change?"

The looks were diminutive and the acknowledgements subtle as the leaders congregated and unified their response. Mr. Donahue finalized the answer. "On this day of Harvest Moon, by 5PM this evening, you will have all five signatures ready to resign our positions. From there, we will put our faith and trust in you not leading us astray on this vision quest of yours. However, we will require a 15% increase in pay, and on Monday morning, we expect nothing less than a full disclosure on what the next steps are and why."

Hook. Line. Sinker. End game. "Excellent." Matthew walked over to the morning sun over the city. The angle of its red light was just enough for him to see his grinning reflection.

From large speaker sets, sounds filled the evening sky: bone-chilling screams, continuous bubbling, creaking doors, and ghoulish laughter. Above those sounds were children whimpering and laughing over their entrance and exit from a large, golden corn maze. The air was crisp with a rush of various smells depending on the moment of the variable wind: spicy cider, rich cocoa, grilled hot dogs, and sugary treats. Off to the side was an oversized model of a wolf shifter complete with torn human clothing, bared teeth, and a blood-thirsty expression. It pointed to the sign which read '*Enter if you dare!*' Although the sign wasn't effective at the time, soon jack-o-lanterns, glowing torches, and spotlights would control the amount of light seen on this vibrant festival, giving it the ominous atmosphere it desired.

"I can't believe on how much costumes have changed since I was a kid." Roman shook his head in amazement as he saw contemporary and modern costumes reflecting current popular trends, celebrities, and motion picture entertainment.

"They've changed even since *I've* done Trick-or-Treating. That was five years ago. But there's still some classics." Mikaél smiled as a few passed by in some of his favorite costumes: a few warlocks, skeletons, vampires, and zombies.

"You stopped going out when you were 12?" Roman asked.

"Well, yeah. Isn't that the magic number these days?" Mikaél returned.

"I suppose it was different for me. I had to take Ryan and Rixen out when I got older. Our dads shipped themselves off to a party once they decided I was old enough to watch the knuckleheads until two o'clock in the morning."

"Ah. Makes sense. Drew never took me out. He couldn't be bothered. Veo always took me out instead. Laycin and I went alone our last year." Mikaél caught his mate looking shocked at a very convincing car accident victim. "Wow! That takes talent."

"Looks like he could use some surgery."

"Good thing they have Dr. Roman Erricson here to save them," Mikaél joked.

"They have us observe surgery for clinicals, not perform them," Roman corrected.

"Don't you get to do anything fun in Sports Medicine and Physical Therapy?"

"Everything is fun in Sports Medicine and Physical Therapy! Rewarding too! To see someone walk for the first time after a bad accident—"

"You mean like prom victim back there?" Mikaél interrupted.

"Yeah," Roman laughed, "or even for the first time. There's a lot of little kids who need therapy before they even take their first step. Getting to be there and experience it with their parents—that's going to be magic right there."

Mikaél's heart warmed. "And just think, after this spring, you'll be circling expected calendar dates on RJ's first steps."

"RJ?"

"Roman Junior!"

Roman's face shifted in confusion. "I didn't know we had named him already."

"Ah, I'm just throwing names out there. Thinking out loud. Seeing what sticks." A few brave souls returned from the exit side of the corn maze. Mikaél picked up several pieces of candy and dropped them in their bags as they left. Since it was right next to the entrance, their position allowed Roman and Mikaél to be with each other the entire time. It was the most alluring part of being convinced by Mikaél's Veo to help volunteer for the annual Spotlight on the Arts Festival fundraiser. It was a safe alternative for inner-city families to enjoy the holiday rather than risk the night in downtown with all the overindulgent partygoers driving or roaming under the influence.

The festival was held each year in Tauris Park which had a generous field with benches, walkways, and built-in shelters. Half of the park disappeared into a moderately-wooded area where Roman and Mikaél stood, guarding festival patrons from entering the dicey darkness which was not part of the festivities. Instead, the festival built the corn maze leading them back to the safety of the field.

"I never asked. Do you like Harvest Moon?" Roman wondered.

Mikaél nodded. "Oh, yes. One of my favorite holidays as a matter of fact. I especially love the lore of it all."

"Really? Scared the sh—"

"Hey!" Mikaél pointed to a young pup and his father entering the maze.

"I mean scared the *fur* off of me when I was a pup." Roman smiled, hoping he appeased the leering Sur.

Mikaél bit his tongue and held his breath until they were out of sight. He exhaled. "I loved scary stories as a kid. Still do. I have a bunch of horror books still in a box at home. I think I even have one or two on Harvest Moon."

Admittingly, most of the secular celebrations surrounding Harvest Moon were still remnants of the primate-descendant's All Hollow's Eve or Halloween. Wolf-descendants weren't intolerant of the culture and traditions celebrated from their primate-descendant counterparts, but they avoided the notion most of the holidays were centered around religious ideals which only included the few and cast out the many who didn't share their belief system. So, most of the pre-existing holidays were altered in the Post-Wolf Era.

Like primate-descendants, wolf-descendants, and even wolves themselves, observed many worldly events based upon the sun and moon. Traditionally, humans used the Harvest Moon in order to collect the final crops of fall in its luminescence.

In culture and lore, on the night of Harvest Moon, Wolf-God sent his Alpha Pack down to earth each year in order to capture or "harvest" weary souls who weren't expected to survive the harsh and fruitless season of winter, thus sparing them a long and agonizing death. Using the brilliance of the moon, the Alpha Pack scanned and picked out every soul they deemed necessary of crossing over to the Spirit World: the old, the lazy, the sick, the unskilled, and helpless pups and adults. Willful humans not wishing to have their lives, or the lives of their loved ones, ended on this earth just yet disguised themselves in animal skin and fur so Wolf-God's Alpha Pack couldn't distinguish between the souls allowed to stay on earth and those needing to leave to the Spirit World. After waiting out the hours of the Harvest Moon, the humans on Earth rejoiced in celebration with the foods they cultivated from the season.

Roman scanned the festival stands from where he stood. The lights were on full display in the absence of the sun, and the essence of the holiday consumed everything in sight. Getting lost in the scent of a food stand, he didn't immediately feel a little boy in a wolf costume poking his leg.

"Hey, mister. Did you see my candy bag?" The young pup couldn't have been older than five. His face was red but not from cool night air. Traces of tears lined his face as he struggled to maintain courage in his inquiry.

The emotion melted Roman to his knees. He came down to the boy's eye level. "You know what?" he replied enthusiastically. "Earlier I happened to find a little pumpkin bag full of candy laying right here at the entrance. Does that sound like it could be yours?"

The boy's head nodded slowly, face unchanged. When Roman produced a cloth bag with a happy pumpkin on it, the pup's expression lit up and he giggled with glee. His smile reflected on Roman's face also.

"Jason?!" A frantic father called out.

"Daddy!" the boy replied. The father turned and saw his little boy jumping up and down with his newly found bag hopping and his wolf's tail wagging.

"I told you to stay with me. You could have gotten lost," the father lamented.

"The man found my bag!" the boy celebrated.

Seeing his son's refreshed holiday spirit kept the father from continuing his scolding. Instead, he looked at Roman with gratitude. "Thank you." Roman acknowledged the father as he took his son's candy bag and hoisted the boy up on his shoulders. The sounds of a parent reminding his son of caution dimmed as they became lost in the crowd.

Mikaél beamed. Roman tugged at his heartstrings.

"What?" Roman asked, taking notice of his mate's expression.

"I can't wait to see you as a father."

Roman's own heart thumped in his chest. He stepped past his post and embraced his Fate with strong arms. A warm kiss cut through the cold night. "You're going to be a great father." The shivers from Mikaél's body were noticeable. "Are you getting cold? I can see if we can leave our shift early."

"No, no! We only have about 30 minutes left. After this, you can buy me a dozen boxes of frosted cookies and a gross of hot dogs."

Roman laughed. "Deal." He went behind Mikaél and bear-hugged him to shield him from the slight breeze. It was one of his favorite places to be. Nothing in the world felt better to an Alpha than pleasuring and protecting their Omega at the same time. Except maybe the birth of their pup. That one weighed heavily on Roman's mind. The joy and energy pouring out of all the kids and parents in the festival was sensory overload. He fantasized, picturing their family walking around as patrons instead of volunteers. Thoughts of creative costumes, overpriced food, loads of candy and chocolate, and memorialized photographs excited him in a way he never expected to experience in his life. He was changing as a person, and it was just starting.

"Are you going to go back to sports this winter? It's your last chance before graduation." Mikaél's question came out of nowhere.

The shift in thought took Roman by surprise. Also, for the first time in his life, it wasn't an experience he was looking forward to. He realized a part of his life was ending permanently. "It's not an option. Clinicals keep me busy either onsite or studying sometimes until ungodly hours. Plus, you and the pup are my priority."

Mikaél's shoulders fell. "Yeah, but I don't want us to take away from your life experiences. You have to live too."

"Hey. Look at me." Roman turned and grabbed his mate's shoulders and his gaze zeroed into Mikaél's eyes. "You two are the best things in my life, and for more than six years, I have wanted nothing other than you and the pup to arrive. You are not a burden to me. Ever. Do you understand me?"

It never got old hearing his forever mate reinforce his love and loyalty. A nonverbal kiss and embrace demonstrated he understood Roman's claim. It meant everything to him and more.

The heavy door shut with an exhale coming from both men as they arrived home.

"Do you want to go to bed early?" Roman asked, throwing the keys on the counter.

"Hmm..." Mikaél scratched his chin. "I guess that depends on what you mean by 'bed.'"

Roman shined his white teeth as he walked over to his mate. "I think I'm willing to expand my initial thought." He licked his lips as he could begin to smell Mikaél's pheromone pallet of lust.

Mikaél turned and walked into the bedroom, waiting to see what his mate would do.

Roman pulled off his jacket as fast as he could and followed the young Omega. When he finally joined him, Mik was already sitting on the bed with his shirt off. "Are you playing the role of the submissive Omega or the wannabe Alpha tonight?"

"Heh. You have a preference?"

"I'm up for anything." Roman stood there like a mountain, ready to show his mate he had the endurance to do whatever was needed to please his mate.

"You're going to regret saying that," the Omega teased.

Before Roman even had time to register what his mate said, Mikaél launched himself on him, pushing his lips against his. The exchange lasted forever in his mind, but he could never get enough. They were soft and sweet like every other part of him. But Roman wanted so much more. He flipped his mate around, grabbed ahold of his neck, and began to take in his scent. It was pure intoxicating bliss. Even better was the fact it belonged to Roman. His mate and his scent belonged to him.

Shivers went down Mikaél's spine as he felt Roman's teeth gnaw on the pheromone gland in his neck. In the infancy of their relationship, Roman had to overwhelm the Omega with his Alpha pheromones to initiate a successful connection indicated by a pupil dilation. After that, Mikaél's own mating response kicked in which brought them the most satisfying lovemaking ever imagined. But that didn't need to happen anymore. Their response to each other was second nature. Reconnecting like this was a return to home and a return to euphoria. And he couldn't wait.

Based upon the increased pattern of moans Roman heard from his mate, he knew Mikaél's gland was getting ready to pulsate an orgasm. In a quick motion, Roman lifted his mate's shirt up and over his head. He returned his sharp teeth into Mikaél's neck and wrapped his arms around his stomach. As the thought of his child growing inside his mate crept into his mind, he expected their exchange to become more sensual and soft. But it didn't. It had the opposite effect. To Roman, knowing Mikaél still had his seed inside him and that he owned both drove him wild. He grunted one more time into his mate's neck and felt the skin break just a bit. The pheromone gland leaked and mixed with blood. Roman sucked on it slowly, then licked it clean, savoring his mate's sweet scent of orange and clove.

Mikaél moaned hard and pushed himself off his mate. Pregnancy had only increased his sensations and it sent him into overload quickly. Turning around, he faced his mate like a beast ready to claim what was his.

Roman had learned quickly his mate didn't have patience for shirts. His clothing budget had doubled since moving in with Mikaél. His mate kept ripping his button-down shirts, no matter how expensive, right down the middle in order to get at his chest. The sound of fabric tearing was accompanied by drops of metallic buttons over the bed and floor. It was the eternal price Roman paid for slashing Mikaél's shirt to bits the first time they met. Now, Roman successfully removed his shirts in record time to prevent the credit card from melting.

Once Mikaél saw Roman's shirt hit the floor, he grabbed hold of the back of his neck and pulled him down to give him a deep lip lock. He nipped at Roman's lower lip which caused him to open his mouth in a gasp. When he did, Mikaél darted his tongue deep into his mouth and massaged his. As he massaged Roman's pecs, even more moans seeped out. Then, he turned his attention to Roman's steamed neck.

Another thing Roman was well-prepared for was the fact Mikaél loved testing his limits on what it meant to be a strong Alpha during mating. Like Mikaél, he possessed the same pheromone gland in his neck, only larger. It also needed to be relieved in the same way—a programmed instinctual response dating back to the origin of wolves. While Roman's focus on gland reciprocation was centered on pleasure, Mikaél's was centered on pain. He wasn't the gentle Omega he once was. Roman knew what his mate wanted to see. He wanted Roman to suffer. Roman wasn't going to make it easy. Mikaél was going to have to work for it.

Licking his lower lip, Mikaél eyed his prize. The endless practice of saving his mate allowed him to know all the nuances on how to get under Roman's skin—both figuratively and literally. It started with a few bites on the collar bone and right under his chin which he performed masterfully. Then it was a few long licks right along the gland. He heard Roman moan which made him smile.

Roman felt his body tensing from the inside out. He was hoping to hold out as long as he could, but it became even more difficult when felt Mikaél's nails glide down his bare back and his teeth tug at his nipples. Finally, he felt a slender hand slip underneath the waist of his pants. The heat of his mate's hand matched the heat of his now half-hard cock which strained to get out of its confines.

Mikaél knew it wasn't these acts which would bring him to his knees; it was what he was about to do. His lips wrapped around Roman's pheromone gland and began licking, kissing, sucking softly then harder, soft again, and then even harder. As he repeated the pattern, he heard Roman's discontent grow.

Contrary to what one might think, not biting down on the pheromone gland when it was ready was a thousand times worse than biting down like an amateur wolf. To deny a Fated Mate the only relief another Fated Mate can provide was inhumane. In this scenario, it was typically an Alpha who denied an Omega their relief out of a show of dominance, wanting to bring them down begging for relief. Roman didn't partake in the barbaric practice, but he didn't stop Mikaél from doing it. Perhaps it was another one of Roman's punishments for putting Mikaél through hell when he Fated him.

That's when Roman felt it. It was like having his heart beat a hundred times in a minute. With it, a dull pain became harsher and harsher. His body was wanting him to cry out and tell Mikaél it was time give him what his body was programmed to do. But he didn't. He chose to show his mate what he was made of. At some point, Mikaél must have expertly unfastened his pants. Before he knew it, they were below his waist and his pre-cum soaked underwear were about to be next.

Mikaél pulled down the last cloth covering his mate's waistline. A large, engorged member lifted to its near potential and dripped its pre-fluid in anticipation. Watching Roman pant like a dog was hot, but it wasn't where he wanted him yet. Latching himself back onto his mate's neck gland, but not too hard, he used a free hand to massage the thick member. Roman's knees buckled which made the Omega hum right on his neck. He heard a growl for that one.

It never ceased to amaze Mikaél just how big Roman's cock could get when he was really worked up. As his hand glided down past the shaft to his egg-sized balls, he felt them twitch and move close into his body; he knew he was getting close to his prize.

This was where Roman couldn't hold his Alpha together any longer. His gland wanted an orgasm, his loins wanted an orgasm, and his body wanted to become one with his mate. The final straw was when he saw Mikaél undo his own pants and slide them completely off quickly. When the scent of his mate's perfumed slick rushed into his nostrils, his mind flashed lightning and his voice became a thunderous roar.

Hearing Roman lose it was music to Mikaél's ears, but it was an acquired taste. With all the other unique traits Type 6's seemed to carry, this was another one. Roman's sexual instincts were also attached to his protective instincts. This was the only explanation as to why Roman nearly mauled instead of courted him upon their first meeting. Since then, sex with Roman was interesting to say the least. Scenting Mikaél's first and only heat in the throes of lovemaking gave rise to a metaphorical beast inside Roman. Unfortunately, it wasn't clear whether or not Mikaél was going to play victim to another uncontrollable assault from his destined mate. But Roman never hurt Mikaél since that first meeting and vowed he never would. That promise had now warped Mikaél into thinking it was an invitation to play with fire.

"Tell me what you want," Mikaél whispered into his ear.

Roman groaned hard at the words and even harder when Mikaél's hot breath traveled through his ear canal. "I want you to claim me. Claim me now!"

It was ecstasy to Mikaél's ears. He bit down with sharp teeth, puncturing little holes into his mate's skin. As he let the first few drops trickle down his throat, he inhaled a deep forest rain scent. Roman's scent drove Mikaél wild, and he could feel his natural slick pulse deep inside, leaking in drops into the fabric of his underwear.

"Yes! Fuck!" Roman held his stance but sounded like a whimpering pup when it came to Mikaél strategically driving him to the edge of insanity. But knowing his mate got off on it made it so worthwhile. Mikaél's slick and pheromones were ten times stronger when he showed his underbelly a little. Whatever points Roman lost in the name of being an Alpha now, he was about to make up in spades in a moment.

He lifted Mikaél up by his waist and pushed him back on the bed. After a slight bounce and a quick assessment to make sure hadn't gone too far with his pregnant mate, Roman attacked Mikaél's underwear until they flew off and were on the opposite side of the room. Stepping out of his own clothes already pushed to his ankles, Roman laid on top of his mate to remind him what it felt like to be under a horny, dominating Alpha. He took Mikaél's cock down his throat to the hilt in a matter of seconds. He felt his hips involuntarily push back on him, sending the throbbing member down farther. When he felt Mikaél's hands try to steady his head, Roman took both hands into his and thrust them back up by his head and held them. Continuously, he let the hard cock massage the lining of his throat. Every full-length retraction painted it in pre-fluid. There was a sweet and bitter taste to it. But that's not what he wanted. He wanted it all. With one final thrust down, he laid his forehead right below Mikaél's belly button and held his head in place, moaning onto the cock deep inside him. The scent of slick grew stronger as he heard his mate cry out louder. Roman could have easily soaked the floor beneath him in a bucket of his cum if he wasn't so fixated on getting his mate's seed. He heard the warnings of his mate screaming out it was happening. He was cumming. Those words pleased Roman, and the Alpha held on and waited in anticipation. Soon, expanding throbs of the Omega's cock head and shaft released shot after shot deep inside Roman all the way down to his stomach. The flood consumed him, and he was in ecstasy, knowing his mate was cumming for him and him alone. Mikaél pushed Roman's hands away and tried to escape after the hot liquid ceased to come out of him. But Roman wasn't having it. He proceeded to bob his head up and down and make sure every drop was gone.

"Ugh! Stop!" Mikaél begged.

Roman pulled his mouth off and laughed. "Turnabout is fair play."

Mikaél groaned. "Now you got yours."

"Oh no, I haven't."

Before he knew it, Mikaél was now laying on top of Roman, the motion happening too fast to comprehend. Underneath him, he felt a solid member wet with its own pre-cum sliding up and down his inner thigh. Then, large hands held him up and placed his body squarely upon Roman's cock. Upon the head stretching Mikaél's opening, a gush of slick dripped down and lubed up the rest of the length. It took a lot less time than it used to get used to Roman's considerable size. But knowing Roman was to know himself and his body wanted to accept him each and every time. Still, Roman let him take the lead until he finally took the full length all the way down.

Owning his mate with sex was one of the most magical experiences Roman ever felt in his life. The thought of it alone was enough to send him over the edge. Doing it was quite another. But the Alpha inside steadied him to make sure he felt his mate's insides came before he did. And he was going to do whatever it took to make sure it happened that way.

The thrusts were slow and short. Roman let the head of his cock almost see the light of day before shoving it back in each time.

The louder Mikaél moaned, the faster his pace went. Feeling Mikaél's hot body clenched around him reminded him of their first time: When Mikaél was on the brink of orgasm, Roman could feel his womb drop. Once Roman pushed himself inside it, he exploded his seed deep.

If he thought about the memory too much, he was going to go first. Luckily for him, he heard Mikaél's groans hit a higher register. He knew his mate was going to cum.

Mikaél's insides were the first to contract. The vibration inside sent lines of flowing slick down onto Roman's swollen sack below his cock and the sheets underneath. Although Mikaél wasn't going to feel an orgasm as deep as when he was in heat, his prostate did an excellent job sending him into euphoria. Another strong pulse radiated out of his own cock and splashed onto Roman's neck and chest.

"I'm going to knot you. Get ready." The words were low and sure.

That's when Mikaél felt Roman's cock expand even larger at the base. The knot was forming as Roman roared. Soon, Mikaél felt continuous throbs of his mate's cock send ropes of cum into him. One final push made his cock go all the way up in him and lock them together.

Roman grabbed Mikaél's body down and pushed his tongue deep inside his mouth. Mikaél moaned on it as he had no choice but to stay there and take Roman's onslaught of love. The moment was so heated, Mikaél felt like he couldn't breathe. He broke the kiss and placed his head on the cool sheet next to his mate's shoulder. In his ear, Roman purred, sending chills down his back. His breathing wavered back to normal as he felt strong hands hold and caress him to sleep.

CHAPTER 06:

TO CELEBRATE AND TO CRINGE

Over the next two weeks, Mikaél fully embraced his Veo's offer to become an apprentice of sorts in his father's professional art studio. As promised, Mikaél was never forced to take boring, mundane headshots of anyone. He did, however, get a perk when he was given the assignment of photographing some very handsome models for a magazine ad. In addition, he taught rudimentary classes for aspiring artists. Mikaél's greatest skills were wide shots of landscapes and large spaces. Alec complimented his work and highly suggested he take this as a potential career opportunity.

Though it had been many years in the making, his Veo had finally achieved his dream. Tonight was the reception for friends and family and other connoisseurs to view his artwork in his own studio. The view from the street revealed tall shining windows accented with lighted trim. The building was pronounced and inviting. Inside, large track lighting bounced off the tall white walls. Various photography of many shapes, sizes, themes, and approaches were on full display. Piano music complimented the voices of several entertained guests. Their formal outfits matched the crystal glasses full of champagne. Occasionally, servers glided on the polished wood floors, bringing trays of pretentious hors d'oeuvres. Tonight, everything was perfect.

The best part of the evening was the endless support from Alec's family—even his own siblings and parents. Everyone was there. As they toured, he and Dustin locked arms. Behind them walked their son Drew and a very pregnant Will. Coming toward them were Mikaél and Roman. At this point in his pregnancy, Mikaél had started showing himself. His modesty had the better of him, so his sweater was bigger than needed, but he couldn't hide it all.

Alec beamed upon seeing his son and son-in-law. "You made it! Oh! I was beginning to get worried." He rushed in for a hug from both.

Dustin chuckled. "Babe, seriously, it's only been 20 minutes." He leaned into whispering space of Mikaél. "He's a little nervous and a little tipsy. Fair warning."

His son nodded his head in amusement.

"I've been waiting because I wanted to show you a surprise." Alec flexed his eyebrows.

Mikaél flashed a look at Roman and then back to his Veo. "Oh?"

"Look around the corner."

Mikaél walked around to another tall display wall. On it were several familiar prints. He held his mouth open. "Dad, are these mine?"

"Mmhmm. I told you they were exquisite. They are worthy of being up here just like any other professional."

"Wow, Mik. These are great." Roman pulled his mate into hearty side-hug.

Will agreed. "What a great accomplishment."

Will was Drew's Omega mate. Although he was a tall lanky man with a commanding presence, he was delicate and soothing soul. His pregnancy made him even more adorable. He simply glowed with his soft blond hair and ocean blue eyes. It was a stark contrast to Drew's dark facial features which he shared with Mikaél. He was shorter than Will but very much a buff athlete.

Dustin and Alec had to look at their son Drew before he stepped forward to make his own comment. In a demure fashion, he acknowledged his brother's work. "Good job, Mik."

Drew cast quite the metaphorical shadow over his younger brother. He was used to being the center of attention, especially when it came to accomplishments and achievements. Seeing Mikaél in the spotlight was new for him. In addition to feeling uncomfortable, he still carried a chip on his shoulder from their last encounter. Months ago, upon the reveal of his own Omega's pregnancy, Mikaél quickly managed to make the announcement all about him. It consumed the rest of the evening, and he still hadn't discussed the event with Mikaél, let alone forgive him for the insult. His also being pregnant at the same time as his mate was the sour cherry on top.

"Look who's coming now!" Dustin pointed out.

Approaching were Roman's parents. Both Jake and Adrian walked up in a bittersweet expression. They were here to support Alec in his moment of glory as a longtime friend and extension of Dustin, but they were also on cautious terms with their own son Roman. Unlike Mikaél, Roman had had no contact with either of his parents since their last failed family dinner.

Adrian stepped forward and congratulated Alec on the evening. He admired the architecture in the room more than the art displays, not that he expressed his personal thoughts. It was Jake who appreciated the art.

The group formed their own circle as Alec shared his success in his self-owned and operated business. He was sharing the sentiments again, along with his eternal thanks for everyone involved, in a short speech. The eloquent words captivated his audience and they responded with a roaring applause.

As the crowds resumed their enjoyment, the Erricsons were surprised when they saw their younger sons and their presumed boyfriend coming toward them. In the limited space, Ryan, Rixen, and Garrace filed in and then separated like a threesome superhero alliance. Like the rest of theme of the dysfunctional family members, Jake and Adrian were shut out of their sons' lives after they exiled them from the house.

Adrian set the tone early by finishing off his glass of champagne while all eleven family members stood there quietly. Deep inside, they were all thankful the guests and entertainment covered up the awkward silence.

In an effort to save face, Jake presented himself professionally, gesturing with his own champagne glass. "Rixen. Ryan."

"Hello fathers, Mikaél, Roman." Ryan's greeting was polite but aseptic. He turned to face Mikaél's parents. "It is nice to see you both under different circumstances. Congratulations."

They both replied in reserved approval. The last time they met, Roman claimed Mikaél as his own in a rage. It made the reunion feel a bit unsettling. "And you must be Mikaél's older brother?"

"Yes. I'm Drew, and this is my mate, Will," he introduced his small family to all three new individuals.

"Ryan." He gestured to his company. "This is my brother Rixen, and this is our boyfriend, Garrace."

All the Cavenbelle family members held an unchanged expression as they shook hands.

Drew replayed the introduction in his head. He leaned into his mate's ear. "Wait. Did he say 'our' boyfriend?"

Alec caught wind of the question. "I'll explain later."

Drew tightened his lips, still lost in the words he heard.

Adrian attempted his own slow approach. "It's great to see you both. I wasn't sure if—"

Rixen cut his Veo off by coming up and giving him a deep hug. It took everything for Adrian not to break down right then and there. He returned every bit of the hug he could in return.

Out of courtesy, Ryan replaced his brother and did the same, although with less enthusiasm.

On an upward track, Adrian went on. "Garrace. It's nice to see you again." A gentle hug ensued.

Jake took his mate's lead in a greeting, but no hugs were exchanged between him and his sons nor Garrace. "I'm glad you three could make it."

Garrace acknowledged the family and then turned his attention to Mikaél. "You look great, Mik. Looks like things are coming along. Are you both excited?"

"Time can't move fast enough," he admitted.

In order to keep the night in a positive light for his mate, Alec chimed in. "Feel free to explore and have some of the champagne and delights. As far as the artwork, my personal favorites are on the east wall and uh, the ones right here." He winked at Mikaél, acknowledging his work like a proud father.

A little later in the evening at the reception, whether out of courtesy or out of spite, the twins weren't sure why their parents chose to split off. Considering their Sur walked away with a purpose, the betting money was on the latter. Hand in hand *and* hand in hand, the three lovers began their tour of the impressive artwork. Roman and Mikaél joined them; Drew and Will ventured out on their own as well.

Garrace noticed Mikaél behind him. "You know, you never told me your Veo was so accomplished."

So many versions of saying the same conclusion went through his head. He decided to stay neutral. "I guess the moment didn't present itself." He snuck a look at Roman who surmised in his head quickly what Mikaél truly wanted to say. A more accurate *You left me before I could* was a close alternative statement he considered.

Roman reached out and touched Rixen's shoulders. The Omega broke the hand-holding chain to look back at him for truly the first time since he left the family home. "How are you doing in the apartment? I hope it's working out for you."

Rixen slowly nodded as if he was simmering on the idea of tolerance. "It's going just fine, thank you."

Garrace pulled Rixen into tight side embrace while he inhaled his pheromone gland. "We've settled the apartment into a nice home for our family."

Neutral smiles were returned. Roman resumed, "How are you going to approach dad on mending fences?"

Rixen was taken aback and offended at such notion. "*Me?* I'm sorry; I don't feel I'm the one who has to approach anyone. If he wants to fix his mistakes, I am more than willing to entertain his sorry ass."

Roman darted his eyes left and right, hoping no one within earshot heard the overt language. The tone in Rixen's voice concluded the terms weren't negotiable. Ryan pulling his brother's forehead into a kiss was the nail in the coffin. Following the family tradition, Roman kicked back his champagne and made a casual excuse for him and his mate to veer off in a different direction.

They made it to a refreshment table near the charming entertainer gliding his hands across the keys of a beautiful baby grand piano. Mikaél carefully participated in the various rich and flavorful options. Roman, on the other hand, had no issue stuffing an entire smoked salmon canape in his mouth.

Mikaél's face lit up with concern. "Roman?" He received an inaudible acknowledgement through Roman's attempt at grabbing another appetizer. "Are you okay?"

Roman decided to nonverbally assure him. He figured it was better than outright lying. It was convenient to avoid his mate's eye contact as he searched for his parents who were no doubt glued to Mikaél's parents somewhere.

Mikaél's sight narrowed. "Roman..." he drew out.

An innocent expression washed over Roman's face. "What?"

"You're up to something."

"No, I'm not."

"Yes, you are. I can feel you thinking." Roman dramatically dismissed the claim which only told him to press further. "You asked me once to look into your eyes to judge whether or not you were telling me the truth about Peyton's contract and pregnancy ending."

"Yeah. So?"

"Would you like to do that again?" Mikaél leaned in with emphasis.

Roman's face moved in thought, and he licked the inside of cheek while weighing his options. "Okay fine. I'm hoping Rixen and Ryan can repair things with our dads before the night's over." He still couldn't quite look his mate in the eye.

"You're not serious? Here? Tonight? At my dad's reception?"

"I know it's not ideal."

"You can say that again!"

"Look, if it doesn't happen here, I fear it's going to be Winter Solstice, or worse, our pup's birth before they even attempt this. And I'll be damned if they're going to have a standoff in the hospital on the day of my son's birth."

Mikaél's eyes went wide. This was quite the positive approach to his family which he hadn't seen in a long time—if ever. "So, am I to assume since you're advocating this so much, you yourself are calling a truce?"

The comment made Roman reflect. As much as he wanted to hold on to his anger, the same philosophy he wanted to avoid with his brothers was also applicable to himself. He also didn't feel like playing the role of hypocrite right now. He grumbled, "Yes. Fine."

"Aww." Mikaél's heart warmed as he gave his mate a tight embrace. "I'm so proud of you." He finished the compliment with a warm kiss. The goal at hand quickly prioritized. He sighed. "The first step is finding your parents, right?"

"Right."

Like two undercover detectives, Roman and Mikaél investigated every corner of the studio. With the maze of several ten-foot-high right-angle displays, many blind spots were created. Fate decided it was funny to put all four parents in the most opposite position from where they were. The four were finishing up a conversation with another couple who conveniently left as they approached.

"Well, hi there!" Alec was still on cloud nine from the success of the evening. "Still enjoying yourselves, I hope?"

"You two thinking about heading out?" Dustin wondered.

"No," Roman replied. "As a matter of fact, I was just hoping to have a word with my parents."

"Of course," Jake said with enthusiasm. He was optimistic about the conversation since Roman had intentionally sought him out. After all, the evening hadn't invoked any issues thus far. Both he and Adrian broke off and joined their sons. "How is everything going?"

Roman cocked his head. "You know the answer to that."

Jake held his patience. "Then what can we do it make it better?"

"Talk to Ryan and Rixen."

"No. Not going to happen." Jake's response was swift and sure.

"Why not?"

"Because this isn't the time nor the place."

That train of thought didn't sit well with Roman, especially since Mikaél had claimed the same just moments earlier. "Then when?!" Roman's voice rose.

Adrian stepped forward next to his mate. "Roman, keep your voice down."

Patience held Roman a bit longer. But it was waning. "You have got to talk to them now. It's not going to get any easier. You're here. They're here. It makes sense."

"*That* conversation—and I'm not even sure what that conversation is—is not something a few words is going to fix."

Roman rubbed the bridge of his nose. "Dad, you have an opportunity to fix this right now. If you walk out tonight and let them slip through your fingers, I'm not sure exactly where this is going to go." Jake didn't respond. "If it makes you feel any better, I'm trying my best to get this family back together and that includes me getting past my issues, too."

"We're very glad to hear that." Adrian smiled.

"Then come on! They have even less to be angry with you about than I do. If you and I can get over this, then so can Ryan and Rixen."

"Get over what?" a new voice asked.

All focus shifted to the mildly annoyed trio who were obviously thinking pessimistically of their family.

Roman gulped. "Hey guys, I was just—"

"—meddling in our lives again?" Rixen finished the thought as he crossed his arms.

"No," Roman corrected, "I just thought it would be good for me to facilitate the conversation between you and Sur and Veo. That's all."

"I see," Rixen replied.

"And?" Ryan waited for this 'unplanned' discussion to begin.

Both parents held their breaths. Adrian took the opening. "We want to apologize for the way we reacted. You're our sons and we love you."

Roman took a deep sigh of relief. *Good so far.*

"Is that what you think, dad?" Ryan asked his Sur. "Did you *overreact*?"

Jake twitched. "I believe the word stated was 'react,' not 'over-react.'" Already the tension was building.

Roman whined. "Let's not do this."

Jake refocused his efforts. "I know our reaction did nothing to help the situation. For that, I apologize."

"Now apologize to Garrace," Rixen commanded.

"What?" Jake pushed his head back.

"Garrace isn't invisible. He's a part of our lives, too."

Like billowing clouds from a volcano, pheromones were starting to pollute the air.

Jake stiffened his lip. "Garrace, I am sorry for the way I reacted once I found out you three were a," a deafening pause came, "were... were... whatever it is you say you are."

Garrace wanted to accept the apology but ended up furrowing his brows instead.

Ryan crowed and shook his head. "Wow."

"What?" Jake pushed back.

"What exactly do you think we introduce ourselves to people as? 'Hi, my name is Ryan. These are my special friends'? Or 'Hi, these are my whatever you want to call them'? They're my *boyfriends*, dad. A five-year-old knows that word."

A grunt from Jake's chest pushed the apology further away. "Fine. That's what you are."

"We need to know you are going to support us," Ryan added.

As a few patrons casually walked by, Jake plastered a smile on this face. "I think we're good now. Do we really need this?"

"Yes!" Rixen's crescendo carried into the crowd.

"Why?" Jake demanded.

Rixen lifted his chin. "New Year's."

The confusion hit Jake as well as everyone else. "New Year's?" he inquired.

Garrace weighed in. "Ryan and Rixen said they'd love to be home for the holidays. And when the fireworks bring in the New Year, all three of us want to be able to kiss each other without having to worry about people thinking we're deplorable human beings."

Adrian clenched his champagne glass and muttered a little too loudly. "Oh dear, Wolf-God!" The reaction wasn't in response to the statement so much as it was anticipating his mate's reaction. The petrified look hit Roman, too. As if they were walking hand in hand, both men knocked their drinks back.

A hushed roar ended any willpower Jake had left. "This conversation is over." Jake pushed his way past them and turned away.

"You're kidding," Ryan responded. "Why?"

Jake faced his son once again with daggers in his eyes. "You three want me to know who you are? Congratulations. I know. When you all are in your own space, you're free to do what you want. But that doesn't mean I have to see it, and I refuse to. If that's what you're going to do when you come home, I suggest you reconsider your plans. Good luck to you."

"Then go to hell!" The anger boiled over, and the words came out with no restraint; neither did the volume. Looks from the crowd focused on a red-faced Ryan and a frozen cluster of everyone in the know.

For the triad, the night was over.

"Come on, guys. Let's go." Ryan led them straight to the doors. Garrace held a tense expression. He hated seeing Ryan so vexed. It hurt him more to see Rixen was barely holding it together.

Rixen took another look at Roman who appeared disappointed more than anything. Not enjoying the reserved criticism, he huffed with watery eyes and followed his boyfriends out.

Roman wasn't going to leave the situation like this. He excused himself from his Veo and Mikaél and chased after his brothers. When he exited the doors, he saw the three a half block away. "Hey!" All turned to face him. "What the hell was that?!"

"What are you talking about?" Rixen's voice carried a harsh attitude.

"You said if dad made the efforts in apologizing, you'd meet him halfway to mend all this."

"I did!" Rixen defended.

"That's bullshit!" Roman yelled.

Ryan pulled Rixen back. He was not going to have Roman attack Rixen after having to deal with their Sur. Garrace intercepted him and held him close. "You have a lot of nerve, Roman! Rixen did the best he could, and you know it."

"It was a set-up, Ryan. How long have you three been waiting to spring that on them?"

"Oh, please! What was it supposed to be, Roman? Were we supposed to wait until we showed up at the house and ask what they're comfortable with while we're making out?"

"Tell me then. Did his response surprise you?" Roman asked.

Ryan smirked. "Of course not."

"Then why, Ryan? I don't understand." Roman's voice was exasperated.

"Look, we both acknowledge and agree this is what Sur was going to do. Saying this now gives him time to deal with what's going on."

"So, your goal was to ease him in so when the holidays do come around, you'll be able to act like you want to when you're there?"

The look on Ryan's face read like he couldn't believe Roman couldn't put the pieces together earlier. "Yeah."

Roman shook his head. "You three have a lot more faith in this than I do."

Garrace spoke. "Showing up on what's supposed to be one of the greatest days of the year feeling like the family's going to blame us for ruining it just because we want to be who we are is foolish at best. We wanted to give us the best chance. This was it."

"And what if this doesn't go as planned?" Roman asked. Ryan looked at Rixen.

"Then maybe the Erricson family will be severed for a while." Rixen's words ended the conversation. All three left Roman in a hot fog of his own breath lit by the streetlight.

Roman walked back to the studio feeling like a failure. All he had wanted to do was make things better. Taking the situation in his own hands did not yield the results he craved. The good deed did not go unpunished. As he reached the door, he suddenly stopped.

His heart sank as he reflected. Knowing he was, in part, responsible for making the situation worse wasn't the hardest to deal with. It was knowing he was slowly becoming his father--that was the most horrific realization of all.

CHAPTER 07:

TO FIGHT AGAINST PREJUDICE

A large circular hall held several conversations between men in business suits and men in turquoise scrubs. Morning rounds had several different professions represented on this Monday morning. One particular team of five was already two weeks into their rotation in Post-Op. The pack was led by an ostentatious Alpha relishing in his superiority and control.

"Satine. Baker. Rooms 1-5." Two young members split to their assignments. "Deserae. Wynn. Rooms 6-10." That left one individual standing alone. "Erricson. Rooms 11-15. That's all."

As best as he could, Roman hid his disapproval. If he wanted things to change, he needed to speak up now. "Dr. Daniels, could I have a minute?"

Annoyed already by the request, the doctor scanned his watch, wishing it was ten minutes later than it already was, so he had a reason to leave. "A minute is all I have, Erricson. What is it?"

"I was hoping for this time, last time, the time before that, or any time actually, I might have a chance to rotate with a partner."

The relationship between Roman and Dr. Daniels had this negative energy about it ever since he was assigned to the Alpha's caseload. On top of that, Dr. Daniels had very strong features, complete with protruding eyes and harsh brows. He wasn't that old, making everyone wonder what kind of god he had to be in order to secure one of the highest positions in the medical field. Several concluded that taking students under his advisement was a mandatory order and not a pleasurable choice. It was a great rationale for his attitude.

Dr. Daniels sneered back. "What's wrong, Erricson? Can't handle it?"

Holding back what Roman wanted to say was difficult enough. Trying to figure out what he could say was even harder. "I feel that I'm missing out on some great collaborative efforts. We're a team of five, but yet, when it comes to this part, I become a team of one."

"You're specializing in PT, are you not?" Dr. Daniels clicked his pen and put it in his front jacket pocket.

"I am."

"When you're starting your lowly practice in some old, abandoned town, like Gemini perhaps, because let's face it, it takes a master to successfully begin a practice around here, and all the major hospitals already have the top practitioners they need, you will be working alone. All I am doing is preparing you for the real world." The doctor satisfied himself with his answer, anticipating no response in return.

"With all due respect, no one on our team is specializing in surgery. In that sense, them being alone is equal to me being alone, and yet, they are given opportunities I am not." It felt like talking to a brick wall.

Dr. Daniels scoffed at the comment. "Do you think you're special, Erricson?"

It took Roman by surprise. "No, sir."

"Oh, I think you do." Dr. Daniels crossed his arms and exuding his strong Alpha scent. "Because I don't see anyone else coming up to me and questioning my instruction. I don't see anyone else expressing their displeasure. Do you know why that is?"

Roman shifted his weight. "I—I couldn't speculate."

"They don't because they are grateful to be here. They know it is a privilege and honor to be chosen from hundreds of candidates to be in this program and under my leadership. Perhaps, if you felt the same way, this conversation wouldn't be happening at all."

The notion Roman wasn't appreciative or lacked perspective on his opportunity was a hammer to his chest. He gasped. "Dr. Daniels, I swear to you, I am every bit as—"

"I've studied you 'round here, Erricson. You garner a lot of attention. People are distracted by the misguided idea you are some sort of celebrity because of your Type 6 Status. There's this idea you must have magical powers or are part of Wolf-God's elite pack in the heavens."

"I swear to you, I don't believe I am, nor do I advocate myself as such to anyone."

Dr. Daniels examined Roman from head to toe. Not that he'd say it, but he was pleased with Roman's passionate stance on correcting such preposterous claims and rumors. "Good. Because there is no cell in my body that believes it. Nevertheless, I *do* believe men like you need every reassurance you will not be treated in such a privileged manner. Therefore, I will do whatever it takes to make sure you get a challenge equal to this overrated impression. In my program, if you stand out like the Alpha leader everyone thinks you are, you'll conquer the world. If you fail at the tasks I give you, or ever come close to second guessing my expertise or orders again, I will dismiss you on the spot."

There was no time to reply to the harsh criticism. The doctor walked around Roman and hurried himself away. Frustration grew on Roman's face from the twisted words he spoke. In addition, there was this feeling in the pit of his stomach as if he had done something wrong, but the feeling was irrational. Deep inside, Roman decided it was Dr. Daniels who should have accepted those sentiments.

Shaking it off as best as he could, he walked to the island station and opened the patient reports. He rested his head on his fist as he paged through the summaries and test results.

"Hey," a voice said coming toward him. In the same scrubs, a very good-looking man approached. His full dark auburn hair and scruff face worked wondrously against his lightly tanned skin. On his young face, he wore stylish, black-framed glasses.

Roman looked up, recognizing Zayne instantly. "Hi," he replied, deflated.

"Didn't mean to eavesdrop. Sounded rough."

"You can say that again," Roman moped.

"Don't let him get to you. He's just riling you up because he wants to see what you're made of."

Roman snorted. "Yeah, well, if he keeps this up, he'll find out it's a whole lotta Alpha and strong muscle."

Zayne laughed, entertained by his comment. "Ain't that the truth?" His expression changed to serious with a touch of empathy. "Really though, if you need any help with your assignments, just let me know. Carlos has a pretty good handle on things. I guess our cases aren't as demanding as others."

"It's just," Roman paused, trying to find the right words, "why does everyone with power get it stuck in their head I'm looking to dethrone them or threaten their manhood?"

"Simple. Their dicks are small."

Roman's eyes widened. Once he knew the coast was the clear, he burst out laughing. "That's a theory I'm not willing to test out."

Zayne joined him in the humor before returning to his empathetic state. "How bad is it, anyway? I mean, do you think it's something you should go to the department head for?"

Roman swayed back and forth. "Not really. Whether or not I want to admit it, he's right. There are a lot of people who would have killed to get into this program, let alone our cohort. Regardless of what I feel is unfair, I can't imagine those who complain about their assignments get very far."

"Hm. You might have a point there." A new train of thought rushed into Zayne's head. "Hey, you knew Siro LaCroix, right?"

The name hadn't been spoken aloud for quite some time. It caught Roman off-guard. He was tested too early; it didn't sit well with him. "Yeah, I did," he confessed. "He and my friend Nico and I were all close. We went through all the specialty Levels together. Siro had a good chance at getting into the program until he fucked everything up this past summer."

"You mean the assault?"

Roman winced as he realized the past still felt fresh like a new wound. "Yeah."

Siro had the visual features of a dashing old-time movie star and the bad boy persona to go with it. It was this persona which led him down a dark path. In addition to confessing his own personal issues with Matthew Whitmore, Siro decided to take on Roman's too. In the same moment Siro decided to become a hero, he fell from grace just as quickly. When Roman first found out Peyton was pregnant, a fallacy from the start, Siro took the issue into his own hands. Rightfully convinced Mr. Whitmore was doing nothing more than manipulating everyone, he brutally attacked Terrence, Matthew's Omega mate. Now, two months later, Siro was sitting in a cell on an 8-year sentence.

"Man, I can't imagine what he was thinking when he went after one of the most powerful Alphas in town. It's one thing to go after an Alpha; it's quite another to go after their mate. Siro's lucky to be alive, I'm sure." Not knowing what to say, Roman repeated his former short response. Zayne continued, "Heh. No way he's getting a career in healthcare after that one."

Roman's voice was low. "No. No, I suppose he won't."

Zayne ran his hand over the counter—trying to act casual as he brought up the next topic. "When you said 'Nico,' did you mean…"

"Hallen. He was in our last Human Physiology class."

Zayne thought for a moment. "That's right. He's so quiet," he pointed out. "Cute guy. I always thought about asking him out. He makes himself so small in a crowd, I worry he won't even speak to me."

That was another friend Roman found himself distanced from, this time not on purpose. Nico didn't get into Dr. Daniels' clinical group. He was successful getting under another doctor's wing, but their schedules differed so much, it was hard to keep in touch. "I think he's worth another look. He's a genuine person. Anybody'd be lucky to have him."

"*You* have someone special yourself. I've heard the name Mikaél get thrown around. Is that right?"

"That's him, my one and only." Finally, a thought which made Roman light up.

"Fated or contracted?"

"He's my Fate, the best anyone could ask for. If Dr. Daniels wants to call me overrated or even insignificant—fine. But if he wants a candidate who's truly special, it'd be my mate."

"Awe, that's sweet," Zayne replied. "Though everyone says that about their mate. I'd be hard pressed to find anyone does not say that about their *Fated* Mate."

There was a solid point in Zayne's claim, and Roman knew it. He wished he could scream from the mountaintop with pride that his mate was the only Type 6 Omega in the world. Or at the very least, talk about it in the same manner his own Type 6 Status was discussed. He wondered if he'd ever get to tell anyone what quality Mikaél possessed. Carrying the burden of secrecy about his mate was going to be hard enough. Should their son be a Type 6 Omega, that was going to present a whole new ballgame Roman wasn't sure he was ready to bat for yet.

"I suppose I better get to it. I'm not going to get any relief like the partner groups today." Roman closed his files and smiled at Zayne.

His tone became heartfelt. "Thank you for your willingness to help. It's nice to have a friend here."

"Anytime, Roman. I'll be here for ya." Zayne watched Roman walk into his first patient's room before sighing and going to his own assignments.

Casual conversations peppered throughout the large lecture hall. Laycin flipped his blond hair back as he examined his best friend filling out his stomach. As a Beta, he was experiencing a pregnancy by proxy. He was never going to be able to experience one himself. He couldn't get pregnant, nor he could he get anyone else pregnant. So, having Mikaél around was a big deal for him to know what procreation was like.

"When are we going to have to sit on the bottom row because you can't do stairs anymore?" Laycin cracked up.

Mikaél rolled his eyes. "You really know how to make someone feel better about themselves."

"Hey, I'm just lookin' out for you, buddy. I don't want you to trip down these concrete stairs with a stomach as large as a beach ball. You'll look like a busted watermelon by the time you get to the bottom. All of Roman's seeds will be scattered around the room."

In slow motion, Mikaél turned to face his best friend with wide eyes. "That was specific and also very disturbing."

"Thanks. I thought of it on the spot." Laycin nodded, proud of himself. "But in all seriousness, I do want to keep you safe. I want to make sure my nephew doesn't come out looking like scrambled eggs." He leaned over to Mikaél's stomach, pouting his lips for baby talk. "Isn't that right, you little pup?"

"You know, it's amazing you don't have a boyfriend yet." Mikaél tilted his head as it became apparent Laycin was ignoring him.

Suddenly, he felt Laycin rubbing his baby bump with his index finger. Mikaél smacked his hand away.

"Ow!" the Beta yelped. "What did you do that for?"

"You don't touch a guy's stomach without asking! I don't understand it when people do that. If I wasn't pregnant, you'd never randomly come over and touch my stomach. It'd be creepy! But all of a sudden because I have a pup growing inside of me there's a neon sign pointing down at my stomach that says 'Petting Zoo' on it," Mikaél huffed.

"It's a compliment!" Laycin defended out of ignorance. "Growing a pup is an amazing thing. Guys wanna touch it because it's adorable and fascinating at the same time. A dude coming up to an Alpha to rub his barren stomach and describing it as 'adorable' and 'fascinating' –*that's* a creepy situation."

Mikaél's face heated red. "And this isn't any less creepy!"

"Okay! Okay! Point made." Laycin relaxed back in his seats with hands up in surrender. There was a boring lull between the two of them after Mikaél reclined back in his desk as well. With a sinister grin, Laycin decided the tease was too much to pass up. In a flash, he found himself inches away from Mikaél's stomach again, speaking in a way he would to a smiling infant. "Who's a good boy? Is my nephew a good boy? Yes, he is!"

"Laycin, if you are lucky enough to still be alive after his birth, I'm going to strangle you with his umbilical cord." Mikaél spoke between clenched teeth. Laycin sat up, pretending nothing happened. "You mean 'nephew' right?" Mikaél reminded his friend he wasn't actually related to his family.

"Oh, I'm going to be better than any other uncle in the family and you know it," Laycin insisted. Mikaél smiled.

"Gentlemen! Good morning!" The professor walked in with a sunny smile on his face.

"Wow, professor! You look like the morning of Winter Solstice. Did you have a hot date last night?" A random student called the question followed by laughter.

The man laughed back, seemingly unphased. "No, sir. I don't dabble in the dating world too much anymore. Not that it's something you're interested in knowing. But I am happy to announce I am the new Director Elect of the Tauris Research Medical Center!" A roaring applause engulfed the room.

"Dr. Johannes," a student raised a hand, "does that mean you're going to leave us?" The boy stared at his professor with bedroom eyes.

"No. Absolutely not," Ken reassured his pupil. "I'll still be here as an adjunct just like Dr. Birowack, for those of you who know him. I will hopefully, now that I have my official title, get to tell Ashershire Preparatory what I *want* to teach versus being plugged into the available position to cover paternity leave." A few laughs came in reply. "But right now, we're making the best of it. In that spirit, I hope you have your career readiness presentations complete. You're going to be presenting these in groups for feedback, so put your best foot forward. Turn them in tomorrow after class."

On any other day, Mikaél would be joining in the brief celebration. After all, he was very aware Dr. Johannes was joining his father's research team. Correction: he was getting ready to *lead* the research team. Mikaél decided he didn't want to put too much effort into figuring out his father's feelings on the matter. Right now, he had more immediate objectives to worry about.

Butterflies flew in the Omega's stomach. Since being pregnant, being nervous or anxious wasn't a friend of his. It reminded him too much of how he felt during morning sickness once he found out he was carrying. The mere thought of having to connect the memory made him nauseous. He willed himself to hold it together; he needed to get through this presentation. After this, the anxiety he'd built up in his mind could release in a welcome wave.

On the main floor, underneath the projector screen, Mikaél found his five-member group circled on the carpet, each with their own paper reports. Whispers were heard all the way up to his arrival. When he approached, the voices died down to nothing. Their cat eyes and smirks staring back it him were enough to confirm his fears. Slowly, he began to sit down, completing the circle of his group.

The Alpha at the head of the circle was a boy of the same age as Mikaél, Charles Brody. He had a full head of brown curly hair which he now hid with a red ball cap. The cap appeared out of nowhere since it was against school policy to wear them. But with Dr. Johannes not instructing and currently out of sight, he used this minimal opportunity to be more like himself rather than the student he was told to be. His hazel eyes flashed as he saw Mikaél approach.

"Uh-oh, barge comin' in! Hold on mates!" Charles plastered a dizzy look on his face while grabbing the shoulders the classmates on both sides of him, pretending to use them as a brace for impact. The boys attached to him joined in holding their breaths as they waited for Mikaél to finally make his landing. When he did, the three blew out air like they'd been holding their breath for a year underwater. The two remaining members responded, mildly entertained.

Mikaél held it together and even managed a controlled smile back. "Very funny." As he pushed up the sleeves of his shirt, he locked onto his report. It glared like a pistol staring right back on his face, his own hand the trigger. "Who's going first?" he asked in a timid voice.

"Charlie!" Wayne toyed.

Charles swiftly came up from his comfortable position and pushed Wayne's shoulder back, throwing him off his equilibrium. "Hey, fuck you." The action was to show dominance more than anything else. Wayne was his friend. Or follower. Mikaél wasn't sure which. It was clear with three Alphas in the group, Charles was positioning himself as the leader. "Go Nate!"

"O-oh." Nate was caught off-guard. "Me?"

"Yeah, you, ya pussy!" Charles's voice indicated he wasn't afraid of anyone else hearing him. "Don't tell me you didn't do the assignment like some sort of Type 1 loser."

"No, no, Charlie. I did it." Nate stood up straight as best as he could. Even sitting down, it was clear Nate was the runt of the group. "I even took your suggestions." He smiled, looking for his approval. It was apparent Nate was easily manipulated by Charles's coveted status. Looking at Nate alone in a neutral setting, no one would visually recognize him as an Alpha. He appeared as if puberty barely touched him. "Why I want to be a policeman by Nate—"

"The fuck?" Charles interrupted.

"What?" Nate jumped.

"What do you mean you want to be a policeman?" Charles snorted.

"That's what you said I should write my report about!" Nate defended.

"I told you write about being a *postman*!" Charles cried. "A policeman? Are you serious? No one is going to trust a Type 3 Alpha who looks like you to police a bathroom, let alone the real world. Stupid." To prove his point, Charles gave a hefty punch to Nate's shoulder. He began to laugh to himself as he saw Nate's eyes sting. "Wayne. Impress me. You better have listened to me more than Nate did."

Although Wayne was a Type 4 Alpha, he hadn't quite come into his own neither. He did however have a presence about him as wide as his waistline. His physical thickness complimented his mental one. "I got this, bro." He cleared his throat. "Imagine me, Wayne Northrop, as a firefighter. With my at—atness... ape-ness... what's that say..."

Mikaél narrowed his sight. "You mean 'aptness'?"

Charles groaned loudly like he was at his wit's end. "You idiot. Did you just look up random words in a dictionary or somethin'?"

Like with Nate, Charles decided to express his disconnect with a firm slap to the back of Wayne's head. "Just get it over with."

Wayne swallowed. "With my ... skills ... I'd be able to rescue an Alpha from a fire with one hand while using the other hand to comfort his Omega mate at the same time."

"Stop. Just stop," Charles commanded. "All right, one of you worthless Betas go next."

Mikaél zoned out the other speeches along with Charles' harsh criticisms. He scanned the room to see where Laycin was. To his left, he saw him balancing himself on a side table half-listening to one of his group members give their presentation. He caught a glimpse of Mikaél and waved, completely unaware of the trouble his friend was about to be in. By the time Mikaél had refocused his attention back to his own group, Charles had chewed up and spit out the other two speakers.

"Okay, Omega 5, let's hear it." Charles smirked.

It became very apparent what Charles was trying to do. Not only did he intentionally place Mikaél last before himself, but he also gave a taste of what to expect when he heard his opinions on the other speakers. Clearly, Mikaél was going to be no exception. Intimidation was not an uncommon practice for a wolf-descendent demonstrating the hierarchy of Ranks. Mikaél was an Omega in the presence of a dominating Type 5 Alpha, and he was set to let everyone know it.

Mikaél began. "Since I was a pup, I've always admired and appreciated the world of art."

"Typical." Charles laid back and crossed his ankles like he was a CEO observing an entry level employee disappoint him.

Mikaél ignored the comment. "In the last couple of months, I've had the privilege of working under the expertise of my Veo in his photography studio and am inspired to grow my talent there. One day, I want to continue his footsteps and own my own studio just like him. Through research, I have discovered—"

"Pfft! Oh, my Wolf-God!" Charles doubled over laughing while his blind Alpha followers joined him. The Betas weren't as enthusiastic, but they visibly shared the same train of thought.

"What's so funny?" Mikaél inquired offensively.

Charles regained his composure. "I'll give you credit for appropriately choosing a mundane job. However, pushing a camera button doesn't make you an expert. A quadriplegic can take a picture by holding a toothbrush with his teeth. But I don't know where you get off thinking you should be owning your own business, Omega."

"A lot of Omegas own businesses," Mikaél defended.

"That doesn't mean they *should*. All they do is take up space and take business away from Alphas. It's disgraceful to all ranks and a foolish venture for any Omega who thinks they're doing their family a favor by wasting money in a failing business."

Mikaél cocked his head. "What proof do you have Omegas aren't successful or are less successful than any Alpha-owned business?"

Charles shrugged. "I'm sure the statistics are out there. My Sur says Omegas who become entrepreneurs are a mess and don't know what they're doing. In the end, they just beg the government to bail them out. That's our tax money. So essentially, I'm paying Omegas to push out defective shops and supermarkets when they should be laying on their backs to push out babies. Omegas who get the notion to act like they're an Alpha who can successfully run the show offends me and pisses me off to no end!"

"My Veo *is* a successful Omega running the show, as you put it."

"Congratulations then. Your family officially offends me."

"And you offend me, you prick!" Mikaél blurted out.

Every member in the group tensed up, waiting for Charles to attack Mikaél like a savage wolf. Instead, Charles creased his forehead as if he was waiting for this moment. "I know you're a Type 5 Omega and all, but do you realize who you are talking to? If your tiny brain forgot, let me remind you: I'm a Type 5 *Alpha*. No one gets away with doing anything to me, and no one gets away with saying anything to me. I will always outrank you and own you in society's eyes."

"Maybe not. I'm not a Type 5. I'm a Type 6, you jerk." Blurting the information out was both empowering and frightening. It was the first time in revealing his newfound Status—no one else knew—not even Laycin knew.

A Type 6 Alpha was a blessing to be envious over. What was a Type 6 Omega going to be?

Starting with Charles, the consensus in the group was to laugh.

"What the fuck, dude?" Charles's shoulders bounced as he thoroughly enjoyed the ridiculous claim. "Ah," he exhaled with a chuckle, "of all the dumb things you've said, that takes the cake. What? Couldn't come up with any other poor comeback?" Mikaél gave Charles a look which cut through the air like a knife. As the pheromones rushed out, Charles's smile, along with the other group members, faded to a dark expression. "Seriously?"

Wayne maintained a nervous chuckle. "Wait. Charles, you don't actually belief that shit, do you?"

"Shut up, Wayne!" Charles's own pheromones displayed a clear feeling of being threatened. He was ready to show Mikaél he wasn't bluffing about his approach to disrespectful subordinates. "If you weren't pregnant right now, I'd deck you so hard that half of your body would be in the ground. After that, you'd bury the rest of yourself to escape the pain of it."

Mikaél mustered the last of his courage. "Why? Because you feel threatened?"

Charles's voice grew. "No, because you're an abomination! The only place you belong is where the worms can feed off of you!"

"What the hell is going on here?" Dr. Johannes stood over the group like a father catching adolescents committing a small crime. As he crossed his arms, the entire group absorbed his anger.

"This Omega is causing nothing but trouble. He's talking crazy; he's preventing us from working; he's threatening us..." Charles pointed his finger at Mikaél as he attempted to cover himself and his dedicated followers.

"Don't even try it, Mr. Brody. I heard it all. By the way, if *you* have forgotten, I will remind you. I may be a Type 4 Alpha, but *I* run the show here. If I even hear of a *possibility* you continue this behavior in the school, I'll make sure you never step foot in it again. Do I make myself clear?"

Charles grimaced. "Yes, sir."

"Good." Dr. Johannes took one last neutral look at Mikaél and walked away.

The ceasefire didn't erase any contention in the group. Mikaél kept a hawk eye on Charles for any possible movement; Charles returned the same.

"So," Nate broke the silence, "are you going to go?" He turned his attention to Charles.

Now Charles grinned. "With pleasure." He picked up his report like it was a proud scripture from a religious book. "This world is constantly changing and so is its problems. What we need is a leader who can keep justice in check. Our territory and state are no exception to the chaos in modern society. Specifically, liberals have taken over detrimental positions which has changed the wholesome fabric of our communities. That is why I plan to run for Supreme Alpha under the Alpha Conservative Party. When I do, I will restore us to the sacred days when Alphas ruled without question and led us to prosperity, good health, safety, and most importantly, protected us from the Omega Liberal Party which plans to undermine every pure intention we have. My reign will make sure Omegas return to their expected role. If they don't, punishment will be swift and sure. My new appointed court will make sure of that."

Sweat formed on Mikaél's brow. He gulped his confidence into the pit of his stomach. Whether Charles had true intentions of running for Supreme Alpha or did it as scare tactic once he found out

Mikaél was in his group weeks ago was irrelevant. The message itself was clear.

The room became hazy as he proceeded to hear the nightmare unfold, the only uninterrupted report in the group.

"Whoa. That's messed up." Laycin shook his head equally in disgust and shock. "What is his issue?"

"I don't know." Mikaél rubbed his forehead. His headache grew with every light bump in the road. As memories flashed in his mind, he realized he needed to level with Laycin. "There's something I need to tell you."

Laycin shot Mikaél a look while trying to keep his attention on the road. He didn't like the tone. "Okay?"

"The same night I found out I was pregnant," he began, "I also found out something else." Mikaél held the moment.

"Are you going to tell me?"

"You know how Roman is a Type 6?"

"Yeah." He laughed. "Everyone who knows of him knows that. For some, that's all they know about him."

"Laycin," Mikaél paused, "I'm a Type 6, too."

The words didn't register right away. As the concept processed, Laycin realized what his friend had revealed to him. "Really?" Mikaél nodded. "Okay." Laycin shrugged.

Mikaél leaned in, waiting for the condemnation. It never came. "That's it? 'Okay'?"

"What else were you expecting me to say?"

"Oh, several things come to mind: get out of my car, I'm going to kill you, you're the cause of the apocalypse, we're not friends anymore..."

"Wow, Mik." Laycin frowned. "You honestly think that little of me?"

"I—I don't know. I'm sorry." Mikaél closed his eyes in regret and sadness.

"Hey... I'm here, buddy. Did Charlie spook you that much?"

"I'm shook, honestly."

"He's not going to do anything." Laycin relaxed in the driver's seat of the shiny red car. "No one else is going to either." Mikaél didn't respond. "So, who else knows?"

"Just Roman and our parents."

"I'm the first person you've told?" Laycin blinked. "Aww, Mik. Now I feel really special!"

"Well, technically it was Charlie Brody and his goons," Mikaél reminded him.

"Nah. You told them in a fit of rage. Doesn't count." Laycin looked pleased with himself, wearing a badge of honor.

"I don't know, Laycin. I just have a bad feeling about this."

"What's there to feel bad about? Roman is as rare as a winning Bingo card, and you're the winning lottery ticket as far as I'm concerned. This is awesome! Dr. Birowack in his classes hasn't even talked about a Type 6 Omega, and he's a god! Hey! Does that mean Laycin Junior is going to be a Type 6?"

"Ha! It has been discussed, that's for sure. Roman's Sur and my Sur think 'Laycin Junior' will be. I don't think there's a reason to think since both Roman and I am that he would come out any different."

Laycin nodded. "Cool." The car rolled up to the front entrance of Mikaél's apartment complex. He pursed his lips in heavy thought. "You know, 'Laycin Junior' is a pretty kick ass name."

Mikaél made his quick exit from the car. "Goodbye. See you tomorrow."

"I'm just sayin'!"

CHAPTER 08:

TO FACE ANOTHER COLD
HARD TRUTH

The continuous sound of feet tapping filled the quiet waiting room.

"If you keep that up, you're going to wear a hole in the floor." Mikaél tossed the magazine he was pretending to read on the open chair next to him. Roman's nerves made it impossible to concentrate on anything else.

"Sorry," Roman replied. He tried getting comfortable in the chair. He sat forward, laid back, then propped a leg up. Nothing worked. He let his frustration out with a groan.

"Roman, seriously. You're not helping anything."

"I'm sorry! I'm just—I'm just nervous."

Mikaél puffed. "Yeah, no kidding. Look, I'm nervous too, but I feel like you're taking this one step beyond what you need right now."

Roman turned his head and faced his pregnant Omega. "You're right. I'm sorry. I should be stronger right now for you, and I'm failing miserably."

Mikaél rubbed his leg. "No. Don't do that to yourself."

"See. That right there. I should be doing that to you!" Roman insisted.

"I'm fine, babe. Really."

Roman tried his best to let the conversation go. A door opened with a nurse holding a clipboard. Like a wolf, Roman's ears perked up. All the same, his head bowed in sadness when the nurse didn't call for them. In the corner, Roman leaned his long body over to the water cooler. He ignored the looks from other patients which were a mix of amusement and disgust as he struggled to pull the cup down and fill the water—too stubborn to get up and do it gracefully. After a few unattractive grunts, he successfully filled the cup halfway and sat back as he drank the contents in one gulp. He smiled with a satisfied grin to his captivated audience. The expression faded however as he turned back to his mate who didn't share his triumph. Instead, he crossed his arms.

"Do you hate me?" Roman asked.

"You could have just walked the two steps over."

Roman peered at the water cooler. "No. Not that. Do you hate how we got pregnant?" That comment made a few heads in the room jump up.

Mikaél's face flushed. "For Wolf-God's sake, Roman! Lower your voice!" he strained in a whisper.

"Sorry," he whispered back.

"What do you mean? Why would you ask that?" Mikaél pressed.

"Because it happened the very first time we tried. Not to mention we weren't actually trying. We didn't expect you to be in a heat. And then there's the fact the heat was an abrupt, emotional one."

"We've already discussed how this wasn't ideal. I'm not sure what you're looking for."

"Do you *resent* me?" Roman's expression fell to shame.

Thoughts danced in Mikaél's head. Roman's sincerity warranted a deeper reflection before answering. "No."

Light came back into Roman's eyes. "Really?"

"No," Mikaél said again. "Do I wish things had been different? I think anyone is capable of coming up with a suggestion on how any situation could be better. But we weren't ignorant, Roman. We knew what we were doing. And that took two of us. So, no, I don't resent you. I couldn't do this without you." He smiled.

Roman shook his head as he playfully dismissed his foolish insecurities. That is, after all, what they were. To have to ask almost a third of the way into the pregnancy should have sent Roman a message. Mikaél wasn't shy about sharing his emotions, and he definitely wasn't good at hiding them.

"They were supposed to be here already." Mikaél turned his head toward the door like he could see miles beyond it. Disappointment shadowed his face.

Roman was frustrated. Another letdown. "They'll be here. Don't worry." As he glided his fingers along his mate's hair, the natural instincts to comfort surfaced. But the accomplishment was short lived as the nurse came out to the waiting room again.

"Mikaél Cavenbelle?" The nurse smiled with his brown eyes and naturally jet-black hair. He guided the nervous couple back to their room. After the pair sat on the subpar quality couch, the nurse went over the usuals: confirming the appointment, vitals, and initial observations of Mikaél's overall health and baby bump. Finally, the nurse put on a stethoscope and placed it on his bare stomach. After a gentle expression, he commented on how healthy it sounded. "Good. We'll have the doctor come in and check you out and then do the sonogram."

Roman's brows furrowed. "Doctor? Don't you mean technician?"

"Yeah," Mikaél added, "I have the appointment downstairs after this."

The nurse hummed. "No, the doctor is having it done right here."

It was only then Mikaél took note of the large machine in the room. Had he paid attention a bit more, he would have recognized it quicker. "Do doctors usually do that?" Mikaél asked, full of concern.

"Doctors do what they feel is needed." The nurse smiled back. "If you'll wait here, Doctor Smith will be with you shortly."

After the nurse left, Mikaél shot a look at Roman. Feelings were turning into anxiety rather than excitement.

Roman tried easing the situation the best he could with the first thought which came to mind. "Doctor 'Smith'? Is he a lawyer, businessman, and a plumber, too?"

"You don't think there's something wrong, do you?" Mikaél's face began to blossom with worry.

"No, of course not. Everything is going to be fine." Sensing his mate couldn't shake the feeling, Roman came up and embraced him tightly. Mikaél rested his head in the curve of his neck. After a generous minute, a knock was heard on the door.

Mikaél's head shot up. "Wow, that was faster than I expected." As the door swung open, he quickly realized it wasn't the doctor but instead four individuals with subtle expressions. "Could you have waited any longer?"

"So sorry!" Alec replied. "We tried getting here as fast as we could."

Jake appeared. "Traffic got the better of us."

"Nothing like waiting until the last minute." Roman's gaze set upon his Sur. The message was clearly received.

"Are you both ready?" Adrian asked.

Roman exhaled. "I think so." He cautiously glanced at Mikaél who nodded and affirmed the sentiment.

"You know, I've heard of everyone being present at the birth, but don't you think it's a bit ridiculous to have the entire family at a sonogram? I mean, are Drew and Will not here because they weren't asked or because they couldn't commit?" It was a question Mikaél had wanted to ask for a while, but given the shaky nature of family dynamics, there weren't any hints of open invitations to have such candid conversations. It didn't make anything better when he noticed the room darken upon his inquiry.

Dustin stepped up to his son. "It's no secret we're all excited for this unprecedented pregnancy. But we've also mentioned concerns we have. It's better we all are in the know to help you in any way we can."

Roman showed his frustration. "You mean so you can study him more closely?"

"It's not like that," Dustin contested.

"Please. I've been an experiment ever since I could cry. Don't tell me what it is or isn't."

Dustin silenced himself upon the response.

Jake's face fired red. "Roman, you do not disrespect him like that. He's telling the truth. We're only looking out for Mikaél and the baby's wellbeing. That's why Mikaél has a doctor initiating the sonogram."

Roman became suspicious. "Hmph. How did this place know to have a doctor do it in the first place?"

"It's *my* doctor, Roman," Adrian answered. "Your father recommended you use him for a reason."

Roman huffed in pleasure. It was a good thing the doctor came in afterward, preventing him from saying anything else he might regret.

"Dr. Erricson! It's so good to see you! Adrian!" Dr. Smith held out a firm hand and commenced a family reunion. After all, it had been almost 20 years since Adrian saw him for his own pregnancy. "You must be Dr. Cavenbelle." Dr. Smith turned and welcomed him and Alec into the fold. "And *you* must be Mikaél and Roman."

Watching Dr. Smith address Mikaél last did not sit well with Roman. It was as if the doctor forgot he was supposed to care about his patient. He appeared more interested in networking. As much as he wanted to crucify him over it, Roman knew he needed the specialist –or whatever he was—so he bit his tongue.

"Roman! Haven't seen you in years!" Roman managed a hint of respect in return for the enthusiasm. "Sounds like Joel was happy with everything he saw. So, I'll just do a quick check and then we'll do what we've been waiting for!" Dr. Smith sounded jovial, like the appointment was a revelation of a new cellphone or car. Keeping with the upbeat disposition, he repeated the vitals from the nurse and moved to the ultrasound machine. He lifted Mikaél's shirt quickly, giving him no time to worry about any self-consciousness.

The baby bump was pronounced but nowhere near what it was going to be. Still, no first-time parent is truly prepared for it until it happens—at least that's what Mikaél's Veo had said. From there, Mikaél felt the cold gel and the wand pressing up against him. And finally, there it was: on a black screen with gray and white lines forming into shapes and curves, an outline of a pup came into view. The room hummed with emotion. It didn't affect Mikaél until he saw Roman's face. The more Roman squeezed his hand, the more his emotions built up a pressure, ready to release tears of joy. When Mikaél saw the first drop casually fall, he felt his own eyes sting from emotion.

"There we are!" Dr. Smith smiled. "Boy, this little pup must have known you were coming in today. What a view!"

"That's him, Roman," Mikaél whispered.

Roman sniffled and nodded his head. "Yeah, there he is." Suddenly, Roman's mind flashed back to his protective Alpha instinct. "Is everything as it should be? I mean, is he healthy?"

"Oh, yes," Dr. Smith replied, "it appears to be showing appropriate growth and vitality. But..." His head turned as he leaned into his screen.

Mikaél's heart jumped. "What? What's wrong?!"

"My Wolf-God," Dr. Smith whispered. "It appears you are correct in your theory, Dr. Erricson."

Adrian grabbed ahold of his mate, unsure if he should be elated or scared. Jake didn't help the situation any.

Mikaél pleaded again. "What's wrong? What's going on?"

Dr. Smith took a deep breath, refusing to take his sight off the screen. "Either your son is lacking his genitalia, or you are having a female pup."

Panic hit Mikaél.

Roman acknowledged it instantly. "A female? What do you mean?"

Now the doctor fully turned around, ready to make sure Roman heard loud and clear. "You are going to have a baby girl."

It still didn't sink in for Roman. The words refused to stick. Looking at the image on the screen didn't make it any more real. This fragile, tiny, and innocent life was a girl? Believing it was impossible. A ruse. A joke—a cruel one at that. Typically, this was a one liner used as a friendly scare or tease geared toward an expecting couple. Roman never heard of a doctor being so bold to join in on the antic. What was even more telling was the fact none of the future grandparents acted like this was a joke.

This wasn't a joke.

This was for real.

***

"You *knew*?!" Roman exclaimed. The need to have decorum wasn't as imperative to him anymore. Dr. Smith had left moments before.

"No," Jake defended, "we did not *know*. It was only a possibility. This was the only way we were going to find out."

"How long did you know this for?"

Jake braced himself. "Dr. Birowack expressed the idea not too long after we discovered Mikaél was a Type 6."

"Your boss came up with this crap?" Roman's question didn't receive a response. "Why couldn't you tell me? Or tell Mik? This is our child! You didn't think it was important to tell *us*?"

"Respectfully, no," Jake declared.

"Why?!"

"This was a *theory*, Roman. Do you have any idea what the world would be like if every time a scientist had a hypothesis, they shared it? It would be utter madness. There was no need to tell you if this didn't exist."

Roman couldn't believe his father's justification. He had just watched his love's face—Mikaél was scared to death. His voice softened, but his heart hardened. "Is that what you think we are? Two people on the edge of madness you have to pet like we're animals?"

Adrian touched Roman's shoulder. It felt stiff like hardwood. The tension was immovable. "We have never thought that about you."

"Yeah, right," Roman scoffed.

"Damn it, Roman! Listen!" Jake took command of the room. "I'm sorry if life constantly throws you curveballs. But the fact of the matter is we are here to support you now—we all are."

Dustin chimed in, looking to present himself as a formidable Alpha. "We don't want you to go through all this alone. We care about nothing other than you and the health of your pup."

Mikaél turned to face his Sur. Eerie feelings began taking over him. Like Roman, the words of comfort did little for him. "Dad, why is the doctor doing my ultrasound? And why did he appear to know all about this before we did?"

Jake took the lead once more, pushing Dustin's efforts back. "I've known Dr. Smith for years and took a chance on the promise we could trust him."

"Trust?" Mikaél inquired, still in disbelief.

"It shouldn't be a surprise, Mik." Dustin treaded lightly. "This news isn't something we need publicized."

Mikaél growled. "Why? Because my child defies every natural law on this earth?"

"Clearly not," Alec replied.

Dustin resumed. "The only words we need right now are of support. Yes, there is a population out there who would see this as a progressive miracle. Probably even a sign from Wolf-God himself. But as you know, there are plenty of conservatives would believe nothing less than the worst."

"What? Like the Wolf-Devil?" Roman spat back.

"Does that surprise you?" Jake probed.

Roman dipped his head to the floor. He had no reason to doubt the claim. Roman heard the same criticism growing up—even though Type 6 Alphas were well established back then.

"I think there's at least one thing we can agree upon," Jake confirmed. "We are all proud of what is happening here. This is our grandchild. However, out of safety, no one outside this room hears of this. The only other is Dr. Birowack. Oh, and Dr. Smith."

"Can we trust him?" Roman asked.

"Yes."

"What incentive does he have not to blast this to every news outlet in the territory?"

Jake understood the hesitation. "The foundation of this is doctor-patient confidentiality. But we also thought he'd be interested in getting updates on this one-of-a-kind experience—not to mention—also attending the birth."

The words hit Roman like knives hitting nerves from his feet to his head. "'Not like that,' huh? That sounds exactly what this is: another doctor getting in on the rarest scientific discovery. Soon, Mikaél will have several pairs of hands ready to dissect every inch of his body while waiting on his every word as if he's going to say something to crack the secret code. That's if the gallon of blood you're going to want to drain from him doesn't tell you first."

Alec rushed over to hold a soundlessly sobbing Mik. "It's okay. Don't cry."

Roman felt the gut punch when he realized he was beginning to equal with his father in originating pain for his loved ones. "Look. I was an anomaly accepted for my Status as an Alpha. If it ever gets out Mikaél is not only a Type 6 Omega but also pregnant with a female child, this will not go without consequence."

Jake entertained the set-up. "I've been by your side ever since you were a newly typed pup. We educated you, protected you, monitored your health, and gave you the best opportunities we could think of. Now, you will be a parent yourself and go right back to square one where your father and I once were with you. So, what is it you want from me right now?"

The angst melted away as Roman's usual nature came forward. This was the Roman of compassion and centered thinking. "Help us."

The words alone had enough power to shatter every piece of glass in a radius. Everyone took notice of the words which weren't natural for an Alpha who had a chip on his shoulder for the last few months. And yet, here he was, speaking honestly and naked.

"We do have another option." Jake's words were cautious as he signaled for Dustin's support. With Dustin assessing Mikaél's now mild state in the care of Alec, Roman allowed Jake to proceed. "You're right, Roman. It's bad enough Higher-Types have issues with mortality rates during birth, but you have this on a whole new level. An entire hospital of medical professionals won't know how to respond—let alone prevent this from getting out into the community."

Roman snorted. "Let's hear what you've already planned for months now."

"Dr. Birowack has a trusted colleague, Dr. Zang, who works in the Western Territory. There's a quaint little town out there which liberally accepts the work of the research facility. It is Dr. Zang's professional opinion that this would be a great place for you and Mikaél to go and wait out the pregnancy. This is far away from prying eyes who would wish to endanger you."

The blood rose to Roman's face. "You *what*?" It took every ounce for Roman not to rip his father a new one.

"You want us to move? By ourselves?" Mikaél searched his Veo's expression for the truth.

"I think we should table the discussion for the time being." Alec attempted to calm the waters.

"Sur?" Mikaél asked. Dustin's sight shifted to his mate and then to his son. "This is true then?"

"We agree this is the best option for your safety," Dustin said.

"Then I don't think we have anything else to discuss," Mikaél replied. "Get out."

Alec gasped at his comment. "What?"

"I want you to leave." Mikaél held his words with as much confidence as he could, his chest beginning to heave.

"Mik, are you okay?" Roman asked.

"No, Roman, I'm not." Creasing his lips and eyeing the ceiling, he carried on, "I'm starting to see the same truth you already knew. We're never going to be respected like human beings—just lab rats."

"That's not what we said at all!" Dustin defended.

"Yes, it is!" Mikaél spat back.

"How do you figure?"

"That's exactly what this is. Last time I checked, dads don't send their kids to a research facility. They send them to a hospital!"

For the first time, Dustin truly felt what the Erricson betrayal motif felt like. He never anticipated such misfortune and anger to come from what was considered a sacred bond between two men. At this point, fate seemed to communicate the pair were star-crossed lovers, not destiny. Having to be a victim of his son's wrath over an example of unconditional love was a proverb in the making. After blubbering failed attempts at more defensive pleas, he accepted in surrender and gestured for Alec to follow him.

Alec himself felt naked in a room with strangers. The son he shared a kindred spirit with wanted nothing to do with him— demanded he leave. Patting his son's shoulder to say goodbye broke every happiness he had for the moment. For a second, he forgot about his grandchild. All he knew was he was being lumped together with a duo of scientists who forgot the humanitarian side of their decisions. Was he a victim himself? Perhaps. He was now equally complicit in attempting to control his son and son-in-law's future. The price of ignorance was bad enough; the price of refusing to stand up and speak out was worse.

It only took a few seconds for Jake and Adrian to follow. They held a tattoo of shame which was so old it was beginning to fade. Once again, they found themselves completely on the outside of their sons' lives.

"Mik?" Roman asked as he heard the door close. "Talk to me?" His voice was soft. None of this was his to blame, but he wasn't convinced Mikaél was going to treat him fairly.

A silence hovered for several uncomfortable seconds. The struggle to hold it together was harder than childbirth—not that he knew. "I don't understand how this all went wrong." Involuntary huffs came from deep inside his chest. "This day was supposed to be one of the happiest occasions of our lives and now... now..."

"It still is," Roman finished. "They're not going to take this moment away from us, Mik. I refuse."

Mik's voice hardened. "I'm not going out there in no man's land, Roman. No way." Roman's face gave no reaction. "You told me of all the horrible things about what it was like to be under the heel of your father for just being who you are. No good came to it." Mikaél wiped away his own stray tear. "Our lives will not be subjected to this anymore. And I will die before I let our..." The pause came fast as he realized what had to come next.

"Daughter." Roman cracked a smile, but the nerves stuck with him just the same. "Our *daughter* will not be a science experiment. I promise."

Relief flooded Mikaél. He needed to hear those words more than anything. They slowed the world back down and centered his thoughts like a laser pointer. He had his Fate in front of him and their child inside him. Nothing else mattered. "Thank you," he whispered.

CHAPTER 09:

TO GO UP IN PRAISE & DOWN IN FLAMES

"So, you are going to make nice with our dads before Winter Solstice, right?" Roman paced the floor of their apartment. The success of the phone conversation was lukewarm, but the tension was just heating up.

"*Me?* Are you kidding?" Rixen's voice carried teeth.

"Rixen, I understand what your point of view is on all of this, but you guys have got to give a little."

Rixen's voice carried on his emotional plight as Roman heard the apartment's door open and close. Mikaél walked in and acknowledged him. He started with a smile, but it faded when he realized it wasn't a joyous social call. He set down his bag and walked to the open living room instead and turned on the TV. After blocking out most of what Rixen had said, Roman jumped in before the monologue got too carried away.

"I think our dads are working on it, Rixen. They'll get their act together. Right now, all of us have a bone to pick with them so it's not as if they're sitting at home proud of themselves."

"Wait. You too?" Rixen's voice perked up with curiosity. "What happened?"

"It's a long story," Roman dragged out. As Rixen began his protest in the dismissal of Roman's latest run-in with all the parents at the doctor's office, he noticed Mikaél sitting like a statue right in front of the screen like a zombie. Not fully able to see what captured his attention so much, Roman listened in with a free ear.

A voice burned into his ear and flowed throughout his entire body. Suddenly, Rixen's words became background noise—an irritant to what truly required his attention. "Rixen, I have to call you back."

When Roman walked toward the living room, he hoped his presence would break the spell over Mikaél. But no such change occurred. Standing near him, Roman studied his face. It was ice cold and pale. Looking down he could see his chest rising and falling with a purpose and his fingers slightly shake. Roman wrapped his hand around him and listened to the determination of an odious statesman.

"...I have spent the better half of my life fighting for what I believed in. I championed the rights of Omegas in order to lift them out of oppression. I challenged any conservative foe who believed Omegas were less than their Alpha and Beta counterparts. My message was for equality including mating contracts, social hierarchy, career preference and hireability, and reproductive rights. Right now, before the city of Tauris and all in the territory who are watching, I can firmly say... I was wrong."

The words pierced Roman through the heart. He knew the man who passionately fought for these rights firsthand. Whether he wanted to admit it or not, Roman was once schooled by the proud man and his liberal agenda. It impressed him to the point where he changed and accepted his changed views. Being contracted to his Fate made Roman believe Mikaél was worthy of every right an Alpha should have. But to hear the man who damn near led a revolution in this city begin to reverse his own crusade was frightening.

"Citizens of Tauris, I stand before you a man in shock and a man in fear. I have the undesirable burden to share with you that what I thought was a fight to encourage equality was truly a fight to overthrow every natural balance bestowed upon this Wolf-God given earth. The righteous movement to have Omegas stand next to their counterparts was corrupted by those who wanted nothing more than to tear the natural fabric apart and destroy life as we know it.

Deep in the heart of our city, the Wolf-Devil's work is being done. Extreme liberalists are seeking to wipe out Wolf-descendants forever in the hopes of placing Omegas on the golden throne. One by one, they will decide who is allowed to pass on their genes and family legacy and who won't. That is why I am in fear. Look at your sons: your innocent pups, your emerging adolescents, and your fearless adults. Do you want them to be the last of your legacy? The last of theirs? I don't want it to be. And I will die fighting to make sure that doesn't happen to my family or yours.

And that is why I, Matthew Whitmore, will be facing off in the election against the incumbent Pack Alpha for the City of Tauris and the Eastern Territory under the proud flag of the Conservative Party. Why? Because I want there to be a tomorrow for you and for everyone else. I am lucky enough to have the support of my entire family. Here, today, I have my mate Terrence standing unconditionally by my side. My son Peyton was not able to make it today. He is busy with his altruistic nonprofit business 'Hope's Horizon.' If he had to miss this announcement, I'm glad it's because he tirelessly works to makes sure Omegas are kept safe off the streets and are given a chance to thrive in this ever-changing world we have. Because *that's* what I fought for and will continue to fight for today. I know I have his support and I hope I have yours. Bless you all. Thank you and goodnight."

A roaring applause from downtown Tauris blared through the speakers. For a second, Roman was convinced he was standing there in person, watching Whitmore give his prophetic speech. The live feed then cut to the news studio with a stunned reporter holding his composure as best as he could.

"For those of you who may have joined us just now, Matthew Whitmore, owner and CEO of Silver Bullet Drilling, has just announced he is running for Pack Alpha of Tauris and the Eastern Territory. Whitmore has had an extensive and successful history advocating under the Liberal Party. Now, it seems here, he has declared he is abandoning that party and their message to join in the *Conservative* Party. Once again, if you were not tuned in, Whitmore is now making extraordinary claims that entities within the Liberal Party are responsible for an unknown plot to control populations to favor Omegas. It is not clear who, what, or how these actions are being carried out or, if it is true, why. We will keep you updated as soon as we hear more details."

What was worse? Whitmore's ludicrous accusations and cause against Omegas? Or was it the fact Roman felt in his gut the city of Tauris and the Eastern Territory were about to change forever? The whimpers coming from his mate told him all he needed to know.

"Mik?" he asked. No answer. "Mik?" ... "Mik!" Jumping out of a trance, Roman finally broke him of his spell. "Hey," he whispered. "Everything will work out." The words flowed out automatically, almost robotic.

"How can you stand there and say that?" Mikaél's voice quivered. Hearing the passion and the determination in Whitmore's voice was the march of a thousand men. Torches. Pitchforks. Chants. All these flooded through his mind.

"I say it because it's true."

"Didn't you hear him? He has an agenda. I don't think he's talking about random people around the world, Roman. He's talking about us."

Roman struggled for the right word. "So?"

"*So? SO?!* Wake up! This is what my nightmares have been about. This is what everything has been about! That man is after us! He knows about me. I feel it. You're right. That corrupt asshole of a doctor must have said something already." Mikaél began to shake. Nothing could appease his frightened state.

"He didn't look like the kind of guy who would betray our dads like that. If they trust him, there's no reason to think we can't trust him." It hit Roman in a funny way knowing he was defending the people who have irritated him so much as of late. Without having proper time to reflect on the statement, he kept going. "I just don't think Whitmore has the bullseye target on us like you're assuming." Hearing the meltdown hurt Roman to no end. All he wanted was to wrap him in the tightest embrace like a bulletproof vest. "Babe..."

"No." Mikaél backed away. "I'm not looking to be comforted. And I'm *definitely* not looking to be told I'm stupid."

"I never called you that! I never will!" Roman's blood began to boil. Mikaél's anger began to shift from a minacious flat screen T.V. to him. The flood of emotion hit him hard.

"Just don't, okay?" Mikaél threw his hand up in defense.

"You can't honestly be holding me somehow responsible for this? I've been here for you ever since the first day I met you!" Roman defended.

"Well," Mikaél scoffed, "not the *first* day."

Roman grunted through his tight jaw. "That's not fair and you know it."

"Really? Because right now I'm feeling attacked at the worst time of feeling the most vulnerable. Thanks for that." The tears were dropping from eyes of fire.

Roman shook his head in disbelief. This time, his voice lowered. "This isn't like you, Mik." He paused and considered his next words. "It's the pregnancy hormones talking. Not you."

Mikaél's eyes widened like he just witnessed a vicious crime. No. Worse. The crime was directly committed against him. "You did not just say that."

"What? How is that so wrong? This isn't you," he pleaded.

"Wrong. This isn't *you*. The mate I know would never dismiss me and push me away like I'm some child. What now? Am I just going to wear a sign on my back that says, 'Watch out, pregnant!' so people know not to take anything I say seriously?"

A headache started throbbing in Roman's head. "Are you listening to yourself? The words coming out of your mouth alone should tell you that you're not thinking straight. You've never said anything like this before."

Mikaél rubbed his eyes as he prepped for his inevitable statement. "I want to go to the Western Territory."

A string of words in a foreign language hit Roman's ear. "What?" His head leaned in, making sure he heard every word.

"I said, 'I want to go to the Western Territory.'"

No. Roman heard the words right. He still didn't recognize the person saying them. "You can't be serious."

"I need someone close to me who is going to advocate for me like they're taking me seriously. Obviously, that's not you." Mikaél turned away from Roman's sight. Although he felt justified in his statement, he knew the words were severing major arteries. He refused to look at Roman to read his expression.

For Roman, the words triggered out emotions in a rush: hurt, anger, confusion, madness, but mostly sadness. His Fate Mate had declared to him he'd rather seek shelter and comfort from an unknown entity over him.

In a similar way, there was a Wolf-God proverb which spoke of a spirit pack gone a sunder. The defecting wolves left on a full moon—one of the most sacred nights in existence. The story goes that the stray wolves roamed the earth and became stained and scarred by the curses from the Wolf-Devil himself: hatred, greed, jealousy, famine, disease, and death. When the wolves returned to their spirit pack, they brought the curses into the Spirit World. In the darkness of the New Moon, the curses slipped into humanity during the night when no one could see them. Ever since, the curses were said to rise up once a Fated couple loses their sacred bond: arguments, violence, relationship challenges, separations, death, and any moment in which a Fated lover can't be reached physically or emotionally.

Now, Roman felt his curse for the first time ever since climbing and succeeding the uphill battle for what he wanted most: his mate. "Mik. Please. I love you."

"I need us to go to the Western Territory." The repeated words were beginning to send Mikaél into a tailspin. Was Roman honestly not listening? "And we need to go now."

Roman puffed his chest. It was a move he never anticipated ever using against his one true love. But he was standing there steaming with Alpha hormones which filled the room. "No."

The one word thrust Mikaél's head forward as he squinted his eyes. "*No*? What do you mean 'No'?"

"You laid on that exam table earlier today and ripped our dads a new one about what they were doing against us." He observed Mikaél's face turn sour as if he interpreted Roman's words as placing blame. "Don't get me wrong—rightfully so. But you were standing your ground fighting for what was right. Selfishly, I thought it was one of best things I ever saw you do. To go back on it now is to absolve any responsibility on their part for what they did to us. But all of a sudden, that asshole on T.V. says he's running for political office, and *that's* what you can't stand up to?" Mikaél stood there, mute and motionless. "So, I'm going to ask you this... which Mikaél should I believe is in his right mind: Mikaél this morning or Mikaél now?"

There was an inability to blink on Mikaél's part. Standing on the scale of reason was a delicate balancing act. On one hand, he would have to concede to his parents and realize they were still in control of his life perhaps now even more so than before in his pup years. On the other hand, he was on his first standoff with his mate since the day they met. The choice to force an Alpha's natural loyalty to their Omega against them was not a gift to take advantage of. An Omega who chose to exploit the power typically found themselves on the receiving end of an Alpha's rage once its effects wore off. But to yield to Roman was to recognize his mate came from an old bloodline of Alphas who still believe Omegas were made to be less than equal—and even worse—made to obey.

A constant flood of vibration filled the room as both of their phones began receiving message after message. Mikaél was the first to pick up his phone and examine the continuous attempts to get through. As he scrolled through the history, he realized both he and Roman must have been so engrossed in their argument, it drowned out any noise they should have heard from the phones earlier.

"What's going on?" Roman asked with subtle frustration as he attempted to unlock his own phone.

A heavy gasp left Mikaél's throat. "We need to go. Right now."

City lights kept the sky bright in downtown every night in the city of Tauris. But their glittery attempts were no match to the dazzling lights of fire trucks, ambulances, and police cars. Huddled in a half circle, the emergency vehicles created a barrier only qualified personnel were able to pass. Beyond them, crowds of onlookers stood staring like moths to flames. And flames they were.

Like a miniature blaze from the sun, a tall, two-story building stood in an inferno, painting everything around it with its billows of black smoke. The fire roared like a vicious animal. It laughed at the attempts water made to tame its wild ways. At this point, professionals had deemed the building a total loss. Now, the goal was to spare its adjoining buildings as best as they could.

Roman's car couldn't penetrate the growing crowds nor the makeshift security line. The car squealed as he pounded the brake.

Mikaél had already attempted his ejection from the vehicle before it had even come to a full stop.

"Mik!" Roman's voice was lost to the sounds of the shouting crowds, blazing sirens, and the hearty laughter of the flames.

Mikaél began an attempt at a slow and steady jog. As he did, he began to notice the limitations of his pregnancy set in. His attempt to test his own limits were stopped quickly by a tall statuesque Alpha officer.

"Young man!" he yelled. "You can't pass this line. We're urging all citizens to clear the area. There are too many people here as it is. You're preventing the personnel from doing their jobs."

"That's my dad's studio!" Mikaél's unguarded emotion sank into the commanding officer. But the moment was short lived as a loud explosion rang out from a second-floor window. The flames crawled out and up into the sky like a demon's arm rising from Hell itself. Observing the officer standing still in awe, Mikaél began to push his way to the side of the officer to gain closer access. The attempt was futile as the officer grabbed his arm, preventing his body from going forward.

"Sir, I need you to turn back now and head to safety before we have a problem!" With a natural instinct, the officer took his free arm and reached back for his handcuffs and contemplated whether or not he was going to actually detain an Omega clearly in an emotional state.

"Hey!" Roman barked. "What are you doing?"

The officer released Mikaél's arm. "Are you with him?"

"He's my mate!"

"Then can you please tell your mate he needs to—"

"Dad!" Mikaél's voice rang out as he saw both of his fathers zigzagging through the onlookers and screaming personnel. The officer eased his stance as he allowed the reunion to commence. "What happened? What's going on?"

"Mik, you shouldn't be here!" Alec held his son close to his chest as he felt his mate wrap his arms around them both. After the embrace, he faced his son, forgetting he was 17 and not 7. "I texted you not to come here. We were going to call you after this got under control!"

"There was no way I was just going to sit by and wait all night for a call! What's going on?" Knowing his parents were safe, Mikaél's mind zeroed in on the spectacle that was before him. All his Veo's hard work was up in smoke. The literal context hurt worse than any artistic expression he could make. But there it was. Everything. Gone.

"We don't know," Dustin began. "We received a call from Sam's Delicatessen next door. He said a customer who was sitting near the windows began seeing flames reflect off the front of the showroom. Next thing we knew..." It was hard for Dustin to continue. He knew what all this meant to his mate. Alec's heartache was so visible, it was hard not to feel every bit of emotion. Not that Dustin would have it any other way. "...we were called and got here about 30 minutes before you did."

Alec's eyes were moist with sadness. He didn't have enough energy in him to go through another breakdown as he had when he first saw the inconceivable scene in front of him. "Well," he murmured, "that's that."

Mikaél narrowed his sight. "What do you mean?"

"I think that does it for the studio dream."

The strings on Mikaél's heart tugged. "No, no. Dad, I know everything in there is lost, but you can start over. You're the best photographer I know."

He grabbed his son in a side hug. "Don't worry about it, sweetheart. Most of my prints are digital. There are some I can't get back, but most... most I can. Luckily, I think all of yours can be saved."

"I'd love to see them in a studio again." The guilt trip was a bit selfish in the moment. But Mikaél didn't quite know which approach to take. Everything seemed hazy. Maybe it was too much stimuli. Maybe it was all the toxic smoke still hurling out of the building. Whatever it was, he found his legs starting to wobble.

"Whoa!" Roman stopped him from making any stumble of consequence, but everyone noticed it. "I think it's time we leave. This is getting to be too much stress."

"I'm fine!" Mikaél lamented. He didn't do himself any favors in how he responded.

"No," Dustin chimed in, "Roman is right. You need to go and get some fresh air. Take some time to take this in and relax."

"Relax?" The word was offensive and even that was putting it lightly. "I can't relax when I know you two are here dealing with this."

Once again, Alec appreciated the empathy and care his son wanted to give him. Instantly, in the moment, he knew Mikaél was going to be a great parent one day. "It's okay, Mikaél. There's not much anyone can do right now. We'll be all right. The important thing to remember is no one was hurt. Go. We'll give you a call tomorrow. How's that?"

If anyone else had requested, even as eloquently as his Veo, Mikaél wouldn't have been moved. But the connection to his Omega father was stronger than it had been in a long time. There was healing without even having to going through the natural process. It was instant and without thought. Still... backing away from it all was difficult. In his short contemplation, he let Roman take him back home.

As he clicked his seatbelt in the passenger seat, an ominous thought crept into his mind. It was one he couldn't get his mind to concentrate on with such chaos happening in front of him. Now, a million thoughts ran through his head.

Was this done on purpose?

"I'm just saying," Roman began as he pushed the car door shut, "if you took the day off from school tomorrow, I don't think anyone would think less of you. You'd have some time to process the trauma. In addition, you'd get to relax and recharge your batteries."

There was that word "relax" again. It was beginning to become a trigger word. Mikaél huffed. "I don't need a day off. I'm good. And why is 'relax' the buzzword of the evening?" Mikaél replied, annoyed.

"Because you're pregnant, babe."

Mikaél sighed. "Yeah. I know, Roman. I was there."

"You're not helping."

"Funny. That was my sentiment about you, too."

"Mik, twenty minutes ago, you were standing in front of your Veo's career burning to the ground. Literally. This is not a small thing."

The truth crawled into Mikaél's skin. "You don't need to tell me that."

"Then can you acknowledge I have some validity, please?" No answer. "I know you view all my opinions and suggestion as a sign of me thinking you are weak. In reality, if you were to take my advice, you'd actually be viewed as a person of strength." That only elicited a sarcastic stare in return. "I'm serious!" Roman struggled as they walked from the parking garage to the high rise. "You know, I grew up with siblings, too. Rixen and Ryan struggled with being told they shouldn't push themselves beyond what might have been too much. They always thought since I could do it that meant they should do it. You grew up with Drew, and from what you told me, it was a similar experience. I know that's hard to deal with. Does that help?"

Mikaél stopped in his tracks and turned to his Fate. "No. It doesn't actually."

Now Roman was lost. "Why?"

"Because in that scenario, you got to be Drew. I don't think it was too difficult for you to grow up as the gold standard. When you take a walk in my shoes of growing up as second best, especially as an Omega, then come talk to me."

Roman swallowed hard and felt his feet sink a foot below his ego. He watched Mikaél walk away in disgust. What was happening to him? How could he have gone from everything his mate wanted just a couple months ago to be the one person he felt agitated the most by? Was this how a relationship was supposed to go?

Roman remembered hearing about contracted mates constantly at odds. The instinctive pull Fates had was nonexistent. Although it was rare to break a contract and survive without social condemnation, it was more common to stay together in the shadows of what once was. But that's not what he and Mikaél had. This was sacred. A bond. A biological need to feel complete only a Fate could fulfill. And yet, here he was left in the dust. The biological need was a blessing and a curse. Alphas were programmed to satisfy their Omegas, in any sense of the word. To have Mikaél at odds with him for so long was beginning a dangerous trend he feared wasn't going away. It was bad enough Mikaél was struggling with his own family. How long was it going to take before Roman was put into the same category? He wasn't going to let that happen. Quickly, he ran just as Mikaél opened the full glass doors to the lobby. He had already pushed the elevator button.

"Wait!" Roman cried out. He made it just in time before Mikaél walked into the open shaft.

"You've made me miss the elevator," he whined.

"I know. But it can wait." He gently held onto Mikaél's shoulders and steadied his eye contact. "You're right." An eye roll shot back at him. "You are. I'm wrong. I'm deciding what you should do. I keep doing it without even asking you what you think or want. For that, I'm sorry. The only excuse I have is that I love you. I want you safe. I want our baby safe. That's all."

Mikaél scratched his head. He appreciated the words. It meant everything to him. However, the frustration was harder to get passed than he thought. "I know. I know. It's just... things are changing *so* fast. Every time I think things are going to get better, or at least normal, they get worse." Roman held his gaze, waiting for the ending blow. It didn't disappoint. "In all of it, I never anticipated you'd be someone making it worse."

If Roman's determination to fix his mate hadn't kicked in his Alpha pheromones, the words could have crushed him. Instead, he chose to not let it affect him. His eyes closed and his stance elevated.

"What do I have to do in order to prove to you I'm not one of those people—that I'm someone who is going to be right there every step of the way—that I'm willing to do whatever it takes to show you I will be the person you expect me to be?"

A sudden crash shattered one of the glass doors leading into the lobby. Roman didn't have to even think of what to do. His instinct kicked in as he grabbed Mikaél's body and shielded him from any potential harm. As the glass continued to fall like a loud rainstorm, the sound of a loud thud followed. A brick. Rubber bands hugged something tight against it.

Roman turned and aimed his gaze like a sniper's rifle to a car barely lit by the building's light. The ancient wolf inside wanted to lunge and jump as if he had supernatural powers onto the car and rip the perpetrator to shreds. Sounds of agonizing bloody screams would be music to his ears. But he had his pregnant mate to protect. The urge to cover him like a bulletproof vest tugged at his ability to make the right choice.

Unfortunately, the decision was made for him. Squealing tires and rushing taillights wiped out any chance Roman of specifically identifying the car or its driver. The leftover silence put his mate's fearful whimpers on display.

"Are you hurt?" Roman gasped.

Mikaél couldn't answer. He shook his head and tried to hold the tiny bits of stabilization he had left from the nightmares of the day.

Roman rushed to the lobby doors. Instead of opening the remaining door, he opted to hop through the gap of the obliterated one. He knew there was no chance in tracing the car, but he couldn't help himself. No clues were left behind on the street. They had won. Roman failed. He failed his mate. With the remaining dignity he had left, he ran back to Mikaél. He examined and touched every part of his upper body including his small round stomach.

"Did anything hit you? Glass? The rock?"

The rock.

Roman picked it up as Mikaél reassured him once again, he was unscathed. He couldn't pull the rubber band off fast enough. There, printed on bright white paper, were the blackest letters reading...

Type 6 Omegas are an abomination.

YOU. WILL. BURN. TOO.

The next day, Mikaél tried to listen to Dr. Johannes's lecture. He could have been asking if he wanted a new car or luxurious vacation and it wouldn't have made a difference. The only thing he could concentrate on were visions of massive flames and the sounds of glass shattering. Needless to say, he didn't get much sleep last night.

Against Roman's wishes, he still came to class. When he tried getting Mikaél's parents to convince him otherwise, it had an opposite effect. They assured them the cleanup and paperwork from the fire would keep them busy for days. They also commented how it was better for him to keep his routine. Mikaél was shocked he didn't use the latter incident of the brick smashing through the lobby window as a wild card to solidify his argument for a "sick" day. Then again, Mikaél begging Roman not to probably had something to do with it.

Although Roman never said anything, it was clear he was not happy about being dismissed by both his mate and his mate's parents.

But what was Mikaél supposed to do? It was better to have a distraction instead of constantly dwelling on the issue alone in the house. That's what he originally thought anyway. If he had known how it was going to play out today, he would have reconsidered.

Mr. Cavenbelle.

Mr. Cavenbelle.

"Mr. Cavenbelle?"

The voice trailed into Mikaél's ear. Finally, the synapses in his brain reconnected and he remembered where he was. His enthusiasm didn't take hold and he lifted his head slowly off his resting hand. "Yes, Dr. Johannes?" he mumbled.

"Answer the question, please."

A silence surrounded him, and his throat went dry. "I—I don't know the question. I'm sorry." His Omega pheromones released subservience—a feeling he wasn't used to as of late.

"I see." He spoke in that professional teacher tone which meant he was going to be made an example of. Dr. Johannes didn't disappoint. "I understand I may be the latest addition to your father's laboratory, but that doesn't give you an excuse to not pay attention."

A few snickers and comments were heard. They held onto Mikaél's temples like a vice grip. "I'm sorry, doctor. It won't happen again." *Is he serious right now?* How could he not know what happened to his Veo's studio? His attitude came off like he was the latest cool kid in a club that only accepted Mikaél because he just happened to be blood related.

"Could someone else who did hear my question answer please?" The doctor searched the small auditorium for a volunteer. He found one all too willing—the worst one possible. "Yes, Mr. Brody?"

Charles spoke to Dr. Johannes directly. "The reason post education is designed to be eight years is to help ensure our most critical occupations are held by individuals who are dedicated to the profession and can be trusted. This weeds out Lower-Types. Completing eight years requires a lot of stamina." Then, he made sure to look back at Mikaél. "Omegas can quickly find themselves unable to keep up with its demands, and they usually tuck their tails and go back to home to the safety of their Alphas." A narrowed stare, "Especially, pregnant ones." As Mikaél looked back, Charles returned a cat's grin.

Dr. Johannes sensed the minor standoff and grunted. "I believe there was some embellishment on several parts to that, Mr. Brody." He then spoke to the entire room. "All right, class dismissed. See you all tomorrow."

Mikaél was seething. He couldn't believe Charles directed the comment back on him so blatantly. Perhaps underestimating him was the mistake. He already knew Charles detested him as an Omega. The accidental reveal he gave him about being a Type 6—whether Charles believed him or not—didn't help. It was the pregnancy hormones. He couldn't explain it any other way. But adrenaline ran through his extremities. As he watched Charles saunter out of the room to the rest of the campus, the urge to pounce was screaming through him. Somewhere in himself, he found the strength to confront the vicious Alpha.

When Charles reached the edge of the open balcony, Mikaél called to him before he could make his dissent to the main floor. "Hey!" he yelled through gritted teeth.

What was he thinking? Omegas never provoked Alphas in this way unless they were prepared for bloodshed—a worthy move for a tall, muscled specimen looking to prove himself in haze of dominant pheromones. Unfortunately, none of these attributes belonged to Mikaél. By comparison, Mikaél was a slim, petite gymnast with no skill standing next to a firm, seasoned professional rugby player.

"Well, well, if it isn't Omega 5. I'm sorry. I meant Omega _6_." He stood a bit taller as he amused himself with the comment.

Mikaél threw his bag down at Charles's feet. The move seemed to entertain Charles more than anything. "When are you going to get it through your thick skull that I am not less than you just because I'm an Omega?!"

Charles snorted, "When hell freezes over, my little Omega."

"I'm not your Omega!" Mikaél barked back.

"Oh, believe me, I know it. If you were, I'd have you locked up in some cage for the rest of your life. The only conundrum I'd have is whether or not I should knock you up during your heats or drug you completely out of your psychotic mind while I make you watch me fuck a worthwhile Omega. If you kept insisting on your elevated Omega Type as you are now, you'd make the decision a lot easier."

Hearing Charles's voice alone made his skin tightened up. All the minute hairs on his body stood up like a wild animal. "What makes you think any Omega wants you if this is the way you talk to them?" Now Charles was *really* laughing at him. "What's so funny?"

"I'm not sure what delusional idea you have in your head about Omega equality, but whatever it is, you need to have your head examined."

"Wake up, Charlie! You're behind the times."

"No! *You* wake up!" Charles's voice boomed. A few bystanders noticed. They could scent the anger starting to build a dark aura around both him and Mikaél. "Your stupid Omega Freedom groups may get a lot of airplays on the news, but that's not how the real world works. When you step outside your privileged and safe neighborhood out there on the hill, Alphas roam and control everywhere else."

"That's not true." Mikaél shook his head as if he knew better. Still, there was a seed of doubt starting to plant deep inside him. Charles was not backing off his overbearing Alpha stance. That worried him more than it should have.

"It *is* true. I don't know if you watch the *real* news, but there's a man out there running for Supreme Alpha who is going to put all you Omegas back in your place. When Matthew Whitmore wins, everything will be right in this world again."

A horrible churning sound went through Mikaél's stomach. "That man is a monster!"

"That man is a saint! And when he wins, every Omega with their head in the clouds is going to get a weight attached to their foot. They will crash down so hard they'll fall through the cracks of the earth and burn in Hell—right where they belong. I, personally, can't wait to wear shades and watch the flames consume you all."

Burn. *Burn?* The words flashed in like lightning. Everything made sense. From the confrontation last week to last night's event, there was only one possible conclusion. It had to be Charles. By the time Mikaél was done with his mental assessment, Charles had somehow begun his descent downstairs.

"You did it. Didn't you?" There was no question—not in Mikaél's mind.

"Did what?" Charles resumed walking down the stairs, finished with the unnecessary aggravation.

"Last night. You burned down my Veo's studio."

The railing on the staircase squeaked as Charles gripped it with ridiculous strength. The blood ran to his hands and up his neck. "What?!" As he slowly turned back to Mikaél, he could see the scared faces and hear the shocked murmurs of onlookers paying too much attention to someone else's business. But he wasn't going to let them deter him from his Alpha disposition—not in the least.

"You heard me. You burned it down, then you came to my apartment and threatened the lives of both me and my mate." On the outside, Mikaél stood his ground. On the inside, he had melted into a puddle of fear.

This time, Charles stood close to Mikaél, close enough to kiss him. That wasn't his goal, however. No. His goal was to make him feel small and make him wish he had never provoked him in the first place. A mere inch away from his face, he spoke in a soft volume, a slow pace, but a sharp tone. "Why would I do that?"

Shifting his eyes in submission was embarrassing. Mikaél swore if he didn't, he'd touch Charles's eyelashes. His swallowing throat was too loud for comfort. Some strong Omega he was. He forced words to come out. "You had quite the opinion of me being a Type 6 Omega on Monday. I remember you saying what you'd have done to me if I wasn't pregnant. The next best thing would be to destroy my dad's studio. After all, he'd fall into your category of 'delusional Omegas,' wouldn't he? After that, you threw a rock through the window with your threatening note attached to it. If you didn't do it, you blabbed my Type 6 Status to someone who carried it out for you."

Charles squinted. Smirked. "You think too much, Omega."

"And why is that?"

"I don't give a fuck about your Type 6 Status. I have better things to do with my time than go around like some dramatic pup whispering idiotic claims about who you think you are." Mikaél stood there. Frozen.

"You may think of me as some conservative, backwards hick who got lucky enough to get into the city but let me tell you something. I'm smart, and I have plans. So, if you think I'd jeopardize all that by carrying out some ridiculous plot about burning down a business and throwing some stupid rock through a window, you're more hopeless than I thought. That being said, if someone did do those things, you might want to heed their message." Charles peered at Mikaél's stomach. "If that pup of yours is lucky enough to be born before someone finishes the job, you better tell him after he's born there are real terrors in this world to be afraid of at night, and it's not just the monsters under his bed."

A tear welled up and streaked down Mikaél's face. His pheromone palette fell to an all-time subservient low.

Mission accomplished.

Charles resumed his final journey down the stairs to the lobby, his feet sounding like boulders with every step. "Give my regards to your Type 6 Alpha—another delusional freak who thinks he's special."

Left by himself amongst a sparse crowd, Mikaél's hands shook, and his knees felt weak. With the remaining strength he had left, he grabbed his shoulder bag and ignored the people staring at him. After turning the corner of a low-traffic hallway, he ran into an empty bathroom and grabbed hold of the sink.

Upon stabilizing, he worried that he made a mistake not going to a toilet in order to throw up every last drop in his stomach. It heaved hard as his face throbbed red. But instead, he repeated the mantra of "calm down" to himself dozens of times. Eventually, his mind won over and his insides relaxed. All that was left were the echoing cries of his voice bouncing off of the old, faded tile.

CHAPTER 10:

TO RELUCTANTLY GIVE A GIFT

One month later...

Mikaél shut the door to the apartment and walked in. The kitchen was spotless and shiny. Red and white candles, pine garland, and a small wintry tree on the center island set the holiday spirit. The smell of a roasted chicken, seasoned potatoes, and fresh string beans filled his nostrils. In his ears, the low hum of guitar and piano music filled the background from surround sound speakers. There was little doubt in Mikaél's mind it was a traditional Winter Solstice song, but he didn't focus on which.

"Roman? Are you home?" He wondered if he was going to have to discover his mate's hiding place like in a child's game, but he showed up around the corner from the living room a moment later. "Hey!" Mikaél grinned. It was tough to not play coy. To think his Alpha mate went all out like this warmed him from the inside out. Mikaél never had someone fuss over him like this on his birthday—not since he was a young pup. "You look like you've been busy."

"You have no idea!" Roman huffed. "I didn't realize just how much work goes into impressing a mate."

"You didn't have to do all this, you know."

"Yes, I did!" Roman beamed as he walked over and wrapped his lips around his mate's. "Happy Birthday, baby."

"Thank you," Mikaél moaned. Unfortunately, it wasn't from the kiss. It was from the weight of his shoulder pack as he slowly shrugged it off.

Roman scooped in to intercept it. "Let me take that." Holding the bag reminded him just how heavy it was. "Why do you carry this thing around? It's going to hurt your back. It's way too much."

"I don't know when I'm going to need a textbook, notebook, reading book, toothbrush, scarf, blanket, a change of clothes, candy bar..."

"Wolf-God, Mik! Did you go to your parents' house, or did you go backpacking in the mountains?"

Mikaél exhaled. "Can we not fight?"

Roman came out of his original train of thought. "Sorry." On the center island, there were two champagne flutes waiting. After scenting one of the glasses, he handed his mate the non-alcoholic sparkling wine. They held up their glasses, clanked, then drank. "How are they doing?"

The thoughts swirled in Mikaél's head. "All things considered, I think it's good. My dad has finally got the color back in his skin you could say. I think now that the insurance has gone through, and the inventory is done, he can finally breathe for a bit. I think the fact that Winter Solstice is next week helps."

"What about your birthday?" Roman added. "I'm sure that put a smile on his face."

"Yeah, I suppose it did. They were sad you couldn't make it."

"I know. I'm sorry. I wanted to be there, but I had some other things to take care of." Roman peered into his glass.

"Obviously." Mikaél beckoned to the spread before him. "So..."

Roman once again seemed to be out of sorts, but he finally saw what conclusion Mikaél wanted. "Oh, right! Eat." He handed his mate a small platter and watched as he took in the sights. When he was finished, Roman followed.

"How did your day go?" Mikaél asked while slowly walking over to the dining room table.

"Good." The word was drawn out.

"What did you end up doing?" Mikaél asked.

"This was most of it. Also did a little shopping."

"Hmm. What for?" Mikaél grinned.

"Guess you'll just have to wait and see." Roman winked back. He sat down at the table across from his mate and took his first bite of mouthwatering chicken. He followed the act with a hearty swig from his glass. "Did things go well at school? I mean…" Roman gestured to Mikaél's now pronounced stomach.

Mikaél chuckled. "Yes. I'm not going to break, dear."

"Doesn't mean I shouldn't worry about my mate. I'm only going to get more protective from here, you know."

"I know. I know." Tonight, the thought of that mate the Omega smile.

"Things still going okay with shithead?"

"You mean Charlie?" Mikaél clarified. Roman snarled at the utterance of his name. "I think we've both agreed to stay out of each other's way."

Roman pushed a small potato around on his plate before stabbing it with his fork and popping it into his mouth. "I still don't understand why you just didn't let me go down there and kick his ass." Roman gripped his champagne glass tightly. Any tighter and it would have been in pieces.

Mikaél shook his head and sighed. "You know exactly why. We've discussed this already a million times. I wouldn't be able to show my face at Ashershire anymore, and you'd lose any credibility you have for your career. No one wants to hire a doctor known for putting people *in* the hospital."

"Ah. You're funny." Roman pointed at him and winked. "How do you like it?" He gestured with his fork to Mikaél's already half empty plate.

"You really outdid yourself here. Maybe you should do this every night." He smirked.

Roman choked on his champagne. "Another funny."

"I guess I'll just have to enjoy this, then."

"You better." Roman smirked. After swallowing his latest bite, Roman lifted his hand and brushed the stubble on his cheek. Mikaél noticed him contemplating.

"What?"

"Is this still surreal to you?" Roman observed his mate thinking.

Mikaél snorted. "What? Being 18 and pregnant? Yeah. I thought it was supposed to set off alarms or fireworks. In my head, I imagined this big procession taking me out of my parents' house and dropping me off in the freedom lands of adulthood. Never anticipated this though."

Roman furrowed his brows. "It's not bad, is it?"

"What? Finding my Fated Mate and carrying our child? Horrible."

"You're on a roll tonight," Roman acknowledged.

"I love you. You're the best thing that has ever happened to me. And in April, this baby girl is going to be the best thing which happens to *us*."

Roman glowed as he studied his mate. Nothing in the moment could have been more perfect. He was celebrating the day of his mate's birth with all the benefits which came with it. His mate expressed sincerity when he spoke of him and their future family. Knowing Mikaél was his was one thing; hearing Mikaél say it was quite another. The thoughts stirred his loins. It was a spell, a hypnotic trance, and it was working. Slowly, he stood up from his chair and walked toward his love. His mate's attention stayed on him, recognizing Roman's changing sexual aura.

Mikaél attempted to speak but found Roman's lips on top of his before he could. The force and the hunger told him this wasn't going to be a passing moment. His mate wanted him, and Mikaél was going to let him take him. Returning the enthusiasm, he held onto Roman's neck and pulled him into an embrace. It elicited a groan which only increased his own sexual pheromones. Suddenly, he felt his body being lifted to a standing position. Gliding his hands across the different textures of his Alpha's body was a puzzle to finding the most erogenous zones on him. Of course, he already knew what they were. That was the fun in driving Roman wild, intentionally avoiding them like death traps in a video game.

But Mikaél's own lust took ahold of him, and he couldn't resist scratching his nails down Roman's neck to his lower back. At the same time, he sank his teeth into his lower lip and moaned in satisfaction.

Roman let his hands cup the small globes of Mikaél's ass and thrust his hips forward into him. As the slick inside his mate became apparent, the smooth wave of emotions was interrupted by a rough, aggressive, dominating desire. Having Mikaél close to him meant everything. His mate was safe and protected in his arms, and he didn't want it any other way. But a hard pit fell in his in stomach as his thoughts wandered into the realm of those times when he couldn't be there to protect his mate. Thoughts of Charlie or Matthew Whitmore controlled his emotions, and he felt the anger soar throughout the blood in his veins. Those thoughts alone made his mouth latch over the crux of his mate's shoulder and neck, and he began to bite down. It had been way too long since he had claimed his mate. The time was upon him. It was happening. Right. Now.

"Yes, yes," Mikaél whined. "Claim me."

"Not here," Roman growled back. "The bedroom."

The voice was dark and commanding. It was evident Roman meant business tonight, and it thrilled Mikaél to no end. As he turned around, his target was locked onto his mate. Roman pressed forward and matched his every step backward. It was amazing he didn't fall over. The sexual tension was a turn-on but also dangerous.

"Well, well," Mikaél smirked, "someone looks like they're out for blood."

"Hmph." Roman smiled. "I'm out for a lot more than that."

"Yeah? Come get it."

Even before Mikaél finished the sentence, Roman was on him, taking his clothes off unceremoniously. Before he knew it, Mikaél was in nothing but a tight pair of underwear sporting an outline of his cock in arousal. His mate's body glowed from the pheromones humming around his body. Roman scented the slick which moistened his outsides.

Without any patience left, he dropped down and squared his face with his mate's pulsing briefs. Pulling them down, he gulped his hot member down his throat. Hearing Mikaél gasp and whimper was everything. He couldn't get enough. His head suddenly was held tight against him, and he felt Mikaél's hands pull him in as far as he could. When he began heaving, Roman pulled his head back.

"Why did you stop?" Mikaél panted.

"This is why..." Roman replied. After pushing his mate's shoulders onto the bed, he lifted his legs and pushed his knees up to his rounded stomach. There, he saw a slow continuous drip of aromatic slick. It was already swollen and open, needing him inside of it. His mouth covered his entire pucker as he darted his tongue deep in his mate. As Mikaél began to hold his own legs, Roman inserted two fingers inside while he used the other to stroke his aching cock.

Heat blasted down Mikaél's spine into his neck. It was as if his heart had moved into his neck. His pheromone gland responded again after the constant stimuli. It wasn't a surprise when Roman stopped immediately—he knew. Suddenly, a wet tongue slurped its way up Mikaél's belly, chest, neck, and finally reached his chin. After a quick lick across his lips, he trailed his mouth down to the pheromone gland pulsing deep dark red. Thankfully, Roman decided to play nice and gave him reprieve rather quickly. It was if water had released from his neck when sharp teeth dug into his skin. He could hear Roman's moans of approval as he took whatever he pleased.

The Omega yelped involuntarily, the euphoria more than he ever had before. He tried to muffle himself by biting into his own arm, but pregnancy had thrown his hormones into overdrive and every feeling, every emotion multiplied again and again. He wanted his insides to cum so bad. But he couldn't help but want to change the game. Knowing Roman was going to be soon satisfied with his mate's anal contractions, he immediately stopped him and pushed off the bed. He looked down upon his Alpha mate who appeared lost on the need for the interruption.

"My birthday. My rules," Mikaél commanded.

"What—" Roman began, but he was assisted by his mate and led to assume the same position he had previously been in. Mikaél attempted to swallow as much of Roman's hard cock as he could, but he was never going to be able to deep throat like his mate could. But he knew trying, even gagging while doing it, seem to produce heavy sounds of approval every time.

"Babe, I want to fuck you," Roman protested.

"You're not getting it until I tell you you're getting it," Mikaél returned, massaging Roman's egg-sized balls in his large sack. Roman's voice was gruff and dark. It wasn't quite the response he expected. Thinking his technique was a bit lacking, Mikaél took his mouth off and licked the open slit which was still producing a generous amount of pre-fluid. But as he gazed up seeking his Alpha's approval, he proceeded to grunt out of frustration.

A loud thump was heard when he let go of his Alpha's cock as it hit his lower stomach. Crawling up his body, Mikaél attacked his mate's soft nipples. As he pinched the right, he bit the left. Roman's body twitched and stretched in response. When the areola became erect, he switched to the other. The voice coming from above him still sounded like he was gritting his teeth from pain.

"You feeling all right?" Mikaél asked.

"You're driving me crazy! I need to be inside you! Seriously!"

Confidence plastered all over the Omega's face. He was doing exactly what he wanted. Now was the time to push Roman to the edge. Leading Roman up by his hand, he was once again a tower over him.

Roman's thoughts and sight were hazy. As he came back into focus, he saw the twinkle in Mikaél's eyes. He gulped as he deduced what his mate's intentions were. But as an Alpha, he wasn't going to show his hesitation or his lack of confidence. Something was off. Something was not right.

Lost in his own ecstasy, and unable to read the signs, Mikaél continued his gratification in watching his Alpha suffer. It empowered him. He was supposed to be the submissive Omega, now carrying their child. But he refused to be. To show Roman his worth, he wrapped a strong hand around the large Alpha cock and grabbed his neck with the other. Pulling him down, he massaged both his hand and his tongue onto him.

Roman's shoulders and chest bounced as he felt the sensation deep within him. His pheromone gland was calling out to his Fated Mate. Blood throbbed up his chest and into his shoulder. The gland was powerful and unrelenting. It screamed like a banshee. This *wasn't* how it was supposed to happen. Not this. Not again.

Large breaths and beaded sweat began to pour out of Roman. With his pupils dilated black, his sight became the clearest it had ever been. It was as if he could count every strand of hair on his mate's head as he stood there. His hearing ability expanded, and he could hear people in the next apartment. The most agonizing was how his scenting skills increased so he could smell the scent of Mikaél's slick as it was producing inside of him. Roman knew it was beginning to be too much. His muscles flexed and veins pulsed to the surface of his skin. He gave Mikaél the look of an antagonized animal.

A new feeling of fear washed over Roman. He knew he had to let go and give in. The fire burned inside him stronger than it ever had before. To let it go farther was going to bring about a consequence he couldn't fathom.

"Mik. Mik, you have to do it. Something's wrong," Roman whimpered.

Mikaél noticed the scent change in Roman which wasn't like the other times. There was always a danger in doing this reverse dominant behavior, but this went to a whole new level. Hearing his strong Alpha become vulnerable like this frightened him. All he did was study him, looking at him like he was glass breaking.

"I can't hold it! Do it! NOW!" Roman began whimpering. He wished deep inside this curse never came upon him. Whatever anomaly Roman possessed as an Alpha Type 6, he didn't want it. It turned him into a reckless, rapid, unrecognizable being. That's not what an Alpha was. That's not who he was. But deep inside him, everything was telling him that's *exactly* what he was. One final growl shook out of him.

Out of fear, Mikaél performed his part on what should have been a beautiful, blissful, intimate moment between him and his mate. He wrapped his arms tight around his tight muscled shoulders and back. His mouth struggled to focus on the protruding gland on Roman's neck. Between his own shaking bottom lip and Roman's body shivering in convulsions, it still wasn't happening fast enough. With one final grunt, he closed his eyes and begged for the ability to hit the right spot. As he felt Roman's skin give out, a gush of sweet-smelling earth scent swept over his tongue along with hints of the tinny sensation of his mate's life force.

In his ear, Mikaél heard the sobbing gasps of Roman's voice like a broken record. The sensation of his body pressed up against the Alpha felt like Roman was burning up from an out-of-control fever;

sweat poured from everywhere. As the throbbing gland began to recede down to a faint outline, he removed his lips and began to tremble from the aftershock. "Roman?"

As if he sprinted ten miles without stopping, Roman panted with half the ominous expression he had on before. Every muscle hurt and he wanted to collapse. But the adrenaline from the trauma was alive and well in him. He was convinced he could pick up a full-size car if he wanted.

That wasn't a good thing. Roman knew it.

"I'm sorry." Roman walked like a robot shuffling his feet to the bed. Once he sat down, he stared at his mate who was white as a ghost. The look back was as if he must have been a stranger to his mate. Roman couldn't blame him. He felt like a stranger to himself. "That wasn't supposed to happen."

"When I said you were out for blood, Roman, I was just kidding!" The words were angry, but the pain flooded in as his eyes began to sting. Roman looked down in confusion. "What happened?" Roman didn't answer. "Does it really tear you apart that much when I want to take control? You could have told me!"

"No, that's not it." Roman tried to comfort his mate's hysterics but a headache began to set in like a hangover.

"Then what is it? Because all I could scent out of you was a provoked, aggressive Alpha getting ready to kill someone. Not just *someone. Me!*"

"I would never hurt you or our pup!" Roman huffed.

"It was going to happen, Roman. I could sense it. I want to know why!" Mikaél's plea fell on deaf ears. It was like his mate wasn't even paying attention to him. Clearly, he was stuck in his own head. "We've done this so many times. What was so different this time?"

Roman forced himself to replay the moment which threw him over the edge. It was a moment which should have made him want to cream himself out of ecstasy, but it didn't. "Your slick."

"My what?" The answer threw Mikaél completely off guard.

"Your slick. It's changed. A lot." Roman was still struggling with his breath. But now that he made the connection, he felt relief begin to run through him.

"Um. How?"

"Your pregnancy. It's not just you I scent; it's the baby."

"You said you scented the change the minute I told you I was pregnant. How is this any different?"

Roman shook his head. "It was never this strong. Apparently, it's been awhile since we've had sex."

"No doubt because you think I look absolutely hideous with a pregnant belly."

"That is not something I've ever said, and I will never say it!" Roman's voice boomed a bit too much. He took a deep breath and contained himself. "You are beautiful and every bit as attractive to me when you carry my pup versus anytime you're not."

Mikaél knew his comment was juvenile. It was said more to hurt than anything else. Shame washed over him. He could have apologized, but he still thought there were more pressing matters at hand. "So, what's going on? What's wrong with my slick?"

"It's not 'wrong.' It's how strong it is. When your body was prepping itself for me to take you, it hit me like a ton of bricks. I wanted to take care of your need and make you mine like I always do."

"What's wrong with that? That should have turned you on, not piss you off."

"Except I couldn't do anything about it. You had me practically on my knees chained to the wall when you wouldn't mark me back. All I know is I wanted to claim you as mine, but I was powerless to my pheromone gland which fucking hurt like hell."

Thoughts danced in Mikaél's mind. "Well, that sounds familiar. *Really* familiar—like the first time claiming me familiar." *How intriguing,* Mikaél thought. "Is that what it felt like back then?"

Roman scoffed. "Multiply it by ten. That was tonight."

"Wolf-God!" That was unsettling. "Have you ever felt like that before?"

The Alpha's face shifted. "Just once. Nothing to do with you." A memory flashed in his sight as he held his best friend Siro up by his neck, his dangling feet practically levitating in the air. Roman knew had Siro not expelled his pheromones to submit to Roman's rage over the fact he almost killed Peyton's Veo, he would have snapped his neck. "All I know is when I sensed you were in distress, the monster inside of me wanted to stop whoever was impeding me from coming to your rescue. Only, there wasn't anyone there. There was just—"

"—me," Mikaél completed. Mikaél took in the information with a deep, slow breath. Although unbelievable, things surprisingly began to make sense. With every passing day, he even recognized his body was changing faster now than it ever had before. His Veo already had told him it only gets crazier from here. Mikaél rolled his eyes as he didn't know the word was so literal and poignant. A hum of amusement squeaked out. "I guess I should feel ecstatic that your instinct is so passionate about taking care of my *sexual* needs, too." He walked over and sat by his mate. Laying his head on his shoulder, Roman's skin felt cold and clammy now.

One final calming sigh escaped Roman's lungs, and he began to purr. Whatever distressful pheromones Mikaél exuded, sexual or otherwise, were completely gone. Of course, he was bummed about the sexual ones. He let his head fall on top of his mate's.

"I believe you, you know." The words escaped Mikaél's lips.

"Hm? About what?"

"That you'd never hurt me."

Roman snorted. "This wasn't the best example for it."

"I think it's the perfect example."

"How?" Roman lifted his head and wrinkled his brows.

"You kept your word. You didn't hurt me. You did whatever you had to do to hold yourself back."

"It took *everything* I had." Roman frowned and bowed his head.

Mikaél lifted his chin back up and smiled. "You're my Alpha. And I'm your Omega." Roman laughed. "What?" Mikaél peered back at his mate, disappointed in his reaction.

"You know, there are things I keep forgetting about you."

"Like what?" Mikaél inquired.

"You may only be 18 years old today, but you are an old soul. You are my center, my equilibrium, and my conscience. You have been since the start. I guess I should trust you more." It had been a genuine statement, but the words felt like sandpaper against his character at the moment. Roman wanted a new focus. "I think it's time."

"For what?"

"Your birthday gift." Roman walked over to his nightstand and pulled out a small rectangular box. It was black velvet with a silver wolf paw print on top. "I should have given you one of these a long time ago."

Mikaél beamed from ear to ear. "What is it?"

"Open it."

Taking it from Roman's hands, his fingers trembled with excitement. Inside the box Mikaél saw a beautiful, glimmering, silver chain necklace and pendant with the Great Gray Wolf's insignia on it. In the center was a small but pronounced diamond glowing over it all. "It's beautiful," he gasped.

Roman removed it from its case. He unlocked the clasp and gestured for Mikaél to turn around. "It is said the Spirit of the Great Gray will protect you as long as you wear it. He'll protect you from the evils of the spirit world, and *I'll*," he grabbed him close and whispered into the back of his neck, "protect you from the all the evils of this world." He planted a slow, deliberate kiss on his mate's neck. "I love you."

Mikaél wrapped his arms around the arms which held him. He turned his head and gave his mate a sweet peck on his lips. "I love you, too."

Holding Mikaél tight against him, Roman forgot one more thing. Moments like this had been way too few as of late. But right now, his mind was transported to an early fall day where he held Mikaél on the cobblestone streets of an art festival. He remembered back then just how much he wanted it to last forever and ever. Now, he didn't have to worry about it. His mate was always here—right where he should be. What if it was too good to be true? The possibility of Mikaél not being there scared him to death.

After finally finding the inner strength to disengage the embrace, Roman was overtaken by a hollow essence. Confusion clouded his thoughts and he felt lost. He needed some sort of decompression—a way to clear the air. After a quick text and confirmation on his phone, he began to get himself dressed.

"Where are you going?" Mikaél watched Roman concentrate on an objective with a clear urgency.

"I'm going to be out for a while," Roman lamented. "I'll be back soon." The Alpha watched as his Omega emotionally fell. He rushed to his mate and calmed his nerves with a deep kiss while caressing his cheek. "I love you."

"I love you, too."

"Holy fuck!" Nico's voice was barely contained inside the cozy coffeeshop this evening. The atmosphere was perfect other than his profanity.

"Um. Yeah, could we chill out just a bit?" Roman's skin flushed like he was getting an immunization deep into muscle. Thankfully, the establishment gave out real coffee mugs. His white knuckles forming around the dark cup weren't going to crush the ceramic—at least not today.

"Well, what do you expect from me? I feel like you've abandoned me in the last two months or so."

Roman couldn't deny the claim. Since finding out Mikaél was pregnant, Roman's life, as he knew it, was over. It wasn't necessarily a bad thing. But seeing Nico live in front of him reminded him of what he missed from his old life.

As Nico drank his own warm treasure in his hands, Roman examined the coveted features he possessed. Flushing red cheeks covered a now fading tan. Dark brown waves of hair were longer and barely staying out his view. As usual, his glassy, hazel eyes were his power. He could spellbind any man who was willing to show their heartstrings. He was close to Roman's tall stature, but not as muscular or defined. It was apparent the stress of the fall semester and the arrival of winter had diminished Nico's blissful routine of working in his dad's shop.

"I'm sorry. I didn't do it on purpose." The Alpha's words were calm but no less guilty.

Come to think of it, Roman hadn't seen him ever since Nico drove him to Mikaél's parents' house. That particular occasion was the night Roman and Mikaél consummated their relationship. The rest was history.

"I'll think about forgiving you." Nico winked. He wasn't going to share it out loud, but the comment had more than one meaning. What also wasn't discussed since that fateful car ride was an acknowledgement; he became opportunistic one night and fooled around with an inebriated Roman who was between mates at the time. Confessing to Roman he had feelings for him for a few years fell on deaf ears. The rejection never settled well after that. As before the incident, Nico found himself engaging only in casual hookups and nothing serious.

Without the trio of him, Roman, and Siro, Nico faded to a loner status. However, an Omega sharing any personal relationship woes to a mated Alpha he once declared an interest in was highly inappropriate—threatening really. Out of respect, he was determined Roman would never hear of his isolation or melancholy existence.

Besides, Roman's world was much more interesting. "So," he set his drink down on the coffee table separating them, "sounds like there's always something going on in the Erricson household."

Roman hummed. "Where do I start?" Where *did* he start? Nico knew just as much as he did about Siro being locked up. Now that he was completely severed from the Whitmore family, there were no updates on Terrence's recovery from the near-death assault or Peyton's status since their annulled contract. Nico knew of the polyamorous relationship going on with his brothers and Garrace. But every time Roman thought of that, unsightly images flashed in his head. All that was left was the continuing saga of him and his mate. There was no shortage of that. Of course, there was the most prominent issue of the night.

"Something is changing within me. It's not good."

"Oh?" Nico sat up, ready for the reveal.

"I'm starting to get overprotective of Mik. It's causing me to be aggressive—to the point where I need to attack someone like a rabid dog. I'm scaring myself and don't know what to do."

Nico relaxed in his chair and waved it off. "All Alphas do that with their pregnant Omegas. Omegas do it back to their Alphas if they feel threatened by other Omegas getting what they consider too close to their mate."

"I get that. But the person my mind told me attack was Mik."

Nico blinked. "Oh. Oh!" He tapped his fingers on his drink cup. "That's a new one."

"Great. Once again, I've found myself on the list of 'firsts.'"

"Maybe it was just a fluke?" Nico attempted to keep it positive.

"I can only hope."

The desire to stabilize and balance the situation intuitively told Nico to switch the subject. "What else is going on?"

Roman sighed. "Mik is still dealing with the loss of his Veo's photography studio last month."

"I can't imagine. Horrible. Do they know what caused it?"

Roman nodded just enough for it be noticeable. "Arson."

"Damn. Do they know who?"

"No..." Roman flashed back to the flames consuming the building. Worse, he flashed to how Alec's dream fell to ashes. That wasn't even considering how Mik took on that emotional burden on himself. Then, there was the attempted attack on them in the lobby. No one but the two of them knew about that. "Mikaél thought he knew who did. He confronted the bastard at school. I could have killed him for doing that by himself." Harsh comment. He wished he had chosen other words. Still, Roman balled his fist and hit the arm rest.

"Yikes. How did that go?"

"Not good." Roman grunted. "The asshole completely denied it, and no one has evidence to prove he did anything. There's no evidence to prove *anyone* did it."

Nico sighed. "I'm so sorry." A conversation change was needed once more. "Other than the obvious, how are you and Mik doing?"

"We're still kind of hot and cold."

"Really? Why?"

"I don't know why. One second I'm the best thing in his world and the next he wants to blow me off the face of the planet." Confessing such difficulties emasculated him.

Nico understood. "Hmph. Pregnancy hormones will do that to a person."

"That's what I told him!"

"Whoa." Nico almost spit out his coffee. "You actually told an Omega all their problems were because of pregnancy hormones? How are you still standing?" he howled.

"It's not funny!" Roman growled.

"Yeah, it is. What were you thinking?"

Roman searched his mind. "I thought it would be good to remind him he was once a bright, centered, romantic, caring, and considerate person."

"Tell him he is now. Just because he's hormonal doesn't mean he's any less of who he was."

Roman leaned his head back, surprised he never thought about it that way. Nico had a point. Ever since his parents decided his life was incomplete without a mate, Roman had plenty of bouts of not being the cordial charismatic Alpha he once was. There was no denying it had changed him as a person. Mikaél was one of people who had seen him at his lowest. How had that affected him? The difference was, in Mikaél's case, his ordeals were because he was getting ready to give Roman the best gift anyone could ask for: their child.

"You're right. You're absolutely right." A touch of hope lit up his face. "I guess I just thought the hormonal stage would have been over by now. We're three months into this. It's the second half—" He was cut off by another round of amusement radiating off of Nico. "Why's that funny?"

"Did you pay any attention to the reproductive class we had, or did you just focus on the sex videos?"

Roman blushed. "Hey, give me a break! I majored in Physical Therapy. You're the one who majored in Obstetrics," Roman defended.

"Be that as it may, I'm telling you now, this 'stage' as you called it is going to be a thing until your boy is born."

Roman shied away. Here it was. The struggle had been planted ever since he made the date with Nico. How long was he going to be able to keep this a secret? And if he couldn't hold it in any longer, who could he trust to tell? There was no one else in his life this close to him. He knew no one else could keep such a secret. But Nico? Surely, he could. The weight of the consequences was balanced against the weight of his mental health.

The roaring fire in the coffee shop sat a good distance away from them, taking the chill out of the air. But now it was beginning to be a nuisance as his body heated from the inside out. Not even the mood lighting and calming instrumental music soothed him.

"Nico, I have to tell you something." Nico's face dimmed. He knew the tone. "Mik's... I mean, *our* pregnancy, isn't a normal pregnancy."

"He's not even 18 yet, Roman. When you have a child that young—"

"—No, that's not what I mean," Roman interrupted. "What I'm about to tell you, Nico, needs to be kept quiet. Can I trust you to do that?" In an instant, Nico confirmed with a gentle flinch of his body in the way which said he agreed. "I'm serious, Nico. If this were to get out to the wrong people... just promise me!"

Now Nico paid close attention. He leaned forward. "I promise, Roman. What's going on?"

Roman still had difficulty with what he was about to confess. "You're going to think I'm crazy. Sometimes, I don't even believe it myself." Nico held his breath and stopped blinking, waiting in anticipation. Roman glided his finger up and down on his now lukewarm coffee mug. It gave little comfort. "Something is going to happen which is going to change the world, Nico. When it happens, I have no idea what we're going to do."

The suspense was dragging on too long. "You don't know what you're going to do when what happens?" Nico assisted.

"When our pup is born..."

"Yes?"

"It's not going to be a boy." Roman said it to the floor, hoping Nico could fill in the blanks.

His friend's mouth popped. "What? Are you going to have a wolf?" Nico amused himself with sarcasm.

"A girl. Our baby is going to be a girl."

For Nico, the music in the shop stopped in his mind. He examined Roman's every gaze, every subtle movement, and every Alpha pheromone he expelled. He waited for the punchline, or at least the pheromone pallet change. It never came. Could Roman actually be telling the truth? He shifted awkwardly. "Uh, Roman. This really isn't something to be playing—"

"I'm not playing." Roman's voice, although soft, carried the Alpha tone he needed to get his sincerity across.

Nico surveyed the room. No one appeared to be within earshot. Still, this conversation was quite dangerous. "How do you know this?"

"My Veo's doctor did Mik's sonogram. In front of an audience of all our parents, my Sur filled him in on what he had been hiding from us for quite some time. Apparently, the doctor isn't a skeptic. He also identified it quickly—too quickly if you ask me."

"Is this the type of guy who's going to blab this?" Nico's heart skipped, thinking this could be all over before it started. With his background knowledge of births and attitudes toward offspring, there were already enough reasons for parents to shun their children. The government did enough to protect them from the worst of crimes, but irrational abortions or abandonment still occurred. As a matter of fact, they happened too often. He knew Roman and Mikaél would never harm their child, even if the claim turned out to be true.

However, extremist groups were granted plenty of attention in the media, spewing hatred for differences. Sometimes, simply being an Omega was enough. The irony. Most of the crusades were against Types. It went both ways: Low-Types against High-Types and vice versa. Nico even remembered one particular group's rallying cries against the births of the Alpha Type 6. The empathy and sadness alone he carried for his once unrequited love hurt his heart enough.

"Roman, how is this even possible?" Nico flipped back his hair and tried to get the fog out of his head.

Roman found himself constantly readjusting in the soft couch. In his head, the cushions became sharp rocks instead, and he couldn't get comfortable. "My dad told me later it has to do with Mikaél being a Type 6." *Fuck.* He cursed himself.

Nico didn't know his eyes could get any wider—but they did. "I'm sorry. What did you say?"

"Nothing. Ignore that," Roman tried to backtrack.

"No, no, no, no, no. You can't do that. I heard what you said. You're kidding me, right?" Now it was Nico's turn to use his natural abilities as an Omega to force Roman out from the wall he built in front of him. "He's a *Type 6* Omega?"

Roman's throat dried up. He couldn't say it again. Nico would have to accept a nod instead.

Frustration built in Nico's head which triggered an instant migraine. The information was an overload. "This is unbelievable. What is happening?"

Watching Nico break down worried Roman. "This is me asking you to hold it together for me, as a friend." Roman's lungs tightened.

"Is Mikaél some mutant or something?" Now it was Nico who wish he hadn't said something. He knew it was wrong, way before Roman's sight targeted his vital organs. "Roman, I'm sorry. I didn't mean that."

"Then what did you mean?" Roman tightened his muscles. Whether or not Roman could interpret the comment as a simple poor word choice was irrelevant. Nico had offended his mate. Had Mikaél been in the coffeeshop with them, he wasn't convinced his friend would still be enjoying oxygen so freely.

"I simply meant—"

"I know what you meant."

"Roman, please, I didn't—"

"Excuse me," a voice broke into the conversation, "is there anything I can get for you? A refill? One of our fresh baked items perhaps?"

Both Roman and Nico stared up at the older gentleman like he'd caught them in the middle of a drug deal. The man's salt and pepper hair glowed as he stood under one of the mood lights. His eyes and mouth never wavered from the pleasantry he showed up with. Had he heard any of the conversation?

Nico couldn't come up with a quick enough response so Roman covered. "No, thank you. I think we're actually going to head out."

"In that case, thank you for joining us. Please visit us again." And just like that, the man walked away and carried on his rounds to the other patrons.

They couldn't believe it. How did they dodge that? For Roman, reality set in quickly that he was the dumbest person in the world divulging this information in a public venue. He wasn't even sure telling Nico was the best decision either.

He swiftly stood and grabbed his bag for a quick exit full of frustration. The hurried steps behind him didn't help. How bad could it have been if he decked Nico right then and there?

After the door opened and he stood outside, the overcast sky brewed a snowstorm. Daylight was now in its final minutes. With only being a week away from Winter Solstice, it was like there was hardly a day at all.

"Can you stop, please?!" Nico begged.

"I don't think you should talk right now." Roman's words were more of a command than advice.

"I screwed up. Give me some credit, Roman. I got dumped on with information you've been dealing with for months. I had five seconds." Roman twitched his lips. "This is a lot. I wouldn't wish the burden of the secrecy on anyone. That being said, this is a special gift. I can't even describe how amazing it is. You have my support. Mikaél, too!" Roman appeared skeptical. "I won't tell anyone, Roman. I promise. I'll take it to the grave with me."

Roman relaxed his shoulders. "Thank you. I know you will. You're a true friend like that."

Snowflakes fell around them, but they would never stick. Instead, the roads and sidewalks were wet in a charcoal gray tint. Some buildings in the area held large greenery and decorations in celebration of the holidays. Twinkling lights barely poked out, but this evening they glowed in a joyous light Roman couldn't quite appreciate at the moment.

Before the double revelation, Nico couldn't stop talking to his best friend in the coffeeshop. Now, standing out here in the cold, he was lost for words. He eased in. "Do you want to grab a bite to eat or a real drink?"

Roman shook his head. "No. I actually need to get back home. Today's Mik's birthday, and I fucked up enough today."

"Oh!" Nico replied. It was the third reveal of the day. "The boy became a man today."

"I think that happened when he started carrying my child."

Nico reflected. "Speaking of, how did his parents not crucify you getting their 17-year-old son pregnant?"

Roman coughed. "You know, I never thought about it before. I know his Veo didn't appreciate me even trying to connect with him after we found out we were Fates. If I wasn't his Fate, they would have jailed me and sucked my parents dry for all they're worth. As a matter of fact, if we weren't Type 6, we wouldn't be here today."

"Hey, let's not forget. If I hadn't dropped you off so you could ninja your way into his bedroom, we wouldn't be here." Nico smiled, hoping it would be contagious.

It was. A smile crept onto Roman's face. "Maybe you're right. Maybe you're the one who made it all happen." He walked up to his friend and gave him a deep embrace. He whispered into Nico's ear. "Thank you for the gift." With that, he gave his friend a peck on the forehead. He adjusted his jacket as he turned to walk down the long city street to the parking garage.

Nico's legs froze more than the temperature. He couldn't move. But his cheeks flushed hotter than the sun. "Anytime!" he yelled.

Soon, Nico saw his friend become a dark blip in the silvery city of Tauris. A snowflake kissed the Omega's nose.

Tonight, Roman had Mikaél. Tonight, he'd spent his birthday with him. No doubt, they'd solve their issues and move on like the amazing couple they were. He'd kiss his mate passionately, speak to him of his unconditional love, and hold him in his muscled arms the rest of the night to keep him warm. In the spring, they'd welcome a beautiful child and become a picture-perfect family.

That's when it hit Nico the hardest. Tonight, he was going home alone. The wind whispered *let him go*. And so, he did.

Mikaél woke from a restless sleep. He constantly felt in the middle of consciousness and unconsciousness. The attempt at reenergizing had been futile. With that, he easily heard Roman walk into the bedroom.

"Hey." Mikaél smiled at his mate.

"Hi," Roman acknowledged.

"How are you?" Mikaél sat up, leaning on his arms.

There was no way Roman could get away with not telling his mate of his rendezvous. "I saw Nico for a bit. I just needed to flush this out."

That warranted an emphasized rise. "Nico?" The name had only been mentioned a couple times in the past few months—almost like an afterthought. It wasn't his to say, but Mikaél had assumed the friendship faded with Siro's incarceration. He didn't know how to respond. He chose neutral curiosity as best as he could. "How is he?"

Roman nodded like it was everyday small talk. "He's good. He's good. Like me, his clinicals are keeping him busy." Like earlier in the coffeeshop, just the slight flicker of a candle made him feel the sweat underneath his collar.

The air didn't smell right. It didn't feel right. Roman wasn't saying something. "Did your talk go badly or something?"

"No." The reply was short and fast. Too fast.

Mikaél's eyes furrowed. "What did you two talk about?"

"Just the update on the family. He knows about the fire. He knows you're 18 today. So, the cradle robbing jokes can stop now." Roman smirked. Mikaél caught it for a moment, but it didn't satisfy him. "I told him the pregnancy was going well."

There it was, Mikaél sensed. "Did you tell him anything else about the pregnancy?"

Roman stood up a little taller and took on his Alpha posture. A million scenarios went through his head. Out of them all, only one played out. "I told Nico you were a Type 6." Roman held his breath, waiting for the onslaught.

Mikaél's shoulders fell. "Oh," he deflated. "I guess that's not so bad. Then don't worry about it so much. Wolf-God, Roman, you looked like it was actually serious. Felt like you were going to give me a heart attack."

Roman's eyes lifted. "Really?"

"Yeah. I mean, the more I think about it, I probably told one of the worst people at school I was Type 6 Omega. And that was out of spite. Nothing happened with Charlie. He didn't even believe me. So, I couldn't see the harm in you telling one of your best friends."

Roman exhaled loudly, feeling like he'd made the winning shot in a game. That's how he interpreted it, anyway. Maybe it should have felt more like getting away with murder.

"Is that all?" Mikaél asked, this time out of concern.

A gentle nod robotically came out of Roman. "That's it." Murder. It was definitely getting away with murder. "Any interest in continuing this birthday celebration with a movie and ice cream? We have mint chocolate chip!"

The Omega smiled. "More than anything."

CHAPTER 11:

TO DEAL WITH DIFFICULT PAST & PRESENT

"Is there anything I can help you with?" Mikaél sat on the stool at the bar watching Adrian walk frantically throughout the kitchen.

"No, no. You are just fine where you are." Adrian smiled.

Mikaél hid his discontent. He knew that was code for "You're pregnant, sit down, and grow a baby." Instead of protesting, he sat there picking at a small plate of hors d'oeuvres and cider. There was a choice to either moan and groan over tonight's impending events or make the best of it. After setting his mind straight, he chose the latter.

The smells were the strongest: holiday roast, garlic, thyme, rosemary, cinnamon sugar, chocolate, and peppermint wafted in the air occasionally. When they didn't blend together, the aromatics were pleasing. The sights were better: fresh greenery accented with red berries and holiday lights, a wood burning fireplace set ablaze, and an enormous tree in the corner of the vaulted living room trimmed to perfection with endless gifts piled underneath it. The sounds were the best: traditional holiday classics pumped into the kitchen speakers and throughout the main floor, all the parents gathered round the large white kitchen island with cider and eggnog delightfully talking over one another. But on the opposite side of the room, Mikaél could hear Garrace, Rixen, and Ryan whispering to one another while standing next to the TV attempting to drown out their conversation with sports commentary.

However, even that was quiet to what he heard loudest of all: Roman thinking on the couch while staring down his brothers and their mate with the awkward stare. He wasn't the only Omega who noticed, because soon after, Adrian called to him.

"Roman, I want you to do me a favor," he called out.

Roman twitched as if coming out of a trance. The TV remote which was once a comfort in his hand did a small flip and landed on the couch. He catapulted himself up and acted like he wasn't dealing with a conundrum in his head. "Yes, Veo?"

Mikaél perked up again. "Something I can do?"

"Oh, no," Adrian reassured Mikaél. "There are just some platters on the top shelves of the hutch in the dining room I need. Tall person's job. Roman knows where they are."

"Sure!" Roman answered.

Both he and Adrian appeared to miss the letdown written all over Mikaél's face. As Roman headed to the privacy of the formal dining room, the Omega used this as his opportunity to say something. Once they both were there, he overdramatically cleared his throat.

Roman turned to look back with furrowed brow. "What's wrong?"

"Why do I get the feeling like I'm invisible in this house?" Mikaél huffed.

"Invisible? You're not invisible," Roman corrected.

"Oh yeah?" Mikaél crossed his arms. "How would you know? You've been so preoccupied on tracking your brothers since they arrived, I'm surprised you'd notice anything else."

Roman exhaled as he stretched his height to open the highest door on the solid wood hutch, revealing shiny silver platters which hadn't seen the light of day since spring. "To be fair, I think everyone has been eyeing them since they arrived. Can you take this?" Roman asked as he carefully lifted an extra-large platter out of its cradle.

Mikaél grabbed it firmly, not expecting it to be as heavy as it was. "Actually, I've been fine with them here. They probably wish they could be me right now, the invisible holiday elf."

"Mik, I swear, no one thinks you're invisible." Roman brought down another platter and examined it thoroughly before setting it down on the dining room table, completely missing his mate's aggravated expression.

"You know, I saw this in a sitcom once where a pregnant Omega felt like this. I just didn't think it was portraying life so accurately."

"What was it supposed to be in real life? A pregnant Alpha?" Roman glanced up, hoping Mikaél would take in the joke. His expression back said otherwise. "Sorry."

"Just because I'm 50% done with the pregnancy doesn't mean I'm 50% of the person I once was. I can still do things, you know. I'm not going to break!" Mikaél spoke down into the platter, enchanted by the glittery light bouncing off of it.

"Good. Remind me of that when we get home and I'll have you chop some wood." Roman grabbed the platter from his mate, hoping to get a rise out of him.

Mikaél pushed his tongue into his cheek. "Fine. It's clear you're not going to take me seriously." As he began to make his ascent back into the living room, he felt Roman pull him back.

"I'm sorry; you're right," Roman pleaded, locking onto his hand. "I haven't done anything except focus on Rixen and Ryan. I'm just waiting for the inevitable to unfold, that's all. And I'm sorry for that too because that's not what Winter Solstice is supposed to be about. It's about celebrating life and family—our family." He pulled his mate into his arms and gently kissed his forehead. "Forgive me?"

Mikaél hummed. "Maybe," he replied as he hugged him back.

"Yeah?" Roman asked. He planted a firm kiss on Mikaél's soft lips. Like Winter Solstice itself, they possessed magic.

"Yeah, I forgive you," Mikaél playfully sang.

"Happy Solstice, baby," Roman whispered.

"Happy Solstice," Mikaél echoed.

"Roman?" Adrian's voice came through the hallway.

"Coming!" Roman loaded up both trays and followed his mate back into the hustle and bustle of the kitchen.

Upon seeing the traditional wares, Adrian sighed as if seeing an old friend. "Roman, there's a polishing pad right next to the sink. Could you buff them out for me real quick?"

Roman flashed a look at his mate and then back to his father. "You know, I think Mik would be good at that." He saw Mikaél smile back at him; he acknowledged him with a wink.

"Sure!" Adrian's expression revealed his surprise.

Mikaél beamed as Adrian handed him the pad. As far as the night was going, this was the best gift of the night, other than his mate's kiss and well wishes. The serving platters themselves were already quite immaculate. There was no need to do even do a touch-up. But Mikaél wasn't about to let his father-in-law down.

"Hmm, looks like they're a few spots you need to clear up there." Dustin gestured with his index finger while the others grasped hard onto a glass beer bottle. The light faded from his son's face.

"Oh, leave him alone," Alec defended. He placed a hand on Mikaél's shoulder for encouragement. "Those spots are your fingerprints, anyway. They'll come out real quick. You should wear gloves."

"They're Roman's fingerprints," Mikaél replied with a smirk.

Roman's head turned from across the room. "Huh?"

"Nothing." Mikaél laughed.

Jake joined the crew while carrying a chilled champagne bottle in from the garage. "I think this should do. I'm very sorry Drew and his mate couldn't make it, Dustin. We could have rescheduled."

Dustin shook his head while he finished the final contents of his current bottle. "No, really, it's good. They're at Will's parents' place. We'll see them in a couple days."

"Plus, I think Will is appreciating low-key gatherings at this point," Alec added. "The pregnancy is taking quite the toll on him right now, I'm afraid. And he's such a gentle spirit to begin with. It's heartbreaking." He rubbed the side of his wine glass gently.

"He's a Type 3, isn't he?" Jake asked as he bargained for room in the refrigerator.

"He is," Dustin replied.

"Ah, he'll be all right. They pull through effortlessly these days—their pups too."

An abrupt silence hit the entire room. Mikaél shouldn't have been able to make out every word of the holiday song playing on the surround sound. Even more, he shouldn't have been able to feel everyone staring at him, including Roman's brothers and Garrace.

With the shut of the refrigerator door, Jake realized what he said, or more specifically, what was left unsaid. "Oh. Mikaél. I'm sorry. I didn't mean it to assume—"

"No, it's fine. I know you didn't mean anything by it." Mikaél set the second and final platter on the little remaining space of the kitchen island. The last thing he needed right now was for Jake to remind him of the dismal mortality rate his own father bestowed upon him and his unborn child. He felt his nerves shoot out from his stomach and could hear the anxious heartbeat in his warm ears. Or maybe it was Roman's heartbeat from across the room he heard. He saw Roman give a death stare to his own Sur.

Jake didn't linger on his son's hatred. Instead, he fumbled with a fancy corkscrew in his hands and struggled for his next words, hoping to save face with his son-in-law.

"When is Will due?" Adrian jumped in.

"January," Alec replied. "Next month already."

"Wow. That was fast."

"I know! Mere weeks away!"

"Exciting!" Adrian gestured with his wine glass. "Are you ready to be grandparents?"

"Absolutely!" Alec replied. "Besides, if we weren't, we were going to have to be for this one." He kissed Mikaél's forehead and then turned back to Adrian. "Which means ... you're not that far behind! Excited yourselves?"

"Of course!" Adrian's confidence wavered as he garnered Jake's confirmation.

"Yes!" Jake affirmed. "We're very much anticipating the arrival of our granddaug—er—um, grandchild." He grunted and surveyed the room.

Roman approached the island. "Dad, come on!" he seethed.

"I'm sorry, Roman. I—I don't know what came over me. It slipped," Jake pleaded.

"What slipped?" Ryan joined the now hollow group. Garrace and Rixen trailed him. No one spoke a word. "You all look like you've seen a ghost or something."

"Yeah, what's going on?" Rixen inquired. He fidgeted while struggling to keep attention on the current company.

All eyes fell to Jake. "I, uh, almost let it slip what Roman and Mikaél were going to name their pup, their *son*."

Rixen was taken aback. "Whoa. Roman told *you* what their son's name is before anyone else?"

"Really?" Ryan pouted. "That's not fair. What is it? It better not start with an 'R.'" His annoyance with the tradition showed.

"We *were* considering 'Roman Junior'" Roman anxiously looked at his mate.

Mikaél laughed half-heartedly. "Yeah, that was a name, wasn't it?"

"Ugh. Barf," Ryan whined.

Rixen squinted, unamused. "Are you sure that's what happened just now?"

"Hey, who is ready for champagne?" Jake held up an expensive bottle with a title on it which was written in another exotic language. All others in on the secret agreed chaotically, successfully stopping Rixen's investigation. Even Mikaél lifted an empty glass sitting near him, forgetting he was with child. Luckily, Alec came to his rescue.

"Do you want that sparkling cider you brought?"

"Yeah," Mikaél replied, remembering himself. "Besides, anything is better than that wine Will drinks."

Alec cocked his head. "You had some of that?"

"They left it at the house the night dad tried it. Remember that, dad?"

Dustin made a face. "That wasn't wine. That was sadness in a bottle."

"I have to agree," Mikaél replied, receiving his first glass of non-alcoholic grape juice from his Veo. A cork burst almost made him drop his glass as Jake poured the first glass of the real deal.

Jake perfected seven champagne flutes for the traditional toast to the holidays. He proudly handed them out to the remaining family members. Unfortunately, the pride was short lived after he handed one to Rixen and Ryan.

"Uh, dad. You're missing one." Rixen spoke awkwardly.

Adrian winced. "For Wolf-God's sake, Jake! You forgot Garrace!"

"Damn it!" Jake hit his fist on the countertop as he dipped his head.

"Nice going, dad. You made my boyfriend invisible," Ryan murmured. Jake's expression gave Ryan a look of warning.

"No, no. Don't worry about it." Garrace held a steady disposition, hoping to balance out Ryan's remark.

"Yeah, we can just share. After all, that's the name of the game with us, isn't it?" Rixen humorously offered.

Jake's focus turned one-eighty back to Rixen who was clearly getting ready to kiss and embrace his lover—one of them that is.

The thought hit Jake's stomach and his words came out involuntarily. "No!" Rixen and Garrace froze their attempt. Their judgement came through instantly. Jake readjusted his posture. "I mean, no, here. Just take my glass." He rushed Garrace like freight train.

Garrace held up his hands to decline. "No, Mr. Erricson. I couldn't do that to you at your own party."

Mikaél hummed. "That's Garrace. Always thinking of others." Garrace glared back.

"You absolutely can!" Jake reassured. "It's not like I haven't had it before. I'll do the toast with wine."

Garrace nodded politely and accepted. He plastered on a smile to help bring Ryan back down from his attack mode. The overdramatic gesture worked as he saw Ryan tuck his tail and walk over to join him at his side opposite his twin.

After delivering his olive branch, Jake returned to the safety of his own mate. He clasped his hands together as he tried to think of the right words to officially start the evening.

"Here." Adrian passed his drink to his mate. "*We* can share."

Jake nodded. "Right." Looking out to a stressed-out audience, Jake took a deep breath and began. "A lot has happened in the last few months."

"Jake..." Adrian attempted.

"No, just listen," Jake interrupted. "A *lot* has happened. As wolf-descendants, we are naturally prone to go into survival mode when too much happens at once. This natural instinct causes us to make quick decisions we later regret. We're human—we're imperfect. Mistakes are the result of those hasty thoughts, words, and actions." Jake paused as he noticed everyone waiting on his every word. "And that's why *I* believe Wolf-God created holidays, including Winter Solstice, for us to finally put the brakes on our fast-paced lives. It's the time we get to reflect and focus on the positives we and remember what is truly important. We have family and we have friends. We have health and prosperity. And we have welcomed not one, but two new members to our family."

"Garrace and Mikaél," Rixen announced proudly.

Jake tried to remain subtle as Adrian's eyes grew big. "True. I was actually referring to the two pups getting ready to be born this coming year." All the parents joined in a quiet roll of amusement. Rixen felt as if he was being put under a spotlight while being laughed at by a jeering crowd. Garrace and Ryan didn't feel any different. "But, what the hell, why not? Here's a toast to the *four* new members of our family and to Winter Solstice!" Jake toasted his glass to the highest recessed light as if it was the sun itself. Without taking a drink, he handed the glass to his mate. A stoic expression remained on his face.

"Here, here!" Adrian shouted. Soon after, the rest joined in the toast.

Garrace hummed. "Wow, Mr. Erricson. That's really smooth."

"Jake," Dustin agreed, "you've never shared this one with me before."

Jake stood a bit taller. "Just something I save for special occasions."

"He's always got something up his sleeve." Adrian smiled, not realizing the words he was saying.

Jake coughed. "Not *always*."

As if Wolf-God himself wanted to save the evening, a timer rang out. Everyone knew what it was for. No one more than Adrian was happy to hear its triumphant sound. "The roast is done! We're ready!"

"Thank Wolf-God!" Roman exhaled.

Delicate silverware and glasses made satisfying sounds as the newly declared family of nine sat at the Erricson formal dining room table. Wolf-God was celebrated with food that could have been mistaken for stately home or catered by a five-star restaurant. Another decorated tree and fireplace brought the visual ambiance in from the den. Occasionally, conversations drowned out the music playing in the background.

"In short, it does sound like I will get some time off when the pup is born so I can be with Mik," Roman concluded.

"That's so good to hear. I know you were a bit worried your direct supervisor was going to be an obstacle." Adrian continued to speak as he held the glass bowl of potatoes for Rixen—a second helping for him.

"Oh, he's still a problem. The thing is there's already an established protocol for this so he couldn't do much about it. Doesn't mean he didn't give me a dirty look when I reminded him of it."

"You're not causing trouble for him, are you Roman?" Jake scolded.

The tone in his Sur's voice sent Roman's memory back ten years ago after when Roman hit puberty. Everyone on his basketball team was convinced Roman was on steroids because he outranked his teammates by strength and stature. Roman found himself in several fights for simply being too rough at practice and during games. But no one could deny Roman's elite ability and MVP status. The question echoed from a conversation on whether or not the coach thought it was worth the risks of keeping their best player on the team. "No, I'm not." Roman's words were controlled and steady— unlike the conversation ten years ago.

"I hope not. The opportunity you have coming up for you is invaluable. Too much to be wasted on a supervisor who only has high expectations of you," Jake reminded him.

"Unfair expectations!" Roman insisted. "He only has them on me because I'm a Type 6."

Jake's expression remained unchanged. "Perfectly good reason to have them." Based on his son's expression, Roman did not agree.

"So, Garrace..." Adrian lifted his glass of courage while opening a new dialogue. "Rixen tells me you work at Brookside Books?"

Garrace nodded his head as he finished and washed down his bite of seasoned vegetables. "Yes, Mr. Erricson, I do."

"Please, call me Adrian," he insisted.

Jake let out a low growl. "No, 'Mr. Erricson' is appropriate."

Adrian's focus fell to the table as he tried to appear undeterred from the comment. "And how is that going for you?"

Garrace himself paused. Scanning the room, some glued their attention to him while others pretended to be focusing on anything else. "Very well, actually. I'm going to start training for a manager position after the holiday rush is over."

"How lovely! That's great! Are you considering any sort of management in your Levels?"

"I guess I should probably choose a few more electives in management now that I think about it," Garrace acknowledged. "But I actually want to be more of an influencer."

"A what, sorry?" Adrian asked.

"Pass the dinner rolls?" Mikaél inserted over the conversation.

Roman reached his long arm over. "How is everything treating you, babe?"

"Good. No issues so far. I'm keeping it pretty plain." Mikaél took the basket carefully to choose his favorite.

Garrace ignored the side chatter. "An 'influencer.' It's a job in a company where they look for someone to inform them of what the next best trends are." Garrace explained it casually as he passed Rixen the roast platter when it was silently beckoned.

"I see." The concept didn't appease Adrian. If it didn't appease Adrian, it was going to have an even worse effect on Jake.

Garrace proceeded with his sell. "Most companies have them. That's how you get new toys in stores where kids go insane, and parents are scrambling to get them for the holidays. Or when the latest features on phones or TVs show up or new types of drama or reality tv shows appear. There's always someone there who dedicates their life to making sure the business is on the cutting edge of fads and trends."

"And I suppose companies are just begging for people to apply for these positions?" Jake intervened.

"Well, no," Garrace confessed. "They're actually very hard to find. They don't necessarily advertise the job that way neither. Most get into positions like that when they get noticed or are famous themselves already."

"And just what is it that you are famous for, Garrace?" Jake locked his gaze on Garrace and didn't flicker once.

Garrace swallowed hard. "I—I don't have anything at the moment."

Rixen dropped his knife and fork on the table. His forehead began to sweat. "Can we switch topics, please?"

Adrian reached out and touched his hand and then his forehead. "Rixen, you're warm. Are you feeling all right?"

"It's just hot in here," Rixen replied while wiping his brow.

Adrian wasn't convinced. "I'm glad to see you're eating well at least."

"He doesn't eat like this at home," Garrace pointed out.

"Maybe he just misses his dad's cooking." Adrian smiled at his own remark. Rixen, however, seemed to ignore all of it as he steadied his focus on his plate. "How is your job going?"

"Dad, I tell people all day that their airline miles won't work on weekends or holidays or that I need to transfer them to a different department." Rixen finished the rest of his wine glass in a couple of gulps and hit it on the table. The flames on the candelabra swayed in the aftershock.

Taking a hint from his son, Adrian finished his own wine glass and set it down on the table. "Anyone else?"

"Yes, thanks for asking, dad," Ryan snarled.

"Problem, Ryan?" Jake intercepted.

"I don't know. At this point, I should be used to being acknowledged last or in this case not at all."

"Listen, bro," Roman pushed in, "just take it easy. We're trying to have a holiday family dinner here. And we have *guests*." He calmly pointed to Dustin and Alec who intently watched the scene unfold.

The words hit Ryan hard like a betrayal. "You've got to be kidding me! I get criticized for calling out bullshit, but Rixen throws out attitude and no one bats an eye?"

"Why the fuck you bringing me into this?" Rixen blurted.

"Ryan..." Adrian tried. It fell upon deaf ears. Ryan kept going on his rant. He tried desperately to make his Beta son focus on what he knew was happening at the table, but it appeared no one else knew what was going on with Rixen. But *he* did. "Ryan!"

"What?!" he shouted back.

"Just let it go," Adrian whispered slowly. "Leave your brother alone."

Rixen shot up out of his chair and slammed it into the table. "Why don't you *all* just leave me alone!"

The room stood still as Rixen successfully captivated all eyes on him. His breathing quickened and sweat fell down the side of his face. Silence set in, making Rixen reflect on his words and actions. But with the clarity came vulnerability and a realization on what was happening to him. Suddenly, his skin flushed red, and he left the room through the door leading to the downstairs basement. He quickly opened and slammed it shut as his footfalls gave his position away to his old bedroom.

"What's his problem?" Ryan criticized, holding is fork up.

Adrian watched his ignorant son one more time. "Ryan. Go to him."

Ryan chewed slowly on a bite of cold meat. The skies cleared in the same way for him as it did Rixen. "Oh Wolf-God." He dropped his fork. After missing the attempt to catch it, he backed out of his chair, placed it back on the table and hurried to the basement door.

"What the hell is going on here?!" Jake demanded

Dustin groaned in disbelief. "You don't know?"

"I knew," Roman confessed.

Mikaél stared back. "You did? When? How?"

"I knew as soon as we came over. You gave off a similar scent when yours hit."

"Oh," Mikaél realized. "That's what you meant by the inevitable. Why didn't you say anything?" He criticized.

Roman winced. "Um. It's not exactly something you just talk about to your brother. And technically it's none of my business. And furthermore, it's not like I thought *he* didn't know himself."

"What didn't Rixen know?" Garrace exhaled. For some reason, he had been left at the table while his two lovers played secret meeting in the basement.

"*It's* here," Adrian answered.

"What is?" Jake asked.

Adrian lost his patience. "Rixen's first heat! There! Did I really have to spell that out?"

Jake finally understood; and then he glared back at Garrace.

Garrace himself drifted between feeling mortified and stupid: mortified about his lovers' Alpha father looking like he wanted a shotgun and stupid for not noticing his Omega's scent change or what he realized now were the obvious signs. "Should I go?" Garrace pointed to the basement door.

"No," Jake quickly replied. "They'll be back any second." For a beat, no one said anything as he stared at the ominous silent door himself. "Or else." Even with his own declaration, Jake's uneasiness spiked. He threw his dinner napkin on the table and heavy-footed his way to the basement entrance. He slammed his hand on the door. "Boys! Get up here now and have dessert!"

"Jake!" Adrian pleaded.

Roman snickered. "Dessert is probably already in the basement."

Dustin stifled a laugh. All three Omegas still sitting at the table showed him their disapproval of it. Quickly, he regained his composure and set his wine glass on the table, looking for his next out. "Can we help you clean up, Adrian?"

"Yes, please let us help," Alec encouraged.

"That would be lovely," he confirmed.

All others at the table joined in —all except Garrace who still sat there dumbfounded.

The air around Garrace grew cold as everyone processioned out of the formal dining room. Once again, the subtle hints of music filtering in from surround sound speakers dusted the room. A few crackles from the fireplace created an awkwardness as Garrace wondered if anyone still remembered he was there at all. Talk and laughter filtered in from the kitchen from all the members in the house who considered themselves official family. He remembered earlier when it didn't bother him. Now, it was damn near an insult. When he finally gathered the gumption to make his way toward the basement to find the twins, he heard an inconsistent pattern of footsteps ascend the stairs.

Ryan opened the door first. Behind him, Rixen appeared small with his skin still flushed. "Hey!" Ryan scanned the room in confusion. "Where is everyone?"

"In the kitchen cleaning up." Garrace's shoulders slumped forward. He tried to get Rixen's attention, but his expression read like he was on another planet. "Is Rixen in heat?"

Ryan observed his brother who only managed to stare at the floor. "Yeah, he is." He shifted his weight. "Rixen and I are going to say goodbye. And then I think we need to head out. How are you?"

Garrace took a moment to consider the words. "I'm good." Ryan nodded as he led Rixen into the hustle and bustle of the kitchen, once again leaving him alone. Garrace exhaled as he held his head in his hands. As he reflected, he couldn't remember what the original intent of the night was. His thought process was broken by a soft vibration in his pocket. He pulled out his phone and saw the bright light spell out the text in beautiful cursive:

[Happy Winter Solstice! Love, Hayden]

Upon reading the text, Garrace's heart skipped a beat and the warmth returned to his body. As he replied to Hayden's text, he didn't even notice the doorbell ringing until Roman announced he was going to answer the door.

The door opened and cold air rushed into the room. There, in front of Roman, stood a familiar boy dressed in a white button-down shirt and tan dress pants. His blond hair glistened in the spotlights of the recessed hallway lights and his eyes penetrated Roman's soul.

"Peyton?"

"Roman!" Peyton beamed. His body thrust forward as he embraced the stunned Alpha. Slowly, he felt Roman's strong arms wrap around him and his body temperature transfer to his own. After what seemed like a minute, they parted. "It is so good to see you!"

"P-Peyton! It's good to see you too." For Roman, the words came out automatically. The moment still hadn't sunk in. "What are you doing here?"

"Roman?" Mikaél voiced. His hands clung to a damp kitchen towel for safety. He observed the ethereal Omega still attached to his Alpha by the hands—smiles plastered on both of their faces.

Roman remembered himself. "Mik! This is Peyton."

Mikaél took the stranger's hand outstretched for his own. "I've seen you on the news before."

"Not as of late, that's for sure," Peyton replied, giving a firm handshake to Roman's hesitant mate. "My father wouldn't be caught dead with me being anywhere near him in public these days." A subtle laugh followed, showing there was still tension between Matthew Whitmore and his outcast son.

"Peyton," Roman shook his head, "I can't believe you're here."

"Yes, why are you here?" Mikaél asked, holding his pregnant stomach.

After a cautious glance at Mikaél, Peyton returned his attention to Roman. "We need to talk."

"I swear Roman, if I knew anything more, I would tell you," Peyton reaffirmed. The privacy of the office behind the den allowed Peyton to let his hair down.

"You honestly have no idea what his campaign is about?" Roman rubbed the back of his neck—the nerves sharp.

Peyton sighed. "I saw the announcement campaign live on T.V. just like you did. It shocked me too. I never thought he'd do anything like that. He had been asked for years to run for office and never gave it one thought."

"Why not?"

"He had all the influence he wanted already. If my Sur had gone into public office years ago, everyone would have been scrutinizing his business ten times more than they did before. He didn't want that."

"The fact that he announced his running on the soapbox of an entity trying to destroy life as we know it so we can be replaced by a superior Omega race doesn't seem a bit odd?" Roman pointed out.

"Roman, I'm sorry I can't be of more help, truly I am. You just told me about Mikaél, but I had no clue about him before now. Other than a few phone calls to my Veo, I haven't had any contact with my Sur, let alone been in the same room as him. I don't know how he found out." Peyton crossed his arms.

"Someone told him," Roman replied.

"How can you be so sure?"

"On the same day he announced, Mikaél's Veo's studio was destroyed by an arsonist and then we had a lovely note attached to a brick thrown right at us through a glass door." Roman's blood heated underneath his skin and the hair stood up on his arms.

"Oh, Wolf-God!" Peyton gasped. "Is everyone alright?"

Roman paused. "For now."

"And you don't have any idea of who could have done it?"

Roman shook his head. "It could be anyone. And worse, it could be more than one at this point. So much time has gone by now."

"That's a good thing, no? A couple of isolated incidents and it's over."

Roman's eyes found his former mate's. "This isn't over."

A knock on the solid office door interrupted the private conversation. "Roman?" Mikaél peaked his head through. "We're setting up for dessert." Once again, his gaze studied Peyton carefully.

"I'll be there in a second." Roman turned his head back to Peyton. "Will you join us?"

"No, I couldn't," Peyton replied. "I need to be heading back anyway." His thoughts danced in his head. "It's good to see you."

Roman's expression softened. "It's good to see you, too. I didn't think I'd ever see you again."

"I knew we'd see each other again," Peyton corrected.

Roman smiled. "I suppose you did."

Peyton crossed his arms, unsure of what to say next. "Congratulations, by the way. When is he due?"

"Thank you. The pup comes in April."

"Are you ready to be a father?" Peyton dared to ask, remembering a conversation where Roman insisted he was waiting to have offspring.

Roman's heart clenched. "I thought I was. Every single time I think I've finally come to terms with what to expect, it all changes again."

"Don't they say the same thing about parenthood?" Peyton chuckled.

Roman stared cautiously. "You don't know the half of it."

The office door opened again, this time a faster. "Roman?" Mikaél asked, with less patience than more.

"Yeah," Roman confirmed as he began to lead the way out.

"I'll text you if I hear anything new," Peyton offered.

"I appreciate that." Roman led Peyton to the front entryway. "I'm sorry you have to go so soon."

"Oh, it's not a problem," Peyton assured. "You were on my way."

"Where are you spending Winter Solstice?" Roman asked.

"At the guardian house. There are a lot of Betas and Omegas there who don't have homes or families to celebrate the holidays with, so we organized a party there."

Roman shook his head in disbelief. "Look at you—all grown up."

"Sounds like you've changed too," Peyton added.

"I'd like to think so."

"Happy Winter Solstice, Roman." Peyton smiled with a glimmer in his eyes.

"Happy Winter Solstice, Peyton."

CHAPTER 12:

TO ACKNOWLEDGE NEW BEGINNINGS

"Drew, quit pacing. You're making Roman nervous." Mikaél cut the silence in the hospital waiting room while eating a granola bar.

"Hm?" Roman lifted his head up from his phone, still barely paying attention.

"Mik, leave your brother alone," Alec scolded. "This is a big moment for him. You and Roman will go through the exact same experience, too."

"No, dad, Mik's right," Drew replied. For the fourth time in twenty minutes, he tried gluing himself to the chair which was now starting to feel like sharp concrete on his spine—hard to accomplish since it was the softest chair in the room.

Roman leaned into Mikaél's ear. "Damn, he must be out of it if he thinks you said something right." A glancing thrust of Mikaél's elbow into his side told Roman his comment was unwelcomed.

"How long has it been?" Drew asked aloud as he peeked at the time on his phone as if he couldn't trust it.

"Well, it's been about three minutes since you asked last time," Mikaél replied, balling up the granola wrapper in his fist.

"Mik, enough!" Dustin scolded. He got up from his chair and sat next to his Alpha son. "Drew, Will is going to make it. The pup is going to be perfect. Just be patient."

Drew sat forward in the chair with his elbows on his knees. His hands were clasped tightly together as if he was sending a direct line of communication to Wolf-God himself in the heavens, praying for his soon-to-be family's welfare. "What do you think, Mik?"

Mikaél paused in the middle of the waiting room from his return journey of getting a cup from the water cooler, his expression wide. "Me? Why me?"

"Because you're the only one I trust to give me the truth." Drew's eyes were heavy and dark. Clearly, the last 24 hours had drained the Alpha of all his strength.

For the first time in a long time, Mikaél gazed at his older brother with empathy. All the bravado, ego, and façade had faded from Drew. The man before him now was a shell of the self-absorbed jock he once was. Instead of returning another sarcastic retort to his brother, Mikaél chose the signature comfort that only an Omega could bring. "They're going to be fine, Drew. Honest. You have nothing to worry about. Soon, you'll be embracing your mate again and listening to your pup babble louder than you can. A welcome change for sure."

Drew returned a hint of gratitude in his sigh of relief. He leaned back in the chair and closed his eyes, trying to distract himself again.

After sitting back down in his own chair, Mikaél felt his Veo's hand squeeze his. "Thanks," Alec whispered to his younger son. Mikaél smiled back.

Roman sat up in his chair. "Did they decide which method they were going to try for the birth?"

Drew kept his eyes closed and wrinkled his brows. "Last the doctor said, he was going to try natural, but they were still monitoring Will's kidneys."

"His chances are pretty good since he's a Type 3," Roman commented.

Drew shot up in his chair. "Pretty good?"

Mikaél glared at Roman.

"Great chances!" Roman corrected. "Awesome! Phenomenal!"

Each word seemed to send Drew backward. He scratched his head and winced. With a grunt, he stood up. "Where are they?!"

Suddenly, a doctor in full scrubs came out. "Cavenbelle?" Drew rushed to him—his heart in this throat. "Everything went well. We did a natural birth, and Will pulled through like a trooper. There was some bleeding, but we were able to control it without any issues. His organs are great, he's in good spirits, and your Alpha pup is awake and already putting those lungs to good use." The doctor smiled.

Drew lit up. "An Alpha? My boy is an Alpha?"

The doctor nodded. "Would you and your family like to see them?"

Drew laughed. "Yes!"

"Follow me."

In a birthing suite, Will sat up in his hospital bed in good spirits considering the toll the pregnancy had on his body. Drew rushed in and gave Will the softest embrace he ever had and kissed his forehead. "And how are you?"

Will gave a hint of a smile. "I have some pretty good pain meds running through me right now." He pointed over to a small bassinet next to him. "Come and meet your son." The words barely came out as emotions flooded him.

Drew glanced over and saw a precious little pup under the golden halo of a heat lamp, arms and legs stretching out in slow motion, eyes barely wanting to stay open. His son had pale skin like his Omega father, but had dark hair like him. Every now and then he heard a tiny breath give off an audible sound—music to his ears.

"You can pick him up," Will encouraged.

As if his body movement alone would disturb the child, Drew carefully picked up his son in his muscular arms. He felt the young body kick. All the stress and worry he felt for the past 24 hours melted as he heard his son coo for the first time. "Hi, Xavier," he whispered. "I'm your Sur. And this is your Veo." His pride bloomed as he spoke to his son for the first time. "Look out world, major Alpha coming through!"

"Have they Typed him yet?" Alec asked.

"They said they're still working on it. Should find out tomorrow," Will informed them.

Jake nodded. "That typically takes a bit more time."

"Wow, these birthing suites sure have changed in 18 years," Alec commented. "Mountain Ridge has really stepped their game up."

"Yeah, this is a lot better than Summerlain," Will added. "Hard to believe I was born in that place." There was gratitude in his voice, knowing he was in a favorable position because of his mate's family.

Mountain Ridge was the premier hospital—connected to Tauris Medical Center. With it came a hefty price tag or the demand of elite insurance not typically held by anyone with less than a Type 4 Status. Betas and Lower Types typically received care here in the same way Will did—by mating contract. Alec chose not to comment on how Will's family was designated for the community hospital and instead chose to concentrate on his grandson.

"He's beautiful." Alec gasped. He stole him away from Drew and presented him to Dustin and the rest of the family.

"Congratulations, son." Dustin beamed with pride as he patted his son on the shoulder.

"Anyone up for a celebratory cigar?" Jake pulled a gold box from his jacket pocket.

Mikaél scrunched his face. "You brought cigars into a hospital?"

Jake laughed. "You can bring them in. You just can't smoke them."

"I think they have heat lamps out in the courtyard patio," Dustin added.

"Perfect!" Jake replied enthusiastically.

"I'll join you," Roman chimed in, then looked to his mate. "Are you going to stay here?"

"Yeah. I have no desire to stand out there in the cold to be your windbreaker so that the baby and I don't inhale that crap. Plus, someone has to stay here and keep Will and Xavier company."

"Splendid! Drew, are you coming?" Alec asked.

Drew shook out of a trance while completely transfixed on his baby boy. "Absolutely!" He meticulously watched Alec return Xavier to Will's arms and melted when he heard his baby coo. Xavier knew his parents already.

After the room cleared out, all that was heard were joyful baby noises cutting into the hums of few hospital monitors.

"Why do they still have you on all these?" Mikaél became uneasy as he began to observe more of an examination room versus a birthing suite.

"Monitoring different things," Will answered.

"The doctors told us in the waiting room everything was good."

"They are," Will reassured. "Just precaution is all."

Mikaél nodded. Thoughts of going through his own experience mere months away made his stomach sink. He had his mind wrapped around being father himself so much, he forgot the dangers pregnancy and birth inherently have for higher Types, especially a Type 5. Oh wait. He was a *Type 6*. What were the risks for him? Better? Worse? There was no precedent for him. Mikaél would be the standard for success; the thought unnerved him. "He really is beautiful."

"Hey. You're going to make it and give birth to a happy and healthy baby." Will's eyes were soft and comforting.

"Hm?" Mikaél's brows twitched.

"I know what you're thinking. I can see it all over your face. When it's your turn, you'll make it just like the rest of us did. Probably better. You've got a strong will and won't give up the fight easily. That much I know."

Mikaél peered out the window of the hospital room. In the far distance, the massive mountains sparkled with its freshly fallen snow. Directly below him, he saw the courtyard and all the family members there, most with cigars, laughing and having a joyous occasion which would serve as a memory for years. Yet, here, in this moment, Mikaél found little happiness in a moment he knew should be shining like the now setting sun for his brother-in-law and new nephew. "You know, it's funny... all throughout school and the better half of my life, teachers, my parents, family, and even my friends all talk about how the higher Status you are, the more dangerous it is to have pups. They always talked about it in the same breath when they said 'Don't talk to strangers' and 'Don't go downtown after dark alone.' After that, it was 'Don't get pregnant unless you know all the risks and your family medical history.'" Mikaél, somehow entertained by the warnings which now held water, broke into a smirk. "Now that I am pregnant and have a front row seat to what everybody is talking about, a lot of things are going through my mind."

Will sat up in his hospital bed as best as he could while still holding his pup. "Like what?"

Mikaél hesitated. "*Did* I make a mistake? Did Roman and I make a mistake? Should we have waited? Should we have adopted or done a surrogate with a Low-Type Omega instead like Sur and Veo wanted?"

"Nonsense!" Will exclaimed. "This baby you're having is a miracle. Miracles happen exactly when they are supposed to happen."

A smile crept on Mikaél's face. He tried to his best to ignore the fact he knew Will and Drew had no clue about the baby girl he was carrying. "I mean, you're right. But earlier I think back to when Roman asked me if I resented him for getting me pregnant when we did."

A pause ensued. "And?"

"I told him 'No' back then—that I thought what happened when it happened was perfectly all right."

"And now you feel differently?"

Mikaél gazed at Xavier who was slowly drifting to sleep, then back to the hospital monitors attached to Drew. "I'm not sure." Several steps returned to the birthing suite, breaking Mikaél out of focus. "You guys are back awfully quick." He scanned everyone, a tad suspicious they may have heard too much of the conversation. No one appeared the wiser.

"With the sun setting behind the mountains, it's getting pretty chilly, even with the heat lamps." Adrian rubbed his hands together to help jumpstart the return of warmth.

"Still, I think we got the job done." Jake stood tall as he patted his jacket pocket.

"It was a very nice gesture. Very grateful for you to be here," Dustin thanked his co-worker.

"I wouldn't have missed it! Your family is our family now. Adrian and I are just thankful you wanted us here for this beautiful moment."

"Exactly!" Adrian agreed.

"We feel the same way." Alec hugged Adrian to confirm the expression.

Will nodded. "We'll all have to do a repeat when it's Mik's turn!" Will's comment caused an unsettling aura to engulf the room. Several sets of eyes scanned each other awkwardly, but no one offered a hint as to why the comment invoked such sensitivity. "What?" he asked.

Alec shifted his expression instantly. "Mik, did you get a chance to hold Xavier yet?"

Mikaél himself joined in on the act, avoiding Will's comment as well. "Actually, no." Mikaél held out his arms and gleefully received his nephew for the first time, now fast asleep.

"What? Has Will been a protective papa bear this entire time?" Dustin amused himself with his own comment.

"No," Mikaél answered. "We were just lost in conversation is all." Mikaél never looked up as he observed the baby, still like a statue, memorizing every feature on his delicate face.

"What about?" Roman asked.

"Oh, nothing. Just baby talk." Mikaél glanced at Will to see how he would react. No words came out nor did his expression change. He once again found himself walking toward the window, now with Xavier in his arms.

Several other conversations began to fill the room as twilight set in. Mikaél heard footsteps approach and stop next to him. "When do Will's parents get here?"

"Probably in an hour or so. Takes them a bit to get up here to Tauris City," Drew replied.

"And how does it feel to be a dad?"

The new Alpha father exhaled in disbelief. "Even though I waited months for this and thought about being a parent for years, I didn't know it'd feel like this."

"What does it feel like?"

Drew paused. "Indescribable." Mikaél's eyes grew wide. "I'm sorry. I wish I could say it any other way. I became a parent the moment he was born."

"Makes sense."

"No, I really mean it." Drew eyed his younger brother with a sincerity Mikaél rarely saw. Then he looked at his baby boy. "The first moment I saw him, I became a parent. I transformed. I will never be the same again. And it's so amazing, I can't even find the word to describe how amazing it truly is!"

"Wow, Drew. I've never seen you like this before."

Drew laughed. "Wait until you're holding your son, you'll see what I mean."

Mikaél's expression dimmed. "Yeah... I suppose so."

"Mik? Are you ready to go?" Roman asked from across the room.

"Yeah, I think now is a good time."

"So soon?" Drew asked.

"I'm a little tired anyway. Plus, you still have grandparents here who I'm sure are itching to hold him again. Isn't that right, little guy?" Xavier turned his head slightly with his eyes still shut. "Time to go back to your daddy." After returning him to Drew's arms, he hugged his brother as tight as he could. "Congratulations, Drew," he whispered.

Drew's heart and face lit up from the emotion he wasn't used to seeing from his little brother. "Thanks, Mik."

A knock.

Another knock.

Several knocks.

Roman stumbled to door with nothing but the moonlight guiding his way. He reached for the kitchen light switch with one eye closed, bracing himself for the impact it would have on his sight. He moaned as his focus readjusted and moaned again as he peered through the eyehole which revealed a familiar figure standing in the hallway, still shivering from winter's grip.

"Ryan, what the hell are you doing here?" Roman whispered as to hopefully not wake up Mikaél.

Ryan's teeth chattered and his voice trembled. "I'm sorry. I had nowhere else to go."

"Shh!" Roman breathed.

"Sorry. Is he asleep?"

"Ryan, it's gotta be 3 AM. We were both asleep. What do you mean you had no place to go? You have a place." Ryan didn't answer. "What's going on?"

"We had a fight. Yikes, Roman, don't you put on clothes when you answer the door? Do you sleep like that?"

Roman peered down and noticed all he was wearing were black boxer briefs. "It's not like it's 30 degrees in here. Out there maybe."

"Try 20 degrees. At least that's what the bank sign said."

In his mind, Roman tried to comprehend what the comment meant. "The bank? The nearest bank is like four blocks away."

"I know!" Ryan barked back.

"What are you doing at a bank at 3 AM?"

Ryan growled. "I wasn't at the bank! I walked past it. I was at the tram station."

The room stood still for a moment. Then, Roman's shoulders slumped as he still saw his brother shivering from the cold, his arms crossed on his chest like he was a pouting five-year-old. "Come in. Sit on the couch and I'll make you a cup of tea." He flipped a switch and turned on the gas fireplace.

"About time! Make it cocoa if you got it."

Roman stopped en route to the kitchen, clenching his fist for a moment and then releasing it. He made his way to the refrigerator and pulled out the milk and then to the cupboard for cocoa powder. Occasionally, he snuck a look at his younger brother, who frantically scanned his phone every ten seconds. The light from the screen aided the fireplace in making the room bright in the dead of night. He was waiting, hoping for something. A text from Rixen perhaps? But judging by the constant depressed expression on his face, no such comfort was coming through.

For Ryan, waiting for Roman to return was agonizing. In part, it was due to the cold, but it was more trying to figure out what he was going to say to Roman and wondering how he was going to take it. Ryan's leg kept bouncing up and down in nerves.

"If you keep doing that, you're going to make a hole in the floor and fall into the apartment downstairs," the Alpha criticized.

Roman's sarcasm was unwanted, but Ryan accepted the peace offering of a large mug filled with steaming creamy chocolate. The heat from the cup rushed through his icy hands faster than the rate of his blood. As he took the first drink, he felt his body start to calm down for the first time tonight. "Thanks."

"Uh huh. So, you wanna start at the beginning?"

"Not really," Ryan puffed.

"Too bad. You woke me up at 3AM and showed up on my doorstep. You better tell me everything."

Ryan stared into his brother's eyes which were reflecting the flames from the fireplace. He wasn't kidding. "Okay..." He took one more generous gulp of the cocoa and set it on the glass coffee table. "The three of us had a fight."

"You said that already," Roman pointed out.

"Okay... the three of us had a really *big* fight."

"How big?"

"I think the relationship is over," Ryan confessed.

Roman massaged his knee as he contemplated his next response. "So, the three of you didn't work out?"

"Not exactly."

His older brother narrowed his view. "What does that mean?" Ryan searched his phone again for an update which he knew wasn't there. A stall tactic if Roman ever saw one. "Damn it, Ryan. What's going on?"

"Garrace and Rixen are continuing the relationship without me. And I got kicked out of the apartment."

The news struck Roman hard. He was in complete disbelief. "What?" Suddenly, the bedroom door opened. "Mik?"

"Roman, who was at the door?" Mikaél yawned as he held himself up near the doorframe.

"It's just Ryan. Go back to bed."

Ryan grunted. "What do you mean '*just*' Ryan?"

"Shut up," Roman spat back.

"Is everything okay?" Mikaél began his walk into the living room. He was stopped halfway as Roman made his way toward him.

"Yes. I think Ryan's going to spend the night here. So, I'll get him set up and then I'll come to bed."

"Sounds good." Mikaél barely got a look at Ryan before Roman kissed him tenderly. "I love you."

"I love you, too." Roman embraced his mate and sent him back to the bedroom.

Ryan's heart sank as the warmth and affection started to become a distant memory of what he once had. "Thanks for letting me stay here tonight."

"You're not staying here until you tell me what you mean by that statement."

"Right." Ryan took one deep breath in and released it. "Rixen is pregnant."

A shock went right through Roman as the words cemented in his mind. "Oh."

"Really? My older brother who has the perfect life, the perfect career, and the perfect mate can't figure out anything better to say other than 'Oh'?"

Roman's eyebrows dimmed. "First of all, my life is not perfect. I don't know where you got that idea from. Second, my career is no famous movie or magical television special. And third, what the hell do you want me to say?"

"You already did. Or rather, it's what you didn't say." Ryan shook his head.

"What the fuck does that mean?"

"You and your *perfect* mate." Ryan's words spewed jealousy as he saw his brother clench his teeth. "Yeah, I noticed you didn't comment about that. Must be nice knowing you have a mate you can rely on to be everything you wanted: honest, loyal, trusting, uncondit—"

"You better shut your mouth before I do it for you!" Roman's body leaned forward on the couch with his fingers aimed right between Ryan's eyes. As he saw his brother gulp down his nerves, he slowly retracted himself back. "Can you finally tell me what's going on? Why is Rixen pregnant? I thought you guys weren't going down that road."

"We weren't! Or at least, that's what we discussed."

"An accident then?"

"No way this was an accident."

Roman rubbed his chin. "Someone changed their mind?"

"Two people if you ask me." Ryan glanced at his phone again. No update. Sick of the constant disappointment, he chucked his phone to the far end of the couch and crossed his arms.

"I'm guessing you didn't know?" Roman asked.

"No shit! What a great detective you are!" Ryan snapped back.

"Will you lay off me! Wolf-God! I'm not the enemy here!"

Ryan rubbed his temples. "I'm sorry. I know you're not."

A million questions raced through Roman's mind. "When did you find out?"

This time Ryan laid his back against the fabric of the couch. Although the heat from the room was finally absorbed into him, and the couch soft like an inviting cloud, he felt little comfort. "Tonight. Rixen sat at the kitchen table and broke the news to me while Garrace stood behind him like he was an Alpha reminding me that Rixen was his property or something. I could have ripped him to shreds for that!"

Roman scratched his head. "Who? Rixen or Garrace?"

"Both at this point!"

"Hey. Lay off Rixen. He's your brother."

"He's not just my brother; he's my ex-boyfriend. One of two of my ex-boyfriends. Both traitors!" Ryan's voice began to echo a familiar scene only a few months ago when Roman outed him and Rixen to their parents. The shock and disdain from his parents weren't ever going away—Ryan knew that now. Reliving the moment briefly in his head was a mistake, as he didn't want to make

Roman an enemy. He needed someone on his side. Right now, he didn't have anyone else. "You remember dinner at Winter Solstice? You remember when Rixen had the onset of his first heat?"

"Um. Yes?" Roman replied uneasily, not liking the mention of the topic.

"Garrace and I had to take care of it constantly after we got home. It felt like it went on forever and ever. No matter what we did or what we tried, he was just never satisfied."

There was no way Roman had any idea where this thought was headed. Ryan couldn't see it in the limited light, but his face was beginning to turn beet red, and it wasn't from the heat of the fireplace. "Okay, I do not want to hear the details of you, Garrace, and Rixen having sex. I'd rather not barf all over my living room right now."

"Would you just shut up and listen?! You said you wanted to know what happened and I'm trying to tell you. I'm not going to tell you about any stupid details on what we did. That isn't the point right now, damn it!" Ryan began huffing; his patience was getting to an end.

"Sorry." Roman stared down at his feet, the details of his skin going in and out with the flicker of light from the fireplace.

"We could barely get Rixen to do anything. He wouldn't eat, and he wouldn't drink. We tried different distractions like watching a movie or focusing on school; nothing would work."

"Wolf-God, Ryan! There are protocols you are supposed to follow in these situations."

"Fuck off."

"I'm serious! If you're not adult enough to handle everything that comes with a heat, you shouldn't be dealing with one. If he's not getting through the heat or not taking care of himself, you're supposed to call a health professional!" The disappointment in his brother began to bubble up inside Roman, his Alpha pheromones ready to dominate his younger brother, a routine in his life he had almost forgotten about.

"Let a professional fuck Rixen while Garrace and I watch? Not happening." Ryan stared down Roman, ready to go head-to-head on responsibility of taking care of a mate, or in this case, two of them.

"No, you idiot! They'd be there to sedate Rixen so he could relax. Or give him nutrients through an IV so he doesn't go into shock or go unconscious from exhaustion. Or, you know, the worst-case scenario, die! This is 'Mating 101,' Ryan, come on! This is like the first stuff they're willing to tell us in school. How did none of you think of any of this?"

"I—I don't know." Ryan stood down as the logic set in. Maybe there was validity to Roman's accusations. Maybe he wasn't ready for the responsibility of taking care of a heat. The more he thought about Garrace's role in it all, the more he wanted to wring his neck.

"No point in berating it now. *That* part is over. Especially if Rixen's pregnant." Saying the words out loud left a bad taste in Roman's mouth. "So, how did this happen?"

Ryan rubbed his leg, aiding the warmth from the fireplace in getting his body temperature back to normal. "From what Rixen told me, it was getting harder and harder to wait for me to come home from work so that both Garrace and I could be with him."

"Why didn't you just tell your job you were taking medical days off for dealing with a heat?" Roman shut his eyes and immediately regretted it after speaking.

"And what? Tell them I was a Beta taking care of an Omega's heat and that the Omega was my twin brother? I'm sure that would have went over swimmingly."

"Sorry. I'm not quite awake yet. Of course, you didn't say that. How about just saying you were sick?"

"No. I haven't worked at this job long enough to have any security. Being sick for four days wasn't going to cut it, especially right after the holidays."

Roman's eyes grew wide. "*Four* days?"

"Apparently, when I was at work, Rixen's heat would subside enough to where the only topic of discussion was the relationship and its future. Rixen confessed to Garrace in those moments that the way I felt about him was not equally the way he felt back to me."

"No way! Rixen said that?"

Ryan nodded. "I had no clue. Nor did I have any idea Rixen was seriously thinking about having pups at all. He never, ever told me he wanted them. Then, suddenly, he talks to Garrace, and it's like he's wanted them all his life."

"I've told you this before, Ryan. Rixen, quite honestly, fears you."

"Why?"

Roman groaned. "Come on, Ryan. Get your head out of your ass. If this defensive posture is how you are willing to talk to me when you know I can kick your ass in two seconds, how do you talk to Rixen when you're upset or the two of you don't agree?"

Ryan bit his thumbnail. "I—"

"Exactly." Roman teetered on disgust. "How is this pregnancy a surprise to you anyway? Four days of Garrace being involved, you three knew what could happen."

"Except when the three of us were involved, we all used protection."

Roman's wheels began turning. "Are you saying—"

"That's *exactly* what I'm trying to say." Ryan hunched his shoulders and let his head fall.

For the first time tonight, Roman allowed empathy to wash all over him. Ryan was a dick. Even he himself had to know that. But he didn't deserve what Rixen and Garrace did to him. "I'm sorry. I really am. But you did mention you got 'kicked out' of the apartment. Just because Rixen doesn't want to be your boyfriend and is carrying Garrace's pup means you get kicked out?"

Ryan raspberried. "Ha! Believe it or not, neither of those were the reason."

"Oh?"

"In their throws of lust and 'pup making,' several discussions came up on how those two were compatible in life and I was not. They apologized for me being at a disadvantage in the first place since the two of them were together first. They claim they didn't like what me being there did to *their* relationship and that I was a shadow on their shining dream. Me staying in the apartment, even platonically, wasn't possible. At least that's what they said." Ryan's voice ruffed with irritation.

"I don't suppose your immediate reaction to all this helped reinforce their point?" Roman tilted his head.

Ryan hinted at a smile, but it quickly fell back into despair. "Yeah. I guess it did."

"Look. You can stay here a couple of days—"

"Really?" Ryan's face lit up like a sunrise. "Thank you!"

"But after that, you are going to have to make nice with Sur and see if you can move back into the house." Roman waited for the volcano to erupt.

Ryan paused. After a brief contemplation, he conceded. "Deal."

Roman silently acknowledged his brother's acceptance. "Well. I think that's enough for tonight. I'll get you a blanket, and you can sleep here on the couch."

"Roman. Thank you." Ryan's gratitude hit his brother strongly.

"You're welcome, Ryan."

CHAPTER 13:

TO PROVE OLD
HABITS DIE HARD

Brookside Books was more stressful today than normal. Or was it that Garrace had less patience? He couldn't be sure as a million thoughts ran through his head. Every angry voice of a customer, every hard slam of the cash register, and every loud thump and crash of a heavy box of books were murder on his senses. Taking pain killers didn't help ease the suffering nor did the joint he smoked on his lunch break. Nothing seemed to ease the headache or the tight muscles in his upper back and shoulders. But still, he pressed on, gritting his teeth into a smile he could barely hold on to.

"It looks like that book was very popular for the holidays. I'm afraid we won't get copies back in stock for another two weeks." Garrace's voice in his head sounded like customer service management perfection, but the face on the customer said otherwise.

"Are you kidding me? Every time I come into this place looking for a book I want, it's the one book you don't have! I thought you guys were a bookstore!" The man clutched his wallet in his hand like it was a stress ball he could squeeze.

Garrace nodded once, his styled hair delicately moving with him. "I'm sorry we don't have that for you right now. If you want, I can put in an order request, and we'll contact you when it comes in. Or is there another book I can help you find?"

"Just forget it! All of you are going to go out of business to online stores anyway!" He spat and began walking away, leaving the burning stench of angry Alpha pheromones behind him.

The soft expression on Garrace's face stuck there like a movie on pause. However, if someone disturbed the trance, even in the slightest, the façade would crash down like glass on concrete. But the next voice he heard surprised him, awakened him, soothed him.

"I hope every customer doesn't talk to you that way." The voice was gentle yet carried a hint of attitude.

A breath of fresh air entered Garrace's lungs. "Most don't. But there are a few standouts. Damn Alphas anyway."

"Ouch! Are you insulting me or insulting yourself?" The young man beamed, his dark hair and dark eyes glistening in the fluorescent lights.

"Maybe at this point, both," Garrace admitted.

"Perhaps I should ask for some customer service and see just how good your skills really are?" A finger lightly scratched the marbled countertop next to the register.

"And just what are you looking for, exactly?"

The Alpha shifted his weight. "Oh, a title you probably don't have," he teased.

"And that would be?"

A pause set in as the Alpha studied Garrace up and down. "*Moonlight Encounters*." He grinned like a wolf on the hunt.

Garrace rolled his eyes. "Hayden, you *know* we don't have that. You're going to have to go to the 'other' bookstore downtown to find that."

"Of course, I know that. Now the real question is, what good customer service are you going to give to satisfy me?"

Garrace's elbow flinched, and with it, several stacked books fell to the floor in a melodic thud. He cursed to himself silently as he bent down to pick them back up, but he was also grateful the moment allowed him to hide his blushing face. He kept his eyes peering elsewhere. "I'm not even going to *satisfy* that with an answer."

Hayden pushed his finger to his own lips. "Hmm. Are you sure your manager would approve of you saying that?"

"Lucky for me, my manager is out today. I'm running the show."

Slight laughter emanated from Hayden. The moment elevated his exotic looks which came from what was once known as the Far East. "You always did like being the master of your domain." He sighed.

With arms overloaded with books, Garrace searched around for onlookers with prying eyes. Then he leaned in and stressed. "This isn't the time, Hayden."

Hayden held up his hands, his smile never wavering. "Fine. We can talk about something else. Like... how about your lovers? Or is it still just 'lover'?"

"Nothing's changed since we last talked. Ryan is back home with his parents, and Rixen and I are..." Garrace's mouth went dry. Hayden noticed the abrupt pause instantly but waited patiently. "... still working through it."

"Sounds like you two are having issues. What's up, buttercup?"

"Don't call me that! Especially at work." Garrace took off with the stack of books he held in his arms and frantically searched for an empty space to set them on display. He felt Hayden's body follow close behind him, giving him no reprieve.

"You always enjoyed the pet names I had for you." Hayden let his hand glide over the fabric covering Garrace's cold shoulder. Upon his touch, he felt Garrace shrug him off as he began to set up a display.

"I'm not yours to give a pet name to!" Books slammed into place as a low growl rumbled in Garrace's throat.

"What's wrong with you? You're not usually like this."

Garrace rubbed his eyebrow. Sweat began to form on his forehead and under his arms. "Rixen and I... we're just... we're just going through a lot of stress right now, okay?"

"Okay, okay!" Hayden took a step back. His sweet Alpha pheromones turned sour. "Must be *something* for you to be acting like this."

A whimper and a sigh. Garrace let his weight collapse on a tower of books sitting on a display table. At this point, he didn't care who saw him. All the other customers in the store faded into the background. He shut his eyes. "Rixen is pregnant."

Hayden's forehead creased. "Um. Congratulations?"

"Thanks." Garrace grunted and took off toward another book display, pretending it needed to be cleaned.

"What? I'm just going off your reaction here. Aren't you supposed to be smiling ear-to-ear with Daddy Alpha pride?"

"I don't know. I think so?"

"Then why aren't you?" Hayden crossed his arms.

"This... this just isn't what I thought it'd be like."

"That what would be like?"

Garrace shrugged. "I don't know. Life?"

Hayden blinked. "Wow. That was specific. Not."

Garrace once again surveyed the bookstore to see if anyone was listening in on the private conversation. But post-holiday shoppers appeared to be way too busy to notice the two of them. Still, he casually walked Hayden over to a section of the store void of any customers.

"Lately, I've felt like my life has been transported into an alternate universe or dimension or something. I used to be the head Alpha walking tall in our class, getting stared at and admired by practically everyone around me. I had the freedom to talk to any Alpha, Omega, or Beta I wanted to and always be greeted with a smile and know by the end of the conversation I'd probably be asked out. Everyone wanted me in their study group, their gatherings, their posse, and their social media page. Getting home at the end of the day was exhausting, but it was nice to just relax in my own room away from it all—knowing I could go back to having the spotlight on me when I wanted or just relax and enjoy being me, by myself, without anyone or anything else to worry about."

Hayden thought for a second. "So, in other words, you're pissed off because being an expecting father with Rixen doesn't give you the freedom to be a ho anymore?"

"It's deeper than that."

"I know how deep you can get." Hayden smiled.

"Shut up. I'm being serious."

"What are you talking about?"

"I don't know. It's almost like being a part of Rixen's life has cursed me somehow. Guys aren't coming up to me and flirting with me, our classmates aren't rushing up to me asking me to be a part of any class project, or even their lunch group anymore. I mean, for fuck's sake, my social media following is even dropping. This isn't normal!" Garrace cried. "Guys don't lose their attraction just because they're with someone. If anything, it increases the desire to be with them."

"Well, you have a point there. But you know the reason why, don't you?"

Garrace sensed the warning. "No, I don't. Would you like to inform me?"

"It's not because you are taken that all of sudden you're becoming an untouchable. It's because you are with Rixen."

"What? You've got to be kidding me!"

"I'm serious. Have you been listening to what's been going on with that family? I mean, you made yourself a spectacle alone once you announced you were in a relationship with two brothers who apparently have been screwing each other since birth."

"That's not true!" Garrace defended.

"How do you know?" Hayden asked.

"Rixen told me. Hell, I was even the first person Ryan told that he was even in love with Rixen. I was there when the whole thing went down."

"So you say. Maybe that was just their story and you got played into it."

"No, Hayden. That sounds more like something *you* would do."

Hayden shrugged his shoulders. "Learned from the best."

Garrace licked the inside of his cheek and pushed a book back onto a shelf which was hanging on the edge. "And what about this curse you claim Rixen has?"

"Not just him. The entire 'Erricson' name is becoming something to stay away from."

Garrace shook his head in confusion. "Why?"

"Come on. Seriously? Where has your head been the last couple of months? Oh, that's right. Between Rixen's legs." Hayden slid his tongue out between his teeth. But he didn't get any positive response from Garrace. Realizing his antics weren't appreciated, he straightened up and went on. "Roman's best friend gets indicted for messing with the Whitmore family, Roman's mate Mikaél claims he's some Type 6 Omega gift from Wolf-God—"

"Yeah, I heard that nonsense getting around at school," Garrace interrupted.

"And then his dad's photography studio gets burned to the ground. And now, here you are, the once teen dream turned teen scream, and nobody wants you." Hayden viewed Garrace squint his eyes and firm up his posture. "Hey, you were with Mikaél once, weren't you? Maybe you're the problem."

In a flash, Garrace pushed Hayden forcefully into a standing bookshelf. Hayden's body slammed against it and rattled several volumes barely able to withstand the impact. In the heat of the moment, Garrace almost forgot he was dealing with another Alpha. The rage balled up in his fists which were full of Hayden's shirt. His face was a breath away from Hayden's with a bloodthirsty expression. Amazingly, the commotion didn't cause a stir with patrons.

"Listen. I don't know what bullshit you're trying to brainwash me with. But the only problem I see here is you." Hayden's gaze pierced back. Despite the Alpha being pinned against the shelf, he began to laugh. "What's so funny?"

"*There's* the Alpha I know. *There's* the fire in you."

Garrace's concentration faltered as he inhaled Hayden's alluring scent. "Damn it!" He released him from his grasp as the fabric of Hayden's shirt slipped from his hands. His lungs began to work overtime as his head processed flashbacks of moments with Hayden where his pheromones were familiar, stronger, and fulfilling.

"When are you going to realize you want what I want?" The light, seductive sound left Hayden's voice. Now he was serious.

Garrace turned his head in shock. "You know nothing of what I want. I'm nothing like you, Hayden!"

Hayden took one step forward and leaned in, his face unchanged. His voice became a whisper. "You and me, we're exactly alike."

The air felt thicker. A haze still clouded Garrace's judgement as he swallowed hard. "Why are you here?"

"Because you texted me and told me to show up? Or do you not remember that part?"

"No. That's not what I meant. Why are you *really* here?"

Hayden flapped his jacket as he readjusted it. The entertained look returned to his face. "You get off work in what? Fifteen minutes?"

"Yeah?"

"Do yourself a favor and use those fifteen minutes to think about why you told me to come here in the first place." Hayden began to saunter off, proud of himself. "When you figure it out, come and find me. I'll be in the food court—waiting."

Garrace's stomach tensed, and his hand trembled at his side. As Hayden walked toward the exit, he saw a silhouette of a proud territorial Alpha wolf who conquered his conquest without even lifting a finger. The thought reminded him of someone. The man he himself used to be.

"Roman!" the older gentleman shouted with glee as he stood up behind his desk. He shuffled over to the Alpha, preparing himself for an embrace from a muscle god. He wasn't disappointed.

"Mr. Snyder!" Roman embraced the balding man, careful not to crush his glasses which were hanging from his neck.

"My boy! It's been too long!"

"Mr. Snyder, it hasn't even been a year. It was just last spring at the championship dinner."

"At my age, a week seems like a year." He reluctantly let go of the hug and hobbled back to his executive chair.

Roman observed the man and winced. "How are you feeling, Mr. Snyder?"

"It's this damn hip. That's what happens when you get old."

"You're not that old."

"Older than you think," Mr. Snyder corrected. "Plus, I'm a Type 5 Alpha. And you know what they say: the higher the Alpha, the harder they fall." Roman's face became visibly uncomfortable. "Ah, don't worry about it, my boy. With you being a Type 6, I'm sure you're the exception to the rule."

Roman's focus shifted. "One can only hope."

"What brings you here? What can I do you for?" Mr. Snyder laid back in his chair and wrapped his hands around his generous stomach.

"Coach said the championship prints finally came in. Just here to pick up my copy."

Mr. Snyder sat back up and snapped his fingers. "That's right. Those came in a couple months ago. I was beginning to fear that you had forgotten."

"Never!" Roman insisted. "That was one of the best moments in my life!"

The gentleman sifted through stacks of papers all around him which appeared to have never been touched in decade. After that he pulled open several metal file drawers. "5th Championship title for the Territory and the second for you. Team Captain to boot. Although, if you ask me, you should have been the captain a few years before that."

Roman chuckled but then fell back into a serious demeanor. "Yeah, well, Level 4s didn't appreciate the idea of a Level 2 being the captain of their team. Talk about emasculating."

"Alpha pride can be the hardest to conquer sometimes." Sitting on the floor next to a metal cabinet was a large, padded envelope. Mr. Snyder peeked in the previously opened package. "Here we are. This should be it."

The young Alpha opened it and exhaled in reminiscent joy. In a beautifully stained hardwood plaque behind clear glass was a team picture of several young Alphas smoldering in a celebratory moment at last year's basketball championship game. Shiny gold medals hung from every one of their necks and several held their index finger up in the "Number one" pose. Standing near the sides were several support staff in team jackets, including the coach and Mr. Snyder. Mr. Snyder appeared misty-eyed in the photo himself, very much proud of the team's accomplishments.

As athletic director, Mr. Snyder had seen many teams pass by Ashershire Preparatory. To still be here in his final years of his career celebrating a championship meant a lot to him. Watching Roman admire the captured moment in history, he clearly thought the same. He stood there and admired the boy. "Seems like it was just yesterday."

"Right?" The pure scent of happiness faded into a guilt. Roman made no attempts to hide the new pheromone profile.

"You know, it's not too late."

"We're halfway done with the season. There's no way I could get back on."

"Oh, please! Ashershire Prep's number one basketball player in decades coming back to round out his third Territorial Championship? Lesser circumstances have been considered before."

"I don't think I'd get the hero's welcome back." Roman scanned the picture of several young men who he knew would be grateful for his return. And a few who wouldn't. "I have bigger things in my life I have to consider now. A career. A pup on the way."

Mr. Snyder shrugged. "You'll never know until you try."

Roman peered out of the glass walls to the double doors on the other side of the hallway. Like x-ray vision, he saw the polished wood floors, the large overhanging lights, the flashing score board, and envisioned in his head the sounds of squeaking tennis shoes, fans in the bleachers, and roaring crowd-pumping music. He rubbed his forehead and thought for another moment as he imagined the end game buzzer roar in victory.

"What the hell are you doing, Josh? You're playing basketball like a pup today." Vincent snickered at his teammates all drenched in exhaustion while he barely broke a sweat.

"Man, give me a break," Josh huffed. "We've been at this for an hour."

"Dude, do you really think Fairmont is going to let up when you start feeling tired? Come on! They're the team to beat this year. We beat them—the championship is ours." Vincent tilted his head back and shot a stream of ice-cold refreshment down his throat from his water bottle. He sighed in relief. Out of the corner of his eye, he saw Josh grab for his. "Nope! I don't think so!" He growled.

"Are you serious right now?"

"You actually start playing like you care, and then you can get a drink." Vincent smirked, entertained by the power of his new position. As his voice echoed across the gym, his fellow teammates slowed to a stop, unamused at his demands. "What? You all got something to say?"

Timothy stepped forward, holding the basketball under his arm. "That's not how you boost morale, Vince."

"I don't really care, Tim," Vincent barked. "I care about results. And right now, I'm not seeing them."

"Keeping Josh, or any of us, from getting a drink until you see what you deem worthy isn't going to get the results you want. Coach knows that." Timothy threw the ball at Vincent's head. It was no surprise, even at the lightning speed at which he threw it, Vincent caught it instantly, a mere second away from his face.

"Well, coach isn't here, pup!" Vincent threw the ball right back at Timothy. "And until he comes back next week, I'm in charge. And right now, if *any* of you losers want a drink, it's ten laps."

Josh began a coughing fit.

Timothy put his arm on his back. "Josh, get a drink of water."

"Did you hear what I just said?!" Vincent yelled.

"LET HIM GET WATER!" The voice rang out around the gym. Roman stood there as a presiding Pack Alpha while whispers were heard discussing his presence.

Vincent clenched his teeth. "Roman?!"

"Roman!" Timothy led part of the team, halfway down the gym to greet the prodigal. Roman stood there at the center and waited for his brothers. "Man! It is so good to see you!" Timothy embraced Roman, forgetting he was drenched in a layer of sweat from practice.

"You too, my friend." Roman witnessed a dozen pair of eyes stare at him in awe, like he just got back from war. "How's practice going this year?"

The entire team peered at each other. Every single one of them had the same thought running through their head. The silence set in. With it was the unspoken communication for Timothy to say something.

"It's ... going." Timothy peered over his shoulder. On the other side of the court, Vincent eyed his entire team with daggers. "We didn't think we'd ever see you again."

Roman nodded in guilt. "Yeah. About that, guys. I'm sorry. I'm very sorry. There's just a lot of things that happened."

"We all know what happened." Several teammates joined Timothy in a subtle hint of laughter.

Roman felt embarrassment wash over him. "You do?"

"Mikaél, right?"

"Right," the Alpha confirmed.

Timothy shook his head, amused in Roman's unease. "Boy, he must be something really special."

"He's the best, guys." Roman beamed.

Jeremiah, one of the team's tallest, stepped forward with a smile plastered all over his face and gave Roman a side hug and a hand-shake. "And congratulations on becoming a dad!" The rest of the team huddled around him, sharing in the celebration.

"Thanks, guys," Roman uttered.

"When is he due?"

"This April."

"We wish you all the best." Jeremiah looked back to Vincent, who still stared back like a cautious wolf. "Even Vince wishes you the best. Isn't that right, Vince?" Vincent only lifted his chin to respond. Jeremiah turned back. "He'll be all right," he whispered. "What would you say, just for old time's sake, join us in a game?" Several teammates cheered in encouragement.

Pride and guilt flooded Roman's head once more. "I don't know about that, guys. You really want your captain here?" The crowd roared in approval.

"You mean *former* captain?!" Vincent's harsh tone cut through the moment like a sharp knife. "A true captain doesn't abandon his team like the way *you* did."

Timothy winced. "Damn, Vince. Ease up."

Vincent began his strut to the huddle in the middle of the court, Alpha pheromones fuming. "You disappeared without a trace! If it wasn't for Siro, we would have never heard anything about you."

"I talked to coach when he approached me," Roman defended, his face heating up.

"Eventually." Vincent eyeballed Roman with a wild wolf's stare. A challenge was clearly brewing. "We were heartbroken. You were our family; we were all a family, and you left us!"

"Vince, quit." Jeremiah tried to reign the Alpha in. Normally, his stature alone could have put the brakes on Vincent. But Jeremiah was an Alpha Type 4, which meant he wasn't going to curtail any higher Type without force.

Roman saw the writing on the wall. He was going to have to let this play out. He cut in front and shielded Jeremiah from the wrath which was clearly meant for him. "It's all right, Jeremiah." Once again, he was face to face with Vincent. He could almost taste the disdain radiating off his body.

"Were two Territorial Championships not good enough for you?" He let the question set in. "You are a traitor, Roman! We all know it. But for some reason, you come in here thinking you are the untouchable Wolf-God bestowing his presence among the common folk. Your stupid Type 6 Status leaves everyone in a cloudy haze and then everyone forgets just how much of an ass you are." Slowly, several teammates bowed their heads as Vincent successfully opened the wound from the day they realized Roman wasn't coming back to the team. "But not me."

Roman pressed his hard chest up against Vincent. "What do you want, Vince?"

"You and me. One-on-one. No one else. First to ten."

The team murmured to each other. Reactions were all over the place. Some were in shock Vincent even had the guts to talk to Roman, their once beloved captain, in such a manner. Others were entertained and snickered in the chance to watch a head-to-head battle between two top Alphas.

Roman held his own. "And what is that going to prove?"

"That you can't have it all, Erricson. Everyone talks about how great Fate is, including the boy wonder you impregnated."

"You got a problem with that?" Roman tightened his fist.

"I don't give a shit about your Fated Mate, and you'll find that most here don't." Vincent shifted his weight, treading lightly on the subject of Roman's personal life. Vincent was a formidable foe. But he didn't want to have to settle the score in a way that would get him injured, or worse, kicked off the team. "And Fate works both ways. You finding your Fate meant it was my time to shine. I'm captain now, and I'm going to lead our team to the first-ever three consecutive championships ever seen in the entire territory. And you are going to be watching from the sidelines as a has been who didn't make it."

An ice-cold shock rushed through the basketball court as anyone could hear a pin drop. All waited on Roman's reaction.

Roman observed his onlookers, some buckling at the knees. "I'm not a 'has been.' I didn't want the career in basketball anymore, so I focused my attention elsewhere."

"That's what everyone says when they know deep down inside, they don't have what it takes," Vincent rebuked.

In a flash, Roman ripped off his jacket and tossed it toward the bleachers. "You want a game? You got it."

Vincent grinned as the former leader of the pack bent to his wishes, completely unprepared for the challenge before him. "Excellent."

"You don't have to do this," Timothy offered, crossing his arms. He watched Roman sitting on the bench in the locker room, putting on his favorite shoes which were still in his locker.

"I'm not so sure this is a good idea either," Josh added, taking a swig of his water bottle.

After tying his last lace up, Roman pulled up his socks as high as they would go. He stood up and stretched out his arms. "You and I know very well I wasn't going to be able to back down from that. Even if I could have, what did you think I would say?"

The light from the ceiling bounced off Timothy's black skin making him appear like basketball royalty. He nodded, amused by his friend and former captain. "You still would have done it."

Roman walked over to the large mirror to make sure he presented himself as best as he could. Looking back at him was a man he barely recognized. To think one year ago, being in a team jersey was second nature. Now he felt like a stranger. His eyes slanted to the left as his mind envisioned an alternate reality where he never met his Fated Mate. That would mean his final year at Ashershire would be exactly this: living the prestige as the number one player on his basketball team and getting all the benefits which came with it...fame, admiration, notoriety, and cement him as a legend. It didn't help that he just so happened to have his coveted jersey in his locker, #22, still fresh from the spring-cleaning last year.

Another former teammate rushing into the locker room broke Roman out of his distant thoughts. "Hey, Roman! Vincent thinks your stalling!"

Roman puffed his chest. "Just wait to hear what he thinks when I beat his pup ass."

Both Timothy and Josh enjoyed the comment, and enjoyed having Roman back even more, no matter how brief it was.

"Let's do this." Roman grinned, leading his former teammates behind him, like the wolf-leader he was less than a year ago.

208

Once reaching the gym, Vincent stood there, mildly entertained as he watched Roman saunter out like a king. His smile broke as he watched the rest of his teammates clap and cheer him on like he was the hero of the day. "Poser," he muttered.

"Shut up, and let's get this going, Vince," Roman growled.

"As you wish," the Alpha sang. He beckoned to a teammate who threw him a ball. "Clear out!" he yelled. Like leaves, the team brushed to the sidelines, yelling words of encouragement to both challengers. "So, Roman, what will be your pleasure? Top? Or bottom?" He flashed his white teeth through his dark facial features.

"Top." Before Vincent could even register the moment, Roman's hands snagged the ball out of his hands with ease. The momentum startled him for a second, unaware of just how much skill Roman still had bottled up.

Both young men did a simultaneous dance on the court until Roman was facing the basket. A familiar buzzer sound filled the near-vacant gym. Once a comfort to Roman, the noise hit his ears like an ominous warning. The scoreboard was set to 0-0. Sweat began to form at the top of his lip. Roman checked the ball to Vincent. Upon its return, Roman held it firm in both hands and shook it lightly as he contemplated his first movie. A bold attempt made Roman hurdle the ball across the court.

Vincent's eyes were wide as he couldn't believe Roman even attempted the half-court shot. But his stomach turned over twice as he watched the ball, seemingly in slow motion, sink into a beautiful weave of pearl white rope and slam back down onto the court. Roman 3. Vincent 0. "Coward!" Vincent gasped.

"What?" Roman shrugged. "You want a free shot?"

Vincent grimaced as he ran toward the ball—Roman coming up behind him. From the corner, Vincent checked the ball back, not out of respect but out of spite, as he chucked it toward his face. Roman managed to control the ball before any injury, but it pleased Vincent to see the sweat collect on Roman's shirt.

The captain maneuvered around Roman with ease. He positioned himself for an easy lay-up but was quickly denied by Roman's long arms. The crowd went wild as they watched Vincent chase the ball back down the court. With the mistake now behind him, he remembered what it was like practicing with Roman. Instantly, he rethought his strategy. He raced to the outer circle faster than Roman could prepare for. Without Roman covering him, he jumped and soared a scoring goal. Several screams and howls were heard from the sidelines as the two appeared evenly matched. Roman 3. Vincent 3.

"Hm. You improved since last year," Roman commented.

"Yeah? You've gotten worse." Vincent was out for blood as he kept his keen eye on him.

With the ball again, Roman zoomed left as he started a traditional lay-up. But at the last minute, he did a fake out and ran to the other side of the basket. A snap of his wrist, and the ball beautifully arched in for the next score. Roman 5. Vincent 3. "Halfway there, Mr. Maunson. Getting tired?"

"Not on your best day, Erricson! Which was *two* years ago if you ask me." Vincent beamed, proud of his insult.

Roman snorted. "I've been out of practice since last spring, and you've been training since November. I'm beating you. So, what's your excuse?"

Vincent growled as hurried down the court with lightning speed. His anger propelled him faster than he had previously which lined him up for a clear shot. The ball sank in for two. Roman 5. Vincent 5. "You were saying?"

This time Roman chose not to respond. He held the ball in his hand for a moment before walking it back to the sideline. Vincent's coverage was getting better as Roman's movements became predictable. He needed to change things up if he was going to get passed this hungry wolf constantly on his tail. Like most, Roman favored his right side on offense. Although it had indeed been over six months since he'd laid hands on a ball, desperation set in as Vincent's pheromone pallet exuded confidence which couldn't be shaken. Roman required a move Vincent wouldn't expect. His beginning stance easily read a drive taken to the right, but as Vincent began preparing for the defense to cover, Roman switched the ball and took off wide left.

Vincent's initial stance was nowhere near ideal cover for a last-minute change. Stretching his right foot out to help compensate the oversight, it still took an extra second to adjust his gait. Time he didn't have. He cursed as he heard his ungrateful teammates admiring the fake out. As hard as he tried, all he could see was Roman two steps ahead of him, and that's all he needed. Another shot in. Roman 7. Vincent 5.

"You screw this up, it's game over." Roman's voice began to take on a persona he'd almost forgotten. This was the scene he was used to for many years, and he'd almost forgotten what it was like. Scenes of many rivals and opponents flashed in his memory as he recalled their shock, awe, and fear whenever Roman found his stride. And boy, did he ever. Everything about being back on the court felt right to him. The air was thicker, the light was brighter, the sounds vibrating off of the slick floors were louder and longer lasting. At some point, one of his former teammates must have gone around the school to see who was still in the hallways and classrooms. Because with each passing glance, Roman noticed more students and staff filtering in and huddling near the entrances. A few even spilled over into the stands behind the rest of the anxious team. The atmosphere was electric. All of this starkly contrasted what was waiting for him at home.

Home.

The word penetrated his hypnotized mind for a moment, and his stomach dropped.

Mikaél.

The momentary pause gave Vincent another opportunity, one he needed to take advantage of his former captain, whom he now considered a weak opponent. Down the court he ran with a gleam in his eye. His satisfaction grew as he positioned himself outside the inner ring. A tall jump and a throw later, he watched Roman leap for it, but his fingertips couldn't reach the ball propelling through the air. After dancing around the inner rim, the ball sank in as a cheer from the crowd welcomed the play. Vincent basked in the moment where he finally heard the glory owed to him. Roman 7. Vincent 8.

"I'm not screwing anything up, Roman. You, on the other hand, appear to be losing your touch. I guess your stamina isn't what it used to be. Wanna quit now?"

"I'm going to make you eat those words!"

"Then let's see it!" Vincent demanded.

Roman checked the ball for the final time. Everyone was yelling and screaming on their feet near the stands. Out of the corner of his eye, he noticed several new fans and spectators who had joined in. Groups of students and even a few staff he recognized were here to see the Alpha return to glory. The stakes were high. He took a deep breath and closed his eyes. All he heard was the crowd chanting his name. It was like he was back in the Championship game last year with his teammates on the final play. And then, a different memory came to him. Last year, a post-season game, a victory lap around the gymnasium, and a younger kid with dark hair and beautiful blue eyes barely noticing the game being entertained by an over-enthusiastic friend.

Mikaél? Was he there? But now, stuck in his mind, all he could see was Mikaél waiting for him alone in their apartment in the dead of winter.

"Are you gonna play or what?" Vincent's voice rang out.

Roman shook his head and began his play down the court. Knowing Vincent wasn't going to let him score easily, he needed to wear his opponent out to get the three points to end the game. He forced Vincent to follow him like an obedient dog trained by his master. Roman could smell the frustration fuming off Vincent as he soared to the front of the court and then to the back again. The crowd voices grew louder than he could imagine possible. With his window fading, Roman found his goal in an unlikely place poised for a three. He zoomed in on the target, took a deep breath in, and began to hurl the ball toward the goal. The world slowed down as the sweaty ball left his strong hands. Everything was poised perfectly in his form and his release. And the ball left with a small backspin which allowed the black lines of the ball to almost smile at him as it soared away from him.

But just when he thought he'd calculated the perfecting ending, Vincent was able to do this time what he wasn't before. He jumped at the ball at precisely the right time which tipped the ball ever so slightly off its course. The sight and sound of it was so faint, Roman wasn't even sure it happened. However, when Vincent began chasing after his prize, he knew he made a mistake. Roman's heart pumped out of his chest as it urged him to follow. In a sprint, he caught up with Vincent as he saw the ball barely out of reach. Roman knew with his long muscular arms, he could overreach Vincent and take the ball back before he intercepted it. He had to take the chance. Allowing Vincent to have control of the ball was too much of a risk.

Roman's momentum pushed his body far enough to where he could lift the ball up and use his height advantage to recover for a rebound. As his body cast a shadow over his vicious opponent, he positioned himself on Vincent's right and lowered his hand to scoop the ball up. But he didn't anticipate Vincent doing the same thing. Suddenly, before Roman realized it, the ball was already heading upward instead of hurling toward the crowd. Roman's mind stopped, but his feet didn't. His body began to trip up over himself and barely missed taking out one of the youngest players on the team. Gasps were heard as Roman's body flew out of bounds and landed on the wooden bleachers. The pain of his body hitting barriers which were immovable was second to the pain he was about to experience.

Ignoring every pain signal he could, Roman leapt up and concentrated on Vincent who was only a second away from controlling the renegade ball himself. He blasted his body back down the court. In the longest strides he could, he chased after the win which was fading with every throb in his head and blur of his vision. In some form of miracle, he managed to barely be behind Vincent, but not before he threw the ball in for classic buzzer-ending goal.

Roman 7 Vincent 10.

CHAPTER 14:

TO WALK IN THE SHADOWS

Roman's vision was blurry. It made driving difficult, especially this late at night. He blasted the music in his car which vibrated off the windshield. It helped to drown out the sounds of his phone constantly buzzing on the passenger seat—at least—when it was able to stay on the passenger seat. At every inconvenient stoplight, Roman had to reach down and pick up the phone off the floorboard which launched itself all the way up toward the engine. In addition to the uncomfortable stretch which sent a shock down his tender ribcage, Roman had to fight the urge to vomit as his entire upper half bent over. Finally, he chose to lodge the phone in between the cushions which withstood the sudden breaks he occasionally completed.

Parking the car in the apartment building's garage invoked a sigh of relief. He used the rearview mirror to examine his worn-out face. Realizing that rubbing his eyes and temples wasn't helping, he exited the car in defeat. He hobbled away from the car and stuck his hand in his jacket. The uncomfortable emptiness of his pocket made him realize he had forgotten the keys in his car. Luckily, it also meant he forgot to lock it. His hand slipped on the first attempt to open the door, but the second was successful. The bright lights hindered his sight, and he squinted in order to track down his keys.

Right before he exited again, he observed the brown package laying on the passenger floorboard. He closed his eyes and exhaled before begrudgingly retrieving it. He pushed the slim package loosely up against his armpit as he found the lock button on his car keys and put them back in his pocket.

Each step vibrated off the concrete in the parking garage and rang through his ears. A memory of the game buzzer going off in a crowd of mixed reactions flashed in his vision like a lightning bolt. A surge of a headache hit him, and he immediately grabbed for his forehead. In doing so, the brown package fell from his arm and hit the pavement with a crash. From the open envelope, a few shards of glass shot out of the tan paper. Roman stared at it, completely helpless. Another memory flashed in his mind; the feeling was the same as when he saw several of his teammates gather around cheering on Vincent in his upset victory. Only a couple members came over to even talk to Roman before rejoining the current team captain's loyalty. Off in the distance, he saw several students and staff look at him in awe and whisper amongst themselves. After a moment of realizing no one else was coming to approach him, he got off the gymnasium floor and dismissed himself like a submissive Omega to the locker room.

For a moment, Roman considered not picking up the shattered remains of his basketball career off the garage floor. But he didn't want anyone else to find it and pin the mess on him. So, he scooped up a few of the bigger shards and tossed them into the tattered envelope. A sting bit his finger. Drops of blood ran out like a drippy faucet and stained the gray cement. He swore to himself and then stuck his finger in his mouth. The tin flavor did nothing good on his tongue and immediately hit his reflexes. His stomach hurled something fierce, but for some reason his body held strong and kept his contents inside.

The ride up the elevator didn't help anything. It sped along too fast, and he wished it lasted another hour. His legs were heavy boulders walking out. Before opening the door, he laid his head on it. Tonight was just beginning. Inserting the key into the door, he turned it like it was an immovable jar lid. It took but a second to begin the inquiry.

"Roman?" Mikaél gasped. He greeted the exhausted Alpha at the door and embraced him closely. "Where were you? How come you didn't answer my calls or my texts?" Roman swayed back and forth until he conveniently slid around his mate and aimed for the kitchen. "Roman?"

Without responding or even reacting, Roman kept going on his mission to the kitchen sink. A shaky hand threw the damaged package on the counter and then carefully lifted a glass out of the cupboard. He filled it with water and chugged it down. "I went out."

"You're bleeding!" A few drips slid down the glass into the grooves of the design. Mikaél rushed a paper towel wrap to his finger. "Out? Out where?"

A million thoughts raced through Roman's head. "Just ... out." The pressure on his finger felt pointless. Delaying the inevitable. "It's fine, Mik!"

Mikaél's face only grew in concern. "What is wrong?" A bright glare jumped off the sticky tape of the package sitting next to the sink. Then, a few light streaks of blood. "What is that?"

Roman wanted to crawl into bed and forget this day ever happened. Better yet, find a time machine and do the day completely over. "Nothing... it's just... Mik ... don't—"

The glass shards slid out of the bag. Slowly, the wood frame revealed the photo of a proud basketball team. "This is your team photo from last year?"

An uncomfortable itch hit Roman, and he scratched the back of his head. "Yeah, it is."

Despite the obvious evidence in front of him, it still took Mikaél a second. "You picked this up from campus?" Roman nodded his head. The words he wanted to speak felt like mush. And the taste in his throat felt like vomit. "*That's* what you couldn't tell me?" As Roman began to reply, his exhale permeated the air and hit his nostrils. "Ugh. Guess that's not the *only* place you went."

Roman grimaced. "Mik, I don't want to do this right now."

"You drove home like this? Damn, Roman. What were you thinking? You could have killed yourself! You could have killed someone else!"

"I said, I don't want to do this!" Roman's voice cut through the silence in the rest of the kitchen. After Mikaél reacted with a hint of fear, he realized his response went too far. His face softened and his voice hushed. "I'm going to bed." He paused for but a moment—expecting to hear some sort of comment from his mate. But none came. Starting in slow motion, he pushed off the edges of the counter and sauntered off into the bedroom.

Mikaél sat there in the stillness. Confusion and hurt stung his eyes as he saw his mate walk away. The only piece he had left of the night was sitting in his hand. There, in the back center of the photograph, in an Ashershire Nightwolves jersey with the number 22 printed on it, was a tall, glorious Alpha full of pride. There was little to no resemblance of the man who was a pitiful display moments ago.

"Whoa! Hold it!" Jake shouted to the elevator about to close.

"Hey. Had I known we were going to arrive here at the same time, I could have swung by and picked you up or something." Dustin adjusted his collar as it began to lightly chafe the stubble on his neck.

"No, no. It's quite alright. I had to help Adrian with—" An abrupt pause hit him as he tried to choose his words carefully. "I had to help him with his 'thing' again." Jake blushed.

Dustin nodded with a smirk. Jake never said it aloud, but Dustin always assumed Jake was helping his mate through his heat. However, in the past couple years, Dustin noticed this vague description of "thing" occurring more often than it should to be a heat cycle. But as close as he and Jake were, Dustin never pried into Jake's personal life. If it was something worth sharing, he knew Jake would come to him.

"Have I ever expressed how much I regret scheduling these department meetings on a Wednesday evening?" Jake asked.

"Oh, only about every month we have them," Dustin replied.

"I did speak to Steve about moving these meetings to during the day last month when we met."

"And what did he say?"

"The same thing he says every time I hint at it. 'I'll look into it.'" Jake spoke in a bothered tone.

"Why don't you just tell Paul to take care of it?"

"I just got the feeling it doesn't matter to him. It's not like he has a mate to go home to or spent the last twenty-something odd years raising a family."

Dustin considered Jake's assessment as the elevator door chimed and both exited. "Why do you suppose he hasn't gone out to find a mate? I know he's a Beta, but even with his accolades, he should be able to find someone who finds his accomplishments attractive."

Jake peered out to the department main door, heavily focusing on Dustin's words. "I would guess over the years Dr. Birowack has just immersed himself into his work so much that—"

Dustin looked up from the floor upon Jake's halted breath. "What? What's wrong?" His companion completely ignored him as he proceeded to stare at the door several feet away. After a moment, Dustin observed the cause of the abrupt change.

The main door had been left ajar. That itself was not cause for alarm—no one could get into the research wing at all without a proper badge. However, the shattered glass in the tall rectangular window above the doorknob shook Jake to his core. Sounds of glass crackled under his feet as carefully approached the door. Gently, he pulled the door open with his fingertips. It opened effortlessly, causing Jake to wonder if it always opened so easily. With his senses on high alert, even the squeak of the door unsettled him. "Paul?"

As Jake's voice echoed in the long, aseptic hallway, Dustin felt his stomach turn. "Steve? Ed? You there?"

Like cops on a distress call, they both slowly peeked their heads out to the "T" at the end of the hallway. To the right, another long hallway led to the conference room which displayed a bright light contrasted against the dark early evening hours. To the left, their lab was dark, and the door appeared tampered with, the metal knob bent in an unrepairable state. Like the main entry door, it swung open without difficulty.

There, on the floor, was a man disheveled, bruised, and unconscious. Without his normal state of perfection, it took a moment for Jake to recognize him. He flipped the light switches and confirmed his fear. "Ken!" He ran to his side with Dustin closely behind him. His voice and the stinging of the lights startled the man as he jolted awake.

"Jake?" Kenneth mumbled. "Dustin?"

Jake pressed Kenneth still with his strong hands. "No, no. Don't move. We don't know what condition you could be in." Jake's head flew up and scanned the entire lab in a mere second. It wasn't hard to observe that the lab looked the same everywhere: like a bomb had gone off. Broken glass, emptied supply drawers, and an inconceivable number of papers thrown about as if a tornado ripped through it. "What happened?"

"I—I'm not sure." Kenneth tried to move his back but even the slightest move hurt. That's when he felt his forehead. In the corner, a small gash left blood stains on his fingertips. "I came off the elevator and saw the door. When I ran into the lab, it was dark. But even then, I could see the place was a mess. When I heard some sort of noise, I called out. No one answered, but a second later, I felt this pain hit my back and then my head, as if someone hit me with a baseball bat."

"You're lucky it didn't kill you!" Dustin rang out.

Kenneth tried to find humor in the statement. "I agree with that assessment." He chuckled.

"Do you have any idea who could have done this?" Jake inquired.

Kenneth groaned in a peak moment of pain. "No!"

"Hey, hey! Don't move." Jake shook his head in exasperation. "Dustin, you need to call for help."

Suddenly, a noise pierced the ears of everyone in the room.

"Jake?" Dustin's voice teetered.

"Someone's here," Jake concluded. The Alpha in him went into overdrive as he felt the protective wolf push through. He lifted himself off the floor to investigate, much to Dustin's protest. Around the corner of a workstation, on the floor, lay a nearly lifeless man in a white dress shirt and lab coat. Blood stains pooled near his head and shoulders with light spatters everywhere like a child carelessly wielding a paintbrush. "No! Dustin, you have to call an ambulance now!"

Dustin glimpsed down to the floor. After only a moment of peering at the horrific scene, it seared into his memory: his boss in a poor state, struggling to move or even breathe. "Wolf-God!" Adrenaline rushed throughout Dustin's body as his shaky hands grabbed his phone as best as he could. His fingers could barely stay still to dial for help. Waiting for each dialed number to pass felt like an eternity as he feared his call would never make it through. Hope came in the sound of soft yet professional tone answering his plea. "Yes, I need an ambulance at..."

Dustin's words faded into the background for Jake as he tried to assess Dr. Birowack's condition. There was no way the man could be dead. He wouldn't, no, couldn't allow the thought to be true. He held Paul's head gently in his hands as he tried to wake him by continuously calling his name. A deep heavy fear blossomed within his chest as it never produced the results he desperately wanted. And then, finally, some hope. A slight twitch and sound emanated from the barely warm body. "Paul, that's it! Wake up!" Several unrecognizable sounds started spewing out of the doctor's mouth.

Dustin stepped back around the corner as he finished his emergency call. "Oh, thank Wolf-God!" His eyes began to water as he watched every movement and tried to heed every sound coming from his employer. "What—what's he saying?"

"Shut up, Dustin! I can't hear him!" Jake's frustration grew as he couldn't figure out how to make the situation better. Finally, he took off his business jacket and carefully pushed it under the doctor's head. As he did so, he leaned in his ear to try and capture any audible word. "Files."

"Files?" Dustin replied in confusion.

"Come on, Paul. What files?" He tried his best to encourage ever last ounce of energy out of the failing man before him. No other vocal response came. The only reply from Dr. Birowack was a weak finger vaguely pointing back in the way of the entrance.

"What?" Dustin asked. "Does he want us to look in the drawer?"

Jake dismissed the answer immediately. "No, Dustin. There aren't any files in the lab drawers." Then, a possible conclusion came to him. "His office. Go check his office!" Jake demanded.

Without another thought, Dustin rushed back to his office, momentarily checking on Kenneth who appeared in much better condition than his boss. Opening Dr. Birowack's office door was equally terrifying. Whoever terrorized the lab wasted no time doing the same to Paul's office. Dustin scanned every space on the unrecognizable back counters, the opened cupboard doors, and then the file cabinet in the back. He rushed to metal file drawer, opened and half-emptied. Whatever the intruder wanted, it would be impossible to find out if he got it for days, even weeks as they attempted to put this place back together one puzzle piece at a time. One last look centered Dustin's attention on Dr. Birowack's desk. One file folder appeared splayed out and completely empty on top of a pile of disregarded patient medical charts. Slowly closing the folder revealed the name of the patient whose file appeared completely missing. With it, Dustin's stomach hurt, and his heart pounded in fear.

"Ken!" A voice called out from the lab entrance. Dustin ran out to see two superiors in shock as they surveyed the scene. "Dustin?"

"Steve! Ed!" Dustin spoke as he heard Jake run up from the back of the lab.

"What the hell is going on here?" Steve's focus wandered in disbelief.

Dustin's shoulders sank as he didn't have to fear about the intruder coming back to finish them off. But there was also the extreme disappointment that help still had not arrived. "I think I may have an idea." Dustin glanced at his partner who was equally lost in his ominous reveal.

———

"Come on, Dustin. Really?" Jake stopped his incessant pacing back and forth in the hospital waiting area. Focusing on Dustin's absurdity gave him relief from having to worry about Dr. Birowack's condition.

"I'm telling you, it's the only one I couldn't find. His file was completely empty." A million worries went through his head. *Why his patient file? Why now?*

"Are you sure it wasn't there? Maybe it was thrown about Paul's office like everything else in there?" Jake desperately tried to invalidate Dustin's conclusion as best as he could. He himself couldn't handle the ramifications if it was indeed true.

Dustin examined the scene again in his head. "I'm not saying it couldn't have been there. I didn't lift and uncover every sheet of paper in that disaster. But for his file folder to be the one on top of it all is no coincidence, Jake. Even you have to admit it that."

Words struggled to come out of Jake's mouth. "I—It...it just doesn't make sense!" The frustration grew as he tugged on his hair with both hands. Slowly, other hospital patrons began to take notice. Out of the corner of his eye, he caught a glimpse of an adolescent looking back at him as if he were a madman. A description he thought he may very well be at this point.

"Dr. Erricson?" A young doctor walked out in surgery scrubs, carrying a heavy expression. Behind him, two officers walked casually, constantly surveying the lobby. "Dr. Rhodes. Nice to meet you." A firm handshake ensued.

"Likewise." Jake exhaled. Relieved to finally get some answers. "This is my work partner, Dustin. We both discovered Paul in the lab. Dustin made the call."

Dr. Rhodes nodded. "Dr. Birowack is very fortunate that you two showed up when you did. Even a minute longer and I fear we'd be having a different conversation."

"What are we dealing with?" Dustin became impatient.

Carefully, the ER doctor examined both Dustin and Jake. Then, he turned around and took in the two police officers keeping a hawk's eye on the meeting. And finally, he began sharing the prognosis. "Dr. Birowack has sustained multiple impacts to his cranium from what appears to be a blunt object. From the officers' notes, there was discussion about a possible bat?"

"Dr. Johannes told us he felt like he was struck with a bat when he entered the lab," Dustin explained.

"It would match the injuries and points of impact on both individuals," Dr. Rhodes confirmed.

"How is Ken?" Jake asked.

"Dr. Johannes will be all right," he assured them. "He was discharged with minor injuries: a couple of bruised ribs and minor contusion on his forehead. We asked if he wanted to stay overnight for an observation, and he adamantly denied the request."

"Wait. Ken said he was struggling with back pain when we found him," Jake mentioned.

"It's not uncommon for patients to incorrectly identify the source of their pain, especially in situations like these where he might have been left disorientated. Plus, several pain receptors are interconnected. If Dr. Johannes tried to move his ribs, it was very likely he was experiencing shooting pain all over the area including his back and hip."

"How bad is Paul?" Dustin's scent began revealing his nerves.

Dr. Rhodes paused for what seemed like forever. "Dr. Birowack is in a coma."

"Oh, Wolf-God!" Dustin covered his mouth.

The doctor went on. "There was a lot of skull damage and significant blood loss from his injuries. He also is suffering from a couple of cracked ribs and a broken wrist."

"Damn it!" Jake yelled out as his foot pummeled a plastic trash can on the floor.

"Jake!" Dustin tried to calm him down.

"I'm sorry. Sorry!" Jake gathered his senses.

"When will we know more?" Dustin felt his Alpha wolf kick in as Jake took a seat and pinched the bridge of his nose.

"Our goal is to just stabilize him as best we can. We'll be on him around the clock, especially considering the extent of the injuries. Hopefully, tomorrow we'll know more about what we're dealing with. But as far as long term, we won't know until he comes out of the coma."

Dustin tensed. "And how long is that?"

"Days. Weeks. Months. We might even have to prepare that there's a chance he won't come out of this at all."

Jake refused to stare anywhere else but the floor. He even refused to blink. His hands clasped together in a fist held his chin up.

"Gentlemen, these two officers are going to be part of a joint effort for added surveillance tonight, but they would also like to talk to you. If you don't mind, I'll excuse myself."

"Yes, of course," Dustin replied.

"Thanks for your help, Dr. Rhodes," Jake added as he stood to greet the officers.

Slowly the officers approached the two doctors. "I'm Officer Davis and this is Officer Gutierrez. We'd like to ask you a few questions."

Jake was perplexed at the request. "We already talked to a couple of other officers on the scene."

"Just some follow-up questions, if you don't mind." Officer Gutierrez took out his notepad and reviewed several lines already written on the paper.

"Sure." Dustin shoved his hands back in his pants.

"Can you tell us what time you arrived on the scene?"

Dustin went through the events in his head again for hundredth time tonight. "I got to the medical center at about 6:30. I met Jake in the lobby, and we went up together and discovered the lab."

"What were you there for?"

"Once a month, the department heads get together and have a meeting."

Officer Davis squinted. "These don't happen during more traditional work hours?"

"Some of the committee members like to take advantage of the after-hours to enjoy a drink not approved in the employee handbook." Dustin stifled a smile as he remembered the entire group around a large mahogany table, laughing and enjoying themselves. Then, a fear that those meetings wouldn't ever be the same again.

"Didn't you ever think to have these meetings at a bar or someone's home?" Officer Gutierrez followed up.

Jake stepped in. "It was at Dr. Birowack's direction. We absolutely enjoy ourselves to a point, but the nature of our discussions sometimes leads to sensitive information about patients which is, of course, confidential. Having the meeting in the lab conference room allows us to discuss these things without worrying about who is listening and keeps any patient files safe in case something gets left behind or misplaced—"

"—or in the wrong hands," Dustin finished. Jake gave him a look.

Officer Davis focused on Dustin's comment. "Is that what you believe was the cause for this attack? You believe the intruder was looking for something specific?"

Even before Jake could dissuade Dustin from responding, Dustin answered, "Yes."

"What do you believe they were looking for?"

"My son's file," Dustin rushed in.

"We don't know that!" Jake interjected.

"Yes, I do!" Dustin's voice boomed as he held his stance and his strong Alpha position. His pheromones telling Jake he wasn't backing down.

"Do you have any idea of who would want your son's medical file, Dr. Cavenbelle?"

"I only have one name," Dustin replied.

"Dustin, seriously don't do this," Jake pleaded.

Dustin ignored him. "Matthew Whitmore."

Gutierrez's pen stopped instantly upon hearing the name. He was almost convinced he heard the name wrong. "Matthew Whitmore? *The* Matthew Whitmore?"

"You have no idea what you just started," Jake seethed in Dustin's ear.

"I don't care!" Dustin roared back.

The two officers shot a look at each other, very intrigued by the spat. Gutierrez resumed the questioning. "And what is in your son's medical file that you believe would have one of the richest and most prolific men in the city commit such a heinous crime?"

This time, Dustin bit his tongue. The rush of confidence slowed down as he considered what he'd be able to reveal to the two skeptical cops before him; it wasn't much. "I'm afraid I can't speak on that."

Gutierrez sighed. "I'm 'afraid' we're going to need more than that, especially if you want us interrogating him."

"My son's confidential patient record does not need to be shared in order for you to find probable cause," Dustin defended.

"That may be true, but right now you haven't given us *any* probable cause other than a man's name and a bad attitude."

Dustin's blood boiled. "I'm sorry. Do you find this entertaining?"

Officer Davis cut in. "Let's focus this back in. Doctors, with all due respect, we're here to get the same burden of proof required by anyone. This was a vicious crime, and we take it very seriously. But under these circumstances, we also take who you are accusing very seriously as well."

"What's that supposed to mean?" Jake grumbled.

"Come on, guys," Gutierrez snorted, "everyone knows who you are. Dr. Birowack is the world-renowned research doctor and Matthew Whitmore is the man who foots the bill."

"And there are plenty of pictures and publicity with you two standing right there next to Dr. Birowack kissing his behind made of gold," Officer Davis added. "So, we're going to need something if you want us to go knocking on his door."

Dustin peered at Jake with a heavy heart. They weren't persuading Jake in the least, but finally he threw his hands up, giving Dustin the wheel. "This isn't the only incident we believe can be traced back to Matthew Whitmore."

"Let's find a more private place to talk," Officer Davis insisted.

***

In a private waiting room off the ICU, the officers had pulled the shades to completely cover the windows. Officer Gutierrez was nearing his last empty page when Dustin finally finished the many incidents which had occurred over the past six months including Roman's original contract with Peyton, the discovery of Roman's

Fated Mate, Mikaél's pregnancy and Type 6 Status, the harassment both Mikaél and Roman faced, and finally, the studio fire.

"That's why we believe Matthew Whitmore is responsible for this—for all of this!" Dustin exhaled as if he'd ran for an hour straight without stopping once. "So, this should be enough to take him down, right?"

Officer Davis shook his head in exhaustion. "Gentlemen, this doesn't even start to scratch the surface of the evidence needed."

"You've got to be kidding!" Jake clamored.

"Look. This is great and all for daytime television, but we're talking about one of the most powerful and richest men in the city. To be perfectly frank, what you have here is nothing more than spec-ulation and a bunch of family drama," Officer Davis concluded.

"What we have here are very serious crimes: harassment, threats, arson, robbery, assault, and attempted murder," Dustin replied.

"Was Whitmore even indicated as a possible suspect in the arson case?" Officer Davis asked. Dustin shook his head. "Why not?"

"At the time, there was no reason to suspect anyone specific. I don't have any enemies in my life to point a finger at, and I never dealt with Matthew Whitmore personally after the grand opening of the new lab. Jake and Dr. Birowack were the only ones dealing with him. And I only heard about that when Jake's son Roman was to be contracted with Matthew's son Peyton."

Officer Gutierrez leaned back in his chair to catch Jake's eye. "How did that end, Dr. Erricson?"

Jake stared back. "Let's just say the events there would be enough to support Season 2 of your 'daytime television family drama.'"

Officer Davis landed his arms on the cold white table. "We need to clear this up."

"So, you can go after Whitmore?" Dustin asked.

"No. So, we can clear *you* two," Officer Davis finished.

"Officers! We're not your suspects! We're your allies! The way I view it, this was an outside job. There must be evidence of someone unaffiliated to the lab coming in. The security cameras would have caught that." No response came from the cops who had answers to everything else. Dustin's tone changed. "Did the cameras catch anything?"

"It's one of our very first protocols to check the cameras," Davis confirmed.

"And?"

Gutierrez stepped in. "Hold on. You're not privy to that information."

"Gutierrez, stop!" Davis silenced his partner while still juggling his own thoughts. "There's an issue with the security system."

Jake squinted. "What issue?"

"There's no record for an hour's time before the event all the way up to when we went to Tauris's security center to investigate."

"How is that possible?" Jake flexed his fist.

"Security claims the entire system was going through an update and then an issue to reboot. Video surveillance, badge stamps, everything is missing." Davis hated admitting the system failed him in the moment. But with the overall predicament the two doctors were in, he hoped showing an Alpha weakness was overlooked.

"You're not serious?" Jake tilted his head.

"Absolutely serious. And now, we're back to you two." Officer Gutierrez pulled out his phone and hit the record button.

Dustin was flabbergasted. "Why?"

"Because from the initial notes, we have two additional prominent doctors walking in on you two already being on the scene. I'm sure you can imagine their shock when they find a department head and his protégé beaten to a pulp on the floor with you two standing there."

"We helped them! They would have died without us there!" Dustin defended.

Jake pushed his chair in and leaned in on the table. "Wait. Steve and Ed didn't implicate us, did they?"

"They gave us a motive," Officer Gutierrez answered.

"What motive?" Jake constantly shifted his gaze between the two officers who had officially change from "good" cops to "bad" cops.

"According to both of them, there was quite the uproar when you, Dr. Erricson, didn't get the department head position." Officer Gutierrez watched Jake for any minute flinch or breathing change.

"Even more so when you found out Dr. Kenneth Johannes did," Officer Davis added.

Jake crossed his arms. "There was no 'uproar.' But I have every right to feel the way I feel."

"Enlighten us, then, doctor," Officer Gutierrez sang.

With a fire still burning from the notion he did this to Dr. Birowack, his shoulders fell. "I was confused. I was hurt. Dr. Birowack and I have worked together in some capacity for fifteen years. For him to easily find an outsider to replace his position... I still don't understand it."

"Did you ever get angry with him?" Officer Davis inquired.

"I think I came off that way when I found out. He told both Dustin and me when Ken came in to view the lab." Memories and feelings began to bubble as Jake reminisced.

Officer Gutierrez pushed. "Did you ever want to do something about those angry feelings?"

"Absolutely not!" Jake barked.

Officer Davis took back over. "Let's go back to you both arriving at 6:30. What time was meeting scheduled for?"

"7 PM."

"Isn't that a little early to show up for a meeting?" Officer Gutierrez's eyebrow shot up.

"The department heads like us to have the room set up with the projector screen, notes, and presentation—"

"—and the booze," Dustin patronized. "As if we're a couple of secretaries."

"You sound resentful, Dr. Cavenbelle," Officer Gutierrez commented.

"It is what it is," Dustin replied.

"Sounds like a great opportunity if I ever heard one," Officer Davis concluded.

Jake's respect for Officer Davis was running out quickly. Now both policemen appeared to be cut from the same cloth. "For what?!"

"You both head into the meeting early to confront Paul Birowack and Kenneth Johannes about how you both are fed up with being underappreciated and underutilized, it goes nowhere, and so matters are taken into your own hands."

Jake seethed. He couldn't believe Officer Davis reduced his loyalty to Dr. Birowack down to this. "That is ridiculous!"

Dustin became the balance to Jake's emotional outpour. "That's a rather foolish conclusion, officer."

Officer Davis tilted his head. "Do explain."

"For starters, there was no guarantee Jake and I would have encountered both Paul and Ken there. Not to mention Steve and Ed could have walked into that lab at any moment."

"Perhaps you previously talked to both and told them to come to the lab early to discuss business?" Officer Gutierrez offered.

"Is that what Ken said?" Jake sat up. Both officers looked at each other.

"Dr. Johannes doesn't appear to recall much at all—much less a previous conversation concerning that." Officer Davis lightly scratched his nails against the table.

"And you won't find any emails or texts about it either," Jake grumbled.

"Why's that?" Officer Gutierrez pushed.

"Because it doesn't exist!" Jake roared. "It never happened."

"That alone should help our cause," Dustin hoped.

Officer Gutierrez killed it immediately. "It doesn't."

"Why not?" Dustin sank back in his chair.

Officer Davis swooped in. "By the state of the entire lab, this looked like a rush job. Either Dr. Birowack or Dr. Johannes could have walked in on the scene. With two of you, it would be unlikely either of them could have stopped an assault, especially Birowack."

"What about my son's file? Why isn't this the focus of the crime?" Dustin lamented.

Gutierrez scoffed. "As far as we can tell, it's a ruse."

"A ruse?" Dustin was offended by the notion.

"A ruse! A cover-up to throw us off the path."

"Especially since we don't have any information on what makes his file so enticing in the first place," Officer Davis tried once more. "Unless you'd like to share that now?" Dustin carefully and slowly shook his head. "If we find it is *that* important, it's nothing a warrant won't take care of." He pushed his chair back and stood up; Officer Gutierrez followed.

"If you wanted the empty file folder, you could have just taken it from his office. You don't need a warrant for that." Jake smirked, delighted at his own comment. Dustin shot back a look which read he didn't share in his sentiment.

"Have a good night, gentlemen." Officer Davis nodded. "We'll be in touch."

"Don't get any late-night ideas of traveling or vacationing outside the territory." Officer Gutierrez scanned the doctors, instilling a reminder in both Alphas to understand the law was above their High Type Status.

When the officers left, the door shut with thud. After that, an unnerving silence.

"You want to finally tell me what's going on in that fucked up head of yours?" Dustin chased behind Jake, both scrambling to get through a mess of people scurrying about the emergency room. At this point, he didn't care who saw them. No answer came to him. "Jake!"

"Not now, Dustin." Jake's voice was soft but agitated. He focused on the exit door in the distance like it was freedom from an eternal jail cell, one he pondered might be in his future.

"Yes, now! And tomorrow, and the next day, and even next month until this all gets solved." He saw Jake completely run into a hospital patron and keep walking forward as if it never occurred. As such, it almost caused a second collision between the man and himself. "Sorry!" he told the startled gentleman. Then his sights went back to Jake. "Will you watch where you're going?!"

Jake burst through the double doors, out into the wintry parking lot. The cold air hit his lungs as he inhaled his first attempt at relaxation. The dark night did little to relieve any pain he felt now. As if he missed a punchline to a joke, his response was greatly delayed. Without even looking at Dustin, he uttered one word. "Sorry." The word was hardly remorseful. He continued his trek through the parking lot, struggling to remember where he parked in his frantic arrival hours ago.

Dustin kept on following behind as he voiced his frustration. "I understand as of late dealing with your family redefines the definition for the words "patience" and "stamina," but this is taking it to a whole new level!"

"Agreed." Jake pressed on, as if Dustin's voice was a trailing sound in the wind.

Dustin's voice grew louder as he huffed in the cold breeze. "I'd appreciate it that when things directly affect me, especially my son, you would use some tact when discussing matters—especially with the damn police!"

"Sure." Finally, Jake spotted the correct row of cars leading to both his and Dustin's vehicles.

"That's his response?! 'Sure'?" Dustin snickered in disbelief. "Perhaps you noticed back there, I had to play the part of Omega just so we didn't give Gutierrez the satisfaction of putting you in hand-cuffs for disorderly conduct or harassment against a police officer," Jake mumbled in response. "I'll forgive you cutting my balls off if you will at least level with me on what the hell is going on!" The lack of respect coming back to him was hitting a boiling point.

Jake finally reached his car, Dustin still breathing down his neck. "I just want to get out of here. Tomorrow—" Jake felt his entire body slam against the car door and then get whip-lashed as he was forcibly turned around to face an Alpha on the brink of tearing him to pieces.

Dustin.

"WHO THE HELL DO YOU THINK YOU ARE?!" Dustin's blood boiled and his hands gripped the shirt of his co-worker, friend, and brother-by-contract. He saw Jake's eyes widen in fear of him. This time, Jake played the role of the submissive Omega, as he had his turn. "I am getting so sick of you!"

Jake barely caught his breath. "Why? What did I do?" He trembled.

"On paper, the world views us as equals, but I can't pretend any longer that in your mind and in Dr. Birowack's, I am just some lowly servant who should be happy I get to play at recess with the big boys!" Dustin stared off into the distance, trying to figure out how he was finding the courage to speak to Jake in such manner. But he couldn't stop. Not now. He stuck his finger deep into Jake's chest. "You only value my opinions when I'm upset, you only take my advice when it's too late, and you only listen to me when I have your back against a wall!"

"Or against a car," Jake added for good measure.

"Shut up!" Dustin successfully put Jake back in his place. He leaned in and whispered so intensely; it could have snapped Jake's neck. "Now, you are going to tell me why you went from acting like Dr. Gray Wolf in the lab to Dr. Hell Hound here while giving two officers of the law the middle finger when I'm trying to tell them my son's life is in danger!"

Jake watched the new-fallen snow—wishing he was buried beneath it. "I—I can't."

Dustin threw his arms up and screeched in frustration. The scream shook Jake to his core. "Are you some psychopath I don't know about?"

"You know what? Maybe I am." Jake's voice grew weary as his voice teetered on losing it completely. His watery eyes stung more than the bitter cold.

Sensing the pheromone change in Jake, Dustin finally removed the teeth from his words. "What are you talking about?"

"There is only so much I can take, Dustin, and I think I'm about there." Jake exhaled as if he'd been held under water for the past six months. "I was that way in the lab because I needed Dr. Birowack to be okay. I intended to do whatever I had to in order to make sure he came out alive. Had I known he lost that much blood, I would have given him my own blood if I could."

Jake looked upon the hospital like it was a revisited nightmare. "But in there, I was about ready to lose it." The former thoughts came rushing back into his head. "If I had let myself go there, I could have torn everybody in that waiting room to pieces." Dustin threw his head back, trying to see if he heard Jake correctly. "If I had been pushed, even just the tiny bit more, I would have gone on a rampage that made that lab look like a minor nuisance."

Dustin didn't know where to go with this new information. "You're just being dramatic."

"No! No, I'm not," Jake corrected. "I had this rage inside of me that was trying to get out and I was failing at keeping it in." He scanned his co-worker's expression, to see if it finally was starting to set in. "I know a kid saw it. Hell, I think a couple of adults saw it. I wasn't the same person in there. It was ... something else."

Dustin treaded lightly. "Look, I get it. When I think back to rattling off all the things which have been going on in our family alone with Mik or with the fire, it's enough for me to go crazy. It's enough for anyone to go crazy." He paused. "But I don't think I'd ever look at innocent people and want to harm them. Don't you think that's a little ... much? Even for you..."

Jake dismissed the notion that he was overreacting. "Everything is different now."

"Everything?"

"Yes, everything," Jake confirmed. "Every pillar I had in my life is completely gone. Roman is dealing with a life I can barely lend assistance to. I don't even know who Rixen and Ryan are anymore. Paul, no matter how much he pissed me off for keeping me in the dark about the Whitmore fiasco or about Ken, was honestly the only constant guy left in my life I could count on. And there's a good chance we're going to get a phone call saying that I can't count on him anymore." His voice began to choke up.

"How can you say that? You have more than Dr. Birowack. Roman and Mikaél still look up to you. Your twins will come around," Jake quietly disagreed. "Even if you feel that's not true, you still have Adrian, your mate."

"I said, *every* pillar was gone, Dustin, and I meant it." A long stare held Dustin's eyes long enough for him to understand what he meant. Without even saying it out loud, however, Jake realized he wasn't getting an empathetic response.

Dustin licked his cold dry lips and stuck his hands into his jacket pockets. "Okay."

"Okay?" Jake replied in confusion.

"Yeah." Slowly, Dustin began to walk backward in the direction of his own car, the snow crunching beneath him.

"Where are you going?"

"Home." Dustin was flabbergasted Jake couldn't come to that conclusion.

"You're leaving?" Jake replied in disbelief.

"You said every pillar in your life is gone, right? Just want to make sure you're proven right … because Wolf-God forbid you're ever proven wrong … especially if it's me doing it."

A dull pain hit Jake's forehead as he saw what his partner was doing. "Dustin, I'm sorry. I didn't mean that. I'm sorry!"

"That's the way our relationship is always going to work, Jake. I get that now. Have fun always being the one at the top of pyramid who's always right. Just know, it's lonely up there." Dustin laughed sarcastically. "That's right. You already know that. You have nobody." Dustin opened his car door, waiting for Jake's words to completely be ignored.

"Please, can we talk about this?" Jake insisted.

"If you're serious about this 'rage' thing, you need to get help. Sounds like you and Roman have more in common than what you once thought." As Dustin secured himself in the driver seat, he tried to shut the door. Jake's arm stopped it as he raced to get his attention.

"I will get help, Dustin, I promise. But right now, I need *your* help," Jake pleaded.

"Me? Why me?"

"Because you're right. I do have a pillar of support left and it's you. It's more than being just a thick-headed Alpha, it's a doctor thing, too. We never want to be the ones asking for help because we're the ones who are supposed to have all the answers to fix everything. If people can't rely on doctors to solve their health problems, who are they going to get help from? Politicians?" Dustin fractured—a good sign. "Give me the chance to ask for help. *Please.*"

The air was warmer around Dustin. He couldn't tell if it was from the lack of wind striking him or Jake's pheromones finally coming back to normal. Playing the part of the eternal loyalist, he chose the latter. "Alright. Where do you wanna meet?"

It took only a moment for Jake to find his answer. "I got a place in mind."

CHAPTER 15:

TO THREATEN ALL THAT IS GOOD

"Well, well, well. South Street Tavern." Dustin slowly took off his jacket as he admired a bar he hadn't been to in months. Yet, when they arrived, it was walking into the past like it was yesterday. "Wolf-God, I missed this place. When was the last time you were here?"

Jake brushed off a bit of snow before removing his jacket and finding room on the coat rack. "Maybe a time or two after we were all there, but not ever since—Alex!" A younger Omega with short brown hair and long sleeve sports shirt came up and hugged him. "I didn't expect you to be here! I thought after—"

"I'm just here every now and then. I cover a few shifts so I can keep an eye on the place." Alexander admired the place looking spic and span as ever. Being half full after 10 PM on a weekday was a good sign for the downtown bar, especially one owned by an Omega.

"Still defying the odds, are you?" Dustin asked with a smile on his face.

"With every single customer who comes through the door as a first timer and leaves as a patron." Alexander placed both hands on his hips, proud of every moment. "What can I get you both? I don't suppose your usual will suffice?"

Jake beamed. "You still remember it?"

"You guys were some of my favorite customers! Although, I must not have been your favorite bar." Alexander coughed for effect.

Dustin put up his hands in defense as he guided Jake to their once regular table. "I promise, I haven't been cheating on you, Alex."

Sitting down, Dustin took in the sight of the beautiful, dark bar, the black wood sparkling from the yellow glow of the bar lights. Drinking glasses, bottles of beer and liquor glistened off mirrors that showed satisfied customers scattered around the room. Faint lighter rock music played through the distant speakers. Had this been a Friday or Saturday night, the ambiance and crowds would have differed drastically. A Type 5 Alpha never ventured into a downtown bar on a weekend in the hopes of having a casual civilized drink. The culture of customers differed drastically—as Low-Types and other boisterous individuals laid claim to the nightlife. High-Types and more "civilized" individuals chose exclusive clubs and restaurants to avoid pointless confrontation. Even being here now on a Wednesday close to 11 PM was risky. The Low-Type crowd looking to mark the bar as their own loved a brawl in what they considered *their* territory, despite Alex's welcoming invitation to all. But right now, Jake was willing to take that chance. Having Alexander here tonight only gave Jake more reason to become comfortable and relax.

"Same! I found myself drinking a lot more at home." Jake laughed which allowed the other two to join in after. "Where has the time gone?"

"It's gotta be two years for *you*." Alexander pointed to Dustin.

He clarified. "The opening of the lab. We haven't been here since then."

"*I* was here a few times after that." Jake regretted the statement immediately as Alexander gazed at him, his memory locating the connection, an awkward recollection.

"That's right," Alexander drew out.

"Uh-oh. What's that all about?" Dustin asked.

Alexander gave Jake a look. Jake answered him with a nod of approval. "Jake used to come here with Matthew Whitmore."

Dustin appeared shell-shocked. "No way!" Jake nodded once again, seeing the reaction he apparently wanted. "Alex, you're going to have make those doubles, I think." Dustin turned to his partner. "What the hell were you doing setting up private meetings with Matthew Whitmore in this place?"

"They weren't private if they were here in the bar." Jake laughed. "It's when he and I began talking about whole mating contract with Roman and Peyton."

"And how did that go?" Alexander asked like curious cat.

Dustin raspberried. "He's getting asked that a lot today."

"Crashed and burned in Hell," Jake responded.

"Hmm. Hate to tell you I told you so." Alexander bit his lower lip as he set out some napkins and a couple of heavy wood menus.

Jake straightened up. "You were right. I should have listened to you." Both Dustin and Alexander stopped and stared at Jake as if he told them something insane. Alexander gave Dustin a look, this time in utter shock.

"He, uh, he's also working on that, too." Dustin's words were going to have to suffice, as Alexander assumed he wasn't going to be privy to this conversation. He smiled and headed off to fill his former patrons' orders.

Jake felt his partner burn into him. "What?"

"I'm waiting." Dustin had his hands folded on the table as if anticipating his son to spill the beans on a childish lie or misstep.

"It was by complete accident. I was here at the bar that evening shortly after the grand opening and Matthew just happened to walk in. Before I knew it, we both were talking like old chums who were looking to make a difference in our sons' lives."

Dustin braced his body. "Boy, doesn't that sound familiar."

"Here you are. Two classics, double as requested, and extra limes." Alexander dropped off the drinks and accepted a generous tip graciously.

"What's been going on in your life, Alex? Catch us up," Jake implored the Omega to share what he already knew—if for nothing else—take the pressure off himself.

Alex pondered for a moment. "If I recall, the last time we spoke, you knew I was dealing with—"

A sudden movement burst through the front door, then a couple of rough characters in a brawl spilled into Alexander's establishment. "Damn it! Bruce! Find James. Tell him we need pest control." He frowned as he watched his two concerned customers. "Sorry, guys. Catch up a different night."

"Do you need help?" Jake asked, getting ready to put on his Type 5 bravado.

"No, no. You know how it works down here. We got it covered. Ah, Wolf-God, James! Glad you're here..." Alexander distanced himself from the table and joined a couple of bouncers escorting two Alphas in a territory battle back out into the cold.

"I don't miss *that*." Dustin laughed.

"Me neither," Jake replied.

Suddenly, a thought crept into Dustin's mind. "Wait. The night of the grand opening? Wasn't that the night I stumbled across the two of you here and Matthew was drunk out of his mind?"

"That's the one," Jake confirmed.

"Wolf-God, I remember that. You two were acting so strange. Not to mention I had been on an hour's crusade trying to find you two in the first place."

Another wave of guilt hit Jake. "I'm sorry. Another thing I kept from you."

"I can understand that one," Dustin empathized. "At least that one's a personal matter." He reconsidered. "Or it *was*." He moaned in defeat. "What are we going to do, Jake?"

"What do you mean?"

"You know, if..." Dustin couldn't say it.

"Oh." Jake stared at his drink, glistening brighter than Dr. Birowack's outlook. "I don't know." Drinking vodka tonic didn't brighten the mood like it once could.

"Ken is going to be on a steep learning curve. He's good, but he's no Paul."

"No one is." Jake took another drink.

Dustin followed. "You are."

Jake scoffed. "We already discussed why that's not true."

"Everyone in the department knows your worth, Jake."

"Like Steve and Ed?" Jake smirked.

"Hey, they threw me under the bus just as much as they did you. They think we're the Yuri Brothers or something."

"Pfft. The difference there being that Simon and Rex actually murdered people, enjoyed it, and got away with it for years." Jake massaged his own arm for comfort as he slowly viewed the bouncers trickling back into the bar, proud of their accomplishment. "We didn't kill anyone, and they seem to want to put us in jail a few hours later! Plus, last I checked, we don't enjoy the idea of killing people. Unless there's something you want to tell me, Dr. Cavenbelle?"

Dustin playfully scratched his chin and tilted his head. "Nah. I can't even fake that one. Like you said, it's the constant need to want to fix people that keeps me going. Now if you talk to the mob or something, their idea of 'fixing a problem' usually involves bullets or cement shoes."

"Do you know any?" Jake squeezed more juice from his lime slice into his glass and then licked the a few drops of juice from the fruit itself.

"Despite my family's background, no."

"Ah, that's right. 'Cavenbelle.'" Jake had flashbacks of social studies textbooks mentioning several historical mob families. Several lesser prominent groups did include Dustin's ancestral name.

"Maybe I should have included you in my Matthew Whitmore woes. You could have called distant connections to help me out."

Dustin gestured with his glass. "You would have been severely disappointed, my friend. My uncle Tony is only known for his mechanic shop up there." Both he and Jake shared in the humorous moment. "Whitmore probably has more connections than I do."

"You actually think that's true?" Jake questioned.

"Isn't that what everybody says?"

More flashbacks. But this time, much more recent. "I remember the first time Matthew Whitmore was introduced to me. Paul brought him into the old lab."

"How was that?"

"It was like Wolf-God had traveled down from the heavens and graced the entire place. He was a younger, vibrant, rich man who attained immortality overnight."

Dustin squinted. "Whitmore's company existed before he took over."

"Matthew's father was nothing like him. Matthew is aggressive. Plus, with Tauris City growing so fast, Matthew taking the reins hit at the right time. The rest is history."

"Including *your* history," Dustin added.

Jake took a large gulp. "I suppose it is." A belch caught Jake off-guard. "Alex!" He gestured to the glasses. Alexander was on the order right away.

Dustin was in awe of Jake's apparent rock bottom catastrophe. "Damn, Jake. I've never seen you like this."

Jake gave a satisfied sound as he swallowed liquid relief. "This is where I'm at right now."

"If Whitmore is really behind all of this... what are we going to do?" Dustin asked. He had been holding the question in for months. Even now, he still knew the answer. Jake was about ready to confirm it.

"There's nothing we can do. You heard Officer Davis and Officer Gutierrez. We don't have anything right now." His tone became harsher. "Not unless someone wants to come forward or find missing security footage," Jake grumbled.

"I just want Roman and Mik and their... our..." Jake patted Dustin on the shoulder. "I just want them to be safe. Is that too much to ask?"

"Of course, it's not." Jake scratched his five o'clock shadow. "And we can do something about *that*."

"Hey!"

Roman's voice made Zayne jump as it broke his concentration. "Hey." His reply was flat, and he went back to staring at his lukewarm spaghetti, hoping it would give him the same distraction as it had before. No such luck.

"I wanted to say thank you for helping me yesterday with the caseload. We were so busy, I forgot to say something." Roman invited himself to the small table in the cafeteria where Zayne sat. The warmth of the room filled with other hospital employees didn't seem to make it to this side of the cafeteria. When Zayne didn't reply, Roman felt the chill instantly. "Something wrong?"

Zayne took one last look at his spaghetti and pushed the plate aside. He swayed his head side to side before finally breaking his silence. "It's my dad."

"Your Sur or Veo?" Roman asked.

Through his thick-framed glasses, Zayne stared Roman down like a hawk. After a couple of seconds, he eased up, forgetting Roman didn't know. "My Sur."

"Is everything okay?" The pheromones coming off Zayne now clearly told Roman things weren't. He studied him as he began cautiously eating his overheated bacon and potato soup.

"He's... he's not well" was all he managed to come up with in the moment.

"He ill or—"

"What's with all the questions?!" Zayne snapped. Roman sat there like a stone. He quickly searched for a possible audience witnessing the outburst. Amazingly, no one else appeared to notice. Once he himself recognized the overreaction, Zayne relaxed his posture and the pheromones secreting off him. "Sorry. I didn't mean to do that."

"No worries." Roman shrugged it off. "Stress of the job. I know I'm feeling it."

"There's that." Zayne pulled his spaghetti plate back closer to him. The silverware sparkled as he twirled the sauced noodles around them. The aromatics filled his nostrils, but they still gave no reprieve at what was eating him from the inside. Once again, he gave up and set the full fork down on top of his plate. "What's your mate like?"

The comment caught Roman off-guard, especially from the latest topic of Zayne's father. But then again, Roman didn't think of the possibility that the source of the problem was mating. A reasonable topic to be stressed out about. "He's beautiful, intelligent, quick-witted, creative, great with a camera, and a very passionate person." Roman's heart thumped in his chest harder thinking of his love.

Zayne rested his chin on his hand in a sea of hopelessness. "Sounds like a dream."

"Hmm. Struggling with a guy you're seeing?" Roman surmised.

Ignoring the question, Zayne countered, "Would you ever leave him?"

Roman nearly choked on a bite of potato, the savory bacon-flavored cream from the soup heading down the wrong pipe. "Um. No?"

"Do you think he'd ever leave you?"

"Wolf-God, no!" Roman took a sip of water, head spinning as to where this all came from.

"But are you sure? Has he ever told you that?" Zayne inquired.

Roman squirmed and centered his thoughts. "I'm happy to say we haven't discussed the possibility of figuring out logistics on how we're *not* going to be together." Roman leaned in. "And ballsy to randomly ask an Alpha about the integrity of his relationship, especially with his Fated Mate."

Zayne flushed red, realizing the lack of consideration in his interrogation. "Sorry." He uttered. "And no."

"No ... what?"

"I'm not having 'guy trouble.' I'm not seeing anyone." Zayne surveyed his neglected lunch, remembering how it once cleared his mind of all the negative thoughts running through him.

"I thought you were considering talking to my friend Nico?"

Flashing back to their first introduction, Zayne forgot Roman knew the handsome young man. "I just haven't gotten around to it. Next time, when we're back at Ashershire, I'll approach him."

"Good." Roman smiled.

"He's not seeing someone already, is he?" Zayne bit his lip.

Roman dug his spoon back into soup. "Your guess is as good as mine. I haven't talked to him in a while."

"Right."

Looking up, Roman saw the sorrow engulf Zayne again. "Are you sure there's nothing else you want to talk about? Your Sur is going to be okay, right?"

Zayne wrenched his shoulders. "I don't know." He paused. "As the years pass, the less I know the man. He's consumed by his career and his goals..."

"Hey, I know exactly what that's like. My Sur has always put career first and family second. I suppose I should be lucky that his career has mostly been about me; otherwise, maybe I wouldn't even know him from John, you know?"

Zayne nodded. "I fear mine's leading him down some dark path I can't pull him out of."

"Have you talked to him about it?"

Tapping his fingers on the table, he replayed last night's conversation with his Sur in his head. "I talked to him yesterday about something ... different." Roman furrowed his eyebrows. "But as far as the 'I wish you would change your career and attitude so we can be a family again' conversation, it's been awhile."

Clearly, whatever was going on in Zayne's life and his father was going to stay locked inside a safe Roman wasn't getting a combination to. He took one more bite of his soup and set the spoon down next to the bowl, then folded his hands and rested his head on them as he gazed upon his friend. "Sounds like you need to again."

"Right," Zayne replied.

Beepers blasting their sharp sound broke the gentlemen from their conversation. Roman longed for the days to where the incessant sound wasn't calling for him. But as an intern, it was always for him and Zayne, too. "Shit."

"Hey, longer lunch than what we got yesterday!"

"You ready?" Roman stood up, almost forgetting to clear his side of the table.

"Right behind you."

"Are you sure you're up for this?" Mikaél stood at the long mirror, harshly critiquing everything he put on his ever-growing body. Out of the corner of the mirror, he could see Roman hunched on the bed, bouncing his knee in anticipation.

Roman rubbed his face. "Why wouldn't I be?"

"From what you said, this sounds like an ominous trap." Mikaél grunted as once again, not happy with his outfit choice. Every shirt and pant combination accentuated everything he didn't want seen and couldn't hide what he did want hidden. The only thought in his head was to prepare for it to get worse.

"What did I say?" Roman played coy in response.

"First off, our Veos aren't going to be there, and second of all, we're in Booth 3." Mikaél peeled off another shirt he didn't find flattering and picked out three more and threw them on the bed.

"What's wrong with Booth 3? Did you want Booth 1? I can call the restaurant and ask." Roman smiled at his comment while trying not to cringe when he scented his mate's growing frustration in his quest for attire for tonight's dinner.

Mikaél scoffed at Roman's innocence as he tried on another shirt. "I wasn't born yesterday. I happen to know a thing or two about restaurants in Tauris City in which you reserve private booths. My Sur liked telling me a few stories of my uncle's business dealings in a restaurant up in 'Big Town' where the only shady thing about the food is the person eating it."

"I thought you said all that mob stuff about your family was made up?" Roman replied.

Mikaél shrugged. "Who knows?" He let out a low grunt as the final shirt didn't suffice either.

"Mik, you look great! I don't know why you think you need to audit your entire wardrobe." Roman prayed his words were viewed as a compliment.

"We should have had this pup during the Fall. I understand pregnancy weight, but then there was Winter Solstice, New Year's, and then Valentine's Day right around the corner. I feel like a food blimp."

"You are not a blimp!" Roman got off the bed, walked up behind his mate, and bear hugged him. He rested his head in the crook of Mikaél's neck and gently caressed his stomach. "You are proudly displaying you are doing everything right to bring a healthy pup into this world. When she comes out, she's going to smile at you, give you a thumbs up, and say 'Good job, dad.'"

"Uh-huh." Mikaél's sarcasm took front and center. "*If* she ever comes out. I still think if you press hard enough, I'll give birth to a ham and a couple of sides instead."

"Mmmm." Roman's voice hummed in his mate's ear. He pecked his Omega's cheek. "Just not asparagus for one of the sides, please?"

"Ha." Mikaél turned and kissed his Alpha deeply. After a sigh, he refocused his conversation. "How bad is tonight going to be?"

"I'm trying to be optimistic. So, let's go in with an open mind. How about that? If I can do that, I know you can."

"Don't I know that!" Mikaél confirmed. As he went in for another kiss, an incessant knock sounded on the door. "Now who could that be?"

"Hm. Not sure. You mind getting it? I gotta take a leak." Even before Mikaél had time to respond, Roman headed deeper into the bedroom to find the bathroom.

Checking himself in the mirror one more time, Mikaél decided the outfit he had on would do for tonight. Then, he made his way to the front door of their high-rise apartment. Unfortunately, the door produced no one. He feared his timing was too late, or perhaps it was the wrong door.

But as he searched the empty hallway, he peered down to see a large white box with an envelope attached to it. In beautiful cursive was his name—spelled and accented correctly—with heart stickers surrounding it.

As he lifted the box, the earthy smell from the box caught his senses immediately. He smiled as he found it ironic he just mentioned Valentine's Day coming up in the bedroom when here, Roman already sent him an early gift. Then he shook his head in amusement. "Had to go to the bathroom, eh?" he said out loud to himself. He anticipated Roman walking into the kitchen any moment so he could see the elation on his face. The moments passed and he didn't show.

Am I supposed to wait or...?

Excitement got the better of him, and he started opening the card without his mate there.

> To Mikaél: I can't find the perfect words to describe when I think of you and the baby girl growing inside you. I'll let these do it for me.

An uneasy feeling fell into the pit of his stomach. *How could Roman do that? Why would Roman do that?* To be so foolish and careless as to divulge that to anyone, even a florist or delivery boy—that wasn't Roman. But then, who was it?

Mikaél stared at the box, which began to lose its luster quickly. As his hands lifted the lid, a rotting smell took over. Opening it slowly wasn't making anything better. So, with one small deliberate gesture, the top flew off and revealed the contents inside. Dead, musty blood red roses were coated in a mess of maggots feasting on the remains of rats sliced open from their necks to their entrails. One of the vermin had eyes looking straight back at him. Another one flinched, its claw kicking off a wasted rose petal.

An involuntary sound emanated from Mikaél's throat which grew louder and louder. His scream raced throughout the apartment and reached Roman's ears. His mate ran out of the bathroom, through the bedroom, and into the hall. His pulse raced throughout his body, and his muscles throbbed in his chest and arms. Upon reaching his mate, Roman instinctively wrapped his arms around him and centered his mate's face on him.

"Mik! Look at me!" Amidst the sobbing coming from his mate's voice, he finally turned and gazed upon the hellish package in front of him. "What the hell is that?"

"Someone sent it. They know, Roman! Wolf-God, they know!"

"We don't have to do this." Roman gripped the wheel as the car stood idle in the parking lot.

"What would you have me do, Roman?" Mikaél looked back—feeling like he was between a rock and a hard place.

"We can use the pregnancy as an excuse. No one's going to question you being tired and wanting to take it easy for a night."

"No... what they're going to think is that there's something wrong with me and then want to practically dissect me." Mikaél crossed his arms as he focused on the traffic whizzing by.

Roman turned his body. "And if you're wrong?"

"Then we're just delaying the inevitable, aren't we? Our dads will be calling and texting us every hour for the next several days until they have this talk with us."

Slowly sighing, Roman ran his thumb under his chin as he considered Mikaél's assessment. It was tough to admit he was most likely right. "What happened back there was traumatic, babe."

"Please don't talk about this right now. I'm going to have a hard enough time sleeping in the place as it is." Mikaél used every last ounce of energy he had to hold back the stinging sensation.

"You're afraid to sleep in the apartment?" Roman felt himself getting worked up. He tried to hold it in, but the more he heard about his mate's suffering, the more challenging it became.

"You're not?" Mikaél replied.

"No," Roman replied confidently. "This was most likely just a stupid prank." Mikaél's face told Roman he thought differently. "Even if it wasn't, there's a bunch of security around. We can talk to them and track down the asshole who did this."

Mikaél rolled his eyes. "Right. Dead of winter with some random guy in full winter gear with a popped collar, scarf, hat, and gloves. I'm sure they'll recognize him on the spot once they see him."

To Roman, there appeared to be no consoling his mate. He reached out and massaged the Omega's shoulder. No reaction. Despite it being rather toasty in the car, Mikaél's expression was frozen. Roman could see it all over his face; his mate was transfixed on the disgusting image on the kitchen counter. And it was going to be there the entire evening.

"There you are!" Jake rose out of the chair to greet his two sons walking in from the bitter cold. His own expression was juxtaposed against the boys.' "Thought maybe you two got lost."

Roman robotically embraced his father before answering. "Just a little hiccup. But we're here."

Dustin's ears perked up. "Everything okay?"

Mikaél's gaze went to his mate.

A fake smile plastered on Roman's face. "We're good."

Reading the signs on his own son's face told Dustin otherwise. But he accepted Roman's words and chose to observe instead—waiting to hear the truth if his intuition was right.

Jake gestured to an assortment of delicatessens on a wooden board near a flickering candle in the center of the table. The flame's light bounced off the sparkling clear glasses and silverware. "Hungry?"

"Starving!" Roman rejoiced.

Mikaél twitched his brow as he observed his mate hamming up the "Nothing's wrong" routine. His legs were like rusted metal as he mechanically found his chair. If he wasn't careful, his own displeasure could counteract Roman's and send the entire evening into a tailspin. But since he wasn't doing a good job of hiding his own personal feelings, he began to realize Roman's idea of using pregnancy challenges as an excuse was better than he originally thought. In his head, he thought to give Roman more credit. However, that wasn't happening at the table now.

"Mik, are you going to eat?" Dustin tilted his head as he scanned the somber contrast, Mikaél's scent saying more than his words.

"Yeah, I'll have something light. I've come to realize the miracle of pregnancy comes with a label in fine print that reads: 'Warning: the pup growing inside you is actually an alien that will take over your entire body.'" Dustin and Jake were amused by Mikaél's claim, obviously recalling memories of their own mates going through the unforgettable ups and downs of carrying offspring. Roman's expression didn't appear nearly as entertained—if anything—it was of disapproval.

In a split second, Roman brought back his jolly persona. "How is Veo?"

With his hands neatly folded on the table, Jake shrugged as if the question bounced off him completely without registering. "Just as good as ever."

Mikaél asked the same of his. Dustin gave a thoughtful response. Afterward, the silence began to take over the secluded room. Now it was easier for Mikaél to take in his surroundings.

Around most of the walls were beautiful dark red drapes which looked like they'd suffocate a man should the heavy fabric collapse and fall onto him. The entrance to the cozy room had its own dual set of curtains as well. This set was tied back with a golden rope around the middle, clinging on a rod iron hook jutting out of the wall. Near the entrance was one waiter who pretended to not listen nor even watch the four of them sitting at the table. Only a few sounds from the main dining hall were able to penetrate the room, although Mikaél was convinced he could hear whispers coming from various rooms surrounding them, all done up in the same fashion. It was in that moment the welcoming ambiance faded. Something wasn't right. None of this was right. He couldn't contain himself any longer.

"Why aren't our Veos here?"

Dustin glanced at Jake, trying to combat the fire in Mikaél's voice with his own soothing tone. "We thought this was a good opportunity to include just the four of us, especially given the sensitivity of..." Dustin paused. His focus shifted to the floor.

Mikaél gestured his head forward. "Yes?"

"Should we order dinner first?" Jake scanned around trying to find the waiter. His frantic voice made it sound more like he was investigating his nearest exit.

"I'm more in the mood to talk actually." Mikaél's voice was authoritative. Whether it was pregnancy hormones or not, an Alpha was clawing its way out of the once meek Omega.

"Mik!" Dustin strained his voice in a whisper. "Don't speak that way to him!"

"This was your idea, wasn't it?" Mikaél spat back. "Coming here to this place?" Dustin winced. "I knew it."

Roman watched his mate unfold before him. It tied his stomach in knots as it transformed his mate into someone he didn't recognize. "Mik, please."

Mikaél's sight never left his father. He kept on his path, ignoring his own mate completely. "I grew up being told Grandpa's stories about our family history was nothing more the ramblings of a senile old man. So, either he's senile or *you* are. And after being here, the answer to that is becoming a lot clearer."

Jake's eyes were stunned opened as he witnessed an Omega son emasculate his Alpha father. He tried to keep the situation in perspective, especially considering Mikaél's current condition. Without the pregnancy, Mikaél wouldn't have a leg to stand on for his behavior in a public place, regardless of how private it appeared. If anyone was testing the limits of Omega equality, Mikaél was doing it right now to his own father. Jake only dared to think how he'd respond to his own Omega son Rixen doing the same to him. Ryan, being a Beta, tested the waters enough as it was already.

"Listen here!" Dustin shifted his weight. The blood surfaced on his skin as the heat radiated off him. With it, the strong pheromones of Alpha dominance permeated the room. He didn't have to say anything for his son to know he was about to take his rightful position in the household as Pack Alpha. And based upon Mikaél's reaction to his father's scent, the message got through. "If you want to talk about your grandfather's misguided idea of what our family heritage is, that's another time. But right now, we're here to talk to you both about something very serious and very important. As a matter of fact, it may be a matter of life and death. So, I'd appreciate it if you cut me a little slack tonight." Despite his words, Dustin's tone grew colder, harsher, and louder with every sentence. "I, for most of your life, have been a patient and understanding man—"

"That's up for interpretation," Mikaél insisted.

"BE SILENT!" Dustin's voice boomed throughout the hidden quarters of the restaurant. The sounds of clanging glasses, tapping silverware, and whispers from the other rooms halted immediately. Out of the corner of his eye, he saw the waiter, once a statue, animate immediately to draw the curtains shut and leave the room for privacy. Facing his son again, he saw the emotions as they welled up into tears which wouldn't fall. Now that his son showed his submission, he lowered his voice to the comfort he was used to. "I don't like doing that. I don't." Dustin slowly closed his eyes as he attempted to gain his composure. "My Sur thought the louder his voice was or the harder he hit his kids, the better father he was. And I *hated* him for it. When I met your Veo, he said, Fated or not, he wasn't going to be with me, let alone raise a family with me, if I was going to be like that. I reassured your father with every breath I took that wasn't going to be me. And I know it wasn't." As his face lifted again, he felt Mikaél ease up on his defensive posture, but the hurt remained. "Does that mean I did everything right? No, of course not. Your brother Drew took the spotlight every single time he was in the room, and I know that. What I thought was a phase turned into a way of life that neither your father nor I did anything about, which in turn kept you from being the center of attention most of the time."

Mikaél exhaled. "Yeah, I know."

"So, now that you are the center of attention, how does it feel?" Dustin's voice was sincere with a hint of attitude.

Now Mikaél's voice was soft, quite the opposite it once was. "I don't know. Did Drew get talked to this way?"

Dustin nodded. "More than you know."

"Really?" Mikaél couldn't believe his ears.

"Just because you didn't see it doesn't mean it didn't happen."

So many thoughts raced through Mikaél's head. So many things he wanted to say. But there was one he wanted to say the most. "I'm tired of being a spectacle and a secret at the same time. I'm tired of looking over my shoulder and wondering if there's someone out there who wants to hurt me or hurt my pup. And I'm tired of being kept in the dark of my own life."

"Kept in the dark?" Dustin asked.

"Not learning about my Type 6 Status until I was pregnant."

"To be fair," Dustin began, "nobody knew you were pregnant, much less knew that you and Roman were copulating in secret."

Mikaél tried not to cringe. "Dad, really?"

"And we didn't know about you being a Type 6 much longer than you did," Dustin defended.

"It's true," Jake confirmed. "We didn't have a clue until your blood test came back for the contract meeting."

Roman jumped in. "That may be true, but you didn't have to go about it the way you did, stripping me away from Mikaél like that during the contract negotiation and deciding single-handedly that he wasn't entitled to know who he was or that we couldn't be together until the powers at be said we could." His gaze fell upon his mate's womb. "Obviously, we know where that went."

Jake cleared his throat to swallow his pride. "Fair."

Dustin agreed. "I wish I could change things that happened, but I can't." He held his breath. "Unfortunately, the role of being the parent means thinking of the bigger picture that their child often can't see or doesn't want to. It makes us the bad guys—more than it should."

"Absolutely," Jake added.

"One day, I hope for all of this to be different." Dustin braced himself. "Today isn't the day."

The comment was lost on Mikaél. "Huh?"

Wheels began turning in Roman's head. "What does that mean?"

Every beat of his heart hurt Dustin's chest. "We know it is a sensitive subject and how unfair this is for us to ask you again but ... we really, *really* need you both to wait out the rest of the pregnancy in the Western Territory and have the birth there."

Mikaél cradled his head in both hands. "Not this again."

"Mik, please!" Dustin begged and plead with both hands out in front of him. The lack of cooperation sent his focus elsewhere. "Roman?" Against hope, Dustin hoped as his son's Alpha mate could persuade his favor, or if need be, demand it be done. For both parents, they were going to have to settle for disappointment.

Roman shook his head. "I'm not forcing Mikaél to do that. He needs to be here, surrounded by the comforts of what and who he knows. We'd be fending off strangers who, for all we know, would be waiting for him down a dark alley or abandoned parking lot. Shit. That's not even to mention the possibility of a mob mentality, waiting to tear—"

"Roman." Mikaél stared back in the same way he did earlier in the evening while being surrounded by a dozen rotting roses with rat corpses.

The Alpha ceased immediately as he realized he wasn't helping the situation any. Not that it mattered as both he and his mate continued to hear their fathers' incessant pleas. "So, Mik was right."

"About what?" Jake asked.

"Tonight was nothing more than another fucked up dinner where you two unleash some sort of ominous doom upon us." Neither Jake nor Dustin appreciated the comment. Both kept mute as they couldn't disprove Roman otherwise. "You know, you've done a swell job giving me a complex that every time we meet for a formal dinner, we need to brace for impact. At this point, I'm a great candidate for PTSD."

"Same here," Mikaél added.

Dustin's frustration grew. "Guys, look. We called you here because things are happening which are telling Jake and me there are reasons to believe this is getting serious."

Mikaél and Roman gave each other a look. "What things?"

On this subject, Dustin couldn't take the lead. He cowered as he let Jake continue.

"Last night, there was an attack on the lab."

Roman pounced on the reveal. "An attack? Is everything alright? Is anyone hurt?"

"The lab is fine. Some minor vandalism but nothing that can't be replaced." Jake swallowed. "Unfortunately, Dr. Birowack and Dr. Johannes were assaulted. No one else was there."

Mikaél gasped as he reached for Roman's hand. He felt it squeeze back as he processed the information. Roman resumed his inquires. "Why would someone do that? Are they okay?"

"Dr. Johannes should recover," Jake assured them. "Dr. Birowack is in critical condition. We don't know enough yet on how he will play out yet."

"Damn it!" Roman whispered out.

"As far as the reason why," Dustin jumped in, "I think I know."

Jake attempted to steer his colleague away. "Dustin, we're not sure—"

"*I'm* sure!" Dustin clamored back. Then he shifted his attention back to Roman and Mikaél. "I think the entire reason for the attack was to get to your file, Mik."

"*My* file?" Mikaél was shocked at the notion.

"Yes," Dustin confirmed. "On a heap of rubble, there was your patient folder completely empty. Whoever wanted your information has it."

"But... but why?" A million thoughts ran through Roman's head. For so many situations to be coincidental at this point, it was getting harder to ignore it wasn't something more.

Dustin carried on as Jake sat there helpless to stop his theory. "I know this is a lot to accept right now, but I truly believe there have been a lot of 'random' incidents which are actually related to this whole thing."

"What 'thing'?" Mikaél asked.

"Your pregnancy. The studio fire, Matthew Whitmore's election run, the attack on the lab, your file missing; I think it's all related because someone knows too much who doesn't like what is happening inside you, Mik." Dustin sighed as he finally felt a weight lifted off his chest.

Jake was nowhere near the same sentiment as he saw the horror unfold on their sons' faces. He was livid. "Are you happy now, Dustin?"

"What?"

"Look at them! They're scared shitless while you just casually unload a conspiracy theory. I told you to leave that part out!" Jake grabbed his glass and chugged it, unable to find comfort anywhere else. Roman followed him in the same manner.

"I'm not keeping this from them any longer. They already hate us for keeping the secrets we already have. This isn't going to be another one!" Dustin defended. "I'm just glad they haven't had anything happen to them in all of this."

Now it was Roman's turn to look back at his mate. However, this time, Mikaél couldn't look him in the eye. While Dustin went on with his ramblings, Jake took the moment to observe both boys.

"Are you two okay?"

It took Roman a second to figure out which answer to say aloud. He decided on what he thought the safest. "Yeah, I am. Mik?" The only response he gave back was a subtle nod.

"That's why we called you here," Dustin concluded. "I think if you don't go to the Western Territory, there may be other unfortunate accidents which happen. And I can't have you two in the middle of that crossfire. So, what do you say, Mik? Will you consider it?"

Outside, the wintry noises against a black sky could deafen a normal man. A storm continued its onslaught as Roman and Mikaél headed home. Inside the car, the lack of any sound was the scariest. The occasional whimper of the windshield wipers unnerved the awkward silence in the car. Finally, Roman couldn't stand it any longer.

"Do you want to talk about it?" Roman offered as he carefully trekked the car slowly through the blowing snow. Mikaél continued to stare at the floorboard as he did ever since they got back into the car from the restaurant. "I'm not mad at you if that's what you are wondering."

"Are you sure?" Mikaél didn't bat an eye as the words left his lips.

"Yes, I'm sure!" Upon uttering the words, Roman instantly realized his tone didn't help the situation. "Why would you think that?"

"Oh, I don't know. I just sat in a restaurant and barreled over two Type 5 Alphas who just so happen to be our fathers while in addition not even talking to my own Alpha mate who is a Type 6." Mikaél's words ran faster than a sprinter in a race. He was surprised could barely keep the sentences straight.

"I'm not sure what being a Type 5 or Type 6 Alpha has anything to do with it."

"Just forget it." Mikaél waved off.

"No! No, I'm not going to forget it." Roman's words finally startled his distant mate, who sat right next to him in the heated car. "What is your problem?!"

"My problem is my Alpha mate just sat there in silence while I gave my speech as to why I'm not going to the Western Territory. You didn't say anything, Roman, not one thing!"

"I didn't know what to say, Mik!" The conversation now was a mere reflection of the conversation back in the restaurant. Roman still felt the loss of words. "I was completely flabbergasted you said no, especially after what your father said. Not to mention you completely acted like the flower delivery at the door never happened or the rock through the lobby door the same night as the studio fire. You didn't even tell them!"

Mikaél took offense to the words immediately. "That was *my* job?"

"It was *mine*?" Roman challenged. "There was the perfect moment for you to say something back there and you didn't."

"Oh, please," Mikaél puffed. "You have single-handedly decided what about my life to share with anyone you have wanted to thus far. What's the difference now?"

"What?" Roman had no clue where Mikaél was getting the evidence for this. "When?"

"Like when you shared at the dinner table that I was having night terrors right after we moved into the apartment—or when you decided to tell Nico that I was a Type 6 in a public coffee shop."

Roman stuttered. "Well, I... I'll give you the Nico thing." His hairline began to sweat as he remembered he told Nico much more than that. "But I only said the night terror thing to impress upon our parents they were being ignorant."

"While acting the same in return," Mikaél spat back.

"Ouch." Roman squinted as the center line of the road began to disappear under thin blankets of snow. "And while we're on the subject, you told Charlie or whatever his name was, and you told Laycin if I do recall."

"So? That's not the point."

"Then what is the point?!"

"The point is," Mikaél breathed, "I didn't get any support once I told my dad I wasn't going to the Western Territory. I felt like I was by myself, a mere Omega, standing among three top-tier Alphas with an audacity which would have had me tarred and feathered in any other circumstance."

"I told your dad earlier in the evening I wasn't going to support the move without your say so," Roman pointed out.

"True. But it was easy to say it at that point. We didn't know about Dr. Birowack yet. After that we found that out, you didn't say anything."

Roman paused. "And?"

"And—I want to know why!"

The nerves swallowed down Roman's throat and into the pit of his stomach. "Because I... because I'm not sure why you said no."

Mikaél shook his head. "That's not true. My answer has always been the same—you even reiterated it. I don't want to be out in the middle of nowhere with a bunch of strangers having a miracle baby with the chance everyone else around me thinks it's a curse—or worse—a sign of the apocalypse."

"Then I guess it must be..." Roman's voice fell. "I don't know if I agree with your decision."

Mikaél scoffed. "There it is."

"Oh, come on, Mik."

"What?"

"Any other Alpha in this situation wouldn't have let you speak at all and just steamrolled you. Between the flowers and the dinner tonight, we should be heading home to pack and leave this place. If it wasn't for this Wolf-God forsaken weather!"

"Don't hold back. Tell me what you really think," Mikaél threw out sarcastically. Suddenly, his body jetted forward as the car screeched to a halt. Roman threw the car into park and turned his entire body to face him.

"Why am I the enemy all of a sudden?" Roman's voice was terse.

"What are you doing? Are you insane? You're in the middle of the road!" Mikaél searched out into the desolate city for an unsuspecting car.

"There's no one out here, Mik. We're the only ones dumb enough to be on the street in this storm. Now answer my question."

Mikaél licked his teeth as he contemplated his words. "It wasn't supposed to be like this."

"I know," Roman responded.

"We just wanted to be together, have a family, and live our lives."

Roman reached out and rubbed the back of his mate's neck. "I know."

Mikaél's eyes began to well up. "I just didn't see that our union would cause so many people so much misery." His entire body was pulled into his mate's. He heard Roman's heart pound hard in his chest against his ear. Roman's body heat warmed him up even more. "Hell, I even made my dad cry tonight."

"My dad didn't look much better," Roman recounted. "It's all just fucked up. I know that."

"Do *you* want us to go to the Western Territory?" Mikaél lifted his head.

Roman released in exhaustion. "As much as I hate to admit it, if my Sur makes a suggestion like that, he usually has good reason to. Despite what you may believe since I met you, he and I used to get along a lot." Roman thought for a moment. "Or at least I used to listen to him a lot more."

"So why didn't you say anything back there?"

"Because at the end of the day, you're the one carrying our pup, Mik. If you're deathly afraid of being there or find yourself under even more stress while being there, it's not going to be good for you, and it's certainly not going to be good for the baby." Mikaél quietly agreed. "Maybe it's just that natural pull you have on me because you're my Fated Mate, I don't know. I'd like to think it's more than just the natural instincts programmed into us."

"Me too," Mikaél whispered.

"Can we be a team again? Please?"

Mikaél's face grew into a smile. "Can we get a milkshake first?"

"A milkshake? In this weather?" Roman scanned the city as saw the object of Mikaél's affection. A Prowler Burger sign lit up in the bleakness of the night.

"Neither of us ate much of anything in the restaurant. We're only another mile from home. Besides, it looks like it's clearing up a bit."

Roman tapped the steering wheel. "We're a team then?"

"We're a team." Mikaél relaxed in the seat for the first time this entire evening.

CHAPTER 16:

TO CRASH A COURSE IN FRIENDSHIP

"Wowzers!" Laycin shivered as the restaurant's heat attacked the chills on his body. "Just when you think it can't get any colder!"

"The storm last night was bad. The weather system made the temperature drop through the floor." Instead of taking his jacket off, Mikaél shoved his hands into the pockets, hoping it would help heat him up faster. He watched Laycin eye him awkwardly. "I used to watch 24/7 Weather on TV."

"What? Like for fun?" Laycin asked as he slowly walked to the host in the restaurant.

"Maybe?" Mikaél slipped out.

"Geek!"

"Takes one to know one." The Omega smirked. Laycin smiled at the restaurant host as if the immediate conversation never took place. "Two for a table, please."

"Right this way, gentlemen."

Laycin smiled as they followed the host through a maze to get to their table. "I was worried we'd have to wait. This place looks packed!"

"No kidding! Though I shouldn't be surprised. It is the best restaurant ever." Mikaél smiled as he waited for Laycin's reaction. What he received was no surprise to him. An "Uh-huh" in a monotone voice if he ever heard one. Deep inside, it made Mikaél smile. "I'm surprised you didn't put up a fight like you normally do when we talked about places to go."

Laycin shrugged. "I hardly ever see you anymore, it seems. I figured I'd be nice." His demeanor changed from considerate to sarcastic. "Besides, this is the opportunity for your pup to tell you they hate soup and salad. They'll kick from the inside and demand a steak or a burger."

Mikaél cracked up as he remembered every moment of why Laycin was his best friend. "I hate to break the news to you, but it's meat in general the pup growing inside me has struggled with the most. Seafood in particular."

"Seriously?" Laycin's face was in disbelief—as most wolf descendants would be. "A pup born to be a vegetarian?" He squinted his eyes and stuck his tongue out like he tasted milk that had gone bad.

"There are worse things," Mikaél muttered as he looked over the menu.

Now Laycin was laser-pointing his focus on his friend, trying to dig through the layers of what he meant by the comment. But the waiter coming to take their order interrupted his investigation. The young man was very good looking: tall, blond, slight muscular build. His plastered smile easily told every customer he was only doing this to take care of college expenses. He was perhaps on his way to be a hot shot lawyer or banker. "I'll do the steak and fries. Medium rare. Lemon-lime soda."

Mikaél stifled a laugh. "I'll do the house soup and salad. Just water for me—thanks."

After the waiter left, Laycin's curiosity got the better of him. "What do you find so funny?"

"Afraid of venturing outside the radius of beef?"

"You should talk. There's meat in the house soup. Thought you said you couldn't do it? The smell alone should drive you nuts. Hmmm. I suppose my steak doesn't help. Do I need to order something else?" Laycin offered.

"No. It's not a smell thing. More of a texture thing. Now that I'm on the downhill slope, things have calmed down." Out of the corner of his eye, Mikaél noticed a couple doting over a young pup barely able to hold onto his chicken tender. Both parents looked like they were in heaven. Then he noticed everyone else in the restaurant paying them no mind. All were heavy into their own meals and conversations, not giving any care to the young pup lightly tapping the window or spilling ketchup on his sweater. Lost in his trance, he didn't even notice the waiter coming back with their drinks.

Laycin caught his line of sight and then watched Mikaél stew in his own thoughts—his pheromone palette saying it all. "What's wrong?"

With a barely visible gesture of his finger, Mikaél pointed at the picture-perfect family. "That." Laycin observed them one more time but couldn't make the connection. "Roman and I are never going to be able to do that."

Now the Beta was thoroughly confused. He scratched his head. "You and Roman can't bring your pup to a public restaurant? Why?" No response came. "This isn't about that whole Type 6 thing, is it? If so, it's not like anyone can look at you and see that." Mikaél couldn't even look his best friend in the eye. "Mik?" The trance appeared to be unbreakable.

"There's something I need to tell you." After another pause, Laycin gave a word of encouragement. "When I told you about the 'Type 6 thing,' I didn't realize what other implications it might have. Still today, I can't believe it. In my head, I create scenarios to where it's all just a dream. But it's not."

"What isn't a dream?"

"Roman and I are having a pup that's going to be..." he hesitated a bit before uttering the words, "...a girl."

The idea didn't penetrate Laycin right away. His mind alone had to reach in and pull the concept out of memories from history books and childhood stories. He watched his friend, waiting for the smirk, the smile, the hint of laughter that he put on a dramatic show just for kicks.

But it didn't show. What did show, however, was Mikaél's expression growing fearful. Instantly, the Beta felt his worry. What did he expect Laycin to do? Get angry and yell? Stand up and walk out on him in a crowded restaurant? No. Instead, he started laughing.

Mikaél felt heat boil inside him. "What's so funny?"

"You just keep finding yourself in positions to make yourself the most unique and prolific Omega in the world, don't you?" Laycin grinned.

The Omega's chest relaxed as he didn't hear the rejection he anticipated. Then, Laycin's claim set in. "Ironic, isn't it?"

"Last year, I think people barely knew your name. Now, you're going to be most known Omega out there."

"You think?" Mikaél grumbled.

"Oh, it's not so bad." Laycin waved off. "You can go on tour!" A lightbulb and dollar signs went off in his head. "I'll be your manager—for a fee—and book you on all the major news networks and talk shows. 'Laycin Vaughn presents the Amazing Omega and his Wondrous Offspring. What will his womb and his Alpha's baby batter produce next? Find out next spring! Advance tickets on sale now!'"

"Advance tickets? To see what exactly?" Mikaél asked with sly curiosity.

"That depends." Laycin smirked. "How much do you want to make?" He flexed his eyebrows.

Mikaél smiled in a way he hadn't for a while. "Thanks, Laycin."

"Anytime, my friend."

"Gentlemen," the waiter came back, "the first order of unlimited soup and salad and one steak medium rare with fries."

Laycin drew in the aromas and savored the moment. His mouth watered at the butter melting on his beautifully grilled steak, flavor seeping out of the blackened hash marks. "So, who all knows this juicy tidbit of information?"

"Believe it or not, practically no one. Not even Drew or Roman's brothers know."

"Yes!" Laycin hissed with a fist drive. "Another score for Uncle Gray Wolf!"

"Just me, Roman, the doctor who confirmed it, and our parents." A spoonful of his favorite soup didn't soothe as much as he hoped. "And someone."

Laycin spoke while chomping on a french fry. "Someone?"

"Some creep out there trying to scare us."

"How?"

Mikaél contemplated his words. "We got an early Valentine's gift of dead flowers and animal parts." Based on Laycin's immediate reaction, he could have been more tactful.

"What the—?" Laycin took a big swig of his drink, as if to digest the information. "Why on earth would someone do that?"

The Omega sighed. "To send us a message that our pup is somehow a sign from the Wolf-Devil, I suppose."

"Crappy, expensive way to do it," Laycin replied. "Knowing places around here, they probably had to pay premium for dead flowers and animal parts."

Mikaél shook his head. "What?" No matter how much Mikaél wanted to be angry at Laycin for making a joke, he appreciated it, needed it. "You are unbelievable."

"I'm just sayin'! A couple of photos done up on a home printer would have done the same. That's pretty extravagant."

As much as he could have dismissed his friend's words as sarcasm, Mikaél couldn't help but wonder if there was validity to his claim. Dark and psychotic as it was, the message was rather over the top, though it was tough to say whether it was a simple task done by someone with means or an arduous task by someone barely scraping by. Or worse—more than one person. He didn't want to dwell on it much more.

"No clue on who it could be?"

"No," Mikaél huffed. "Whoever seems to be doing all this shit lately does a good job of covering their tracks."

"What about the doctor who examined you and told you of your miracle baby? That would be my first guess." He looked down at Mikaél's side of the table. "Aren't you going to order another? You seem a lot slower than normal."

Mikaél hummed as he weighed his options. "I was assured left and right the doctor could be trusted. Not that it means anything at this point. But yeah, he's the obvious guy in my mind." He stared at his half-eaten bowl. "Anyways, no, I think I'm good. Not that hungry."

Laycin gave a melodramatic gasp. "The salad gods are in disbelief! Aren't you supposed to eat since you're eating for two?"

"Oh boy." An eyeroll ensued. "Number one, 'eating for two' is not a real thing. If that were true, Omegas carrying three or four pups would be left at the buffet table and never allowed to leave."

Laycin bit his lip, hoping he didn't offend. He really was out of the loop on the facts of pregnancy. More than just being a sterile Beta, he surmised.

"Number two," Mikaél pointed out, "believe me, I've been told to eat, relax, calm down, and any other iteration reaching to the same conclusion: shut up and grow a pup."

"I have an idea!" Laycin put on a sinister grin. "How about you shut up and grow a pup?"

A firm middle finger on display showed Laycin what Mikaél thought about that idea. Both burst out in laughter. Mikaél let his body slump to the wall of the booth, propping his head up on his hand. "Wolf-God, I missed you!"

"Hey, I wasn't the one who decided to change half of his classes to fit a photography career. If it wasn't for that career class, we wouldn't see each other at all this semester." Laycin frowned, reminding himself he was still bitter.

"I know." Mikaél deflated. "Between my Veo asking for help in redesigning his next studio, Roman's crazy clinicals schedule, doctor appointments, and dabbling in online courses from home, I don't have any recollection of my former life."

Laycin's expression grew worrisome. "It will be worth it in the end, right?"

Despite the noise of all the customers in the restaurant, it became quiet in Mikaél's head. After a moment, his face softened. "Yeah ... it's worth it." Simultaneously, both crawled out of the booth to begin their exit. "When are you going to find yourself a man?"

"Me? Date? Ew. No. Never! I would never! I would never find a guy online and start dating him..." Mikaél cocked his head, "...this past weekend."

"What?!" Mikaél couldn't believe his ears. "And I'm just finding out about this now?!"

"Finding out about what?" Laycin played coy as he finished out the bill and led the two out of the restaurant.

Mikaél gawked at the cash thrown on the table. "I was going to take care of that!" He realized he had taken the bait as his best friend kept walking on without a care as if he wasn't with him. "Oh, I don't think so!"

Walking outside, Laycin zipped up his jacket and took a deep breath. "Man! I think the temperature dropped! Good thing I parked close."

"Listen you! As your best friend, I think I deserve practically live updates on your love life!" Mikaél walked carefully to the car parked on the side street only a half a block away. Falling on the ice, especially stomach and face first, was not what he needed in his life now. As he reached the passenger door handle, relief washed over him.

"I did!" Laycin claimed. "Texted you and called you."

Scrambling for his phone, Mikaél was frustrated he missed them. He scanned both his messages and missed calls; no such notifications came through. As confusion set in, he caught Laycin stifling his enjoyment as if he was a kid successful in pulling a prank. "Ugh! You!"

The car went into gear as their warm breaths sent fog up to the windshield. Wheels revved as they struggled to gain traction on the pavement layered in glossy white ice. Once they successfully glided onto the road, Mikaél resumed his interrogation. "If you think I'm getting out of this car, Mr. Vaughn, without some details, you are severely mistaken."

Laycin still tried to play the whole thing off as if it was simply a daily occurrence that a young, loner of a Beta found a companion, or like it was yesterday's news. "What interest do you have in a Beta dating another Beta anyway?"

"A Beta, is he?" Mikaél sang. Laycin shot a look over, regretting and savoring the experience at the same time. "And what do you mean by that? You're my best friend; of course, I want to know."

Laycin hummed as he carefully guided the car on the frosted streets. "I guess you are worthy of hearing a *little* bit."

"That's right, Uncle Gray Wolf, I do!" Mikaél affirmed.

Laycin's eyes lit up. "Well, now you're talkin'! Where has that been?"

"Maybe I'm just—"

An ear-splitting skid roared toward their car. Before either Laycin or Mikaél could react, the oncoming car slammed into them, crushing the front of the red convertible. Bodies rushed forward from the impact; glass shattered and metal screeched as it obliterated any resemblance of the car's sleek shape and pristine condition.

As fast as it happened, it ended. The deafening noises faded to nothing. A harsh cold breeze snaked into new cracks and holes of the windshield and windows. Voices surrounded the vehicles, but inside, it was quiet.

Sirens. They pierced Roman to the core. Lights. They flickered red everywhere. As he weaved through the crowd, the worst thoughts went through his mind. As onlookers and emergency vehicles became more of an obstacle, Roman flexed his muscles and roared as he pushed anyone out of the way he needed to. He completely ignored the side comments coming from crowds for his rude, erratic behavior. The Alpha didn't care about any of it. All he cared about was getting to his mate.

Automatically, without even thinking, his voice called out to his mate, hoping against hope Mikaél would respond back. But he heard nothing in reply. With a final grunt and shove, Roman finally made it to the front line of the accident, guarded by ominous yellow tape. The sight frightened Roman to his core. A red convertible's front was smashed in like an aluminum can—debris scattered around everywhere like confetti. Airbags were easily visible as Roman noticed the passenger door completely missing. No one was in the vehicle.

Roman felt his knees weakened and his chest tighten. A strong urge to take the remaining rubble of the car and break it into pieces with his bare hands came over him. Even more, he wanted to break every bone in the body of the person responsible for the accident. That was when he scanned the entire scene and noticed what was disturbingly absent: the other vehicle involved.

An officer watched Roman and anticipated his move to breach the perimeter and prepared to stop his attempt. However, a paramedic rushed to the line and called for Roman by name. After the officer allowed him to pass, the paramedic brought Roman to the back of an ambulance truck. There inside sat Mikaél upright on a gurney, holding an ice pack to his forehead. Underneath, a butterfly bandage held together a top layer of skin which tore upon impact.

"Mik!" Roman gasped as he rushed forward.

"Roman!" Mikaél tried to return the hug as best as he could while half of his body was wrapped in a blanket and one hand pre-occupied with the icepack. "Ow! Ow! Easy!"

Roman heard his mate wince as he attempted a full-on bear hug. "Sorry! Sorry!" He took one more look at his Omega, praying to Wolf-God he wasn't an illusion. "Are you okay? What happened?"

"I don't know. I don't remember," Mikaél moaned, partly from the pain, partly from not being able to recall anything about the accident.

Roman was on high alert as he addressed the paramedic off to the side in the ambulance. "He can't remember?!"

"We did a standard test on him. He remembers his birthday, today's date, who *you* are, and what he had for lunch. His eyesight is good, and all his extremities are working fine. Looks like whiplash, a moderate contusion on his forehead, and slight memory loss from impact. Not uncommon." The paramedic finished putting all the sensors on Mikaél and turned on the monitors.

"A contusion from what?" Roman examined it. It took all of his restraint to not want to touch it, examine it, and write up a report he knew Dr. Daniels, his supervisor, would be proud of.

"Apparently, my head hit something," Mikaél mumbled.

"What is all that for?" Roman asked, very suspicious of the paramedic's calm demeanor.

"We want to make sure we have all eyes and ears on his condition. Since he's pregnant and so far along, he'll be on these monitors all the way to the hospital."

"The hospital?!" Roman was about ready to go insane from this dichotomy of a calm persona and the prognosis being told to him.

"Protocol." The paramedic beckoned to Mikaél. "One more check on the eyes, if you please." The young man lifted his pen light against the Omega's eyes and hummed on the positive response. "Good. No change there."

Roman gulped. "And the baby?"

The paramedic smiled. "You got a good one here, Mikaél. I could smell the protective pheromones from the sidewalk." He turned to face Roman. "We have a normal heartbeat on your boy, and all other vitals seem to be in order. Unfortunately, I can't give you anything beyond that. That's what the doctor will have to do."

"My *boy*?" Roman didn't understand the need for the moniker to describe his mate.

"Your pup!" the man clarified.

"Oh." If it wasn't for the bitter cold, the paramedic would have easily clocked Roman's flushed cheeks as foolish embarrassment. *Of course, he doesn't know.*

"Pardon me." A patrol officer knocked on the open door of the ambulance. "Are we able to get a statement before we head out to Mountain Ridge?"

The paramedic scanned all the monitors on the screen. "Make it quick."

"Should only take a second," the officer assured.

Mikaél dropped the ice pack into his lap, tired of holding it. "I've said it three times to three different people. I don't remember anything."

"Do you remember telling *me* you don't remember anything?" the officer asked.

Mikaél dimmed. "No."

"Good. Then let's begin." The officer took out an electronic pad and pen and scrolled to a bunch of notes already entered. "According to the restaurant, you and Laycin Vaughn left at 12:43 PM."

"Laycin!" Mikaél exclaimed. "Where is he?" As soon as Mikaél attempted to stand, everyone around him emphatically encouraged him to stay seated.

Once Mikaél was safely seated, the officer attempted to begin again. "Mr. Vaughn is—"

"Mik!" Laycin bowled into the officer, practically knocking him over and ignoring the policeman's curse. "Wolf-God, are you okay? What's wrong with your head? Did you break anything? You're bleeding! Do you need a tourniquet? How's the baby? Is anyone watching the baby? Shit, I'm never going to be able to forgive myself!"

Initially, Roman planned on biting Laycin's head off for the accident. But as Laycin continued to unravel before everyone, he realized he was doing a good job to himself already.

"Damn, Laycin. Chill out. He's okay." Roman made sure Laycin saw a good look of disapproval—still placing some of the blame on him.

"How would you know?" Laycin dramatized.

"Because I'm a doctor, too," Roman responded.

It was then, Laycin's engine slowed down to a normal speed. "Oh. Right." He whimpered. "Mik, I'm so sorry. I don't know what happened. I was talking to you and all of sudden this truck came out of nowhere and hit me."

"Wait. The truck hit *you*?" Roman asked.

The officer nodded. "We have a couple witness statements who say the same. According to some bystanders, they came at you at a rather high speed for the intersection, not to mention the poor winter road conditions."

Roman's demeanor changed. A darkness flooded his face. "Where's the driver?"

"That's just it," Laycin began, "the other truck is gone. Hit us head-on and then the bastard drove away!"

"What?!" Roman wanted to break the driver in half. He instantly knew what his goal was after making sure his mate and unborn pup were safe. Before he could continue to press the issue further, Mikaél interjected.

"Laycin, your arm!"

Laycin, along with everyone else, fixated on the Beta's arm now held in a sling. "It's nothing!" he dismissed.

"Is it broken?" Mikaél's face fell, devastated by the thought of his best friend being injured in the crash or worse.

"I don't think so. They told me to put it in here as a precaution until I get it checked out." Laycin gently used his free arm to massage the one in the sling to show Mikaél there was nothing to worry about, conveniently avoiding any area of concern which would cause him lose face.

"We already have your statement, Mr. Vaughn," the officer refocused.

Mikaél felt useless. "I'm sorry, officer. I don't have memories of anything."

"Nothing comes to mind? Anything about the vehicle or perhaps a glimpse of the driver who hit you?" the officer pressed. Mikaél shook his head in defeat.

"Wait," Roman interrupted, "you don't have video surveillance or witness video or anything?"

The officer glided his pen on his screen to notes he'd taken earlier. "From Mr. Vaughn and a few bystanders, we have a black, late-model, Canis Pinnacle, 4X4. That much metal could have run over Mr. Vaughn's convertible like a monster truck if it struck just right."

Roman's muscles tensed and his vision streaked red as he visualized the officer's claim. His heart pumped and his lungs flexed again and again. The only thing which kept him from going postal was his mate's hand squeezing his in a soothing, calming pattern. The patrolman continued his report.

"Unfortunately, the nearest light cam was another block up, and it doesn't appear the assailant took any of the monitored streets for a few blocks. Our investigation will track down the truck eventually, but we're going to have to piece together the street cam footage. With no witnesses turning in a license plate number, we may be a couple days out from narrowing it down. And even then, we'd have to make sure we have the right vehicle."

"You've got to be fucking kidding me right now!" Roman let out.

"Roman, please," Mikaél whispered.

Roman gaped at the officer. "Probably a half dozen witnesses around and millions of dollars of infrastructure into this city, and no one can turn up a mother fucking, Wolf-Goddamned license plate?"

Everyone within earshot froze and took in the sight and scent of the Type 6 Alpha on the verge of something ominous.

Out of decorum, the Alpha police officer decided to ease the situation down versus showing Roman by law and by force that he needed to tone it down. After all, he was sympathetic to a man who almost lost his mate and unborn child. "There are some inconsistent reports of the license plate being unreadable either by the accident or from it being snow covered. Possibly both when considering the front and rear license plate."

"I can't believe this shit! I don't believe it! FUCK!" Roman turned and slammed his fist into the swinging ambulance door.

"Roman!" Mikaél yelled out, pleading for his mate to calm down in front of the growing crowd.

The EMT stepped in. "Okay, officer, I think we're good here." He turned toward the front. "Collin, we need to move out!"

"You got it!" The driver flipped on the lights which flickered off the snow and ice on the ground.

"Are you comfortable here if I follow?" Roman asked Mikaél.

"I'm good, Roman. The baby is too. We'll be safe," Mikaél assured his mate.

"They're in good hands, Alpha daddy!" The EMT smiled, signaling for Roman to move of their way. Then, he turned his attention to Laycin. "And you—you need to get back to your ambulance or get clearance to get a ride home if you are refusing services."

"What *are* you doing?" Roman asked Laycin.

"I called my Sur. He's coming to pick me up. No doubt, he'll be lecturing my ear off the entire ride home," Laycin grumbled as he knew the trouble he was in.

"Sounds like it wasn't your fault though," Roman reminded him.

"Yeah, but you know how dads are."

Roman nodded. "I definitely do."

Laycin stood there, awkwardly. "I really am sorry. I hope Mik knows that."

"I know, Laycin, and Mik knows it, too. I'm just glad it wasn't worse."

"You and me both." Laycin slowly backed away toward his own ambulance with an EMT impatiently waiting for him. "Keep me updated on how he and the pup are doing?"

"Of course." Roman gave a wave as he heard an ear-splitting siren lead the ambulance carrying his mate to the hospital. He hurried back through what was left the crowd to his own car. After getting in, he stared at his black steering wheel. He imagined it to be the psychotic perpetrator before pounding it several times with his fists and roaring and cursing the man who would do such a heinous act. The only solace he had was knowing his mate and pup were safe and that he would make sure whatever coward did this would pay dearly for messing with him and his family.

CHAPTER 17:

TO VOTE FOR A
BETTER CHANCE

66 I t's a clean bill of health as far as I'm concerned." The doctor finished signing off several medical reports. Roman let out the biggest sigh he ever had in the past six months. The words were music to his ears. "The nurses keep telling me you're not interested in doing your next sonogram now since we have you here. Are you sure?"

Both Roman and Mikaél looked at each other in horror. This time Mikaél decided to be the voice of reason. "No, no. We're good. We're just happy to hear all the vitals seem to be in order. We'll schedule the sonogram when we get home today."

The doctor nodded, thinking nothing of it. "I hope you found the accommodations last night sufficient?"

Mikaél swayed his head. "Hospitals are only so comfortable."

"I hear ya." The doctor chuckled. "You're mated, but it also looks like you are currently in school. Are you under family insurance or your mate's?"

"I'm still under The Pact Act, so I'm still under my parents' insurance."

"That works for us. I'll just get these forms to its rightful place, and we'll get you checked out." The ER doctor clicked his pen and whistled on his way out of the room.

A weight was lifted off the couple. The afternoon sun shined in like a beacon from heaven. So much could have been different, and yet the family had been spared from the worst. Blessings were counted that day.

Roman saw the bright sky in his mate's eyes. Without having to say a word, Mikaél leaned up and gave his mate a deep kiss, the one that he wanted to give him yesterday when he met his Omega at the scene of the accident. Just then, it was like a pipe ruptured, and he began swelling with tears.

"Babe, what's wrong?" Mikaél softly spoke.

Roman sniffled and held back most of the water works. "Just caught up with me, I guess. The thought that I could have lost you there or our pup. I don't know what I would have done."

"I think I know what you would have done." Mikaél's voice told Roman all he needed to know. A rage was building in Roman, one he had seen before when he and Roman tried to make love. It was still a conversation neither of them broached. The fear of what was there scared them both. Quickly, Mikaél changed his tone. "But, luckily, that's not the case. I'm here. You're here. And our daughter," he glided his mate's hand over his extended stomach, "is right here." This time Roman came down and gave him one more passionate kiss to seal the most beautiful words spoken in a long time. "But damn, can't we get out of here?!"

"Almost. Just be patient," Roman reiterated.

"That's what I've been told ever since I got in that Wolf-God-forsaken ambulance," Mikaél grumbled.

"Has it actually been that bad knowing everything turned out okay in the end?" Roman traced his finger around the bandage on his mate's hand where an I.V. port once was.

"No. I guess not."

"Good." Roman smiled. "Because I think, when we get home, we need to have a little fun..." Roman's hand crept up to Mikaél's nipple on the outside of his hospital gown shirt. The pregnancy changed them to where they were more swollen and sensitive, an advantage for his mate.

Mikaél giggled and squirmed in the hospital bed as he tried to maintain his composure. "A nap! What I need is a nap in my own bed!"

"We'll take a nap afterward." Roman licked his mate's ear.

"Okay! Okay!" Mikaél pushed the Alpha off him. "Wait until we get home then!"

"Hmph. Fine." Roman pouted. Unfortunately, his mind was completely immersed in pleasing his mate, intensified by the possibility of losing him no doubt. "So, what am I supposed to do while we wait?"

"Watch TV or something. Don't you have your daily dose of WOLF News to take in?" Mikaél playfully mentioned.

"Oh shit!" Roman exclaimed. "The election!"

"The election?"

"The Pack Alpha runoff! Yesterday, I was all the way back in our voting district. That's why it took me so long to get you; I was waiting in line to vote against Matthew Whitmore's run for city office."

"Wow, I had completely forgotten about that." A flood of memories came back, a barely pregnant Mikaél staring into a TV screen, hearing Matthew Whitmore switch from the Liberal to Conservative Party, vying to be the next city leader under the pretense of shutting down a conspiracy theory that Omegas were going to overthrow the government and "natural" balance of Alphas controlling their Beta and Omega counterparts. "Did you get a chance to cast your ballot?"

Roman looked up from the remote control with dismal look on his face. "No. Once I heard about the accident, I ran out of there. Everyone looked at me like I was literally on fire."

An uneasy feeling came over Mikaél. "I bet."

The Alpha sensed the worry in his mate and reached over to comfort him as he found the channel he was finally looking for. "Hey, it's okay. There's no way Whitmore won this thing. You know how politics works. You must have years of being in this system to actually get a foothold. From most of the reports I listened to yesterday, they still view this as some radical ploy for attention or to widen his business's scope."

"Only one way to find out," Mikaél followed up. But even before Roman could turn up the TV's volume up loud enough, there in bold letters at the bottom of the screen told them both what they wanted to know—or rather—didn't want to know...

"For those of you just tuning in, the runoff race for Pack Alpha of Tauris City was decided about an hour ago. In a surprising result, Matthew Whitmore narrowly won his very recent campaign under the Conservative Party and will be the face and voice of Tauris City for the next four years. We are at 99% reporting right now which has Whitmore winning at a close 92—yes—92 votes. Of course, ever since Whitmore finally overcame Liberal challenger Jesse Minh last night in the tally, we were waiting to hear whether those results would be challenged. Shockingly, instead, Minh conceded and congratulated Whitmore on what he considered an upset and what he anticipates will be a shake up to 'politics as usual.' We here at WOLF News resonate Jesse Minh's words and congratulate Matthew Whitmore on his victory and are also on standby to see if Whitmore *will* shake things up *or* if this will be politics as usual. Coming up next, what does Whitmore's victory mean for the territory? And does Whitmore have larger aspirations than just Tauris City? Find out with our exclusive interview tonight at 6..."

"Mik, talk to me!" Roman demanded as he cautiously followed his mate into their apartment. His previous attempts had gone unanswered.

"I don't want to hear it!" the Omega spat back. Instead, he rushed to the TV to try and drown out the thoughts screaming in his head. But upon hitting the power button, the haunting of Whitmore's victory returned front and center. He growled at the large, flat screen, shut the box off, and threw the remote so hard it smashed into pieces against the wall.

"What are you doing?!" Roman exclaimed.

"Just leave me alone!" Mikaél continuously huffed his breath like he had jogged for thirty minutes without a break. He snatched up a book he gave up reading months ago from the side table. The words on the book slowed to a crawl as he could hear every syllable of the words he attempted to read in a crisp slow motion in his mind. Mikaél blamed his mate as he could feel his stare burning into his skin. Unable to control himself any longer, he fisted several pages of the delicate paper and ripped out several passages as they scattered toward the floor. Out of the corner of his eye, he saw Roman approach but decided he would not be deterred from his goal of making sure he could win the battle between himself and what was left of the book in his trembling hands.

"Stop it! Stop it! Stop it!" Roman gripped his mate's hands and what was left of the book fell to pieces. In addition to his mate's pain seeping into his soul, Roman could smell the sour scent of iron. Several small cuts from the torn paper on Mikaél's hands left a light splatter of blood on his palms and fingertips. The Alpha felt his adrenaline pump and his eyes quiver at the thought of his Omega in pain. In the back of his mind, he heard the screams of two separate people blinding his entire train of thought. One was much younger than the other, but both were in inconsolable pain, although neither shared the same ailment. Suddenly, his mind refocused and he saw

Mikaél in front of him, holding back the torment going through him as best as he could. "Talk to me!" Roman demanded.

"It's you! It's all *you*!" Mikaél yelled, his voice harsh yet full of emotion.

Roman instantly let go of the grip he had on his mate as if he was touching a hot stove. "*Me*? What did *I* do? I haven't done *anything*. This isn't about me. This is about a car crash that happened yesterday and the downward spiral you've been on ever since we heard Whitmore's announcement on TV back in the hospital. What do you mean this is all me?"

"No, no, no. You don't get it!" Mikaél held his head as his temples throbbed.

"Get what?" Roman yelped, completely lost.

"I can *feel* you. The emotions inside you. They're running through me like a fire. Your anger, your bloodlust—it's all in my head!" The Omega yelped, crying as a tear fell down his cheek, wanting to look everywhere except at his mate.

Roman frantically tried to make sense of what his mate was saying to him. "But... but I'm fine. I'm just worried about you!"

"Liar!" Mikaél stood up and walked toward the large floor to ceiling windows, placing his head firmly on the cold glass, the heat from his head instantly fogging up the glass.

"I'm not lying! I'm only thinking about you right now. I want you to be okay," Roman pleaded.

"The only way that works is for you to finally let out what you're *really* feeling," Mikaél clarified.

"What do you mean?"

"You're bottling it up, and it's somehow transferring to me. It's like I'm an empath or something." Mikaél turned around to finally face Roman. The pain only seemed to grow as he was now forced to look at it. "What's wrong with me?" he pleaded.

"Baby, nothing is wrong with you." Roman's voice quivered as he wrapped his arms around Mikaél. "It's our child; it's our bond. It's making us grow stronger together. You only have about two months left, and it's only building the connection we have between us."

"Why does nobody else talk about this happening? What is going on?" Mikaél buried his head into his mate's chest as if his life depended on it.

"I don't know. But we'll make it through this." Roman exhaled. "Together."

Mikaél balled up his hands and pushed Roman back. "No!"

"What? Why?"

"Not until you say it!" Mikaél pointed at his mate like he was being caught in denial red-handed.

"Say what?"

"What you are truly feeling!" The Omega eyed the Alpha from across the room. No change in his demeanor. "Let me help you paint the picture, then." A terrible feeling hit the pit of Roman's stomach. "I'm lying in a hospital bed, almost crushed to death by some psycho who tried to murder me, my friend, and our daughter."

"Babe, don't do this." A deafening blow hit Roman's ears as his muscles spasmed in his neck, shoulders, and arms. Veins began protruding out of thick tanned skin on his biceps and above his clavicle.

Mikaél resumed, "And just when we think we're in the clear, the Wolf-Devil himself appears on TV, basking in his glory, knowing very well his goal is to come after us and our baby girl."

"Mikaél!" Roman roared. An imaginary strait jacket surrounded Roman, and he couldn't escape free because escaping meant he was going to turn into a beast without remorse or a sense of when to stop.

"And you know he is going to stop at nothing in order to make sure me and our baby girl are locked away forever, or even worse, dead!"

Two heartbeats locked into Roman's psyche which weren't his own. The smaller one was already beating quite fast; the larger one continued to quicken its pace. A horrific thought of both heartbeats ceasing to exist shattered Roman. The sound of the hearts was replaced by a loud voice, Roman's own voice, yelling something even inaudible to himself.

When the noise completely stopped, and silence fell, Mikaél had his hand covering his mouth. His eyes weren't locked into Roman's eyes, but on his right arm, which was now halfway through the living room wall connected to the bedroom.

It took Roman a moment himself to look away from the horror on his mate's face. A stinging sensation tore his gaze back to his arm, trembling among wooden slats and drywall. As he pulled his hand out of the wall, debris continued to fall on the floor and in the space between. Roman studied his arm in awe, barely remembering he had even done it. The skin on his fingers and knuckles were torn open and caked with dust. "I..."

"Are you crazy?!" Mikaél hustled past Roman, frantically searching for a clean kitchen towel.

Roman walked up to his mate near the kitchen sink. "What? This is *my* fault?"

"Well, *I* sure didn't put your hand through the wall," Mikaél sang sarcastically. He grabbed his mate's wrist and shoved it under the cold running water.

"Ow! Easy on that!" Roman hissed.

"If you think it hurts now, just wait until later." Mikaél gently wiped away the foreign objects still clinging to the back of Roman's hand. "Feel better?"

"About what?" Roman scowled. "About what you incited?"

Mikaél dropped the cloth in the wet sink. "Incite what?"

"If you hadn't—" Roman stopped himself. He fell into a trap. This wasn't the conversation he wanted to have right now.

"Don't stop there. If I hadn't done what?" Mikaél stared down his mate and crossed his arms.

"Why didn't you just stay home?" Roman slammed his good fist on the countertop. "Fuckin' A!"

Mikaél chortled as he shook his head. "Yeah. There it is."

Roman scowled. "What's so funny?"

Once again, the Omega found himself rattling off a continuous list of rhetoric he was beyond tired of. "'Why don't I just stay home? Why don't I just stay quiet? Why don't I just do what everyone tells me to do?' When did I get the tattoo that tells every Alpha in my life to control me? And when did I get the branding that gives you the right to tell me what to do?'"

"When you decided to carry my offspring!" Roman shouted, his lungs heaving in his chest.

Mikaél's head cocked back. "*Your* offspring?" He was flabbergasted the phrase was uttered by his Fated Mate. Growing up, Mikaél always knew and heard the stereotypical rhetoric Alphas spouted, claiming their mates and their offspring as property. But to have Roman join the ranks of those he despised was beyond his comprehension. "I never thought I'd hear *you* of all people say that. Anything else you have a problem with?"

Roman felt himself being put on defense—a position an Alpha inherently abhorred. "As a matter of fact, yes."

"Go for it," Mikaél scoffed.

"How on earth could you forget that Whitmore's election was yesterday?"

Mikaél squinted as he connected the dots. "Woah. Wait a minute. You're not honestly thinking I'm somehow responsible for Whitmore getting elected, are you?"

"If you had just stayed home like I wanted, I would have picked you up during my lunch break, and we could have gone down together to help make sure his ass stays out of politics!"

"Really? Really, Roman?" Mikaél stared at his mate in disbelief. "Were you planning on picking up the other 91 voters on the way down to the precinct to make sure Whitmore lost by one vote, or did you forget about that little detail?"

"I don't know how you think any of this is entertaining. This is totally serious, Mik. What that monster is capable of doing now is completely serious!" Roman began walking up to his mate, placing but a narrow gap between them.

Mikaél eyed his mate. "I know that! Don't you think I know that?!"

"Then how in the hell could you say in the hospital you forgot?" Now Roman gawked in disbelief at Mikaél as he looked down upon him. He only caught his mate's view for a second, before it left him.

"I... I don't know." Mikaél's voice fell. "I had a lot of other things go through my mind that day when I was with Laycin. I was dealing with enough; I didn't have room for that, too."

Roman didn't find it a worthy excuse. "Like what?"

The Omega received the attitude and gave it back full force. "How about my Fated Mate getting caught in a pregnancy conspiracy with his former contracted mate? Or the cops out for blood as they tried to pin the assault of Whitmore's mate on you?"

Roman's brows furrowed. "None of that has to do with any—"

"Then my Veo's photography shop getting burned down conveniently after I find out I'm a Type 6 and having the first ever female for the human species in centuries, a brick hurling toward us with a threatening note attached, Charles Brody confirming small-mind, backward discrimination of yesteryear is still very much alive, Whitmore declaring Omegas are somehow a superior species when most powerful positions are always given to an Alpha to prevent the ludicrous idea in the first place..." The more Mikaél began building the list in his head of everything he had to deal with, the more his voice trembled, his eyes watered, and his anger transformed into hopelessness that radiated off his body.

Roman instantly inhaled the Omega's true feelings as his wall broke down. "Mik..."

"...How about receiving a bunch of dead flowers and rotting animal parts specifically indicating our daughter as some unholy comparison? Or our dads' co-worker and boss getting assaulted and nearly killed in the very place in which they discovered what 'blessings' you and I really are?"

The Alpha sensed his mate on the verge of a breakdown and calmly tried to prevent the dam from breaking. "Mik, it's okay."

"Let's not forget that I completely gave all of our parents the cold shoulder when they wanted to help and support us the day we found out we were having a girl. And then I did it all over again, even with my Sur's tears falling down his face. He begged and pleaded for us to get out of here after his boss was attacked, and I just sat there like nothing happened." He finally gazed back at Roman who showed empathy for first time today. "Who does that, Roman?"

"It's not your fault, Mik. You were just trying to be strong. There's nothing wrong with trying to be a person of strength." The Alpha touched Mikaél's shoulders, hoping it would center him.

"The worst part about it is if I had listened to my dad in that shady restaurant, maybe the accident wouldn't have happened. Maybe we would have already been gone."

Roman shook his head. "There's no sense thinking about what might have been. That's not what happened, and you walked away from the accident. We don't have to worry about that now."

Mikaél sniffled as his voice became nearly inaudible. All he could do now is focus on his Sur's dismal expression, the one he gave Mikaél when he had refused to listen to his request to leave Tauris City. "I just wanted out of that restaurant. I didn't want to see my Sur with that expression or that hurt. I've never seen him look that way, and I never want to see that again. Ironically, if the car crash had ended differently, I would have gotten my wish because if it had... if I had..." The Omega broke down as he felt his body being pulled into his mate's chest. The tears ran constantly as he sobbed uncontrollably.

Roman held his mate close and cursed himself for his own responsibility in this. "I'm sorry, Mik. I should have just told you how I truly felt back at the hospital. I didn't know it would manifest inside you."

"Well, it did," Mikaél squeaked out.

"I know. Which is why we need to talk when you're ready."

"Talk about what?" Mikaél sniffled.

"The Western Territory."

The young Omega lifted his head and read the sorrowful expression all over his Alpha's face. He found the answer as he walked back to the living room couch, greeted by the tattered remains of his book. "You want to go there?"

Roman sighed as he sat on the couch. "*Want?* Of course not. I feel like we have to."

Mikaél nodded, understanding the point of view. Roman continued, "For the longest time, I thought maybe relocating to the heart of Tauris City would keep us out of the limelight if Siro's assault went viral on the news should it ever get linked back to us. After that, I thought maybe us being here would be hiding in plain sight after the incidents with the fire and with you at Ashershire. But after the attack on the lab, the flowers, and the car accident…" Roman observed his mate's unwavering concentration. "You think the same thing I do."

Mikaél's shoulders fell, and his view focused on the floor. "That they're all related? How could I not?" A single tear ran down his face. He felt his mate, his lover, his keeper, his protector wipe it away and gently kiss him.

"So, you're willing to go out there? And most likely have the pup there?" The Alpha scanned his Omega for even a hint of hesitation. Mikaél nodded.

"I don't want to lose our baby. And I don't want to lose you."

"Don't worry about me. I'm not going anywhere," Roman touted.

"Don't be so sure, Roman," Mikaél added. "With all the things going on lately, there's no reason to think something won't happen to you."

Roman's face grew serious, and his eyes pierced his mate's. "I will always be here to protect you and our pup. You got that?"

A slight smile crept onto the Omega's face. "I hope so."

"Oh, come on, seriously?!" Nico burst out in the auditorium.

"Calm down! And yes. Seriously." Roman scanned the emptying classroom, students and advisors way too busy to eavesdrop in on their conversation. Luckily.

Nico pouted. "I've barely seen or heard from you in nearly two months, and this is how you repay me?"

Roman felt the sympathy. But still, he felt there was only so much he could do. He returned a toothy grin. "Happy Valentine's Day?"

"Bitch."

"Aww, don't be like that," Roman sulked.

Nico crossed his arms as he reclined in his seat. "Blow me!"

"I—" Roman blushed as he still prayed no one else, especially a doctor, was listening in. He leaned in. "That wasn't very nice."

"Erricson!" Dr. Daniels stopped halfway and addressed his student. Roman stood at attention as Nico nearly flew out of his seat, his books and pencils flying everywhere as he tried to regain his composure. The doctor gazed upon Nico, not entertained in the slightest by the boy's lack of dignity. "You." He pointed at Nico. "You're one of Dr. Phoung's pupil's?"

"Ye-yes, sir!"

"What's your name?"

The Beta stood at attention and offered his hand, though none was offered back. "Nico. Nico Hallen, sir."

"It's *doctor*!" Dr. Daniels sneered back.

"Yes, sir! I mean, doctor!" Nico gulped. Roman observed his friend like his head was on the chopping block.

"Pity." Dr. Daniels scanned Nico up and down, then peered at Roman. "Honestly, Erricson, how on earth do you expect to get the respect of the elite world when you hang around individuals like this?" Once again, he gestured to Nico who looked like he was about ready to shit his pants.

"He's my friend, Dr. Daniels."

"Hmph. Take my advice. If you ever get established in your profession, buy a few friends, ones who actually come to class dressed like they're here to make a difference in modern medicine, not rotate a tire or change oil." Another glare at the poor Beta. "And don't be late for your shift tonight, Erricson! I don't care if it is Valentine's Day."

"Um. Yes, sir," Roman muttered. Now, Dr. Daniels' eyes were wide, looking upon him. "I mean, doctor!" Roman silently cursed himself.

"Kids these days." Dr. Daniels shook his head and began walking down the remaining steps to the floor toward the exit. "Mr. Hallen, I suggest you come to class in the future wearing more appropriate attire!"

"Yes, doctor!" Nico yelled down, not even pausing the doctor's descent out the door. "Yeesh! *That's* your advisor?"

"The one and only," Roman murmured.

"And here I thought *I* was the unfortunate one, not getting into your team."

"Uh-huh," Roman voiced in monotone.

"There's no way Siro would have been able to deal with him. His mouth would have gotten him kicked out of the program in a heartbeat!"

Roman flinched at Nico bringing up Siro's name so casually. Losing Siro behind bars was bad enough. But now, practically abandoning Nico felt worse than he had anticipated.

Nico felt the pain of his friend's news as well. This was the last thing he expected to hear today, especially on Valentine's Day. "So, when do you leave?"

The Alpha swallowed hard. "Tomorrow."

"You're an asshole, you know that?" Nico huffed. "I suppose a goodbye party would be out of the question?"

"Leaving tomorrow does prevent such things. Besides, the goal is to keep this secret. Not even Dr. Daniels knows yet."

"How are you gonna manage that one?"

"My dad is going to take care of it." Roman pinched the bridge of his nose and shut his eyes in disgust. "I can't believe I'm doing this. But that's how serious this is, Nico. You can't tell anyone!"

A voice crept in. "Can't tell anyone what?"

Roman instantly turned to find Zayne innocently looking back at him. "I, uh..." He glanced toward Nico who was no help as far as coming up with an answer. "I'm going away." His answer was vague at best.

"What?" Zayne couldn't believe his ears. "Where? Why?"

"To my uncle's house in the Southern Territory." Roman thought on his toes. "The doctor said it would be good for the rest of Mikaél's pregnancy if he was relaxed. And apparently, the cold weather isn't doing it for him."

"Oh, no. I hope he's all right," Zayne voiced, full of concern.

"He's good!" Roman assured. "It's just that he's struggling with the leaving part. I am too, to a certain extent."

"Do you need help packing or getting down there?" Zayne offered.

"No. We've been packing now for a week or so—"

"You've known this for over a week?" Nico snuck in. He quickly was silenced with an elbow stuck underneath his rib.

Roman went on as if nothing happened. "And I'll be driving us down there."

"Just you? Surely, I could be of help. I could be an extra driver for you or follow you two down there in case something happens with Mik or—"

"No thanks." Roman started feeling anxious.

"I really think that given Mikaél's condition—"

"I said, no thanks!" Roman rushed. The air grew still and thick as the awkwardness set in. "Really, Zayne. Thank you. But this is something we have to take care of by ourselves."

Zayne examined Roman's discomfort. Something wasn't right. He appeared to be hiding something. In a flash, he changed his demeanor to a peaceful, content state. "Just know I'm here if you need me." Then he peered at Nico. "Hey, Nico."

Nico smiled. "Hey, Zayne. Happy Valentine's Day!"

"Same to you." He saw Nico's face flush red, which told Zayne it was time. "It's actually the reason I wanted to talk to you..."

"I'll let you two talk this out." Roman squeezed by Zayne and walked down the stairs, softly hearing him invite Nico to dinner, on the most celebrated day of love for the year.

CHAPTER 18:

TO MAKE A MOVE IN THE RIGHT DIRECTION

" And then Wolf-God created Valentine's Day to send us on the journey to find our long lost Fated Mate, just as he himself did to find his long lost Fated Mate. Ugh. Makes me sick." Grant roamed around Brookside Books, trying to find his selected treasures on which he'd happily get 40% off sticker price, a gift Garrace promised him.

"That's why we're supposed to light a red candle on Valentine's Day, to remember Wolf-God's journey of finding his one and only." Ryan walked behind Grant, tagging along on his adventure.

"If I recall, he never found his mate," Grant pointed out.

"That's why some believe Wolf-God is a Beta and not an Alpha," Ryan proudly replied.

"Heh. Don't say that in front of an Alpha."

"No, shit! You think I really want to be in the middle of that argument?" Ryan was well aware of how Alphas dealt with hearing about counterculture. Growing up, Roman always found it funny, listening to him and Rixen discuss theories which placed Betas and Omegas in a better position than society already did. Their Sur, however, did not find the conversations funny whatsoever. Ryan remembered many conversations shut down in the name of blasphemy, not to mention blatant disrespect to the rank of Alpha.

"Hmm... no... no... no." Grant flipped back his red hair as his hazel eyes gawked at shelves of new releases.

"Are you looking for something specific?" Ryan asked.

"I have some things narrowed down, but I haven't found that one item that says, 'Pick me!' If I'm getting 40% off, I want to make sure it's worth my value."

Ryan shifted his weight. "I thought Garrace only promised Tyler that."

Grant smiled without looking away from the new releases in the science fiction section. "You didn't think I'd let Garrace get away with only giving that to Tyler, did you?"

Ryan responded flatly. "No. No, I suppose not."

The response broke Grant's concentration as he noticed his fellow Beta rank. "Are you sure you're fine with being here? I mean, you don't have to go to the checkout with me if you don't want to." Grant only imagined what it would be like with Ryan there, waiting on Garrace to finish Grant's order. Part of him imagined just bashful, awkward stares. The other part of him saw two ex-lovers battling it out like they were in the wild jungle. Good thing he charged his phone, in case he needed to post any of the action on the internet ... or turn it over to authorities as evidence.

"Don't worry. Nothing will happen," Ryan reassured. "Besides, I'm going to have to play nice with him anyhow. He's going to be in the picture for quite some time."

"That's true." It was common knowledge at this point that Rixen was pregnant with Garrace's offspring. Nobody in their inner circle, however, ventured into talking to either Rixen or Ryan on how it had affected their relationship, at least to Grant's knowledge. He thought for a moment. "He did you wrong."

"Huh?" Ryan looked up from reading a synopsis on a book he had lukewarm interest in.

"Garrace. Whether or not you hold any responsibility in why things ended, you deserved better than how it ended."

Ryan was stunned; it was difficult to let the words sink in. He couldn't remember the last time someone intentionally cared about his feelings, not to mention his perspective. The closest was Roman when he first told him of the breakup. However, Ryan recognized the situation could have forced Roman under duress. But here, Grant was completely offering his empathy of free will. "Thank you."

"Of course." Grant beamed. "Ah, there we go!" Grant picked up a special edition release of a popular novel.

"You found one?"

"Yeah, what do you think?" Grant showed the cover as Ryan walked close to investigate.

Ryan scanned the book. "A science fiction *romance*?" He looked up at Grant. "Didn't think you'd be into that."

"And what do you think I'm into exactly?" Grant asked.

Ryan smirked. "We're still talking about books, right?"

Grant's eyes sparkled. His concentration broke a moment later when the man with all the power walked by. "Garrace!" Ryan's face instantly fell as he caught a look at his former lover.

"Hey, Grant!" Garrace replied. His face also relaxed when he saw Ryan was present. "Hey, Ryan." His voice slowed with less confidence. "How's it going?"

Ryan pursed his lips. "It's going."

Grant's focus played ping-pong as he constantly volleyed between the two. When neither said a word, he jumped in to save the encounter. "I picked out the ones I wanted."

"Great! Follow me and I'll open up a register on the other side, so you don't have to wait."

Ryan added silently, *Or see me longer than you have to.*

The trio walked to the back. There, in a near abandoned section of the store, were a couple of registers reserved for the holidays or high-volume days. Garrace walked behind the counter and opened up the register, occasionally peering at Ryan, trying to gauge his temperature. "You're going to pay with a card, right?"

"Yeah, sure," Grant replied.

"Great." Garrace scanned the few items Grant had picked out. Two were very much what he expected Grant to pick: a commentary on social hierarchy and a biography on a well-known political figurehead on Beta rights. Like Ryan, the third choice of the romance novel entertained Garrace. As he grinned, he observed Ryan's completely empty hands. "Were you getting anything, Ryan?"

"Me? No." The offer was kind but also too little too late. As a matter of fact, while Grant struck up a commentary with Garrace, Ryan thought back to the day Tyler begged and pleaded for Garrace's discount. It was then he realized neither he nor Rixen were ever offered the same benefit, even after Tyler's fit in the restaurant.

"Thanks for stopping by!" Garrace sang. "What are you two doing for the holiday?"

Grant and Ryan gave each other a look, wondering if the other was interpreting Garrace's words in the same way. Ryan was the first to speak as he gestured with his hand between them.

"Oh. *We're* not doing anything..."

"We were just here for shopping and then probably just heading home..." Grant finished.

Garrace's eyes creased as he witnessed his friend and ex-boyfriend act very strange. "Guys. I know you're not together." He chuckled. "I just meant in general." He cocked his head as he proceeded to look at both of them as if they were poorly attempting to steal something or display a lewd act in public.

"Right." Grant laughed.

Ryan pivoted. "How's Rixen?"

Grant studied Ryan as he thought about the question. He realized now just how much the breakup had damaged the brothers' relationship.

Garrace nodded casually. "He's fine. We're fine."

Ryan slowly acknowledged the answer himself with a casual nod. "Okay, then. I guess I'll see you around."

Once again, Grant peered over at Ryan, this time with a heavy heart as he saw Ryan walk away defeated. Garrace was obviously putting on an act. Whether he was doing it as a customer service representative or just being a plain asshole, Grant didn't know. But he wasn't willing to stick around to find out. He bid farewell to Garrace and followed Ryan out to the mall, where he was already several steps ahead of him. Finally, he caught up alongside him.

"Hey."

"What?" Ryan responded coldly.

Grant wasn't going to be dismissed so easily. He hopped in front of Ryan and grabbed his shoulders to get a good look at the Beta as he leaned in. His eyes magnetized Ryan's so he couldn't look away. But the more he stared, the more he sensed the hurt drip from his pheromone pallet. "You're not Garrace!"

"What does that mean?"

"You're not a dick!" Grant clarified. "So, talk to me."

Ryan felt his bottom lip quiver. He didn't feel much better than Garrace. He remembered Rixen describing how much hurt he had caused him before the three of them consummated their relationship. Then, Rixen did it all over again as he explained why the three of them weren't working out, with Garrace adding a cherry on top with his own anecdotes. Thinking of it all made Ryan's eyes water. "Feeling like the world is constantly against you sucks."

"The entire world is not against you. I'm not against you," Grant pointed out. "What else?"

"Being alone sucks."

"You're not alone. I'm right here. And?" Grant pressed.

"Being alone on *Valentine's Day* sucks," Ryan followed up.

Grant kept on him, without even blinking, "Again. I'm right here."

Ryan stifled a laugh while he wiped away a stray tear. "You know what I mean."

With a sigh, Grant stood tall as he let go of Ryan's shoulders. His focus trailed to the left and to the right. After a click of his tongue, he took in a deep breath. "You want to go out on Valentine's Day, then let's go out."

"You want to grab a burger or something?" Ryan threw out.

"Not a burger. A *real* restaurant. You know, where a waiter comes to your table, and you have to look at your watch for forty minutes, wondering where your food is at?"

Ryan finally understood. "Ah. I see. No, I'm good, Grant. I don't need a Valentine's Day date out of pity. Thanks, though."

"Don't be an idiot, Ryan," Grant lamented.

Ryan jerked his head in offense. "Excuse me?"

Grant cursed to himself before laying into him. "Do I really need to remind you that Valentine's Day is the number one holiday where us Betas are the loneliest? They have extra staff today on suicide hotlines because of us."

"This isn't helping."

"When was the last time you actually heard of two guys coming together in Fated bliss that wasn't a fairytale story in a book or in a movie? Or even besides Fates, that two guys just magically find one another, and they live happily ever after without issues, doubts, challenges, or things they have to work through?"

Initially, Ryan wanted to respond. But as he caught himself on the verge of telling Grant details of the perfect mating, he realized all the ideas in his head were fiction. Even the stories of his parents' mating glossed over the details on how their relationship started. The most recent Fated Mate story he had was of his brother Roman. And he didn't need a reminder on how that went down—no matter how unique it was. A memory of pain hit his side as he relived the moment Roman pushed him into the side of the couch with a force he hadn't experienced in a long time. Even if he didn't have Roman's account of claiming Mikaél, nobody's other first encounter story matched any made with movie magic or storybook glitter. "I don't know. I guess I don't have one."

"So why don't you just go out with me and see how it really works?" Grant rushed his response to where he didn't consider the words coming out. For a man who prided himself on being calculated and precise, he didn't think this one through. He swallowed hard as he thought of a way to backtrack. "What I meant to say is... my intention was... I—"

"Okay, Mr. Wellington."

Once again, Grant was lost for words. His tongue swelled to double the size in his mouth. "Okay, wha—"

"I'll let you treat me to a Valentine's Day dinner so I can see how a 'real' date works. Wolf-God knows my only track record is Garrace and my ... brother." Ryan's body squirmed. "Boy, that sounds bad when you say it out loud."

"It does." Grant laughed. "Well, great! It's a date then!"

"If you honestly think you can find a place last minute."

Grant squinted as he considered this one of the worst days of the year to plan an impromptu date. "Actually, I do have a connection. I think I can get us in." Quickly, he pulled out his phone, scanned his contact list, and stopped on a name. He happily waited until the ringing was replaced by the sound of a rather crowded place. After several exchanges, he hung up and put his phone in his jacket pocket, satisfied with himself. "And done!"

Ryan stood there, not quite sure what to think or do. "What?"

"The restaurant. I got us booked."

"Now?" Ryan asked.

"Yup. You ready?" Grant watched as it now appeared it was Ryan's turn to be at a loss for words. "Unless you have other plans that is." Grant moved into a grin. "Or maybe you're just chicken."

Like a pup in grade school, Ryan reacted to the latter comment. "Really?"

Grant shrugged. "I'm ordering wine." Grant's eyes sparkled in delight as Ryan cautiously displayed his softer side

"Excellent."

"Wolf-God, Grant!" Ryan's face was in awe as he took in the ambiance of the elegant restaurant with its redwood interior, mood lighting, and noticeable elite clientele. He leaned in as he whispered to Grant on the other side of their table. "Damn, I knew this place was fancy, but I didn't think it was *this* fancy."

Nerves hit the pit of Ryan's stomach as he examined his own attire. His black button down and dress shoes worked well, but his tight jeans stuck out like a sore thumb. It was then he noticed Grant looking posher and more put together, which was normal for him. His white dress shirt had a collar which popped out of a nice dark colored vest complete with a tie. The dress pants complimented him well, too. Ryan began to wonder if Grant dressed this morning with high aspirations to search for a last-minute Valentine's Day date in the wild. With capturing him so easy, Grant must have been an Alpha howling on the edge of the mountaintop, proud of his accomplishment.

Grant ordered a bottle of red wine with a name Ryan could barely pronounce, let alone spell from memory. The waiter spoke with an accent which gave the impression he was more proficient in a different language other than English. After Grant tasted and approved the selection, the waiter filled both glasses, took their orders, and left the two of them alone. Suddenly, he shook his head in disbelief.

Ryan began to worry. "What? Something wrong?"

"You look so out of place here." Grant spoke boldly.

Ryan faded. "I haven't really involved myself with ... this." Using his wine glass, he gestured to the ambiance of the restaurant.

Grant was shocked. "You're kidding!" Ryan shook his head. "Your Sur is one of the top research doctors in Tauris City and your family lives in Ridge Hills. How does your family not have nightly dinners at places like this? You have a private chef or something?"

Ryan turned his face in annoyance. It was true that their family lived in one of the elite areas of the city, but compared to several other families in the neighborhood, they were low-hanging fruit. Regardless, this was one of the many misconceptions people had of the Erricson family. All three sons had to battle off constant fallacies that they lived in a castle with servants or had eternal wealth. While the wealth was notable, as most Type 5 families experienced, it wasn't anywhere near the grandiose imaginations of ignorant individuals. To a certain extent, the comment bothered Ryan since Grant had been a friend of both he and Rixen for years. Then he remembered that it was actually Grant's family who held the elite status he presumed the Erricson family had. And it wasn't as if Grant came around to the Erricson household as of late to compare lifestyles. Almost no one did.

"No, we're not *that* well-to-do. I mean, we live upper class, but we're not as lucky as some people in our area. Besides that, whatever wealthy prestige my family portrays usually doesn't involve Rixen or me. It's all for Roman." Ryan sipped heavily on his crystal glass as he regretted making the comment. The last thing he wanted tonight to be about was how he and Rixen played second fiddle to their Alpha Type 6 brother. But Grant was all too willing to entertain such conversation.

"So, what, then? You guys would just stay home while your parents paraded around with Roman?"

Ryan gestured with his head. "Couldn't have described it better myself."

"Wow. That's tough," Grant surmised.

Ryan disagreed. "Not really. It wasn't that hard to stay home and do whatever we wanted while Sur and Veo meticulously planned Roman's life." He snorted. "Actually, it was easy."

"Man. Sounds like a lot of pressure."

"Right? It's definitely the reason I'm glad I wasn't Roman."

Grant furrowed his brows. "No. Not Roman. You."

"*Me?*" Ryan responded confused.

"Well, yeah. I mean, think about it. Not being Roman comes with a lot of pressure, too."

Ryan hummed. "I'm not so sure I follow."

"Think of it like this. It's easy to rest on the idea that you and Rixen are the younger brothers trying to live up the precedent that Roman set, if that's what you two ended up doing. But what about your own individual needs and desires?" Grant paused as he collected his thoughts and viewed Ryan intently. "Trying to establish what is uniquely yours including your goals, interests, triumphs are bad enough. But I can't imagine having a brother in the family who *has* to be that prodigal."

"You still lost me," Ryan lamented.

Grant cut to the chase. "What if you are better than Roman?" Ryan nearly choked on oxygen as if it was his first breath. "Maybe not in everything, but some things? What would that have done to your family's status if it was common knowledge your Type 6 brother was less than his younger brother, a Beta no less?"

Ryan blinked. "I could only imagine."

Grant continued, "Instead of believing you grew up being 'second best' because you weren't good enough, what if you grew up 'second best' because otherwise you wouldn't be Erricson family everyone knows? So, in effect, you were taught to know your place and stop your potential so Roman could shine and bring your family into the quasi-celebrity status you know today."

The information had Ryan adjusting in his seat. This wasn't exactly how he imagined the night going. "I have to admit that I've had similar thoughts before. The problem was I was alone in the unpopular opinion... I think."

"Really? What happened the last time you openly spoke to your family about your Status as the Beta son and Roman being the Alpha Type 6?"

That question flashed memories in Ryan immediately. He chuckled. "Last time I did that, Roman kicked my ass."

"What?"

"It's a little more complicated than that." Ryan conveniently left out his role of inciting his older brother by ridiculing his then defunct relationship with his Fated Mate and his secret of knowing Siro brutally attacked one of the most prolific men in the city.

Before Ryan knew it, both young men were greeted by plates of truffled potatoes, winter vegetables, and a seared steak in the shape of a heart. "To the lovely couple," the waiter announced to them both. In any other restaurant, Ryan would have immediately corrected the server, but the atmosphere of the place made it very inappropriate to do so. With Grant also choosing to not say anything to the contrary, it didn't bother Ryan. In fact, the feelings were quite the opposite.

After the food was delicately placed and the service scattered to several other patrons, Grant placed his napkin and resumed his side of the conversation. "So, what do you think of what I said?"

The beef melted into Ryan's mouth. It only intensified the stimuli from the experience of the evening. "I think you're listening to too many of your favorite social commentators."

"Come on. You know I hit some truth in what I said."

"So? What does it mean if you did?"

Grant scented the change in Ryan. "Wow. You haven't been around a lot of Betas lately, have you?"

"You're my only friend who is a Beta. I have a Beta cousin who I haven't seen in years, and I don't see Laycin even though he's Mikaél's best friend. My free time is conveniently spent at the gym since I work there. Otherwise, I don't do much anymore." Time passed by in a flood of mental images as the sounds of a baby grand piano carried him away. "My life has changed a lot in the last few months. I don't even see Rixen anymore."

"You miss him, don't you?" Grant concluded.

"He's my brother. Of course, I miss him."

"That's not what I mean."

Ryan snorted. "Yeah. I know." He paused. "I miss him as my brother. That's it. Whatever happened between us is over. I know it's not easy, but we're going to have to figure out a way to move on like we did before it all happened. I can't just not have him in my life anymore."

Grant nodded. Inside, he was relieved to hear Ryan take the philosophy with such confidence. "You will. That's why family is there: the constant you can always come back to."

"I hope so," Ryan added.

Almost as if someone switched on a light, Grant observed the restaurant in a more prominent way he hadn't before. Suddenly, the place felt cramped, and the overall volume was loud and obtrusive. "You ready to get out of here?" he asked.

"Yes," Ryan beamed.

The drive home went by quickly as Ryan and Grant enjoyed strolling down memory lane of simpler times during their adolescent years. The sentiment was ironic since they remembered how at the time they thought their lives were stressful, and in some cases, traumatic. If they only knew then how things would turn out down the road, they would have appreciated the simplicity back then. For the most part, they laughed about classroom disruptions and afterschool antics.

Then, Grant rolled up in his car to the Erricson's driveway. "Do you like being back home?"

Ryan peered out the window to view the picturesque estate. It didn't please him like it used to. The years of it being magical faded in his mind. "I don't know. It's weird more than anything. At one point I thought I'd only be visiting this place on the holidays. Now it's where I live again... like I failed somehow."

"Hey... that's not true," Grant protested. "You left home before most unmated High-Types even consider walking out the door. That means something. Besides, just because it didn't work out—" Grant found himself silenced as his head was pulled in to meet Ryan's. Their lips pressed tight up against one another. Nothing but the sounds of their breaths and the hum of the car heater were heard as the world instantly became smaller. Before Grant knew it, Ryan pulled back and carefully studied him, trying to get a read. Slowly, Grant caught his breath, and for the first time this evening, found himself at a loss for words. "There's that," he whispered.

For Ryan, the moment made his heart race. Feelings and sensations that he thought would never resurface came flooding back. Taking that risk frightened him, but with Grant not revolting against him, the experience was refreshing. When Ryan inhaled Grant's pheromones, a very faint yet pleasing spring flower scent, he decided to take another risk. "Maybe one day *that* will mean something."

Grant was captivated and felt his heart pump in his throat. "Do you want it to?"

Ryan smirked. At least he learned one thing from his last relationship. "Let's take one day at a time." Grant appeared equally satisfied with that answer. He began to close the space between them again when he heard a knock on the passenger car window: his Sur. He grumbled as he lowered the passenger window. "Dad, really?"

"Sorry, guys. I need you to move the car." Jake spoke pleasantly as he observed both boys failing to recover from their previous engagement. If he hadn't had other things on his mind, he would have enjoyed teasing them in their caught moment. Instead, Jake kept his composure as his focus went to Grant. He waved gently. "Hi, Grant."

"Mr. Erricson." Grant blushed. His complexion made it impossible to hide any reaction.

"Are you going to come with me and your dad or stay here?" Jake wasted no time in trying to push the moment forward.

Although Ryan was grateful his Sur played it off as if nothing happened, the invitation was equally unwanted. "Go where?" he asked in a suspicious tone.

"To say goodbye to Roman and Mikaél."

Ryan sat up, full of concern. "Say what?"

Four separate cars paraded into the underground parking lot, one right after the other. If Mikaél wasn't expecting them, he'd think a planned assassination was about to happen. "Wolf-God, did they alert the newspaper?" He finished adding a light cardboard box to the top of the organized piles in the trunk of the SUV.

Roman shut the back passenger door as he observed several family members get out the various vehicles—too many in his opinion. "He didn't..." Roman mumbled. If it wasn't for the natural echo in the parking lot, he'd yell at his Sur for including such a fanfare. He saved face as he embraced him and used the opportunity to whisper into his ear. "You told them? I thought it was just going to be you guys and Mik's parents?"

"Your Veo wasn't having it," Jake answered. "He wanted them here."

"Do *they* want to be here?" Roman asked as he observed his brothers exit two different cars. Both Rixen and Garrace took one look at Ryan and Grant exiting the car and made their own conclusion. Rixen clung to Garrace as if sending a message to Ryan.

Ryan watched as the two silently walked by him and Grant who were innocently standing by the car, waiting to see if the couple would say anything to them. "Rixen—" he began.

"Now's not the time, Ryan," Rixen replied coldly, practically ignoring his brother completely. His expression switched on a dime as he hugged his Alpha brother. "Roman!"

Roman hugged his brother—something he hadn't done in quite some time. "I didn't think you'd be here."

"And miss you leaving? No way! Though ... I must say ... I'm not too pleased on having to hear about it through our dads," Rixen pointed out.

"Sorry," Roman replied, "it's not personal. Just taking precautions."

Dustin joined the conversation as he and Alex neared their own son. "Is that why you decided to leave tonight instead of tomorrow?"

Mikaél hugged both of his parents. "I'm not going to be able to sleep tonight anyway."

"That's one hell of a Valentine's Day." Alex kissed his son's forehead and held back tears as best as he could.

"Don't cry!" Mikaél commanded. "If you do it, I'll do it."

"I'll try not to." Alex sniffled. "Your brother and Will send their love. They apologize they couldn't make it last minute."

"Tell them thanks and give my nephew a kiss for me."

"Of course, we will," Alex answered.

Ryan finally got the courage to ask what he wanted since Winter Solstice. "Is someone going to finally say what's been going on with you two? Why do you need to have your pup in the Western Territory? What the hell is in St. Capricorn that you can't get in Tauris City?"

Roman looked at his Sur, who finally showed an expression which read the secret wouldn't be a secret much longer. "Privacy. What we need out there is privacy."

"*Privacy?*" Rixen replied. "Why?"

Roman wrapped his arm around his mate and felt his heart pump out of his chest as the nerves swallowed him. "Mikaél and I haven't told you something about our pup. And it's been the reason why things have been different lately. We're ready to tell you, but we need you all to keep this in great confidence. You got it?" Roman spoke out into the crowd who waited on his every word. Mikaél squeezed his hand and nodded in approval. "Our pup isn't going to be normal."

Garrace piped in. "What? Are you gonna have a wolf?" He laughed at his own joke but quickly silenced himself as everyone, including Rixen, gave him a look that read he wasn't amusing.

"It's going to be a girl," Mikaél finished.

For the part of the group that didn't know, they gawked in disbelief that Mikaél would make such a claim. The rest heaved their chests as they prepared for an inquisition.

Rixen, who was biting his fingernail in order to deal with Garrace's faux pax, dropped his hand immediately at the utterance. "Are you serious?"

"This is some sort of prank, right?" Ryan added.

Both Roman and Mikaél shook their heads as they gazed back at their respective parents for help. Jake jumped in while holding Adrian closer to him.

"They're not kidding, Ryan. When the pup is born, *she* will be the first female born in this world that we know of in centuries."

Grant exhaled in elation. "I can't believe it! It's finally happening!"

"What are you talking about?" Ryan asked him, stunned at his reaction.

Grant initially stumbled as he tried to remember previous books he'd read on the subject. "One of the biologists I follow, he talked about this once."

"Talked about what?" Mikaél asked, looking at Roman who was equally glued to Grant's announcement.

"You guys! *This*." Grant joyously gestured to Mikaél's stomach. "That our evolution would eventually see the return of the female species."

Mikaél lit up as he took in Grant's enthusiasm. "People talk about that stuff?"

In addition to stifling a laugh, Grant rolled his eyes. "Yes, of course, they do! You don't think they just constantly theorize about Type 7, 8, 9, and 50 all the time, do you?"

Dustin stepped forward and addressed the small crowd. "As much as we are grateful for your attitude on this, we need you, *all* of you to keep this to yourselves."

"I don't believe this." Rixen shook his head.

"Problem, Rix?" Roman grimaced.

"Why didn't you tell us sooner? You're giving us five minutes before you leave to the Western Territory to announce you're having some miracle baby while also telling us to keep it a secret?"

Ryan concurred, "Yeah, not cool, bro."

"You better call us after you get to there so we can talk about this," Rixen demanded.

"No." Jake waved his hand as he stood next to Dustin. "No phone calls, no texts. Not until things settle down. The only way Roman and Mikaél will be able to communicate is through a hospital line. And no one will know where to reach them at except Dustin and myself. From here on out, the idea is to keep this between us and on the down-low until their pup is born and they are safely home."

"Damn," Ryan replied. "What's the reason for all secrecy?"

"There are horrible people out there, Ryan." Adrian bowed his head. "People who don't want Roman and Mikaél to have their pup."

"What?!" Ryan was in disbelief.

"Oh, come on, Ryan." Rixen walked over to his brother, the closest proximity he had been to him for weeks now. "Is it that hard to believe? Haven't you been paying attention to politics lately?" Even before Ryan could respond, Rixen carried on. "Of course, you haven't." Rixen gave his Beta brother a look of disgust.

"Wait a minute!" Ryan snarled.

"Can you two figure out your lovers' quarrel later?" Roman barked.

Both his younger brothers fell silent as Rixen walked back to Garrace's side, now pretending Ryan didn't exist. "So, what happens now?"

Roman relaxed his posture. "Mik and I will leave. We'll keep in touch with dad as we progress in the next couple of months. And hopefully, this spring, we'll come back ... with a healthy baby girl."

A tear fell down Alec's cheek. Instead of walking up to his own son, he walked up and hugged Roman instead. In the embrace, he whispered in his ear. "You take care of my boy and my grand-daughter. Do you hear me?"

"Absolutely. You can count on me," Roman assured him. Everyone said their goodbyes until it was time for Roman to embrace his Alpha father. "I can feel you thinking," he commented. "What is it?"

"I'm proud of you," Jake answered.

Roman was shocked. What did his father just say? He gave his father a look he hadn't done in years. "Why is that?"

"Today, you officially became a man."

"*Today*? Shouldn't that have happened when I turned 16, 18, or hell, when I found my mate? What's so special about today?"

"Because now you finally get it." Jake rubbed his son's shoulder and looked into his eyes, not seeing the immature boy, self-absorbed teen, or contrarian son he was used to. "You choosing to take Mikaél and your unborn pup to the Western Territory for the safety and survival of your family means you see the bigger picture. When a parent makes decisions, Roman, it's so easy for a child or an out-sider to look at it and say they're being mean, irresponsible, a bad parent, or overprotective. But the truth is, it's all done out of love." Jake's bottom lip began to quiver as his eyes watered. "It doesn't always come off that way. But that's what it all is. That's what it's all about." Jake looked away to help gain his composure. "I don't know what Mikaél thinks about all this, but I know it's not going to be perfect out there. Wolf-God knows anyone in your situation would go crazy. You two will probably have a fight or two and say things you don't mean. But this is the time to keep in the back of your mind that one day he will understand why this happened, and that you were there to love and protect him. Until then," he looked back at his son who was equally on the edge of an emotional release, "Wolf-God is going to give you Alpha strength to weather this out. And I'm only a phone call away." Roman nodded, unable to say a word. "You remember the number?" Roman nodded again and managed a verbal affirmation. "I love you, Roman."

"I love you too, dad." Roman gave his Sur one more hug before he saw his Veo come up for his own goodbye.

Adrian sighed. "I knew one day you'd be destined for something great, Roman. None of us knew it was going to be this. Maybe if we did..." Adrian paused. "Maybe things would have been different."

"Different how?" Roman asked.

Adrian shrugged. "I'm not sure. I know your father had great expectations of you and that caused us to be heavy handed sometimes. Hopefully, we didn't make too many mistakes."

Roman saw a shadow of his Veo. The year had not been kind to him. Dark circles under his eyes emphasized his pale face. The distance in his gaze and in his scent became all too clear. "Veo, what's wrong?"

"Hm?"

"Something has been going on with you. What isn't dad telling us?"

Adrian knew his son had a great sense about him, but his neutral face contrived into a smile instead. "Nothing, Roman. Everything is fine."

Dustin's voice permeated the private conversation. "Okay! Well, we don't want to keep you guys waiting any longer."

"Shouldn't we be going with them?" Rixen lamented. "Or at least somebody?"

"Rixen is right," Garrace chimed in. "The people out in the Western Territory are the closest to our next of kin you'll find out there. Nothing but wild animals."

"They're not like that!" Dustin cast a warning look at Garrace. He was stunned to hear himself defend the citizens of the Western Territory as he remembered saying something similar to Dr.

Birowack himself. "It's nothing but a baseless fear that the people out there must be uncivilized cannibals. They are people just like us."

"Then why don't we ever see people from there?" Garrace asked. Rixen elbowed him in the rib, causing him to wince in pain.

Dustin resumed, "They lead different lives out there. You won't find large cities racing to be the next-best-thing like Tauris out there. Their values are centered around preserving family and loyalty. Roman and Mikaél are going to have to learn how to be accepted as outsiders from a world they don't respect."

Mikaél's nerves began to kick in. "I thought we were staying near the hospital with Dr. Zang's family?"

"Well, you do plan on leaving the house at least once or twice during your stay there, don't you?" Jake hummed.

Roman wasn't amused at his Alpha's father condescending tone. "I think we're ready to go."

"Good luck to both of you," Dustin spoke firmly. "Remember, contact us through the number we gave you if you need us." Roman nodded his head.

"We love you," Alec whispered before giving Mikaél one final hug.

Ryan and Rixen both gave their Alpha brother a farewell embrace as well before the two got in their cars and drove out of the underground garage into the night.

"We're doing the right thing, Jake?" Dustin asked his friend and co-worker.

"We're doing the *best* thing," Jake corrected.

Roman and Mikaél will return in *Aria's Arrival*!

AUTHOR BIO:

Lucas LaMont lives near the mountains of Colorado and has been a storyteller since childhood. Throughout the years, he has dabbled in fiction and poetry and in his adult writing, most of his focus has been in gay fiction. Recently, he discovered the Omegaverse genre and is obsessed with it! During the Covid pandemic, he found his favorite series to read: *The Adrien English Mysteries* by Josh Lanyon (But he is very much a fan of several noteworthy Omegaverse authors). When he's not writing and reading, Lucas loves traveling to fabulous Las Vegas to gamble or staying near the rustic lakes of Minnesota to go fishing. His current focus has been the creation of Boy Love Visual Novels, starting with his first one *Fated: Type 6*. The goal of his writing has always been to focus on the power of relationships and the journey they take. You can find Lucas Lamont on Facebook, Twitter, Instagram, and Wix.

Discover more at
4HorsemenPublications.com

10% off using HORSEMEN10